FOR THE HONOR OF THE AGENCY

Book 1 of
The Honor Trilogy

by

Andrew J Harvey

A Novel of the
Cross-Temporal Empire

FOR THE HONOR OF THE AGENCY

Copyright 2025
Hague Publishing
PO Box 451
Bassendean, Western AUSTRALIA 6934
Email: contact@haguepublishing.com
Web: www.haguepublishing.com

Identifiers:
eBook: ISBN 978-1-922984-09-8
softcover ISBN 978-1-922984-08-1

Cover Art: Jade Zivanovic of Steam Power Studios.
Cover Photograph: Bory Var, castle, Hungary
Bory Var and other images used under license from Shutterstock.com.

Acknowledgements

My thanks to the following people without whom this book would never have been completed:

- Members of the Bassendean Writer's Group including, but not necessarily limited to: Inez, Julie, Ken, Mena, Punito, Sandi, and Theo.

- To Isobelle Carmody, an amazing person and a fantastic writer, who provided feedback on the first chapter.

- Wikipedia, which provided me with an initial start on many of the vignettes.

- My editor, Sally Odgers, and my wonderful beta readers: Alan and Bianca.

And lastly, my wife, who put up with me burbling about the latest issues with my two protagonists while they fell in love, fought villains, and generally ignored the plot I had so carefully created for them.

Table of Contents

1

Prologue

A century ago, Iapura led 53 survivors through a portal to escape a dying Earth. They had expected to emerge on Alpha Centauri but instead found themselves on an alternate Earth. An Earth where in 1884, Russian and English armies faced off across America's Great Plains, unprepared for the technological prowess of the conquering Nayarit.

Within six months, the 53 refugees had seized control of the Mainline, and over the next 100 years expanded their empire across the multiverse, eventually including 54 alternate Earths within the grandly titled Cross-Temporal Empire (C-TE).

Over the next 90 years, Iapura's empire expanded steadily across a series of parallel Earths, absorbing and conquering until it included over 53 separate lines Finally, however, with its technology stagnant and its ruling council riven by dissent, the Cross-Temporal Empire descended into five years of civil-war. A civil war that pitched the C-T E's ruling families against each other in a bitter, internecine feud that almost destroyed it.

Five years later, the Empire struggles to rebuild itself under a new dynasty, the Clemhorns. But now the Empire is under attack from an external enemy – they just don't know it yet.

2

My Nurse Will Bring the Bill

(Tuesday: New York, Commonwealth of America, Mainline)

As the limousine turned into the street, Markus pulled back further into the shadow of the massive oak. A raccoon, disturbed in its feeding, glared at him in warning, while behind it, Central Park drowsed on in the evening's summer air. Markus risked an anxious glance round the trunk to confirm it was the same vehicle he'd seen leaving the redbrick mansion earlier. There was no mistaking the Rolls, and his breathing quickened, knowing it was almost over.

A tram screeched past, the catenary lines sparking as it turned east toward Lexington Avenue. He watched the Rolls pull into the driveway of the mansion across the street and bent to wake the child curled up at his feet. The sooner he delivered his message, the sooner he'd be able to leave this damn country.

"Come on, Liebchen," he whispered.

His daughter roused sleepily. "Is it time to go home, Daddy?"

"Not quite. We just need to talk to the lady I was telling you about."

"All right."

She slipped a trusting hand into his, and he hoisted her up into his arms.

As the two crossed the street, he flicked a nervous glance at the two men loitering on the corner and wondered what they were doing there.

The Rolls' quiet purr had stopped as Markus turned into the mansion's open gateway. He glanced behind him. The two men were walking purposefully toward them, but the rest of the street was still clear.

A little faster now, but trying not to worry his daughter, he started up the neatly raked driveway, pea-gravel sliding under his boots.

"Is that the lady?" his daughter asked, craning her head to look over her shoulder at the tall, statuesque woman with long, raven black hair easing her way out of the Rolls in an elegant, ivory ball gown.

"Yes, Liebchen," he said, placing Jessie back on the ground, wondering as he did so when she had got so heavy.

The scent of gardenias filled the air as he straightened his back and took a deep breath. For the first time, he worried that she, like all the others, might refuse to listen to him. It was too late to worry now, though. "Ma'am," he called. "Miss Peric!"

The lady in question looked round, startled to see him, as the other passenger door slammed open and a shorter woman with a bob of dirty-blond hair, dressed in a scarlet tunic and dark-blue trousers, almost fell out of the vehicle.

"Stop right there!" the bodyguard commanded; her revolver aimed in his direction.

Markus started to lift his hands but found that his right was still holding his daughter's. Carefully, he lifted his free hand – this hadn't been in the script.

Running footsteps sounded from the gravel behind him. He was turning when something slammed against his spine, driving the air from his lungs, and he toppled forward, face-first into the gravel.

Oh Liebchen, I'm so sorry, was all he had time to think before darkness took him.

***

Margaret Peric forced her feet back into her stilettos as the Rolls turned onto Fifth Avenue. They were almost home. Through the vehicle's open window, she could just make out the darker shadows of Central Park's elm trees in the distance.

She noticed Jade smiling at her from the other side of the vehicle and grimaced. "Be thankful you get to wear sensible shoes," she told her bodyguard.

Jade sniffed.

A moment later, the Rolls turned through the mansion's gates, crunching its way up the pea-gravel drive that led to the six-story mansion she presently called home. Jade sneezed as the cloying scent of gardenias filled the vehicle's interior, and the Rolls eased to a halt at the foot of the mansion's stairs.

Ignoring her bodyguard's muffled protest, Margaret opened the car door and swung her legs out – Jade was sometimes over-protective.

"Ma'am," someone called, startling her. "Miss Peric!"

Margaret turned and frowned at the sight of the stranger standing in the middle of the drive, clutching the hand of a small girl.

Behind her, she heard Jade's door slam open. "Stop right there!" Jade ordered.

"Softly," Margaret warned her, as the stranger lifted his free hand. The child looked as though she was on the verge of bursting into tears.

And then her attention snapped to the two men running up the drive toward them, gravel crunching under their feet.

"Jade –" she said, as she caught sight of the knife one of them was holding, but they had already reached the stranger and she watched horrified as the one with the knife thrust it into the stranger's back. As he plunged face forward to the ground, the small girl let out a piercing shriek.

Margaret scrabbled in her shoulder-bag for her revolver as one of the men bent over the body. Damn, where was it, she thought, as the second man grabbed the other's arm and pulled him away, back down the drive. A moment later, both were running for the street.

Margaret was still scrabbling fruitlessly in her bag when she heard a shot and looked across the top of the Rolls to see that Jade had fired her pistol in the air.

"Shit," Jade said, taking off after the two men who had already disappeared around the corner.

Shit indeed, Margaret thought, dumping the contents of her bag onto the back seat to find the revolver. She grabbed it, pulled up her gown and started after Jade.

She'd only taken three steps when the stiletto heel of her left shoe slid on the gravel and she almost twisted her ankle. With a grimace, she slid her shoes off.

Upon reaching the girl, she crouched next to her, swearing as she saw the handle of the knife protruding from the stranger's back. "Jade," she called out after her bodyguard. "We're going to need a doctor."

"What's your name, sweetheart?" she asked the child, resting her ear on the stranger's back. She was almost sure he was still breathing, although his coat made it difficult to be confident.

"Jessie," the girl said. "What's wrong with Daddy?"

"Your father's been stabbed and needs a doctor," Margaret said, lifting his head carefully to get a hand under his ear to clear his mouth. She wondered if that had been the right thing to tell a child. How was she to know though; it wasn't as if she'd had much experience with them. Besides, she'd never been one to sugarcoat the truth.

Jade appeared beside her. "What's wrong?"

Margaret jerked her head toward the protruding handle, and Jade let out a muffled oath.

"James," Jade called to the house. "Phone for a doctor, then get a couple of people down here. We need to get him inside. And get something to use as a stretcher!"

Margaret looked up to see the butler, who had been heading toward them at the run, turn around and head back for the house. "I'm fairly sure he's still breathing," she said.

"Good," Jade said, nervously looking round. "Perhaps you should take the girl inside?"

Margaret frowned but nodded. Although Jade was probably just trying to get her principal out of danger, it made sense to get the girl indoors. Standing up, she brushed the gravel off the bottom of her gown, frowning when she saw the damage. She'd only worn it once!

"Come on, Jessie," Margaret said, offering the child her hand. "Let's go inside and wait for Daddy."

Jessie looked at her father, tears forming in the corners of her eyes. "Will Daddy be all right?"

"I'm sure he will," Margaret said, mentally crossing her fingers. "Do you know why Daddy was here?"

"He said we were coming to meet you," Jessie sobbed.

Margaret and Jade shared a puzzled look.

"Perhaps you can tell me what he said while we go inside and wait for him," Margaret said.

Trustingly, Jessie took her hand. It felt so small resting in hers, Margaret thought. Looking up, she could already see the first of the cavalry starting down the steps toward them. She would have been more comfortable if they were her own staff, but Serge had insisted on her staying at his house while she was in New York, and they seemed efficient enough. The house was certainly cheaper than a hotel or renting her own property. Particularly as she didn't know how long she'd be staying, or whether she'd even keep the job her cousin had foisted on her.

"Come on," Margaret said, drawing the child away from her father. Slowly they made their way back up the driveway, with Jessie reluctantly looking back over her shoulder at her father's limp body as they did so.

"Do you know why your daddy wanted to see me?" Margaret asked, trying to ignore the gravel pinching her bare feet.

Jessie shook her head.

"Can I call your mother?"

Jessie shook her head again. "Mummy's dead."

"Oh." That was a conversation killer, if ever there was one.

"She died when I was six," Jessie added.

"And how old are you now?" Margaret asked.

"Eight," Jessie announced proudly.

Two of the footmen rushed by; one carrying a couple of rolled up blankets. It was probably a good thing she'd left the fundraiser early. If she'd waited until the event was due to finish most of the staff would have been asleep. The children's hospital was a good cause, but she hated having to make small talk and she'd cried off as soon as she decently could.

At the top of the staircase, she paused for a moment to look back to where Jade and the two footmen were sliding the blanket under Jessie's father. She looked down and noticed Jessie was also staring worriedly at them.

Mrs. Mack, the tiny housekeeper, was hovering uncertainly in the doorway. Despite her diminutive size, the housekeeper ruled the domestic staff with a will of pure iron. According to Serge, his father had brought her with him from the Dontfrey Line when he'd returned to the Mainline fifteen years ago. Which sort of made her family, Margaret thought, as she'd lived on Dontfrey herself until a year ago.

"Has someone called the doctor?" Margaret asked.

"Yes, ma'am," the housekeeper said, looking up at her. "James sent the boy next door for Mr. Castles. And who's this?" she asked, barely needing to bend her head to place her face at the same level as the child's.

"This is Jessie, Mrs. Mack. They're going to be bringing her father up in a moment, but I need to get out of this dress and find some shoes."

"Certainly, ma'am. Will you come with me, Jessie? You can help me get some hot water ready for your father."

Jessie nodded solemnly, and confident that she was in safe hands, Margaret started up the stairs to the bedroom. She'd got about halfway up when she remembered what she'd been thinking about in the car on the way back from the fundraiser. "Mrs. Mack," she called, leaning over the balustrade. "Has there been any word from my sister?"

"No, ma'am, nothing from Miss Louise."

Margaret frowned. It would be so much easier if her mother could have done the job herself rather than delegating her eldest daughter with the task of tracking down her youngest child. She understood why she couldn't, with Father's health being so delicate after his heart attack. But just what did Louise think she was doing walking out on her fiancé to traipse all the way to New York? "All right, let me know if you hear anything."

"Of course, ma'am."

"Ma'am!" It was the butler.

"Yes, James?"

"The police are here."

She rolled her eyes – of course the police were here. "Show them into the front room. I'll see them in a moment. And ask Jade if she can make herself available."

It didn't take her long to change into silk pajamas and dressing-gown, and to grab some slippers.

Jade was waiting outside the room for her.

"How is he?" Margaret asked, dropping her voice.

"Alive. Mr. Castles was just starting his examination."

"Then let's see what we can do for the gentlemen in blue."

The two uniformed representatives of New York's finest were standing uncomfortably in the center of the room.

"Gentlemen, what can I do for you?" Margaret asked politely.

"We've had a report of someone firing a gun," the senior officer said.

The other, who looked barely old enough to shave, jerked his admiring gaze away from Jade.

There was a knock, and James stuck his head around the door. "I'm sorry to interrupt, ma'am, but Imperial Security are here."

"Show them in," she said with a sigh. Perhaps she could try to deal with them in bulk.

"Miss Peric," the Imp-Sec Officer said politely when she was shown into the room. "Special Agent Kostello, Imperial Security." She held her identity card up with the all-seeing eye etched into the mother-of-pearl background in black.

Margaret caught Jade covetously eyeing the Special Agent's black and silver uniform and turned her attention back to the Special Agent.

"I was just passing," Kostello said, "and I wondered if I could provide any assistance."

Just passing – as if! Imp-Sec had parked themselves outside the house for the first couple of weeks after she took up residence until she'd put her foot down. After a heated conversation with her cousin, they'd compromised, and Imp-Sec had established a control post in an apartment around the corner at 5 E Seventy-Eighth Street. It was 120 yards away, plus stairs, but at least she could now pretend to be a big girl.

"Thank you, Special Agent Kostello," Margaret said. "My bodyguard was forced to discharge her pistol in the air when we witnessed an attempted robbery."

The three looked at Jade, who gave a short, decisive nod.

"The victim is not known to me," Margaret continued, "nor to anyone else in this house. At this stage, he is being examined by the doctor. If I subsequently decide that the matter is one that should be drawn to the attention of either the local police, or Imp-Sec, I will ensure this occurs."

Special Agent Kostello swallowed whatever she was going to say and pasted a fake smile on her face. "Of course, ma'am. Thank you. Come, gentlemen."

The younger police officer opened his mouth to say something, but the senior shook his head at him warningly.

Margaret rang the bell, and James appeared to escort them out of the room.

"So, let's see what this was all about," Margaret said to Jade, when they'd been shown out of the house.

The lobby was deserted, but they followed the sound of talking into the kitchen, where they found the stranger lying facedown on the large wooden kitchen table. The doctor was carefully cutting the fabric of the stranger's coat back from the knife wound. A strong smell of antiseptic wafted through the air toward Margaret.

For a moment, she froze, the smell overpowering her. Then the patient lifted his head and Margaret could move again.

"Hold still," the doctor told him curtly.

She'd only seen her neighbor once, in the distance, but there was no mistaking him. The doctor's thick, ginger, bushy sideburns stuck straight out from his face like a Cheshire cat's. The round, wire-rimmed glasses he wore emphasized the similarity.

"You're not taking him to the hospital?" Margaret asked, staying outside the door. With four staff, the doctor, and now Jade, all standing around the table, the kitchen looked crowded enough. And there was the fact that the stink of antiseptic brought back too many unpleasant memories.

"Not unless we need to." The doctor did not bother to look up. "The knife is too close to the spine. Too much risk the trip might aggravate the wound."

The cloth had been cut through now, and the surgeon peeled back the coat and shirt to expose the knife sticking up from his back. There was a lot less blood than Margaret had expected.

The doctor opened a small tube of ointment, and smeared some onto the skin around the protruding handle before picking up a small portable scanner. The scanner was about the size of a packet of cigarettes and had a wand attached. As he deftly ran the head of the wand over the skin around the wound, he studied the image on the screen.

"Well?" Margaret asked impatiently.

Mr. Castles ignored her, and she felt a surge of irritation at his manner. He might be good at what he did, and the fact that he owned a house facing onto Central Park showed he probably was, but as the daughter of a Continental Leader she was not used to being ignored.

After replacing the scanner, Castles checked his watch, then carefully placed one hand on the handle of the knife, and the other on the skin around the wound. "Hold your breath," he told the patient before, in one smooth movement, he pulled the knife free.

There was a yelp, and as the knife's blade emerged, Margaret could see it was a single-edged blade about eight inches long. The blade itself was black metal, about three inches wide, with a strip of brass inlaid along its back, and a curved portion cut into the back of the blade near the tip.

Holding the knife up with one hand, the doctor pressed on the wound with a gauze pad as he inspected the blade with the other. "No nicks," he said finally, after he'd finished checking it.

"Which means?" Margaret raised an eyebrow.

"Nothing left in the wound."

"May I?" Jade stepped forward to take the blade before he could place it on the table next to the scanner.

Mr. Castles looked surprised, but handed her the knife.

Jade inspected it for a moment, then nodded, pleased.

"What?" Margaret asked.

"It's a Blacks and Sons' Bowie."

Margaret frowned. Sometimes Jade had a bad habit of simply assuming people could read her mind. "Which means?"

"It has a serial number?"

"And that means?"

Jade sighed. "It means we can trace the person who bought it."

"Ah."

The doctor ignored this conversation as he removed a short piece of black cable from his bag. He screwed an eyepiece onto one end, smeared the cable with more ointment, then clicked the eyepiece over his glasses and carefully inserted the other end of the cable into the wound.

"Well?" Margaret asked after five minutes of watching the good doctor stare into the eyepiece.

Without looking up, the doctor gestured for silence.

Margaret folded her arms, vexed at being ignored. She caught sight of Jade suppressing a grin at her reaction and couldn't help smiling at herself.

Finally, the doctor removed the cable, stood up and stretched his back carefully. "You, sir, are a very lucky man. The knife missed all significant organs, and so long as it hasn't damaged the spine, which it doesn't appear to have, you should be up on your feet within two days. You'll need to remain here for a couple of days. I presume that will be all right?" he said, apparently realizing he might have gone just a little too far.

"Oh absolutely," Margaret said dryly. "The house certainly has enough rooms."

"Good, my nurse will bring the bill when she comes to change the dressing tomorrow morning."

"Of course," Margaret said.

"Give me fifteen minutes to glue everything back together and clean up here and I'll be out of your hair."

"Thank you," Margaret said, feeling she'd been dismissed, and in her own house too! "I'll see about getting a room made up for Mr. . . ." she paused, suddenly aware she didn't know the stranger's name.

"Ackov," the stranger said, turning his head to give her a wan look. "Markus Ackov. I apologize for any difficulty I may have inadvertently caused you, Miss Peric."

"No difficulty at all, Mr. Ackov, I'll see about your room. Your daughter can wait for you there. Is there anyone we should tell where you are?"

"No, no one." His Serbian accent definitely betrayed his background, even if the name hadn't. "I have a room booked in the Casuarina Hotel. The key is in my coat pocket."

"Jade, perhaps you can send someone round to pick up their belongings?" Margaret suggested. "I need to find Mrs. Mack."

"She was going to take Jessie to the parlor," Jade said.

As Jade had suggested, Margaret found Mrs. Mack in the parlor. Jessie had been watching the door and stood up as Margaret came in. "Is Daddy all right?"

"Yes, sweetheart. You can see him in a couple of minutes. Mrs. Mack, it appears Jessie's father will be staying with us for a couple of days. Can you prepare one of the guest bedrooms? Perhaps Jessie would like to help you get it ready."

"Of course, come on Jessie."

With a sigh, Margaret watched them leave, wondering how long it would be before life would return to normal. She had enough problems at the Department without having to worry about two unexpected guests. The latest figures on the impact of the outbreak of red rust in the wheat crop in the American Midwest were getting steadily worse. If they couldn't do something about it, they could be facing famine. And just where was Louise?

3

I'll Try and Keep the Costs Down

(Tuesday: New York, Commonwealth of America, Mainline)

Margaret knocked gently on the bedroom door.

"Come in," came the soft reply.

Markus was lying on his stomach, his head cradled in his arms. As Margaret opened the door, Markus craned his head round to see who it was.

"Ah, Miss Peric. I apologize for all this." He waved weakly.

"Margaret, please," she said, taking the chair near the head of the bed so he could watch her without having to twist his neck. A faint scent of antiseptic rose from his bandages.

"Then you must call me Markus," he said, tight-lipped with pain.

He had beautiful eyes, she thought, struck by their amber softness. There was a brief silence, not uncomfortable, but long enough for Margaret to remember there was a reason she was there.

"So, Markus, what is this about? Jessie told me you were coming to see me?"

"I . . ." He stopped. "I had practiced what I was going to say, but I was not expecting to be in this position. I'm not sure what to say," he admitted.

"Then perhaps you should simply start at the beginning."

Markus nodded. "I work . . . worked for the Department of Agriculture and Food as a field agent."

Margaret raised an eyebrow at this – Ag and Food was her own Department. It still felt strange to say that. She'd been its director-general for less than two months, and still felt she was floundering, with no hope of ever getting her head above water. She'd already tried resigning once but her cousin, Donald, could be very persuasive when he wanted to be.

"I never realized the role of an Ag field agent could be so . . . dangerous," Jade said from the doorway.

Margaret waved her in.

"It isn't," Markus said. "Well, not normally."

"And yet here you are." Margaret raised an eyebrow.

Markus nodded. "I was leading a team that was tracking the path of the infection vector for an outbreak of potato blight on Clyde. The problem was the evidence indicated that there wasn't just one originating source, but three. Three widely separate sources all occurring at exactly the same time."

"Three?" Margaret's brow furrowed in confusion.

"Three. I spoke to my supervisor, but he told me it was impossible; that I must have made a mistake. I showed him the evidence, but he refused to listen, and when I demanded the opportunity to speak to his manager, I was transferred back to head office."

Margaret nodded noncommittally, wondering how legitimate his complaint was. It had surprised her, the number of people working for the Department who'd approached her for help, believing they were being victimized by their supervisor, and yet who couldn't provide any sort of evidence or corroboration of their claims. And without evidence, there was nothing she could do.

"Here?" Jade asked.

"Yes, in New York."

"Trying to speak to me is a little more than raising it with your manager," Margaret pointed out.

"I know, that came later."

There was a pause.

"Well?" Margaret prompted.

"They moved me into records. I started to look at the data we were getting about the outbreak of wheat rust in the Mainline's American

Midwest in my spare time. There was absolutely no evidence of affected crops two years ago. Last year, however, we had five separate identified instances of infected crops over an area of some 2,000 miles. And this year, well, it's pretty much across the entire Midwest. There had to have been a human agent."

Margaret frowned, wondering why she hadn't heard anything about that. Something like this was a little more important than the petty complaints the system was supposed to filter out before they got passed further up the line. It was starting to sound as if some of her fears about the Department might have some credence. "So, who did you report those concerns to?"

"My manager."

"And?"

"She told me to leave it with her and, when I asked her about it a couple of weeks later, she told me she'd passed it on."

"You didn't believe her?"

Markus shook his head. "If she had, someone would have spoken to me. I asked for an appointment with my Director."

"Which one?"

"Director Jones."

"And?"

"And, when I appeared at his office, I was told my services were no longer required and I was escorted off the premises."

"Were you given a reason?" Jade asked.

"No. I tried to see the Executive Director, but he refused to see me. Told me I was lucky to get off as lightly as I had been." He sounded genuinely perplexed.

"The evidence you found. Do you have a copy?"

Markus looked embarrassed. "I did, but it was in my desk, and when I was shown the door . . .." He shrugged, wincing as it pulled at his wound.

Margaret tapped a finger on her chin, wondering if he was telling the truth.

"You believe me, don't you?" Markus asked plaintively.

"It does sound a little far-fetched. That there's someone out there involved in environmental terrorism on a continental scale. And without evidence . . ."

"But why would I lie about something like that?" Markus said.

"I can think of several reasons," Margaret told him. "Revenge for losing your job, or delusion. The list could go on and on. The problem is, however, that someone wanted you silenced enough to try and kill you, which adds credence to your claims." And it would certainly explain some of her own hidden fears, that there were people in the Department, *her* Department; working against her. If that proved the case, they were going to discover what it was like to piss off a Peric.

"We'll talk some more in the morning." She rose to her feet. "Jade, can I see you for a moment?"

Outside, Margaret moved far enough down the hallway to speak without Markus overhearing. "What do you think?"

Jade ran her hand through her hair. "I'm not sure about the story, but the stabbing was real. And they were definitely aiming for him. Whoever they were, they were trying to prevent him talking to you."

"I agree," Margaret said. "Tomorrow I want you to track down the owner of that knife."

"You don't want the local police to do that?"

"No." Margaret didn't even have to think about it. "The police don't have the staff to treat this as a priority."

"It's a priority then?"

"If Markus is telling the truth, then yes, it's a priority."

"Who's paying?" Jade asked. "I mean, is it a personal expense or do I bill the Department?"

Margaret considered the question. "It probably should be the Department, but I'm not sure I'm allowed to commit to that type of expense, so you'd better bill it to me. I'll worry about how I'm going to pay for it later. Unfortunately, my brother's new responsibilities as a World Leader are acting like a bottomless pit for the family's finances."

"I'll try to keep the costs down."

"I'd appreciate that. And I think I need to speak to my cousin tomorrow. If, and this is a really big 'if', if what Markus says is true, I've got to pass it up the line. This goes way beyond Ag and Food."

"I hadn't thought of that," Jade admitted. "If Markus's story is true, and someone *is* trying to hush it up, once they know he's spoken to you, you may become a target too."

Margaret sighed. Bodyguards had been a part of her life since she'd been five, but she'd hoped that with the new job, and her move to the Mainline, they'd become a little less necessary. Unfortunately, it appeared that was not going to be the case. "What do you suggest?"

"I'll speak to the Agency and get someone around first thing in the morning for twenty-four-hour live-in. Between the two of us, I'm fairly sure that will give us enough coverage at night. I'll also see about getting some additional protection during the day."

"Good, I wouldn't want anything to happen to Jessie."

"No," Jade agreed.

"And Jade, thank you," Margaret said.

"Why, thank you, ma'am," Jade said, touching a finger to her forehead. "We aim to please."

4

A Hôtes Non-payant

(Wednesday: New York, Commonwealth of America, Mainline)

Markus groaned as the morning light pierced the heavy curtains over the window. Thanks to the tablets the doctor had left for him, he'd slept heavily for most of the night, but he hated the dead, lethargic feeling sleeping pills gave him. They reminded him too much of the months after his wife's death when it was the only way he could sleep.

"Daddy?" a quiet voice said from near the door.

"Jessie?" He lifted his head just enough to see what appeared to be a nest of blankets on the floor. As he blinked, trying to focus and work out what they were doing there, the tousled features of his daughter appeared over the side of the blankets.

"What are you doing down there?" Markus wanted to know.

"Protecting you."

Markus allowed his head to fall back onto his pillow. "And how were you going to do that?"

"Jade gave me this."

Startled, he reared back up, feeling a bite from his wound as it pulled against the glue holding everything together.

He'd been expecting a gun, or a knife, and at the sight of the whistle she was holding up, he let out a sigh of relief.

"I did ask for a gun," she said plaintively. "But Jade said I was too young."

He wondered who Jade was, because he definitely had to thank her for that one.

"Have you seen her gun, Daddy?" Jessie's eyes were like wide saucers.

"No," Markus said. "Did you?"

"I did," she said sincerely. "Jade said it was a Westinghouse '.303'."

Markus nodded into his pillow, trying to appear knowledgeable, but feeling completely out of his depth. Show him a plant and he'd be able to give you its Latin name, but guns? They were as much a dark secret to him as women usually were.

"I should get up," he said.

"Do you need me to help?" Jessie asked.

"I can manage," he said, adding a muttered 'I hope', under his breath.

Trying to hold his back straight, he swiveled so he was sitting on the edge of the bed. The world threatened to take a swan dive, and he paused for a moment before getting to his feet.

Coming back from the toilet he found Jessie sitting on the end of the bed, and noticed for the first time the long, cotton nightdress she was wearing. "Where did you get the nightdress from, Liebchen?" he asked, as he sat back down on the bed.

"Mrs. Mack gave it to me. I'm almost as tall as she is?" she said, sounding surprised.

"And who is Mrs. Mack?" he asked.

"She's the housekeeper. Did you know that Lady Margaret doesn't own the house? She's just staying here. Mrs. Mack said she's a *hôtes non-payant*. That means she's a friend of the family."

"Oh," he said, trying to keep up with the conversation. He had a dim memory of someone who might have been the housekeeper, but nothing solid. "It was nice of her to lend you her nightdress."

"I thought so."

There was a pause, during which Markus tried to work out the best way of lying back down without hurting his back.

"Daddy?"

"Yes Liebchen?" Deciding there wasn't going to be an easy way, Markus allowed himself to fall sideways onto the bed, and then rolled onto his back. He sighed with relief as he settled into the soft mattress.

"When can we go home?"

"I explained we had to leave the apartment."

"No, I mean home, home," she said, as though to another child. "Constantinople."

His eyes teared at the question, remembering the house they'd rented near the University there. He'd accepted the job with Agriculture and Food while he was struggling to cope with the death of Adriana, and still learning to be a single parent. He'd thought that coming to North America was the chance for a new start. Now . . .

"You don't like America?" he asked.

"I miss my friends."

"I know Liebchen. I do too."

"Do you like Lady Margaret?" Jessie asked suddenly.

"What? Where did that come from?" His mind suddenly remembered the scent of roses, raven black hair, and curves.

Jessie shrugged.

"I don't think it's important that I like her. I certainly think it's very nice of her to allow us to stay here."

"I think she's nice." There was a hint of loss in her voice and Markus' heart ached for his daughter. And then, as though she needed to balance the books, she added, "She's very bossy though."

Markus rolled his eyes. "She's definitely that."

5

Oh Wow! She Thought

(Wednesday: New York, Commonwealth of America, Mainline)

Jade looked round, surprised, as someone rang the bell on the front door. She'd asked the Agency to send someone around at about six, but – she caught sight of the time and swore. It was already ten-past. Giving up on trying to fasten the top button of her jacket, she took the stairs to the foyer two at a time, just beating James to the front door. She gave the butler an apologetic grin as she opened the door to find a tough-looking woman with bright red hair cut short into a skull-hugging buzz-cut standing on the top step. The high-collared scarlet uniform she wore had obviously been personally tailored, given the way it showed off her physique, and the Agency's distinctive brown felt campaign hat with its highly unofficial pinch front crease was worn rakishly low over her forehead.

"Karen," Jade said, pleased to see her old Academy classmate, and quickly pulled her into a hug. "Where have you been? I haven't seen you for ages!"

Karen gave her a wide grin. "I've been off line, heading up a security detail on Chikyù for a couple of months. I just got back, and the brass said you had a job for me."

"I do. Here, let me take that." Jade accepted Karen's duffel bag and stowed it behind the umbrella stand next to the door. The bag clinked slightly on the yellow marble floor. Not entirely unexpected, given Karen's preference for automatic shotguns. "Come on, I've arranged for tea to be served in the library."

"Nice house," Karen said, admiring the mural on the ceiling of the foyer.

The mural displayed the Greek God Hermes bestowing a wreath of laurel on a group of naked male runners.

"It is," Jade agreed. "Unfortunately, our principal doesn't own it. It's a loaner from a friend of the family."

"So, who is she?" Karen asked when they were ensconced in the library, each with a mug of sweet, black tea in hand. "The Agency said you'd brief me."

"Margaret Peric. She's the new director-general for Food and Agriculture. She's also the sister to the new World Leader of Notway, and first cousin to our esteemed First Leader."

Karen let out a low whistle.

"Yeah, that's what I thought, but she's pretty grounded despite all that."

"So why the need for extra security?"

"A Mr. Ackov tried to speak to her last night and two people attempted to silence him. We're concerned they may try again."

"An immediate threat?"

Jade shrugged. "Possibly."

"And Mr. Ackov, I presume he's still here?"

"Yes, with his daughter. The Agency told you we need a live-in for a fortnight?"

Karen nodded. "Already packed," she said, jerking her head toward the front hall and her duffel bag. "So, what will you be doing?"

"I've got something to do in the city today, but my role will be to continue to provide primary protection for the principal."

"You'd better fill me in then . . ."

By the time Jade had completed briefing Karen, shown her over the house, and finished introducing her to the staff, it was almost eight o'clock.

"Margaret should be down for breakfast by now," Jade said, checking her watch. "Do you want me to introduce you to her now or wait until after breakfast?"

Karen shrugged. "Whatever you think is best."

"Let's get it out of the way then, and you can unpack and start with your duties."

"Fine by me."

Margaret was in the dining room. Normally she would eat breakfast by herself, but this morning Jade was surprised to see Jessie perched on the seat next to her.

"Good morning, ma'am," Jade said as Margaret looked up at their entrance. "May I introduce you to Karen Carter from the Agency. Karen, this is our Principal, Margaret Peric, and Jessie. Jessie is Markus Ackov's daughter."

Margaret rose to her feet, wiping her hand on a napkin. "I'm please dto meet you, Karen."

Karen took her hand uncertainly, and Jade suppressed a grin. Margaret was indeed an unusual member of the Empire's elite.

"Ma'am."

"Would you care to join us for breakfast?" Margaret asked, gesturing at one of the empty seats at the table.

Karen looked at Jade, who gave her an almost imperceptible nod.

"Thank you, ma'am," Karen said.

"Jade?" Margaret asked.

"No thank you, ma'am. I need to get to the Agency. I've arranged for a driver and guard to arrive in half an hour to take you to your office. Karen can confirm their identity when they get here."

"Fine, I'll speak to you later tonight."

"Bye, Jessie," Jade said.

"Bye, Miss Carvello," Jessie said, looking up and giving her a dazzling smile.

Outside, the unusually smoke-free sky promised a hot summer's day. Jade paused on the doorstep for a moment to admire the sight of New York's Princess Helena's Central Park across the street. The dark green of the trees in their summer foliage dappling the turf under their canopy.

Jade had grown up in the tenements of Brooklyn, and to open your front door and to look out onto the greenery of the park was something she was sure she'd never tire of. But she was also a city girl, and after the Agency's two-week basic survival training course in the Catskills, she was convinced she never wanted to leave New York again.

Automatically she checked the flap to her holster was safely buttoned, then, adjusting her messenger bag more comfortably over her shoulder, she started down the steps with just a hint of a skip.

On the corner of Madison Avenue, she stopped to buy a hot dog from the cart on the corner.

"Morning, Miss Carvello," the seller said. "Same as usual?"

"Yes please, Bert," Jade said, handing over the one-pound note and accepting change with the hot dog.

She stood for a moment, simply enjoying the taste of the mustard on the red sausage. "Have I told you that you make the best hot dogs, Bert?" she asked, taking another bite.

"Several times, Miss Carvello," Bert said cheerfully, as he added another couple of wieners to the saucepan.

"Have a good day Bert," she said brightly around a mouthful of bun, and with a nod, she headed off to the metro that would take her downtown to the Ruckers' building.

At seven floors, the building was one of the tallest in New York, and the Agency occupied all seven, as benefited the headquarters of the largest private policing and security firm in the Cross-Temporal Empire. Jade paused, as she always did before entering, to stare for a moment up at the massive police badge that hung over the front entrance. Her hand unconsciously rising to touch the smaller version of the shield on her own chest. It was a constant reminder that she was now a member of an organization with a proud history , one that ran without interruption from its creation in 1854 as the North-West Territory Police.

"Miss Carvello," the receptionist said, looking up, as she stepped out of the lift on the fifth floor.

"Morning, Mr. McGovern," Jade said. "Is Inspector Terrance in yet?"

"He arrived five minutes ago. Do you want me to let him know you're here?"

"Please."

The receptionist phoned through. "Miss Carvello is here to see you." He listened to the reply, then nodded. "You can go in."

Jade's boss had a small office at the back of the building. It was hardly larger than a broom closet, but the Agency ran a very lean ship. 'Cheap' was the word Karen had used to describe them on more than one occasion.

"Jade," her boss said without looking up from the report he was reading, almost hidden behind the piles of files that covered his desk. "Take a seat."

Inspector Terrance was a small, rather stout man who, unusually for the Agency, had never been a field agent. Instead, he'd moved into Investigations from HR, where he'd been an auditor. Karen made no secret she despised him as a paper-pusher, but Jade quite liked him. He gave her a long rein and let her get on with her job, which wasn't the case with some of the other bosses she'd had over the past five years at the Agency.

He finished the page he'd been reading and placed the open file facedown over two of the stacks in front of him before looking up and giving her a nod. "Miss Carter arrived I take it?"

"Yes, thank you."

"So perhaps you can explain to me what all this is about."

"Of course." Jade quickly ran through the stabbing, and Markus' claims regarding the possible source of the potato blight.

"And you believe him?" the Inspector said.

"The stabbing does seem to provide compelling support for his claims."

He sighed. "I suppose so." He looked distinctly unhappy at the thought.

That was one thing Jade had noticed about Terrance, he preferred things to remain low-key and very quiet.

"Miss Carvello," he said with a wry smile, as though he could read her mind. "You may find excitement in this activity and the potential for a bonus and advancement. I, on the other hand, only see an increase in paperwork. Paperwork that I undoubtedly will be responsible for filling in, duplicating, and filing as I have found you constitutionally unable to do it."

She grinned back at him, unabashed.

"Is there anything else you need?" he asked.

"Yes, the knife." She pulled it out of her handbag. "I'm hoping you can ask records who purchased it."

He eyed it unhappily. "I'm afraid not. The recent cutbacks have halved their staff and they are presently about six months behind. Unfortunately, peace has not been good for the Agency, and we have all had to tighten our belts."

"Oh." She was unable to hide her disappointment.

"I can, however, offer you the temporary use of an empty office and a phone to assist you in making your own inquiries."

"Gee, thanks."

"My pleasure, Miss Carvello. Now if there's nothing else you need, I have some paperwork to do." He waved at the files that covered his desk.

"Of course."

"Please report to me by telephone at least every second day. And if you need additional resources don't hesitate to ask."

"I thought we had tightened our belts."

"Only in office staff at this stage, Miss Carvello. We are trying to hold on to our field agents. As you would be aware, three months training at the Academy does not come cheap."

"Two hundred pounds," Jade said, parroting her instructors at the Academy. At the time, it had served as an inducement for her to excel, to prove that the faith the Agency had had in her had not been misplaced.

"Which is precisely why we would like to keep them employed," Terrance pointed out. "And don't forget you need to check in regularly."

"Every two days," she promised, getting to her feet.

"Room 512, Miss Carvello," Terrance said, as she opened the door.

It took two hours of patient phoning before she got the information she wanted. But finally, she leaned back, satisfied. She had a name and an address. It was amazing what people would tell you when you said you were with the Agency; things that they often shouldn't have said – but this time she wasn't complaining. She checked the address she'd been given against the road map. West 132nd Street put it slap bang in the middle of Harlem, close to St. Nicholas Park. It was, from memory, an area that was pretty much under the control of the Anarchists.

She rolled her shoulders, trying to reduce the tension, as she pondered her next move. An Agency uniform would not be popular there, and certainly wouldn't open any doors for her. Rather it might have them slammed in, or into, her face. That meant plain clothes.

She checked her watch. She should have time to get back to the flat, change, and be out again before lunch.

6

Vignette: The Agency

'The North-Western Policing Agency' is the C-TE's largest, and premier private policing and security firm. More familiarly known as The Rucker's Agency, or simply 'The Agency', its long and distinguished history began in the 1850s. When, in 1852, Edward Rucker (a Chicago attorney) and Allan Pinkerton (a Scottish American detective) formed the North-Western Policing Agency.

A significant boost to the Agency's fortunes occurred in 1871 when the Commonwealth of America's Congress appropriated 25,000 pounds to create the Department of Justice. Intended to "detect and prosecute those guilty of violating British law in the Americas", the amount proved insufficient to create an investigating unit, and the Department contracted the services of the Agency.

With the establishment of the Cross-Temporal Empire, the Agency expanded rapidly to provide close protective and detective services across the C-T E. With its motto 'Semper ille nostram' (we always get our man) and its distinctive high-collared scarlet uniform, the Agency remains a much-loved institution.

The North–Western Policing Agency Media Relations Unit.

7

A Gift Basket

(Wednesday: New York, Commonwealth of America, Mainline)

As Jade opened the door to her single bedroom flat, the scent of lemon and lavender, from the potpourri positioned in the center of the dining room table, wafted out around her, reminding her of home and her mother. Once again, she made a promise to herself to phone her mother as soon as she had a spare half hour.

A quick look round confirmed that her next-door neighbor, must have been dusting when she came in to open the windows and air out the flat.

There was the sound of scratching from the door opening onto the back balcony and the fire escape and she opened it to find Spencer, her neighbor's huge tabby, waiting to greet her.

"I'm sorry, fatso, I don't have any milk. I'm only here for a couple of minutes."

He ignored her and stalked into the room.

She raised her eyebrows, but it wasn't worth arguing with him. He'd leave when he'd convinced himself she wasn't lying about the absence of food.

She changed quickly into the maid's dress she had in the cupboard; an ankle-length, striped patterned split-dress with a sloped waistline, stiffened bodice, high neckline, and a small straw bonnet. She replaced the service revolver with a mousegun that went into an ankle holster on her left leg. A knife and her lock picking kit went into a pocket on the inside of the dress. She checked nothing was visible in the mirror, then took a moment to give her bobbed hair a quick couple of brushes. Her skin was browner than was thought quite proper and she considered powdering her nose, before deciding against it. Jade thought her snub nose one of her best features, even if it did make her look younger than she was. She'd been about ten when she'd read that only five percent of people had a snub nose and she smiled, remembering her mother's reaction when she told her. The reaction had involved a ten-minute lecture on the risks of pride.

She took a moment to adjust her dress. By the time she was ready, Spencer was waiting to be let out. He gave her a snooty look as she opened the door for him.

"I told you," she told him as he stalked out, nose in the air.

The train carried her back uptown, and she stopped long enough at Macey's to buy a small gift basket which she had wrapped, before grabbing a pastie and hot chocolate for her own lunch.

She got out of the train at West 131 Street, climbing the steps out of the subway with what remained of the morning crowd. This area of Haarlem was fairly run down with vacant apartment blocks and grass pushing its way up between its pavings. The Anarchists' black flag hung from several tenements' balconies.

She had to suppress the urge to spit. There might be a lot wrong with the way the Empire was run but the Anarchists were so far up their own asses they couldn't see that their solutions would be worse than the problem they were trying to fix. And the entire premise that people were naturally good and would just work together was pie in the sky. All you had to do was look around to see that without the State, and the protections it offered, society would collapse.

Just great, she thought, when she got to the address she had. It seemed every single apartment in the building in front of her had a black flag hanging from its balcony.

There were two young toughs in new camouflage uniforms lounging by the apartment's front door. They carried rattan canes, similar to those used by the Police. One of them moved to block the door.

She held up the gift basket. "For Hermandez Cortez," she said.

"Let her in," the one who hadn't moved said.

The other tough took a step back, just far enough to let her know she was allowed in, but close enough to mean she had to push past. Prick, she thought.

Inside, she looked back. "Second floor?" she asked.

"Flat 201," he confirmed.

The walls on the second floor needed a fresh coat of paint, and the floor was dirty. Mud had been tracked in after the last rain, which must have been, when, three weeks ago? That just confirmed in her mind the weakness in the whole Anarchist thing.

Flat 201 was the closest to the lobby and she knocked, hoping it would be unoccupied. Automatically she checked the lock. A Lockwood; good, she already had the bump key for that.

There was some sort of rhythmic thumping from inside, which abruptly stopped. A moment later, the door swung open, and she jumped back, startled.

"Oui?" the person who'd opened the door said with a strong French accent. He was about her height, unshaven, with short, brown, frosted hair. He was shirtless, and his jeans were missing their knees.

"Yes?" the person prompted again, swapping to English.

She lifted her gaze back to his face, her face flushing as she realized she'd been staring. But goodness, with a stomach as flat and as muscled as his . . .

"Hermandez?" she asked.

"No, Carlos."

"Pardon?"

"I'm Carlos Babineaux. Hermandez isn't here."

"Oh, can you tell me when he'll be back?"

He shook his head. "Sorry, I'm not sure."

"Can I wait inside until he returns?" she asked, hoping for the opportunity to have a look around the apartment.

"You'll be waiting a while. He won't be back for at least a couple of days."

Interesting, she thought. She waved the package she was carrying at him. "They asked me to deliver this to Hermandez and I don't think it will keep."

"What is it?"

"A gift basket. The tag says it's from an admirer."

"An admirer? Well, you could give it to me," he suggested hopefully.

He really had a nice smile, she thought. And it wasn't as though she actually wanted to take it back.

"And who do I tell him delivered it?" Carlos asked, taking the basket from her, and at the same time giving her an obvious once-over.

"Jade," she said, trying to ignore the impulse to check her hair.

"Well, Jade, would you like to help me open it and have a mug of tea before you head back?"

Jade pretended to consider the matter. "Thank you," she said.

Carlos stepped back, holding the door open for her. As she entered the small vestibule, the unmistakable odor of fresh solvent stung her nostrils.

"I'd better put a shirt on," he said, as he closed the door behind her. "We have to keep the windows closed because of the dust, and it gets boiling in here."

"It would help," she admitted. She was finding it difficult to concentrate.

The vestibule opened into a small room filled with two trestle tables. A mimeograph duplicator was set up on one trestle, the table's pine wood surface sagging under its weight. Piles of paper were placed in ordered stacks on both trestles. A tiny kitchen was built into an alcove along one side. There were three closed doors on the other side of the room, and a small stack of used placards in the corner.

Carlos picked up the tee shirt that was draped over the back of the seat and pulled it over his head.

Jade had the feeling he was teasing her, but even so was unable to avoid watching the play of his muscles under his skin as he did so. However, when he gave her a wink, she turned her nose up at him and turned her attention to the pile of papers on the trestles.

"So, what are these?" she asked, picking up a sheet. It looked like some sort of newsletter.

"Be careful," Carlos said quickly. "The ink's still wet."

"You could have told me that before," she muttered, as she examined the purple ink now smearing the tip of a finger.

Carlos handed her a rag, and she wiped her finger carefully, trying to avoid adding more ink. The rag was not exactly clean.

"We've got a public meeting Wednesday night," he explained. "I don't suppose you'd be interested in attending."

"I might be," she said, thinking it was probably her best bet to find out more about Hermandez.

"It starts at 8 p.m., at the Central Mission."

"Sure, why not."

"Is English Breakfast all right?" Carlos asked as he stuck the kettle under the tap and turned the gas hob on.

"Have you got anything else?"

Carlos peered uncertainly into a cardboard box on top of the fridge, stirring the contents around with his finger. Finally, he pulled out a tea bag. "I appear to have an Earl Grey."

"English Breakfast will be fine. Bergamot makes me sick."

"One English Breakfast coming up," he told her.

8

Not Just a Figment of Someone's Imagination

(Wednesday: New York, Commonwealth of America, Mainline)

Margaret was trying to make sense of the files she'd had her secretary, Michael, pull for her from records when the phone rang. She'd asked for all the files on any major outbreaks of crop disease in the last fifteen years and had been presented with three full boxes. From the summary Michael had attached it appeared there had been five major outbreaks in the past two years; one outbreak of wheat rust, another of potato blight, and three of bacterial rice blight. Before that the only significant outbreak appeared to have been the epidemic that had wiped out the potato crop in Russia twelve years before.

"Yes Michael," she said, picking the phone up.

"It's the First Leader for you," Michael said.

Margaret rolled her eyes. Somehow Michael managed to put a degree of disbelief into each word. Perhaps if it had been the first time, but this would be what . . . the third time Donald had phoned her at work.

"Put him through, Michael," she said.

There was a click. "Margaret here," she said.

"Just putting you through to the First Leader," came the reply from Donald's Executive Assistant.

"Hello Margaret, what can I do for you," Donald said.

"Hold on a moment Donald." Getting up, she poked her head out of the door. "Michael, could you take a fifteen-minute break?"

"Of course," he said, looking up, surprised.

"Thanks."

Back at her desk she picked the receiver up again. "Sorry about that, I just needed to clear my secretary out from his desk."

"Oh?" She could hear the edge of uncertainty in Donald's voice. "What's wrong?"

"What's not wrong," she said, and felt ashamed at the whine she heard in her voice. "Sorry, I'm still feeling as though I'm drowning here."

"That's not what I've been hearing."

"And how would you hear anything over there on the West Coast?"

"I have my sources."

"They're obviously not very good if they didn't tell you that my Director of Science and Research resigned last week without giving me notice."

"Actually, they did, and they mentioned he'd been undermining you every chance he could, ever since you arrived."

That was the truth, and Margaret had never been so happy to see the back of someone in her life, even if his departure had meant she'd had to move a couple of her directors around to cope with the sudden hole in her management team.

"Hold on a moment," Donald said. There was a muffled conversation in the background. "Sorry about that," he said when he came back on.

"That's all right. The reason I called was to find out if you had heard of any instances of environmental terrorism."

"No . . ." Donald said doubtfully. "Should I have?"

"I'm not sure." Margaret described what Markus had discovered, and the subsequent attempt on his life.

"And you believe him?" Donald asked.

"Given the three boxes of files I'm looking at right now I don't think I can do anything else. From what I can work out there's been something like five major outbreaks of diseases affecting crops in the last eighteen months, compared to just the one in the previous fifteen years."

"How do you define major?"

"Continent wide at least."

"Where were they?"

She could hear the frown in his voice.

"Mainline, Clyde, Huis, Kleng, and Notway."

There was a silence.

"Are you still there?" she asked finally.

"Yes. It's just those were all Clemhorn allies during the civil war."

"Oh." She pursed her lips.

"So – why haven't we known of this?"

"I don't know. The reports all appear to have been signed off properly, but there's no mention of any action. It might be sloppy work, or it could be something else."

"Gods."

"Exactly."

"Hold on." There was another muttered conversation finishing with, "give me ten minutes."

"All right," Donald said, back on the phone.

Margaret shook her head, wondering how Donald did it. "It seems we've got two problems," she said. "The first is that we appear to have some documented instances of environmental terrorism. What we don't know is how much of an issue it actually is or who might be responsible."

"And secondly."

"Secondly, there may be some sort of conspiracy within the Department to hush it up. And until I've established the extent of that conspiracy, I can't just throw everyone onto the task of trying to find out the extent of the first."

"That does sound like a bit of a problem," Donald admitted. "But the second might be something I can help you with. Have you heard of the Office of the Comptroller-General?"

"No," she admitted.

"Neither had I until a month ago." She imagined him grinning at her at the other end of the phone. "It turns out they're a para-military agency attached to the First Leader's Office. I attended a medal ceremony for them three days ago."

"So, what does this Office actually do?"

"As I understand their role, they're basically auditors, but they tend to focus on monitoring income at the World Leader level."

"And they're a para-military organization?"

"I know, accountants with guns, how cool is that!"

"Careful Donald," Margaret said, unable to help a smile. "Your inner nerd is starting to show through."

She heard him laugh.

"Anyway, if you're interested, I can get the Comptroller-General to speak to you."

"I'd appreciate that," Margaret admitted. "I wouldn't know where to start, or more importantly who to trust. It might simply be a case of someone being too timid but . . ."

"Perhaps, but this attempt on the life of your informant . . ."

"Markus, yes, I know."

"Of course it might turn out to be a case of using a sledgehammer to smash a walnut, but if I can't have a little bit of fun now and then why am I doing the job? Besides, it would be helpful to have my other director-generals a little worried about their own jobs. Too many of them seem to think it's still a matter of business as usual."

"In which case I am happy to help."

"How are your parents?" Donald asked, suddenly changing the subject.

"You'd know better than I would. I understood they were in Naisre last month."

"Yes, but I thought you might have spoken to them since then."

"Only a letter from my mother, who's asked me to try and locate Louise."

"Louise? What's happened to her?"

"Apparently she walked out on Daniel, her fiancée. I've got an address in New York but she's not answering my notes."

"Do you want me to ask Imperial Security to help?"

"No, I can manage. So, how's Defella?" she asked, referring to Donald's partner who was from the Dynand Line.

"Resting at the moment. The pregnancy is proving more tiring than she expected."

"You're pregnant?" she exploded. Talk about unexpected!

"Well not me, but yes we're expecting."

"And you didn't tell me?"

"I thought I had."

"Donald, you've got a mind like a sieve," she said crossly. "How's Artos taking the news that he's going to have a half brother or sister?"

"I'm fairly sure he doesn't know yet. School's on at present and with him in Charleston, and me here, well . . ." He trailed off. "Anyway, he's due to fly out in a week." He sounded much happier at that piece of news.

"And Matija?" she asked, referring to Artos' mother.

"She'll be coming out with him. I thought I might tell her when she's here."

"How do you think she'll take the news?"

"Oh, she'll be ecstatic. If there's another heir there's less pressure on Artos."

"I suspect you're right," Margaret said. Matija was someone who valued her privacy. Something she'd had very little of as the mother of the First Leader's only heir.

"Look, I've got to go," Donald said suddenly. "Business calls and all that. I'll get the Comptroller-General to call you."

"Thanks, and please give my congratulations to Defella. I know how much she wanted a child."

"Will do. Take care."

***

It was nearly six when she knocked hesitantly on the open door to Markus' bedroom.

"Ah Miss Peric, come in," Markus said, looking up from the Doctor Seuss book Jessie had been reading to him.

Jade, who was sitting on the chair in the corner, gave her small nod. "Mrs. Mack found some of the children's old books. She thought Jessie might enjoy them."

"And does she?" Margaret asked, giving Jessie a smile.

"Very much Miss Peric," Jessie said sincerely.

"May I ask how your day went?" Markus asked.

"Perhaps later," Margaret suggested, giving Jessie a significant look.

"It's all right Miss Peric," Jessie said. "Mrs. Mack said I can help the cook prepare dinner. We're having *boeuf au vin rouge avec du fromage de chou-fleur*." She pronounced the French with exaggerated care.

"Bright girl," Margaret said, as Jessie closed the door behind her.

"Very," Markus said, proudly.

Margaret frowned. "But beef in red wine with cauliflower cheese?"

"I like cauliflower cheese," Jade protested. "We used to have it every Friday when I was growing up."

"At least it sounds better in French than it does in English," Margaret conceded. "So, how did your day go?"

"I've been asked on a date to attend an Anarchists' meeting on Saturday night."

"I presume that's part of the investigation?"

"Of course. I think I've found the owner of the knife that was used to stab you," she told Markus. "He's an Anarchist, but he's not around at the moment so his flatmate is taking me to the meeting."

"An Anarchist? What did I do to upset them?"

"Possibly nothing. But they did seem better off and more organized than I would have expected so they may be raising money by providing guns for hire."

"I had an interesting conversation with the First Leader," Margaret said. "Followed by an even more interesting conversation with the Comptroller-General."

Jade frowned. "And just who is the Comptroller-General when they're at home."

"Apparently, he leads a para-military agency linked to the First Leader's Office responsible for dealing with financial crime and the smuggling of technology off line," Margaret explained. "In my cousin's words 'Accountants with guns', but then he's easily impressed."

"And what did the Comptroller-General say?" Jade asked.

"He'll have a team here early next week. He's agreed to keep my name out of it for the time being. After all, if no one in the Department has done anything wrong, and they find out I called the auditors in my standing in the Department is going to be shot. They're operating under a cover story that it's a request by the First Leader to begin a rolling audit of all Departments."

"Makes sense, I guess," Jade said slowly. "I'd have just gone in and kicked some doors down."

"If it's any consolation, according to the Comptroller-General, they will arrive equipped to knock down as many doors as necessary." She turned to Markus. "And how are you feeling today?"

He shrugged, and then winced. "Bored," he admitted. "But I do need to thank you again for putting up with Jessie and me. I am very much in your debt."

"If we find what I'm afraid we'll find then I'll be in *your* debt," she assured him. "Which reminds me, did we pick up your personal belongings?"

"They arrived this afternoon," Jade said. "Karen said the team who picked them up reported the room had been ransacked though."

"I'm sorry to hear that," Margaret told Markus sincerely.

Markus shrugged. "Jessie and I are safe."

"I must say you are remarkably composed," Margaret said. "If it had been me, I'd have been spitting chips."

"I think I would have been seven years ago, but after the death of my wife I've realized that property isn't the most important thing in life."

Margaret nodded. "I understand. My parents were never the same after the death of my brother." She looked at her watch. "I'd better have my bath if I want to be ready in time for dinner."

"Wouldn't want to miss *du fromage de chou-fleur*," Jade said.

"Absolutely not."

9

I Didn't Know Netball Was That Dangerous

(Saturday: New York, Commonwealth of America, Mainline)

It was a humid Saturday evening as Jade approached the Central Mission; a large, imposing brown brick building that dominated New York's Union Square. She'd dressed down for the meeting in denim trousers and a brown waistcoat over a simple cotton blouse. An oversized cloth cap completed the outfit. She wasn't expected back at the house until Sunday night so being free until then, it felt more like a date than she had expected.

She was unsurprised to see police stationed around the five entrances to the square. They clustered around their vans, with the steel grills already lifted into place over their front windscreens. There had been increasing tensions between the city's police and extremist groups over the past year or so. The Anarchists were only one of many such groups seeking social change after the war, and Jade could name another four without difficulty. For the moment they seemed to spend more of their time fighting each other than they did the police, but that could change at any time. And if it ever did, it would probably bring the city to its knees.

There must have been ten Anarchists in their new camouflage uniforms hanging around the main entrance. Like those at Carlos' apartment, they carried rattan canes, and empty holsters on their belts. The absence of guns didn't reassure Jade. If they needed to, they could probably arm themselves inside five minutes. For a group that believed in the supremacy of the individual and the overthrow of the State they appeared remarkably organized.

A young lady, about Jade's age, stepped forward to block her entrance.

"I'm sorry miss, this is a private function," she said politely.

"I know," Jade said. "Carlos invited me."

"Babineaux or Denis?"

"Babineaux."

"It's all right Petra," said a familiar voice, and Carlos came down the steps. "She's with me."

"My apologies ma'am," Petra said, stepping aside to allow her to pass.

Jade barely gave her a nod, mesmerized by the half-grin Carlos was giving her. His short, brown frosted hair was tousled and she wondered how long he'd taken to get it looking just like that. He was every bit as cute as she remembered him, she thought, looking him up and down appreciatively. Returning her gaze to his face she found him watching her knowingly.

"I see you've changed your trousers," she said dryly.

"Pardon?" He looked genuinely nonplussed.

"No holes in the knees."

"Ah . . ." he looked down. "They were old ones. I didn't want to get any ink on these. It's impossible to get it out." He held up his hands to show the ink ingrained in blotches on his hands. He had long delicate fingers and she wondered why she hadn't noticed them before. "We'd better go in," he said. "The meeting is about to start."

"I didn't know if you were going to show up," he confided as he led the way up the steps.

"I said I would," Jade said.

"You did," he admitted, holding the door open for her. "I'm going to have to leave you once I've got you a seat. But I would like to buy you a coffee or something after the meeting."

"Thank you."

Inside the main hall the auditorium was almost full, the quiet hum of conversation filling the air as Jade took a seat in the back row. She watched Carlos head toward the stage. He took the steps two at a time, and joined the other four already waiting for him behind the table set up on the stage. He did have a good body she thought, watching the flex of his muscles under his trousers as he took the steps. She wondered what he'd look like naked. It didn't take much imagination, given what he'd been wearing, or rather not wearing, at the flat when she first saw him. Feeling her face start to flush she fanned it with the flier that had been sitting on her chair.

A young lady two rows in front of her and on the opposite end of the row caught Jade's attention as she was also fanning herself. Though probably not for the same reason, she thought with a small snicker. The room was quite warm. As the woman turned to say something to her companion Jade caught her breath. It couldn't be! She quickly turned her face down and pretended to study the pamphlet.

The sound of someone tapping on the microphone and the sudden stilling in the room alerted her. Looking up she saw that Carlos had risen and taken the front microphone. More importantly, the young woman had also turned her attention to those on stage.

The meeting wasn't as bad as she'd thought it would be. Carlos, as MC, kept things moving along quickly. And the main speaker, who apparently was a representative from the Anarchists in London, was entertaining, even if the stuff he spouted about the rights of the common worker was idealistic claptrap that had as much in common with reality as flying pigs. She was impressed with Carlos' summing up at the end of his speech. He worked the crowd cleverly, and his request for volunteers to staff the voting booths for local council elections in two weeks' time almost had her on the verge of volunteering herself. The young lady two rows in front of her, however, was one of the first forward to add her name to the list.

As the screen to the kitchen on the far side of the wall was rolled up displaying the tea urns and plates of small cakes, Jade got to her feet and checked her watch. Only an hour and a half – impressive.

"Here you are!" Carlos said, unexpectedly appearing at her shoulder. He held out a hand with two teacups, one balanced on top of the other. In the other hand he carried a plate with two slices of what looked suspiciously like iced lemon sponge. For a moment she felt an urge to giggle at the thought of all these dangerous Anarchists sitting round genteelly sipping tea and carefully taking small bites of sponge.

"What?" he asked at her smile.

"Nothing; just can't picture you sitting around cooking sponge."

"Ah – there you'd be wrong. I originally trained as a pâtissier."

"Really! What made you give it up?" she asked, as she accepted the cup and the plate and allowed him to guide her back to one of the chairs.

"That would be telling. I hope you like your tea white? And I didn't add sugar, I thought there'd probably be enough in the icing."

"That will be fine," she reassured him. "But seriously, why did you give up cooking?"

He shrugged. "Honestly, I'm not really sure. I came down to New York for a change and just sort of fell into the movement. It certainly offers me more of an opportunity to make my mark on the world. My pastries were never going to let me to do that."

"You're Canadian?"

"French Canadian."

"French Canadian," she said, accepting his correction with an answering smile. She caught herself raising her hand to check her hair and decided to give it something to do and picked up a slice of cake.

She took a bite. It took a moment for the flavor to hit her, and then she almost swooned. The sponge was actually melting in her mouth, the mix of flavors was . . . whatever it was she loved it, the tartness of the lemon perfectly balanced by the icing.

She caught his self-satisfied grin, and a crumb went down the wrong way. "You bastard," she said, when she'd finished coughing. "You did cook them."

"Not all of them. Just that one. I take it you like it?"

"Like it, I love it! What do I need to do to convince you to come home with me?"

"Have lunch with me tomorrow?" he offered. "I take it you do have Sundays off?"

She couldn't help smiling back at his small-boy grin. "I think I could be persuaded," she said. "Oh, hold on. I'm sorry, I can't. I have a game."

"Poker? At lunchtime?"

"No, netball," she said, punching his arm lightheartedly. "The Bellvue Bombers. We're undefeated so far this year."

He frowned uncertainly. "I'm not sure I've ever seen a netball game," he offered.

"You're quite welcome to come and watch. Although I'm not sure that it's much of a spectator sport."

"If I turn up I'll be able to tell you whether it is afterward."

"We play on the North Meadow."

"Central Park?"

She nodded, realizing as a Canadian, sorry French Canadian, he might not be as familiar with New York as she was.

"What time do you start?" he asked.

"The first game starts at eleven."

"How many games are you playing?"

"Three."

"I'll be there then."

Jade checked her watch. It was getting on for nine. "It's time I headed back. I promised my mother I'd phone her before ten."

"I'll walk you," he offered.

"It would probably be more dangerous for you than it would be for me. You being an Anarchist in a city of Republicans."

He smiled back but didn't correct her. "I'd still prefer to walk you home."

"You can walk me to the subway," she allowed.

***

The first game had just ended when Jade spotted Carlos sitting on the bottom row of the bleachers.

"I'll be back in a moment," she told Holly, who was acting as the team's captain while Joyce was on her honeymoon.

Holly followed Jade's gaze. "Nice," she said.

"Keep your eyes to yourself," Jade said. "That one's mine." She was surprised to realize she meant it.

"Spoilsport. I don't suppose he has a brother."

"Holly, what would your husband say if he heard you say that!" Jade said, scandalized.

"We'll just have to make sure he doesn't hear."

Jade grabbed an orange and a cup of water, draped her towel over her shoulders and sauntered over to the bleachers.

"Hi," she said to Carlos sunnily.

"Hi yourself," he said, returning her smile, his gaze pointedly traveling over the uniform of blouse and short dress. She pretended to ignore the inspection.

"So, what did you think of the game?" she asked, starting to pick at the orange, realizing she'd forgotten to get a knife.

He reached into his waistcoat pocket and pulled out a flick-knife. Locking the blade, he handed the knife to her handle first.

"Is that legal?" she asked, knowing it wasn't.

"I guess it depends on whether anyone actually knows about it," he said with that disarming grin. One she could picture him practicing as a young boy in front of the mirror.

She took a bite out of the orange slice she'd cut and looked up to see him watching her.

She raised an eyebrow. "What?"

"Sorry," he said. "What was the question?"

"What did you think of the game?"

"I thought it was supposed to be non-contact?"

"Nah, that's just what we tell the guys so they don't want to play."

He shook his head. "I don't understand why the referee didn't penalize you for that elbow you gave that shooter in the face."

"It was an accident," she protested.

"Sure!"

Jade smirked. "The bitch deserved it. Look," she tilted her shoulder so he could see the three long scratches that ran down her arm.

"How did that happen?" he asked.

"She'd sharpened her fingernails," she explained.

"Is that allowed?"

"Of course not, but it happens all the time."

"That gives me a new appreciation of the gentler sex."

"It might be worth remembering," she said, handing him the knife back.

He flicked it between his fingers so that it passed from one side of his hand to the other, before closing it with a flick and putting it back in his pocket.

"Goodness," she said impressed. "Can you teach me that?"

"It might take some time."

She wiped the sweat off her face and swallowed the water as she caught sight of Holly waving her back.

"I've got to go," she said.

He frowned. "Unfortunately, I can't stay. When are you off next?"

"Saturday night. I'm in service."

"Can I take you out for dinner?"

"I'd like that," she said, standing up.

"So where do I pick you up from?"

"How about I meet you at your place?"

He raised an eyebrow. "If you're sure?"

She nodded, suddenly feeling the need to keep some distance between them. "I'll see you there. About six?"

At his nod she bent down and gave him a quick kiss on his cheek, then, grinning at his sudden flush, she turned and headed back to where Holly was now making hurry up gestures. As she did so, she put an extra swing into her hips.

"Did you have to be quite so forward?" Holly said, taking the bottle of water off her.

"And what were you talking about earlier?" Jade said. "At least I'm single."

Holly harrumphed, and Jade looked back over her shoulder to see Carlos still watching her with a look of consideration. She was in trouble she realized, then with a mental shrug, she turned back to join the team on the court. They had another game to win.

10

Vignette: New York City's Princess Helena Central Park

Settled by the French in 1600, New York was surrendered to Britain as part of the Settlement of Brest in 1664. While renowned for the beauty of many of its original public buildings, the Great Fire of 1905 left few standing, New York's City Hall being one of the few exceptions. Finished in 1815 the hall is the oldest city hall in the Commonwealth of America that still houses its original governmental functions.

Unlike other major cities of the Commonwealth (such as Memphis, or St. Louis) New York City was never provided with the massive fortifications that other cities gained because of the Russian threat. Despite this, as the Commonwealth's premier city on the East Coast, the city has much to offer the visitor, including the must-see attraction of the city's Princess Helena's Central Park. This park covers 843 acres and is the most visited urban park in North America, with about 5.2 million visitors every year, exceeding even the 3.5 million to the Russian Empire's much vaunted Yellowstone Park.

The Backpacker's Guide to the Mainline: New York.

11

An Unwelcome Package

(Monday: New York, Commonwealth of America, Mainline)

Jade had finished her breakfast and was enjoying her second cup of tea in solitary comfort before the others arrived when Margaret appeared. Despite the sun being barely up, she looked immaculate in a business suit which gave more than a nod to the current male fashion, with its military frogging and epaulets.

"Good morning, ma'am," Jade said, starting to rise to her feet but settling back into her seat when Margaret shook her head.

"How did the games go?" Margaret asked, heading for the coffee percolator, and pouring herself a cup.

"We won all three."

"So, still undefeated?"

"Still undefeated," she confirmed, surreptitiously trying to do the top button of her jacket up without Margaret noticing.

"Oh, don't worry about that," Margaret said taking a sip and giving a slow sigh of pleasure. Putting the cup on the table, she was turning back to the bain-marie to get some sausages when Mrs. Mack appeared.

"I'll do that, ma'am," she said taking the plate out of her hand.

"Thank you, Mrs. Mack," Margaret said resuming her seat and taking another sip of her coffee.

"You're up early, ma'am," Jade said.

"I got a message from the office last night. There's been another outbreak of potato blight."

"Where?"

"The Chikyù Line." She shook her head. "The Byre family is furious and demanding action. The thing is this is the first instance of potato blight on the line."

"So, Markus is looking increasingly correct?"

Margaret nodded. "I spoke to him last night. He gave me the name of someone in the Department I should speak to who's been investigating mitigating strategies for potato blight. I thought I'd ask Director Saito to talk to him for me. After that, she can start pulling together a team to begin planning for a worst-case scenario. She's new to the Department; came in from Naisre a couple of weeks before I started. She's bright, driven, and an early starter – which is why I want to be there before eight. And I also spoke to the Comptroller-General again. He's pulling together a local team who'll be on site by the end of the week, but the team leader will be flying in from Naisre by rocket plane today."

Jade whistled. "He seems to be treating this seriously."

"And so he should. The Chikyù Line was seriously affected by the war, and apart from the risk of famine it could seriously affect its whole balance of trade."

Jade hesitated, not really wanting to pass the next bit of news on. "I think I saw your sister at the meeting I attended on Saturday night."

"Louise?"

"I'm fairly sure it was her, from the photograph you showed me."

"What meeting?"

"The Anarchist's meeting."

"What was she doing there?"

"I'm not sure. I know she volunteered to help staff the booths for the council elections in two weeks' time though."

"Oh, great. That's all I need." Margaret shook her head despairingly. "I just hope Mama doesn't hear about this. I suppose I'd better try and visit and find out what all this is about." She looked at Jade enquiringly.

"You want me to put a tail on her?"

"Can you?"

Jade nodded. Inspector Terrance was going to be very happy with her, she thought.

"Just make sure it's unobtrusive," Margaret added. "I don't want to give her any excuse not to talk to us."

"Of course, ma'am. And I'll be coming into the office with you – I want to check your security there. I'm starting to get a bad feeling about all this. I can head on into the Agency afterward."

"Of course."

The lobby was deserted, and they rode the elevator to Margaret's office on the top floor in silence. On the fourth floor the elevator attendant opened the grille doors for them.

Michael, Margaret's secretary, had his feet up on the desk and was leaning back in his chair talking on the phone as they walked through.

"Morning, Michael," Margaret said, causing him to start, and almost fall off his seat.

Jade suppressed a snicker.

Margaret had just taken her seat behind her own desk when Michael appeared at the doorway carrying a package about the size of three large books tied up neatly with string. "This is for you, ma'am," he said, placing the heavy package on the desk in front of her.

"Ma'am!" Jade said warningly, her eyes fixed on the parcel as Margaret leaned forward to take it.

"What?" Margaret said, hand paused in mid-air.

"Michael, do you know who sent it?" Jade demanded.

"No, ma'am. There's no sender's address on it."

Oh shit, Jade thought. And there were way too many stamps on it for the package's weight and size. Carefully she picked it up. The contents felt bumpy inside the thick brown paper packaging, and there was something greasy on the underside of the package. She felt her heart beating harder against her chest.

"What!" Margaret demanded again.

"I think it's a bomb."

Margaret stared at the box; eyes wide. "What do we do?"

Jade didn't want to risk the elevator, and walking down four stories using the steps seemed a very bad idea. "Have you got a safe?" she asked Michael.

He nodded. "Behind my desk."

"All right, empty it, then get everyone out of the building."

He nodded and left.

"Is it safe putting it in the safe?" Margaret asked, then shook her head. "I can't believe I just said that."

Jade shrugged. "I don't know. What I do know is that it's unsafe to leave it here. Look, it would make me a lot more comfortable if you weren't here."

Margaret nodded. "In a moment. So, who's best to try and disarm it? The Police or the Agency?"

"Try the Agency," Jade said, carefully picking up the parcel and walking slowly out of the room after Michael. "They've probably got the most recent experience."

Michael had already emptied the safe and confidential files were strewn across the floor like confetti. Behind her she could hear Margaret in her office speaking to someone on the phone. After carefully placing the parcel in the safe she closed the door and engaged the latch without locking it.

"Okay?" she asked, looking up as Margaret appeared. She frowned as she realized that Margaret was carrying three archive boxes of files.

"They're on their way."

"Then we should leave," Jade said, standing up, and feeling a sudden need for urgency she started to usher Margaret toward the doorway.

They had just reached the door when a flash of light and a shattering explosion slammed her into the wall. Struggling to open her eyes she found herself lying on the floor, and Margaret bent over her, yelling worriedly at her.

"Why are you shouting?" she demanded, her ears ringing, as she started to raise her head.

Margaret frowned uncertainly. "English, Jade," she said. "And don't move."

Jade frowned as she ran through what she had said, before realizing she must have asked the question in Nayarit. It was a bit of a wasted language, but her mother had insisted on her learning it because of her great-great-grandmother, who had been one of the fifty-four to come through that first portal from Nayarit. The Nayarit Line was long dead now, but her mother had been so proud of that heritage, and so like the dutiful daughter, Jade had learned the language.

"What happened?" Jade said, realizing she was woolgathering. Her vision was blurry, and the slight movement had sent a knife of pain through the front of her forehead.

"The safe exploded."

"The safe? Oh, the parcel. It *was* a bomb."

"Afraid so."

Jade's eyesight cleared enough to see what looked like the door to the safe embedded in the plaster wall next to the door. Suddenly she started to shiver.

"What's wrong?" Margaret asked.

"Cold," Jade managed through chattering teeth.

"Hello?" someone called from outside.

"In here," Margaret called, and then Jade blacked out again.

She found herself drifting in and out of consciousness, watching with occasional professional interest as the medics checked her over. When Margaret insisted on having them take Jade home, rather than the hospital they seemed intent on, the argument became rather heated.

She finally emerged from the state of confusion and cottonwool that had enveloped her to find someone shining a torch into her left eye. She blinked, before working out that the red filling her vision was actually Mr. Castles' sideburns.

"Ah. You're back with us," he said, putting the torch away. "How many fingers am I holding up?"

"Three," Jade said, patting his hand away. "Where am I?"

"Miss Peric's residence. Lady Margaret insisted on my attendance. I must say that since your arrival things have been much more interesting. A stabbing, and now a bombing. Whatever will be next?"

"I sincerely hope nothing," Margaret said, coming into view, and resting a hand gently on Jade's shoulder.

Jade felt a sense of warm comfort from the touch.

"Yes, well, I really must leave now. I do have my own patients." He paused. "Keep her as still as possible for the next couple of hours. You have a headache, yes?" He held up a hand to forestall Jade's nod. "I will send one of my boys around with some tablets. Also, something for nausea if you need it. Don't eat or drink until I see you again. She can suck an ice-cube if her mouth gets too dry," he told Margaret. "And an icepack is fine for her headache. She is to rest for the remainder of the day but can get up tomorrow if she feels up to it. Possibly even return to work on light duties if I'm happy with her progress, but now, I really must go."

"Thank you, doctor," Margaret said, escorting him toward the door.

"So how do you feel?" Margaret asked, as she returned to Jade's side. "Do you want an icepack?"

"I think that might be an idea," Jade said carefully, feeling that she might just fly into pieces. "Um, ma'am," she said as Margaret turned away. "I'm sorry for putting you to this trouble."

Margaret arched one carefully manicured eyebrow. "Jade, I need to clearly state that this is nothing compared to the debt that I owe you. If you hadn't spotted the bomb, well . . ."

Jade suddenly saw real fear in Margaret's eyes. She had always admired Margaret's calmness and control, as representing the epitome of the ruling class she had committed her life to protecting. Now, for the first time. she saw that facade start to crack, and Margaret's humanity expose itself.

"It was nothing," Jade started to say. After all she had only been doing her job, but Margaret held up a hand to interrupt.

"No, it wasn't. And when you are recovered, we will need to discuss your future as I hope you will consider a permanent posting to my personal household."

"Ma'am," Jade started to protest but Margaret shook a finger warningly to stop her and Jade saw again the power that so enshrouded her principal.

"Ma'am." It was one of the household staff. "The First Leader is on the phone for you."

Margaret rolled her eyes, and reaching over to the phone next to the bed picked up its handpiece.

"Hello?

"Yes Donald. No I'm fine. The only casualty was Jade, my bodyguard. It could have been a lot worse, but the doctor has just diagnosed concussion." She gave Jade a reassuring smile.

Jade closed her eyes at the thought of her name being bandied round so informally with the First Leader. She just wanted to shrink into the ground. She had always worked hard to stand out, to get the grades she needed in the Agency, to steadily work her way up the career she had marked out for herself. But this, this was just too much.

"Yes, a letter bomb."

Even Jade could hear the oath that followed from the other end of the line.

"Look, I'm fine."

There was a moment's silence and Jade opened her eyes to see Margaret listening intently.

"If you think it necessary," Margaret said stiffly.

There was a pretty emphatic agreement from the other end of the phone.

"I've got to go," Margaret said. "Give my best to Defella."

"What was that about?" Jade asked, as Margaret placed the phone gently back into its rest.

"My dear, demented cousin is detaching a section of Imp-Sec to beef up my personal security."

"Oh." Jade felt disappointed. If Imperial Security was on the job there'd be little need for the Agency to be involved.

"I need to get back to work," Margaret said, pulling herself together. "I still need to speak to the Comptroller-General's team leader, and I've got to speak to Director Saito about setting up that task force." She checked her watch. "Assuming I can find them. The whole building is still a crime scene."

"Make sure you take Karen."

Jade simply lay there after Margaret's departure. The job was coming to an end. No reason to see Carlos again, and she was surprised to find just how disappointed that made her.

12

Sisters and Auditors

(Monday: New York, Commonwealth of America, Mainline)

Margaret had finished changing into a fresh suit that didn't smell of dust and explosive and had just picked up the lipstick when her hand started to shake. She stared at the hand as the shaking got progressively worse until the lipstick dropped from her fingers. The stick left a deep smear of red across the porcelain bowl. Lifting her eyes, she stared mutely at her reflection in the mirror.

A sharp knock on the bathroom door made her jump, and she looked round to see Mrs. Mack.

"Yes?"

"Your sister is here, ma'am."

"Sister?"

"Miss Louise."

Louise? What was she doing here? She checked her watch and saw it was almost twelve – so much for an early start.

"Is she in the parlor?"

"Yes, ma'am."

"Tell her I'll be down shortly."

Retrieving the lipstick, she considered the slight tremor in her hand for a moment before capping the stick and replacing it in its drawer. It would just have to do she thought, wondering how she let herself get talked into these things.

She stopped at the door to the parlor and watched her sister pace nervously in front of the small window that looked out onto the street. Good, Margaret thought, it appeared her sister might be even more nervous than she was. She stepped forward, then paused as she realized her sister had cut her hair. When had she done that? She tried to remember when she'd last seen Louise. Gods – was it actually two years?

"Louise," she said with fake brightness, striding in. "How nice to see you."

"Margaret," Louise squeaked, before recovering quickly, and giving her elder sister a nervous smile that showed her perfectly proportioned, white teeth.

Margaret suppressed a wince. Why did Louise always make her feel so gauche and . . . large. Her sister was thinner than she remembered, though the fine bones, high cheekbones, and small, pert nose and gloss-red lips remained unchanged. Her blond hair had been cut short and trimmed so it was shaped against the nape of the neck.

"I like the haircut," she said as she rang the bell. "Two teas," she told Mrs. Mack, when the housekeeper appeared.

"With canapés?" Mrs. Mack asked.

Remembering that it was almost twelve, and breakfast had been some time ago, she nodded. "And churros, please."

"Of course, ma'am."

Margaret studied Louise as her sister tried to affect indifference. "Take a seat," Margaret said.

Louise was wearing practical day wear, not cheap, but not the sort of quality she normally wore. And she was wearing less makeup than she'd worn since she'd put her hair up.

It seemed strange she had chosen to visit at lunch time on a workday, Margaret thought, until she realized that Louise had chosen this time because she had expected her sister to be out. She allowed a small smile to appear, which caused Louise to look worried, and slightly guilty.

Margaret raised an eyebrow. "So, little sister. What can I do for you?"

"What can you do for me? I'm returning your many requests to visit."

"Ah yes," Margaret said. "Mama asked me check on you. She was worried about you."

Louise rolled her eyes. "Of course, she wouldn't be prepared to tell you that I walked out on Daniel."

"And why did you walk out on your fiancé?" Margaret asked, deciding not to correct her sister about what Mama had said.

"Ex-fiancé."

They paused as Mrs. Mack appeared with the trolley.

"Thank you, we can serve ourselves," Margaret said.

They both watched Mrs. Mack pull the door closed behind her.

"Shall I pour?" Margaret asked.

"Oh, why not," Louise said, throwing up her hands, and taking a plate loaded it with several canapés.

"So why did you do it? What did he do wrong?"

Louise had already taken a canapé, and waved her hands, unable to say anything with a mouthful of food. "These are good," she said, when she was able to swallow.

"I know," Margaret said, taking a small bite on hers. The food settled in her stomach like lead. "So, what did he do wrong?"

"Wrong, nothing. That was the problem, he did nothing. There's a whole world out there and he was content with his little corner of it. Wasting his life, wasting *my* life. I wanted to do something."

"And joining the Anarchists *is* doing something with your life?"

"How did you know about the Anarchists?" Louise asked, freezing as she was starting to pour a cup of tea. "Have you been following me?"

"No, but a friend of mine recognized you at a meeting."

"I didn't expect you to mix in those sort of circles."

"I don't, but my friend . . ." She paused, recognizing Louise's attempt to divert her. "You haven't answered my question."

Louise sighed. "Yes, joining the Anarchists is achieving something meaningful with my life. Look around Mags, almost a quarter of the Empire live their entire life in poverty. The Anarchists are the only ones genuinely interested in lifting the living standard of the workers."

"I would imagine our esteemed cousin would disagree with that," Margaret said, trying not to rise to her sister's use of the diminutive, which she had always hated.

"Perhaps," Louise agreed. "But there's so much protocol surrounding Donald it's almost impossible for him to do anything."

"And me?"

Louise shrugged.

"And you're all right, physically, mentally . . ."

"I actually am," Louise said, sounding surprised. "For the first time in my life I feel I'm achieving something that's important. That's . . . genuine."

Margaret acknowledged the depth of her sister's feeling with a small nod.

Louise had finished her plate now and was studying the tray again, obviously wondering whether she could load up again. Given the way the canapés had been disappearing perhaps she hadn't been eating regularly.

"Do you need any money?" Margaret asked suddenly.

"Gods no," Louise said. "Didn't Mama tell you – I cleaned out Daniel's checking account when I left. It wasn't much," she said defensively. "And it wasn't as though he'd miss it. But I've probably got enough to last me twelve months, which should be enough time to get something sorted out before I have to come back to the family with my tail between my legs. Anyway, I've got a job interview in –" she looked at her watch. "Oh shit," she said, jumping to her feet.

"What?"

"I've got to go."

"Do you need a lift?"

"No, no, it's fine." She was already heading toward the door.

"Louise!" Margaret said, and her sister paused at the snap in her voice. "I'll tell Mama that you're fine on one condition."

"Which is what?"

"That you come by for tea sometime this week."

Louise flashed her a grin. "If the food is up to the same standard, I wouldn't miss it. Would Thursday be all right?"

This should, by all things fair, get Mama out of her hair, Margaret thought. "Fine, Thursday."

"Thank you."

Margaret stood, listening until she heard the door close, then with a sigh she rang for the chauffeur. She still had an auditor to meet.

***

Back at the building that housed the Department, the increased security was obvious, with three Imp-Sec officers in heavy body armor checking the passes of all those entering the building.

The concierge opened the door for her as she reached the top of the steps, and Karen followed her closely up the stairs.

Margaret paused, looking up at the top floor, and the shattered windows that yawned like empty eyes along the outer wall. She felt the tic jump in her right eye and tried to ignore it. "I don't suppose you know where my office is?"

The concierge held back a smile. "Yes ma'am, they're moving you to Jeffries' office."

"I'm not sharing it am I?" Margaret said warily.

Deputy Director-General Jeffries was twice her age and had a disgusting habit of chewing tobacco, a habit which had left his teeth badly stained.

"No ma'am. He's bumped the Director of Off Line Agricultural Services. They've been playing musical chairs ever since they were allowed back into the building."

"Thank you," she said, finally stepping through the door, and allowing Karen to visibly relax. "I have an appointment with Special Agent Aife Schneider from the Comptroller-General this afternoon. Could you let Michael know when she arrives?"

"Already here ma'am. She's waiting in your office."

Her new offices were considerably larger than her old ones, and she tried to hide how much she was enjoying this as she passed the Imp-Sec officer standing outside the office door. Jeffries must be really hating this, even if it was only another month until he was due to walk out the door and retire. Ag and Food, while one of the larger Departments was not one that ordinarily attracted the attention of Naisre. Now, with the cousin of the First Leader in charge, it was attracting a certain political interest that was not conducive to the quiet life he was used to, particularly given that as far as she could work out, he'd been in pre-retirement mode for at least the last two

71

years. That was one reason she was going to be glad to see the back of him. Well, that and his tobacco. A visit from the Comptroller-General was really going to ruin his week. Still, Donald had assured her this sort of thing was good for the public service, kept them on their toes and all that.

Michael had already taken his place behind the secretary's desk in the antechamber and rose to his feet as she entered. "Ma'am, you have some visitors." He waved at the two people who had risen to greet her.

The taller was male, and despite the very expensive dark navy woolen business suit he was wearing, he seemed very much like hired muscle. Very fit hired muscle, Margaret quickly amended, after assessing the way he filled out the suit. The shorter was . . . the opposite and was wearing a pink dress that made her look like a tiered wedding cake. Despite that, she carried a very businesslike, and extremely large briefcase.

"Aife Schneider, I presume," Margaret said, extending her hand to the vision in pink.

"Ma'am," Aife replied. "My aide, Agent Georges McGunn, from the local New York office."

Margaret acknowledged Georges' introduction with a nod. Despite his bulk there was no way he would be able to provide cover for his boss if someone started shooting at her. They were probably about the same weight, but he was at least twice Aife's height. She felt her lip start to quirk at the thought of him trying to a stop a bullet, a little like a goalie at an ice hockey match, and sternly told herself to behave.

"Please come through," she said. "Michael, tea, coffee, and chocolate, if you would."

"Of course," Michael said as she waved the two agents into her new office and followed them in, taking a seat at the head of the conference table that filled half of the open space. She gazed around consideringly – the table wouldn't have even fitted in her old office. She might have to consider keeping it.

"I heard about the bomb," Aife said, opening her brief case to remove a notepad and pen. "I understand your bodyguard was the only person injured."

"Fortunately, just concussion. The doctor said she could be back at work in two days," Margaret said.

"And do you think the matter is related?" Georges asked.

"I'm not sure," she said. "But it does seem too much for a coincidence."

"I do have a plan of attack," Aife said, indicating the neatly handwritten notes that filled up the first couple of pages of her notepad. "But my departure from Naisre was a little rushed and I am more unprepared than I would prefer to be at this stage of an audit. As a result, I would be interested in any suggestions you might care to make about where we might start."

"Of course," Margaret said sympathetically, feeling that Aife's description of her departure as a 'little rushed' was probably a gross understatement. "You might want to start by talking to the whistle-blower, Mr. Markus Ackov. You're aware he was an agricultural scientist at Ag and Food? Beyond that I have no idea. My own background is horticultural and military, not investigations."

"Of course, and where can we find Mr. Ackov?"

Margaret held up her hand in warning as Michael appeared and placed a tray carrying the requested drinks on the table. After serving everyone he retreated, pulling the door closed behind him.

"Mr. Ackov is staying at my house with his daughter for the moment, Michael can give you the address." She caught their glance. "Given there's already been one attempt on his life it makes security much simpler."

"I see." Aife checked her watch. "Perhaps we could talk to him after this meeting? We don't really have much time before the rest of the team arrives."

"Of course. And when do you think you'll be on site?" The tic in her eye spasmed and she swallowed.

"I'm planning for the day after tomorrow." Aife looked at Georges, who gave her a nod. "We'll initially have two teams. The first will be matching staff records to local banking accounts and looking for transfers of large, unaccounted sums. The second will be backtracking on what Mr. Ackov tells us. Trying to see where the trail goes."

"How many people will you have?"

"I expect twenty people on site initially, with perhaps another twenty or so by the end of next week."

"Sounds like a big operation."

"It is, but when the First Leader says jump —"

Margaret stood on the walls of the family palace on Dontfrey as dawn slowly eased its way over the city on the other side of the river. Behind her she could hear the subdued murmur of voices and the occasional jingle of harness as the troops below her waited for their signal. There was a hint of honeysuckle on the early morning breeze, and she took a deep breath, trying to settle her nerves. Abruptly the peace was shattered as the first of the howitzers on the terrace below opened up, and plumes of the thick, yellow, smothering gas started to rise from the red bricked blocks of the city. Once again, as she had for so many times since that day, she was checking the fit of her squad's gas masks. Then finally, as the dull thud of howitzers fell silent and the gate was opened, she was leading her squad across the river and into the city, the thick lenses of her mask casting her surroundings into a swirling fog of yellow murk; a murk that killed people, not gently, but in jerking, spasmodic convulsions.

"Ma'am?"

She blinked, for a moment still lost in the memory, not knowing where she was.

"Ma'am?" It was Georges, crouched in front of her, his face concerned. "Are you all right?"

She shook her head, still trying to collect her thoughts. "Yes, sorry. Just lost myself there for a moment."

"Here." It was Aife, holding a glass of water out to her.

Margaret took a sip and waved them away. "It's all right, I'm fine now."

Georges looked unconvinced and Aife raised an eyebrow. "Are you sure?"

"Positive," Margaret said, nodding, and tried to sound more confident than she felt. She'd never zoned out in front of anyone before.

"Then I think we're finished here for the moment," Aife said, looking to Georges. "We'll go and see Mr. Ackov."

Margaret watched Georges close the door behind them as the tic on her eyelid pulsed angrily. "Why now?" She hadn't had a flashback as bad as that in years.

Michael poked his head round the door. "Did you want me, ma'am?"

Margaret shook her head. "Sorry, just talking to myself."

"Then if you're ready, ma'am, I have some files for you to sign."

"Bring them in Michael," she said. She was damned if she was going to let this ruin her life. "And if you could let Director Saito know that I need to see her at her earliest convenience . . ."

"Of course, ma'am."

***

"Director-General Peric, you wanted to see me?"

Margaret looked up to see her newest Director standing in the doorway. She waved her in. "Sylvi, I hope I didn't drag you away from something important."

"Nothing that can't wait," the small blond said easily. Immaculately made-up and dressed in a pants suit that gave her a carefully cultivated appearance of professional competence, Sylvi was the Department's newest Director of Finance. There were times when Margaret wondered what the hell she was doing as the director-general in the face of Sylvi's calm professionalism. She certainly wouldn't have coped without her. She had come to rely on Sylvi's advice and guidance in understanding the Department's finances. Organizing the finances for a Battle Group of 915 people was no preparation for the skills required to manage a department of 95,000 people spread over 3,456 continents on fifty-four lines.

"Close the door," Margaret said, standing up and moving to the end of the conference table and the three boxes of files now waiting, dusted and cleaned of the worst effects of the letter bomb.

"Ma'am?"

75

"Margaret, please," Margaret reminded her. "Take a seat," she said, seating herself at the head, and gesturing for Sylvi to take the chair closest to her. "Before I start, I need to inform you that this meeting is confidential and comes under the *Official Secrets Act*. You are only to discuss the matters raised here with others on a need-to-know basis."

Sylvi's eyebrows rose.

"First off, a team from the Comptroller-General's Office will be on site for an unannounced inspection the day after tomorrow. Initially they'll be a team of twenty, but I understand that they'll have up to forty people on site within a fortnight."

Sylvi winced, and Margaret grimaced in sympathy. Having that many auditors going through the finances was sure to throw up all sort of discrepancies, let alone the disruption and additional work they'd cause even if everything was perfect, which it never was.

"The cover story is that it's part of a regular audit the First Leader has ordered for all Departments."

"But it's not?"

Margaret grimaced. "No, it's not. And this is not to be discussed with anyone. I have recently been made aware that someone, or a number of someones within DoAF have been actively involved in hiding the existence of significant outbreaks of diseases affecting food crops across the C-T E. The Comptroller-General's team will be working with Imperial Security to identify and arrest those individuals."

Sylvi swore. Then her eyes narrowed. "And you think they're working in my Department?"

"It's possible, but no, the reason I'm telling you is that I'm temporarily moving you out of Finance and putting you in charge of the team responsible for developing a plan on how to deal with the outbreaks we *have* identified, and their consequences."

"How bad is it?"

"There's been something like five significant, continental-wide, outbreaks of diseases affecting crops in the last eighteen months, and as far as I can see nothing's been done about any of them."

"Is the Rice Blast outbreak on Notway one of them?"

Margaret's eyes widened. "Yes. How did you know?"

"My family's on Notway. They're quite concerned. I've been surprised that I hadn't heard anything about it around the Department though."

"So now you know why."

"Where are the others?"

"Wheat rust on the Mainline, rice blast on Clyde and Huis. And Kleng's been trying to deal with potato blight for over a year, while the Chikyù Line's just come down with it."

"Why me?" Sylvi sounded puzzled. "I'm still learning about how the Department works. You've got any number of Directors, hell, even Assistant Directors who could do a better job than me."

"At the moment I don't know who I can trust. And frankly I'm not convinced that any of them *could* do a better job. Jeffries has let the Department slide for too long, and we can't let this continue – if we do people are going to starve."

Sylvi took a deep breath. "All right, what do you want me to do?"

"You need a team. Twenty, thirty people. You've got carte blanche to grab anyone you want from within the Department – just let me know who you want, and I'll get Michael to shake them loose for you. But don't strip Finance, remember they're going to have to deal with the audit team."

Sylvi pulled a face.

"You're also going to need to find office space, and furniture. I'm going to want daily updates and a draft action plan within a week." Margaret raised her hands at the expression of horror on Sylvi's face. "If it were merely difficult, I'd expect the plan by Wednesday; for the impossible you get a little longer. Look Sylvi, we need to get on the front foot with this one. Someone has been busy poisoning our food supply for the last eighteen months and I want them to discover they've got a tiger by the tail."

"Eighteen months!?"

"Yep. And there's two other things."

Sylvi's hand was rubbing the back of her neck. "Which are?"

"Let me know who's going to be doing your job tomorrow and I'll give them the good news about the audit team."

"And the second?"

"You're going to need to speak to Mr. Markus Ackov. He's the whistleblower, and is now staying at my house with his daughter for security reasons. Better make it tomorrow though, he's still recovering from being stabbed. Oh, and you can take these." Margaret stood up and pushed the three boxes across the table. "There'll be a test on their contents tomorrow morning." She smiled at Sylvi's hard sigh. "Sorry, bad joke. Michael pulled them together for me. I only managed to scan half of them last night but it's bad enough." She shook her head in disgust. "When I find out who's responsible –"

Sylvi nodded. "I'll get back to you tomorrow."

"Good, thanks."

***

Margaret got home around five to find Markus writing in the dining room as his daughter colored in a picture on the table beside him.

"You're looking better," Margaret said.

"Ma'am," he said, startled, starting to rise to his feet, then freezing as the blood drained from his face.

"Are you all right?" she asked.

"I just have to remember not to straighten like that," he said with a grimace. He slowly finished straightening, and then gave a small, careful, bow of his head. "Ma'am."

"Margaret," she reminded him.

"Margaret," he said with a smile. She was startled to realize he had a very nice one.

"Please," she said, waving him back to his chair as she took one on the opposite side of the table. "That's coming on well," she told Jessie, as Markus gingerly resumed his seat.

Jessie looked up and gave her a beaming smile before turning back to her task.

"What are you doing, if I may ask?" Margaret asked Markus.

"Agent Aife asked me to try and note down anything I could remember."

"You've spoken to her, then."

He nodded. "I wanted to thank you for believing me. When I was talking to the two agents it did seem unbelievable. I was surprised at how well she took it."

"After the attempt on your life, and the letter bomb this morning it would be a bit difficult for anyone to simply ignore your claims."

"Letter bomb?" He sounded shocked.

"You haven't heard?"

He shook his head. "Was anyone hurt?"

"Ms. Carvello was," Jessie piped up.

"What?" Markus demanded.

"Slight concussion only," Margaret said reassuringly. "The doctor said she had to take it easy for forty-eight hours."

"Ms. Carvello said the 'b' word when Mrs. Mack told her to get back in bed," Jessie said brightly.

Margaret raised an eyebrow. "And did she?"

"Of course she did," Jessie said. "You'd do what Mrs. Mack told you to do, wouldn't you?"

"I rather think I would," Margaret agreed, looking at Markus.

Jessie looked at the clock on the far wall and stood up, pushing her seat back. "Mrs. Mack said I could help prepare the table for dinner."

"Then you'd better not keep her waiting," her father said.

"Jessie seems a remarkably level-headed young lady," Margaret said, as Jessie disappeared through the doorway. "You must be very proud of her."

"I am. If it wasn't for Jessie, I'm not sure how I'd have got through Adriana's death."

"How did she die? I'm sorry – you don't have to answer that," she said, suddenly realizing how rude that must have sounded.

He shook his head. "It's all right. It was nineteen months ago. Heart attack. She'd gone out to teach; she was a dance teacher. She'd actually supported us while I was studying, and then I got a phone call from the hospital saying she'd been brought in but by the time I got there it was already too late."

"I'm sorry," Margaret said sincerely, seeing the pain on his face as he remembered.

"The funeral was the worst day in my life. All I wanted to do was to curl up in bed and pretend it wasn't happening, but I couldn't do that because of Jessie. She's the one who kept me going. I really thought this job with Ag and Food was going to be a new start. But now . . ." He gestured around helplessly.

"That can hardly be considered your fault."

"That doesn't help much," Markus said wryly.

"Perhaps not, but it is true. And now if you'll excuse me, I should go and see Miss Carvello. I'm interested to find out what the "b' word was that she used on Mrs. Mack."

"You mean there's more than one?"

"I know at least seven."

"Please, please don't tell Jessie," Markus said in mock horror.

"I have no intention of telling Jessie," Margaret said with a smile. She stood up, quickly resting a hand on Markus' shoulder to keep him from rising. "I'll see you at dinner."

13

Letter Bomb Injures One

(Tuesday: New York, Commonwealth of America, Mainline)

Carlos was perched on a bar seat inside the all-day diner, dunking his morning churro in his hot chocolate, when the first of the sedans pulled up across the road. He watched the three suits climb out of the vehicle. All were carrying briefcases, and from the way they were standing, they probably had shoulder holsters under their jackets. When the officer in charge of the Imp-Sec detachment on the front door simply waved them through, he raised an eyebrow.

Now that was interesting, he thought, not recognizing any of the three.

There was a folded broadsheet on the bar table next to him and, reaching out a long arm, he snagged it and opened it to the front page. Idiots, he thought, as he read the headline: 'Letter bomb injures one at DoAF.'

He scowled. Just what had those idiots in the Armed Action Wing thought they were doing? He risked another glance across the road. A second vehicle had drawn up and a short, rather round woman in a pink dress was being helped out of the back seat. If he'd been asked to describe her, the word 'blimp' would have come to mind, and he couldn't help smiling at the thought of her being towed into the building at the end of a rope. Her companion, who was helping her out the car, was definitely the one to do that. The man looked six feet of pure muscle.

He turned his eyes quickly back to the newspaper when he saw Margaret Peric step outside the building to personally welcome the woman. Behind her, partially hidden by an Imp-Sec Officer, was a female Agency bodyguard, obviously a replacement for the one injured by the bomb two days ago. He could just make out a bob of short, blond hair and frowned as something nudged at his memory. Everyone was ushered inside, and the glass door closed behind them.

He scowled at the newspaper. He'd warned them against trying to use a letter bomb. They were notoriously dangerous for all concerned. But no, they thought they knew better. And for some reason they thought that taking out the Director-General of the Department would disrupt the Department enough to finish their 'grand plan' to bring the C-T E to its knees. And perhaps, given Jeffries' incompetence, it might have. But what were they thinking about targeting the First Leader's cousin!

Shaking his head, he turned his folded broadsheet over and refolded it to read the sports page. Apparently, the Red Sox looked set to claim their third National series in a row. Not that he followed baseball, but the Red Sox had been so dominant this year it had been impossible to ignore them – even in a city so fixated on the Mets. For Carlos, the most interesting part of the season had promised to be the launch of a competing league to the Majors with both the Mets and the Yankees threatening to decamp unless they received a better deal. The politics and political backstabbing over the course of the year had even flowed out of the sports pages and onto the cover of the major newspapers on several occasions. He still remembered one memorable headline – 'Majors Beanballed' on the Washington Post, although he'd had to have that one explained to him.

Unfortunately, it seemed the Majors had managed to survive the year, and World Series Baseball was now firmly back in the bin. That was a pity; sports politics was so much more interesting to read about than the real thing.

Putting five cents on the plate for a tip he replaced the newspaper on the bench and stood up.

"Thanks, Sally," he called.

The waitress, who was drying glasses at the bar and talking on the telephone tucked under her ear, waved the cloth at him.

Outside, he replaced his hat, and without a glance at the building opposite headed downtown. He needed to speak to his contact in the building, try and find out who warranted being met at the front door by Margaret Peric herself, but in the meantime, he had a couple of errands to run for the Movement.

It was lunch time before he had the opportunity to find out who the DoAF's visitors had been.

"Adeline," he said, with no hint of a French accent, and a careful degree of surprise shading his voice as he came up behind the young lady in the payment line at the cafeteria two buildings down from the DoAF building. "What a surprise to see you here."

"Christos," Adeline said, turning to greet him with a brittle smile.

He gave her a reassuring smile in return, pouring on the charm. His contact was a junior clerk in records whose boyfriend ran a safe house for the Action Wing. She'd been a member with her boyfriend for several years, but had never really demonstrated any deep, personal passion for the Movement.

"Can I buy you lunch?" he asked.

"Of course," she said flustered.

He frowned at the hint of a bruise he could see over the top of the high-collared dress she was wearing.

She waited for him as he paid then they walked down to the small park on the corner together. Despite the weather, not all the benches were taken, and he chose the one tucked into the corner under the statue of Peter Stuyvesant.

"What can you tell me about the visitors that arrived this morning?" he asked, as he unwrapped the end of his roll, not looking at her as he did so, allowing his mouth to be hidden from observation.

"They're from the Comptroller-General. Apparently the First Leader has requested an audit."

He was pleased to see the way she tried to copy him.

"You're sure?"

She nodded. "We were all called into the main foyer to be told. Apparently, it's routine."

He doubted that very much. He nodded, though, and took another bite of his roll. "Don't do anything suspicious; you're too important to the cause where you are."

"Of course."

He doubted Adeline would be under any danger, but others . . . Ah, yes, that was the rub. At least it wasn't going to have to be his job to sort it out. Those idiots in Armed Action had stuffed things up with that botched attempt to silence Markus. In his view the better approach would have been to have snatched Markus' daughter. He'd been very careful not to suggest that, however – they might have tried it, and he hadn't wanted that on his conscience!

But now, to try and bomb the First Leader's cousin . . . it was going to be their job to try and get their coals out of the fire. And he was going to enjoy watching them try to do it. He had enough on his plate arranging the electoral campaign. And none of this was going to help that.

Suddenly he lost his appetite. He re-wrapped the sandwich and tossed the package into the bin.

"I'll see you around," he said, standing up.

"Of course," Adeline said, surprised at his sudden departure.

14

Dinner with the Enemy

(Saturday: New York, Commonwealth of America, Mainline)

Jade chewed at her bottom lip as she stared at the door to Carlos' apartment. It was six o'clock and she'd been staring at the door for the last five minutes, trying to work out if she should knock or simply walk away. There was no doubt she liked Carlos; the fact she'd caught herself singing in the shower as she got ready would have told her that, even if she hadn't spent the ten minutes before that shaving her legs. The problem was it would never work – they were simply too different. She was on the side of law and order and he – wasn't.

And let's not forget you come from Brooklyn and he's from Canada, a little voice chimed up sarcastically.

The mention of Canada brought back a memory of the cute way he rolled his r's. Behave, she told herself sternly.

Of course, the same little voice pointed out, it wasn't as though she was investigating Carlos, he wasn't the person of interest in this case. Well, not in that way!

She was still dithering when a young man taking the steps two at a time burst out of the stairwell and came to an abrupt stop when he saw her.

"Hello," he said. "Can I help you?" He had swarthy skin, with a heavy five o'clock shadow and a small tattoo of a teardrop under his left eye. He was wearing the unofficial uniform of the Anarchists: heavy denim jeans with a thick leather belt, and a red-checked flannelette shirt. The shirt had its sleeves rolled up and showed the hint of another tattoo on his right arm.

"I'm here to see Carlos," she said.

"Oh, you must be Jade."

"Yes," she said, startled to be recognized.

"Carlos hasn't stopped talking about you," he explained with a smile. He thrust his hand out. "Hermandez."

Ah, the owner of the knife that had been used on Markus, and *the* person of interest for her investigations. "Carlos' flatmate?" she said.

"That's me."

"Carlos mentioned you were on a trip. I hope it went well?"

"Very well." He pulled his keys out of his pocket and unlocked the door. "Carlos," he called. "Look who I found lurking outside."

Carlos appeared from the small kitchenette. "Jade!"

Her heart gave a little jump when she saw him. This was definitely a bad idea, she thought.

Picking up his wallet and sliding it into his back pocket Carlos draped an arm possessively around Jade's shoulders. It felt good, and it took her a moment to consider that perhaps she shouldn't be allowing him to take such liberties, but then again if it got her away from Hermandez without any questions all the better.

"Don't wait up," Carlos said edging her toward the door.

"Wouldn't dream of it," Hermandez said, a broad grin on his face.

As Carlos guided her toward the stairs she tried to work out what she should do about Hermandez. If she tried to bring him in it would blow her cover, and the ownership of a knife used in a crime wouldn't be enough to have him charged, especially as there wasn't anything else to link him to the assault. The best thing to do was to continue as she was doing and use Carlos as a cover to get closer to Hermandez. She suppressed a small jump of excitement at the thought. This was purely work she told herself sternly. But that didn't mean she couldn't enjoy it the little voice pointed out.

"Behave," she muttered to herself.

"Pardon?" Carlos said, even as she thought she heard the echo, 'in your dreams.'

"Nothing important," she said. "So where are you taking me?"

"It's a surprise," he said, releasing his hold to allow her to take the steps.

She felt a surge of disappointment, and ruthlessly suppressed it.

In the foyer at the foot of the stairs he put his arm round her shoulders, and held the door open for her. The two Anarchists lounging on the steps outside the front door touched their fingers to their caps as Carlos led her down the steps.

"So, where is this surprise?" she asked.

"Not far," he promised. "How did the games go?"

"The games?"

"Netball. You had more games after I left."

"Slaughtered them," she said, cheerfully.

"Not literally, I hope?"

"No, 57 to 20. I got twenty of them."

"And no injuries?"

"Not to me," she said with a grin.

"Actually, I meant to the other team."

She squinted at him, but he just grinned back unrepentantly.

He turned into a lane she didn't recognize and then he knocked on a door lit by a lurid green, flickering light. The door was opened by a bouncer wearing a suit and wide, white tie and she heard a saxophone in the background playing a jazz riff.

"A Jazz Dive?" she said unbelievingly, taking in the stale stink of cigarette smoke.

"You don't like jazz?"

"I love jazz, I just didn't think you would. My father used to adore it. He'd save up for months to buy the latest record by the Prince. Used to drive my mother crazy."

"Would you like me to introduce you to the band during a break?" he asked.

"Who's playing?"

"Tonight, Flash Daddy and the Fabulous Four."

"Yes please."

"You ever heard them play?"

She shook her head. "I haven't kept up to date with the scene since Dad died, but I recognize the name. They're supposed to be good."

"They are," he said.

The maître d' approached. "Your normal table, sir?"

"Please," Carlos said, allowing the maître d' to escort them to a table only a short distance from the stage.

Jade paused to watch the saxophone player as he finished his warm-up.

"More importantly," Carlos said, holding her seat out for her, "this place serves the best gumbo north of Louisiana."

"I'd never have placed you as a jazz aficionado," she reiterated as he took his own seat.

"You'd be astonished at what we pâtissiers get up to in our spare time."

"I'm astonished you have any free time given your other . . . political interests."

He shrugged. "It's not an *all*-encompassing passion. I do occasionally make time for the rare date with a very pretty woman."

She gave him a smile that caused him to blink, and when the waitress appeared with the menu, she waved it off. "I've been told the gumbo is good."

The waitress looked at Carlos who nodded. "Two gumbos. And for entrées could we have the coco rice with turkey, and a white beans and rice with shrimp." He looked at Jade enquiringly.

"Coco rice?"

"Basically, fried rice with cheese, onion and avocado. If you haven't tried it before I strongly recommend it."

"Sounds good to me."

"And two glasses of the house white," he added quickly. "Water?" he asked Jade, holding up the carafe.

"Please. So how did you find out about this place?"

He shrugged. "Would you believe me if I told you I had shares in the restaurant?"

She looked around at the surroundings, the subdued lighting, and the number of serving staff who were setting up.

She looked back at Carlos who raised an eyebrow at her. "How many shares?"

He leaned back in his chair, and she realized he'd been worried she wouldn't believe him. It pleased her that her view was so important to him.

"Half," he said.

"Being a pâtissier must pay pretty well," she said.

"I wish. No, I got left an inheritance from an uncle in France. It was just enough."

"So, the Anarchist has a capitalist side."

He shrugged. "The other half of the restaurant is owned by the staff. And all of the profit I make goes to the movement."

"A person with principles, and rich relatives." She raised her glass in a salute.

"No rich relatives in your past?" Carlos asked.

She shook her head. "No rich relatives that I'm aware of. Although my great-grandmother was one of the fifty-four Hraffor who accompanied Traek through the portal from Nayarit."

"Really!" His eyes opened wide. "I've never met someone who can claim to be a descendant of the original founders of the Empire."

"That's not surprising," Jade said with a laugh. "I worked it out one day that there's only about 240 of us."

He shook his head. "And no rich relatives . . ."

"Absolutely none. My great-grandmother was apparently of the Ejejatl caste; the caste that included the priests, artists, teachers, and scientists. Being a research facility, about half of the group were Ejejatl, but according to my mother, my great-grandmother was the only one from the priestly sub-caste. And the priests definitely believed in adherence to the duty of poverty, though luckily not to chastity."

Carlos had just been taking a sip of his water and burst out coughing.

"Do you need me to thump you or something?" Jade asked.

Carlos shook his head, gesturing with his hand that he was fine. Their waitress chose that moment to appear with the two entrées and Jade immediately transferred her attention to the plates. She inhaled deeply, the aromas making her stomach rumble.

"Are you happy to share?" Carlos asked, still short of breath.

"Can we?"

"Of course; two plates, Yvettia."

"At once, Carlos," the pretty waitress said with a smile.

Jade felt a sudden surge of jealously and put her hand on Carlos' arm possessively.

When the waitress returned Carlos' attempt to split the entrées between the two plates was stymied when Jade speared a piece of turkey with her fork. She chewed on it blissfully.

"What?" she asked when she caught sight of his expression.

"Nothing, it's just I've never seen anyone get so much enjoyment from eating turkey before."

She shrugged. "What can I say . . . I like food."

"Try the shrimp then," he suggested.

She decided to take his advice, swallowed the rest of the turkey, and stabbed her fork through the shrimp. The shrimp dissolved in her mouth. "Oh, that is good," she managed around her mouthful. "Here, you have to try it." She speared another shrimp and offered it to Carlos.

Carlos gave up trying to move the entrées onto their separate plates and, leaning forward, took the shrimp off the end of the fork with his teeth.

"Do I get more Brownie points if I introduce you to the chef?" he asked.

"Oh, I think you'd probably get me for that," she said.

He coughed explosively, and waved away her offer to help, covering his mouth with a napkin until he'd recovered enough to take a careful sip of water.

"You need to warn me if you're going to say something like that," he said when he could.

"Say what?" she asked, plastering a look of total innocence on her face.

He gave her a look that promised he would undoubtedly get her back for that and took a forkful of the coco rice.

"So," she said, deciding to ask the question that had been bugging her for the past week. "Why an Anarchist?"

He considered her thoughtfully. "I take it you disapprove."

"I didn't say that," she said, spearing another shrimp and avoiding his eyes.

"But you do?"

She shrugged. "It's just . . . look," she looked up to find his eyes fixed on hers, a small smile playing on the edge of his mouth, and it took a moment to remember what she was going to say. "I know the Empire's not perfect but the whole idea that by getting rid of the State everything suddenly becomes tickety-boo has to be the biggest pile of horse shit I've ever heard. I mean, seriously!"

"Cards on the table?"

"Of course."

"You're aware that before the Nayarit invasion the industrial revolution was driving an increase in the wealth of a small proportion of the population, forcing significant numbers into poverty?"

"And the pandemics that followed their arrival killed over seventy-five percent of the world's population, driving up incomes due to the scarcity of labor. I'm not stupid!"

"I didn't say you were," he said calmly. "But are you aware that in the C-TE the top one percent controls over sixty percent of its wealth. Against that, the bottom fifty percent owns less than two percent. That is grossly unfair, particularly as it's getting worse."

Jade stared at him, a piece of turkey stuck on the end of her fork, halfway to her mouth. Carlos leaned forward and took it himself. That action shook her out of her shock, and she speared the last shrimp on the plate with a triumphant glare. "No, I didn't."

He made a placating gesture. "If it makes you feel any better, I agree with you that simply removing the state and its machinery of governance would probably make things worse. But there does need to be some limit placed on the Empire's leaders. And in my view the Anarchists have the best chance of achieving that."

The band had settled into a jazz version of the latest dance hit and Jade's body began to move unconsciously in time to the music.

"Enough talk," he announced, standing up. "Would you care to dance, Ms. Carvello?"

"Why thank you, Mr. Babineaux," Jade said accepting his hand. "I believe I would."

An hour and a half later, the gumbo now a recent memory, Jade was leaning back trying to work out if she'd left enough room for dessert when there was a disturbance at the door. Several waiters were already moving toward it as Carlos started to rise to his feet. He paused and looked apologetically at Jade.

"Don't mind me," she said, waving him away.

He moved confidently around the tables, and Jade took the opportunity to watch him as he worked his way across the floor. He moved with a dominant, easy grace, and Jade's mind immediately flashed back to how he had felt as he'd led her into the first dance – smirking at the memory of the look on his face when she'd demonstrated her own moves. Four years with Miss Michelle's School of Dance had not been wasted.

The voices from the door had started to rise as Carlos arrived.

Grimacing, Jade got to her feet. She had plans for Carlos later that night and having him nursing an injury was not included in any of them.

Her view of the door was blocked by those filling it but as she approached one of the waiters was suddenly shoved back into the room. She sidestepped him as he fell back against a table. He grabbed at the tablecloth to try and keep his feet and the plates and cutlery slid to the ground around him to the sound of smashing crockery.

She heard Carlos' smooth, measured tones but she couldn't see him. Her path was blocked, and with a hand on the blocker's shoulder she pulled him subtly off balance to the right and went around him on his left. There were three men just outside, drunk, wearing leather jackets. She frowned when she noticed the emblem of the National Syndicalists, the *fasces,* the bundle of rods tied around an ax, on the patch on their left shoulders. Not good, she thought. The NS were even worse than the Anarchists., being utterly opposed to democracy. At least the Anarchists were at least willing to work within the framework to achieve their own goals until the State had withered away. She hid a smile as she realized how intently she must have been listening to those talking at the meeting she'd attended.

She glimpsed a knife being drawn, and one of the men grabbed Carlos to pull him out onto the street. A sharp elbow in the side of the waiter blocking her path and she was through.

"Knife," she called in warning. She hoped Carlos had heard as he gave no sign, but she was too busy to worry. All three had turned to face Carlos.

Aikijujutsu was not exactly an aggressive form of combat, so instinctively she swung her handbag. It did better than she'd expected as she'd forgotten the handgun in its concealed enclosure. The handbag struck one of the Fascists on the side of the face. As he turned, slightly stunned, she moved in, and struck hard for his neck while another hand moved for the grab on his arm. She felt her hand contact his elbow and knew she'd nailed it. The hold was perfect, and she drove him to the ground, pushing him forward so that he contacted the one with the knife on the way down. On the ground she brought a knee down on his neck, leaving her hands free to grab the shirt of the attacker with the knife, pulling him back and taking him down with a closed fist. She started to swing him round, but his head suddenly snapped back as the toe of a shoe caught him under the chin and he collapsed back against her.

She looked up to see Carlos standing there, glaring belligerently at the one he'd just kicked. Behind him, the third attacker was lying unconscious in the street. Maybe he hadn't needed any help, she thought.

"Sorry," he said. He placed a boot carefully on the open hand of the attacker she was kneeling on and ground his heel down on it.

"So, where did you learn to fight like that?" he asked, offering her his hand to help her to her feet.

"Would you believe the netball court?"

He raised an eyebrow at her, and she sighed, realizing he deserved an honest answer.

"My father. He was a black belt in Aikijujutsu and thought I needed to learn how to defend myself. I've been practicing off-and-on since I was five."

"A jazz aficionado *and* a black belt. I wish I could have met him."

There was a moment's uncomfortable silence.

"What are you going to do with these three?" she asked, to change the subject, and suspecting the answer wouldn't involve the police. She was not surprised to find she'd guessed correctly.

Carlos looked at those clustered round the door. "Boris, James, you need to take these three round the back while I telephone Hermandez and get a cleanup crew here. Chop-chop people, we have a restaurant to run."

She took the arm he offered her, and he led her inside.

"My apologies for the disturbance," he told those closest to the door, most of whom appeared to have been trying to follow what had been happening outside. "Nothing to worry about. A simple misunderstanding." He made wind-up gestures to the band for them to start playing. "Make sure everyone's offered a free drink," he told the waiters quietly as the band launched into their next song.

There was no doubt he was very smooth, Jade thought as a happy murmur swept around the restaurant.

Carlos bent down to her ear. "You'll excuse me for a moment, I need to make that phone call."

She nodded, but he was already making his way to the back of the restaurant, and the door marked 'Staff Only'.

Back at her table she arranged her skirt, frowning at the stain on the hem. She was still bent down, trying to work out how she was going to get the stain out when Carlos reappeared. He kneeled in front of her. Lifting the hem out of her hands he looked at the damage.

"You'll need a professional cleaner to get rid of that," he said, looking up.

He had the most glorious amber eyes, she thought. Lost in his gaze she was surprised to find their lips almost touching. Leaning forward she allowed her lips to press against his, lightly running her tongue over them.

"I'll send you the bill," she said suddenly remembering where she was and straightening up.

He stared at her, stunned, and she almost laughed at his expression. He looked completely poleaxed.

He blinked, and gave her a slow smile that sent a slow burn to her stomach. "What was that about?" he asked.

"I just felt like it."

"And do you always do what you feel like?"

"Sometimes," she said.

"And what do you feel like doing now?"

A picture of a naked Carlos in her bed sprang to mind – unfortunately not something she could tell him in public, she decided.

"I think I want to go home," she said.

"Oh," he said, disappointment clearly audible in his voice, but already starting to rise to his feet. Definitely a keeper, she thought.

"With you," she added.

"Oh," he said, enthusiasm flooding his voice. He held out his hand.

At the flat, as she opened the door, Carlos stood politely behind her waiting to be invited in.

"Would you like to come in for a coffee, or something stronger?" she asked, hoping he could stay.

"A coffee would be nice," he said.

Inside the flat, the welcoming scent of lemon and lavender filled the air. "I have Brazilian, Indonesian, and Hawaiian Kona," she said. "What would you prefer?"

"How did you get hold of Kona? I've heard about it. I've never drunk it though."

"One of my friends lives in Hawaii. He sends me a package every Christmas."

"Kona, then," he said, a smile quirking the corner of his mouth.

"This shouldn't take long," she said, turning the percolator on, and reaching up to get two mugs from the top of the china closet. "Take a seat," she said, indicating the two chairs at the kitchen table. "I just need to change."

"Of course."

With the door closed the dress went onto a hanger and back into the wardrobe. Then the small revolver and knife were unstrapped and placed into the bedside drawer. Retrieving the pack of condoms from the bottom drawer she placed them under the pillow. Making sure both drawers were fully closed she wrapped a silk robe around her, tightened its sash, then paused to take a deep breath.

Upon opening the door, she found Carlos pouring coffee into the two mugs she'd left out for him. He looked round as she opened the door, and froze, the look on his face leaving her in no doubt what he was thinking. The coffee continued to pour unobserved, and she was just about to call a warning when he remembered and replaced the percolator on the bench.

"Beautiful," he said, crossing over to her and taking her in his arms.

She looked down at the robe, a hand unconsciously smoothing it. "Thank you. It was a present from my mother."

"I meant you."

"Oh."

His hands framed her face, and with a thumb under her chin he tilted her face up to his and then his lips slanted down over hers.

15

Do Sisters Grow Up?

(Thursday: New York, Commonwealth of America, Mainline)

Margaret looked up from the report she was reading at the sound of the front door, and the quiet murmur of voices. The curtains were still open, but it wouldn't be long before one of the maids would be around to close them and turn the lights on. Her eyes ached with the strain of reading, and she pinched the bridge of her nose as she checked the contents of the box on the floor. Only two more files to go.

At least Sylvi's team was starting to take shape, and she'd commandeered the Department's main conference room for them while she tried to find a more permanent facility. Leaning back, Margaret closed her eyes for a moment to enjoy the aroma of the room's lavender scented beeswax polish.

"Ma'am?" It was the butler.

"Yes, James," she said opening her eyes and straightening back up.

"Miss Louise is here."

"Show her in," Margaret said as she put the completed files back into the box, pleased her sister had actually turned up.

"No need," Louise said, breezing into the room.

"Louise," Margaret said, rising to her feet. "I'm glad you could make it."

"I thought it was a condition of my parole," Louise said, taking both of Margaret's hands in hers and giving her a quick kiss on the cheek. Margaret suddenly felt her age, Louise must be what . . . twenty-four. The eight-year gap in their ages had never felt so vast.

"Have a seat," Margaret said, refusing to acknowledge her sister's gentle dig. "Would you like some tea?"

"Or something stronger?"

"Two sherries, James," Margaret said, acknowledging the hint with a smile.

"Of course, ma'am," the butler said, imperturbably.

Margaret hid a grin. James had the professional butler persona down to a 'T'. She settled herself back on the couch, looking across at her younger sister who had removed her shoes and was burying her feet in the thick piled rug that covered most of the floor. "Unfortunately, I can't make any claims on having chosen the rug. It comes with the house," Margaret told her.

Louise looked up, startled. "You're just renting it?"

"It's Serge's."

"Romanov?"

"You didn't recognize his father?" Margaret asked, with a jerk of her head to the massive portrait of Serge's father staring down at them from over the fireplace.

Louise stared at the portrait and shook her head. "I don't think I ever got to meet him."

She frowned, looking down at the carpet. Then she glanced around the room, which would have made the rug at least twenty feet square. "This isn't Chinese, is it?"

"No, I don't think even the Romanovs could have afforded an original this size," Margaret said. "It's from Birmingham. An expensive copy, but a copy all the same. Markus almost had a heart attack when he saw it for the first time – he was worried his daughter would spill something on it. He seemed to calm down a little when he found out it was only a copy."

"Markus?"

"Someone staying with us for the moment. You'll meet him at dinner."

Margaret found Louise watching her interestedly and froze when she realized she'd called Markus by his first name.

Louise raised an eyebrow enquiringly.

"So," Margaret said. "Did you get the job? You said you had an interview."

Louise beamed. "I start on Monday."

"So, what is it? Tell."

"It's at Macey's. I'm the second assistant fitter, women's lingerie."

"A shop assistant. Really?" Margaret was unable to hide her surprise. She hadn't had any idea of what Louise might have been trying to get a job as, but a shop assistant . . .

"You don't have to look quite so surprised," Louise said.

"Sorry. It's just I can't picture you as a shop assistant."

"And what could you picture me as?"

"Ah . . ." Margaret floundered.

"I thought so," Louise said triumphantly. "Well, for your information there were at least four other girls going for the job, and I was the one they offered it to."

"Congratulations," Margaret said, finally able to remember her manners.

"Thank you."

James reappeared at that moment with a tray bearing the sherries and a small selection of shortbread biscuits.

"Thank you, James," Margaret said, as the butler carefully placed the tray on the table.

Louise took a cautious sip of the sherry. "Oh, that's nice."

"It is," Margaret agreed. Viscous, and very sweet, the sherry tasted like liquid Christmas cake.

"I wouldn't have placed Serge as a sherry drinker," Louise said taking another sip. She studied the glass in her hand. "Any chance of another one?"

"Perhaps with dinner."

"Spoilsport," Louise said, dimpling prettily.

"It's the role of the older sister."

"I've missed you, you know," Louise said.

Margaret wasn't sure how to respond to that. She'd never really been close to her two sisters – the age difference was simply too great. "Are you still staying in Brooklyn?" she asked.

"For the moment. I'm sharing a bed sit but I've already started to look for an apartment now I've got a job."

"And you're happy?"

"Probably the happiest I've been for years," her sister said. "The only thing I've been missing was a big sister who has access to some unbelievably good sherry."

"I'm glad I know where I fit in your life then."

Louise took another sip of her sherry. "So, what have you been doing?" she asked. "I had no idea you were in New York until I got your message."

"Donald asked me to head up the Department of Agriculture and Food."

"And you couldn't say no?"

"Not easily," she admitted. "To tell the truth, the farm hadn't satisfied me since I got back from the war. Even so; when Donald offered me the job it wasn't something I exactly jumped at. I thought working in an office all day was going to be awful."

"And it's not?"

"No. It's actually a lot more interesting than I thought it was going to be. And now I'm getting the hang of it I think I can actually make a difference." Remembering Louise's links to the Anarchists Margaret decided she better change the topic. She didn't think Louise would pass information on on purpose, but even accidentally might risk the operation. "Come on," she said. "I'll show you the gardens. They're pretty amazing."

"If you're going to drag me around the gardens, I definitely want another sherry," Louise said, pouring herself another glass before Margaret had a chance to stop her.

Margaret rolled her eyes but offered a hand to help her sister to her feet.

Entering the dining room on their return from the garden they found Markus and Jessie already at the table – Jessie perched on her cushions next to her father. As Margaret and Louise entered, Jessie slid off her cushions while Markus carefully rose to his feet.

"Markus, Jessie; this is Louise, my sister. Louise, my guests Markus and Jessie, who are staying with us."

"Good evening, Miss Peric," Jessie said politely.

Margaret flicked a glance to Markus who simply beamed down on his daughter.

Margaret worried that Markus might withdraw into his shell, but Jessie gave him no chance to do so, burbling on about her day: which had started with her helping Gwendelyn, one of the under-maids, to clear up after breakfast; then Randolph the gardener weed the gardens; then Rolf the chauffeur wash the limousine. And that was only before lunch. If Margaret hadn't already been exhausted, she suspected the long list of tasks Jessie had undertaken would have made her so.

And when Jessie found out that Louise had got a new job as a shop assistant, her excited questions kept the conversation going right through dessert.

After dessert Louise made her apologies, and as Margaret watched Louise walk across the yellow polished marble of the entry hall to the entrance she couldn't help thinking there was an unexpected maturity in her baby sister's steps.

"Louise," she called.

Her sister looked round.

"Same time next week?" Margaret asked.

Her sister looked at her, her expression uncertain.

"Sherry?" Margaret said, miming taking the drink.

Louise's face lightened. "Sure, though I'll need to check my shift."

"Of course."

"And what's my price?"

"No price. I know Mama wants to hear from you, but you're a big girl now. If you don't want to contact her, that's your choice."

"All right, I'll let you know," Louise promised. Outside, at the top of the steps she paused again, turning back. "Tell Mama I will write," she said. "It's just . . ."

"You need some time," Margaret suggested, which Louise acknowledged with a small shrug. "All right," Margaret said, "but –" She held up a finger in warning. "Don't take too much time. You're not the one having to put up with Mama. And you do know that once Papa has recovered enough, she'll be here herself. It might be better for you to have re-opened communications before she turns up on your doorstep."

Louise looked worried at the thought and nodded. "Not too long," she promised.

"Make sure you don't," Margaret said, already starting to plan her letter to their mother.

16

The Pink Python

(Monday: New York, Commonwealth of America, Mainline)

It was eight on the Monday when Jade wearily climbed the steps to the front door of Margaret's house. Carlos had ended up spending the entire Saturday night, and after breakfast together at the diner on the corner they'd taken a walk through Central Park. After lunch, Carlos had accompanied her to netball, and then they'd taken a picnic meal back to Jade's apartment. Carlos hadn't left until after midnight, so she hadn't had much sleep.

Karen, who was sitting on a chair in the foyer and reading what looked like a lurid romance book from its cover, looked up as Jade let herself in.

"Look what the cat dragged in," she said.

"Thanks for taking over my shift last night."

"No worries. You said you'd be here by seven though."

Jade checked her watch. "I'm only an hour late," she said defensively. "I slept through the alarm."

She'd run most of the way here and had been hoping for the chance to freshen up before she had to face anyone.

"Our principal wants to see you," Karen said, destroying that hope.

Jade suppressed a sigh. "Where is she?"

Karen glanced up at the grandfather clock marking time in the far corner. "She should still be in the dining room. She only got down half an hour ago."

"Thanks."

She found Margaret where Karen had said she would be. Margaret's plate looked as though it had barely been touched. The clear glass teapot in front of her was almost empty and she was morosely studying her half empty cup, slowly swirling the dark amber liquid round and round its base.

"Morning boss," Jade said cheerfully, trying to stifle a yawn. "Have I got time for breakfast?"

"Of course," Margaret said, looking up, then catching sight of the time. "You haven't eaten yet?"

"No." She started to load up her plate from the buffet.

"Hard game yesterday?"

"It was definitely hard last night."

Margaret's eyes twinkled. "And might that have something to do with the hickey on your neck?"

"What!" Jade exclaimed, swinging round to inspect the mark in the mirror hanging over the mantelpiece. "Shit," she said when she saw the large purple bruise visible over the top of her collar.

"Oh, leave it alone," Margaret said, as Jade vainly tried to pull her collar up to hide it. "You can use some of my foundation on it after breakfast."

Jade gave one more fruitless attempt to pull her collar up then turned back to filling her plate.

"Well?" Margaret asked, as Jade took her seat.

"Well what?" Jade asked, hoping she'd be allowed to eat. She was starving.

"The hardness you experienced last night."

"Margaret!" Jade said, embarrassed, looking around to make sure no one else was sharing this conversation. The dining room remained vacant apart from the two of them.

"You were the one who started it."

Jade couldn't help smiling at the memory. "It wasn't just last night, it was Saturday night too," she said, slicing off the end of the sausage, wiping up some baked beans and placing it in her mouth. Oh God, chicken sausages. Mrs. Mack had excelled herself this time!

"He must have been quite impressive?"

"Oh, he was," Jade said, unable to keep the grin off her face.

"So tell, who was it?"

"Carlos."

"Your little Anarchist?"

"Not so little," Jade said, this time round a mouthful of potato fritter.

"But you've only known him a week!"

"A week and a half," Jade said defensively.

"Oh, you tart," Margaret said affectionately.

"I know," Jade said, giving her a smug smile.

Suddenly Margaret's face fell. "I envy you, you know?"

"Why?" Jade couldn't hide her surprise. "I mean, look where you live. It's not as if you're short of a crust or anything. And the food!" She waved her fork in the general direction of the buffet for emphasis. "I used to dream of stuff like this."

"But no one to share it with," Margaret pointed out.

Jade frowned. She'd never seen Margaret like this before. "I'm sure things will change," she suggested carefully, uncertain of the social niceties of providing advice to one's principal, especially to one so far above her in social ranking.

"I can't see why they would. They never have so far."

"You've . . . never . . .?"

Margaret shook her head.

"Why?" Jade asked, before realizing that it was probably not the most diplomatic thing she could have said, however, it was too late.

"I don't know," Margaret said with a heavy sigh, eyes fixed on the tea she was still swirling around in the bottom of her cup. "I missed my debutante ball because Papa was too ill to travel, and by the time he'd recovered I was too busy managing my farm. And then of course there was the war. Although that never seemed to stop Michelle and Louise," she added, referring to her two sisters. "They seemed to have a new beau every week." She shrugged. "It's not a big deal. It's not as though I was ever that attractive."

Jade snorted. Margaret had the type of tall, elegant, statuesque beauty that often made Jade frustrated with her own lack of height. And Margaret's long, raven hair made Jade green with envy when she compared it to her own short dirty-blond bob. "That's horse-meat.

If you wanted company all you have to do is go and stand on the corner. You'd have men queuing up around the block. Maybe you've simply never met anyone you're interested in."

"Maybe," Margaret said, obviously not agreeing. She looked up and grinned. "So, has Carlos got a brother?"

Jade grinned back. "I don't know. Do you want me to ask?"

"Better not." Margaret's face was suddenly all business again. "I had a telephone call from Aife last night. She thinks they've got someone."

"Who?"

"Director Jones, Markus' director. There have been several rather large deposits made to his bank account over the last six months. Imperial Security are bringing him in. I want you in on his questioning."

Jade raised an eyebrow. "Where and when?"

"Imperial Security headquarters. They're expecting you at ten."

"Why me?"

"I trust you," Margaret said. "And unfortunately, I have another meeting I can't cancel."

"Okay . . ." Nothing like jumping in at the deep end, she thought. She'd never been involved with questioning a suspect before, and now she was doing her first at Imp-Sec. Suddenly, the food she'd been chewing lost its taste.

Margaret didn't seem to have noticed because she swallowed the last of her tea and stood up.

"I'll see you tonight," she said. "You can tell me how it went then."

Jade nodded silently, swallowed, and mechanically put another piece of sausage in her mouth and chewed. Despite the churning in her stomach, she had to eat something.

***

She presented herself at Imp-Sec's New York offices feeling totally unprepared. She'd tried freshening her uniform as best she could, but the run to the house that morning had left her hot and sweaty. At least she had managed a shower before leaving the apartment.

They were expecting her, which was a relief. She'd had a fear that she would be turned away or be left standing in the waiting area.

106

The receptionist had simply sighted her ID and at her nod the officer who'd been standing patiently next to the inside door opened it for her. "Ma'am."

Jade stepped through, eyeing his uniform. It was definitely more spiffing than the Agency's, all black leather and silver facings, very chic.

"This way. They're expecting you," he said, leading the way down the hall.

It looked remarkably normal, she thought.

"The interview rooms are on the second floor," he said, pausing in front of the elevators.

"So, no dungeons?" Oh shit, she thought, where did that come from?

"No dungeons," he said, not even cracking a grin.

The elevator arrived and they made the trip to the second floor in silence.

Special Agent McGunn, Aife's second in command, was waiting for them as the lift door opened. A female Imp-Sec Officer standing behind him.

"Officer Carvello," McGunn said. "They're just about to start. If you follow me, I'll show you where we can observe the interview."

Jade nodded, irrationally disappointed that she wouldn't actually be involved in the interview. As she stepped forward the elevator door closed behind her, taking the officer who'd brought her up back to the ground floor.

"This way," McGunn said, ushering her forward.

The female officer followed them silently.

McGunn opened a door and waved her in.

Jade found herself in a darkened room. Four chairs were set up facing a large, one-way mirror set into the far wall. Through the glass she saw a small man, with dark slicked back hair, and a small mustache. He was sitting alone in the room which had three chairs and a single fixed desk. His clothes were rumpled as though he'd slept in them. There was a faint sheen of perspiration on his forehead. Director Jones, she presumed.

"If anything occurs to you during the interview," McGunn said, "tell Officer Mathews here and she'll pass it on."

Jade nodded again, confident that wasn't going to happen.

As the door swung closed behind them the door into the interview room opened and Aife entered. She was wearing a pink dress suit with a small pink, pill-box hat. Jade was unsurprised to see that she was accompanied by a male Imp-Sec Officer in the ubiquitous black and silver.

Aife was breathing hard as she sat down, and as she did so Jade noticed that the chair with which she'd been provided was missing an arm to fit her width. Carefully, Aife placed the manila folder she'd been carrying on the desk, while the Security Officer took a position by the door, where he stood, arms folded, simply observing.

"Director Jones," Aife said politely. "I am Special Agent Aife Schneider from the Comptroller-General's Office."

"What is all this about? You have no reason to haul me in for questioning like – like a common criminal."

Jade thought it was mostly bluster. He looked a lot more worried than an innocent person should look.

"Oh, we are certainly not treating you like a common criminal," Aife said with a small smile as she opened the folder and slipped the photograph on the top across the table. "Do you recognize this man?"

Jones picked the photograph up. After a moment studying it, he nodded. "He was an employee in my division. I'm sorry. I can't remember his name."

"His name is Markus Ackov. You sacked him two weeks ago and can't remember his name?"

Jones rocked his head from side to side. "Unfortunately, I have a bad memory for names."

"But you can remember what you sacked him for?"

"He was fixated on the wheat blight in the Midwest. He was disrupting the work of his section and failing to do his own work."

"And you weren't worried about his claims?"

"Of course I was," Jones protested.

"We've spoken to Markus' supervisor, Miss McAlister. She states that Markus' claims that the dissemination vector wasn't natural were real."

"Which is why he had to go. Miss McAlister's sections work dealt with fertilizer production. It had nothing to do with wheat, or disease vector analysis. He was disrupting the entire section, diverting them from their real work."

"You claim to have been worried by his claims, yet you failed to pass the information onto the section concerned with trying to control the blight, or onto Imperial Security to investigate." She gave a small nod to the Imp-Sec Officer standing behind her who stared stonily at the flustered Director.

Jones opened his mouth to say something, then closed it. He repeated the motion again. It seemed to Jade that Aife might be prepared to have mercy on him because she opened the folder again and slid the next three sheets of paper across the table to him.

"Your bank statements for the last six months," she said.

"How, how did you . . .?"

Aife indicated the Imp-Sec Officer with a small nod. "I am particularly interested in the amounts that are circled in red. Five hundred pounds each month. Where did this come from?"

"Those are income from investments."

"Paid in cash each month? Would you like to provide information on the investments?"

Jones remained silent.

"Perhaps I could help you. It turns out that the Comptroller-General's local agents are very thorough. The teller who received the money last month recognized the individual who made the payment. It was one of the local Anarchists." She considered her notes. "A certain Carlos Babineaux."

Carlos? Jade was shocked. Why would Carlos be involved?

Aife continued her relentless line of questioning. "Now why, I wondered, would an Anarchist be paying you money? It was particularly enlightening when my colleagues in Security informed me that you had once been a card-carrying member of the movement."

"That was twenty years ago!" Jones protested.

"And yet, given the magazines you subscribe to, it appears your personal philosophies have remained, shall we say on the 'libertarian' side of politics."

"You had no right."

Aife banged a large, fleshy fist on the table. "We have every right."

The Director looked uncertain. "Look, I admit it. I used to be an anarchist. People should have a right to select the people who rule them. You just need to look at the consequences of the last war to see what happens when people don't have any control over those who set the political direction of the State."

"The State is the enemy of the people," Aife commented dryly.

"Yes, it is, but that does not mean that I would assist them in spreading a wheat blight that will kill millions."

"And yet that is precisely what I believe you have been doing," Aife said. "The payments were made to ensure that you blocked or covered up any investigation if someone, such as Markus, detected what was happening."

"That's ridiculous," Jones spluttered.

"I wish it was," Aife said sadly. "But unless you can provide me with an explanation . . ."

"I need to talk to my lawyer."

"Ah, that's the rub, isn't it? You might remember I told you we were not treating you like a common criminal. In fact, you're being held under the *Treasons Act*."

He looked puzzled.

"No lawyers." She showed her teeth.

Replacing the photo and the bank statements into her folder Aife levered herself to her feet. "He's all yours," she told the Imp-Sec Officer, before leaving the room.

"I'll be back," the officer said, before following Aife through the door.

McGunn didn't make any effort to move for a couple of minutes and then with a sigh he hoisted himself to his feet. "That was short and sweet," he said. "I can see why they call her the Pink Python now."

Jade nodded absentmindedly as she gnawed at her bottom lip, wondering what she should do about Carlos. And then there was Hermandez, she thought as she followed McGunn out of the room. She'd really wanted to collar Hermandez herself, but this seemed to be bigger than anything she would have expected.

Aife and the Imp-Sec officer who had been conducting the interview were waiting for them as they left the observation room. "Officer Carvello," Aife said with a smile. "I'm pleased you could join us."

"Special Agent Schneider," Jade said politely. "I have the name of someone who may have been involved with the attempt on the life of Markus Ackov."

Aife held up a hand. "Please, Officer Carvello. I think that information is better directed to my colleague." She waved a meaty hand to her companion who turned cold eyes on Jade.

Jade swallowed. "Hermandez Cortez. He's an activist with the Anarchists' Armed Action Wing."

"And you suspect him? Why?"

"He bought the knife that was used in the assault."

"And why haven't you reported this previously?"

"Because there's been no evidence to actually link him to the crime. He bought the knife five years ago; all he has to do would be to claim that he lost it several years ago and our whole case evaporates. And there's been no motive. But with Jones' money apparently coming from the Anarchists . . ."

The Imp-Sec officer nodded, apparently satisfied. "Do you have an address?"

"Apartment 23, 75 West 132nd Street."

The officer raised an eyebrow and Jade shrugged. There was no way she was going to explain how she'd remembered that.

"Do you want to be in on the interview?"

Jade shook her head. "I'm undercover at the moment and it would be better if that could continue. I'm happy to give you a copy of my notes of course and answer any questions you might have."

The officer nodded. "I understand. Agent Mathews will accompany you for the notes." He indicated the female agent who had stood silently behind them for the whole interview. "In the meantime, I'd better see about arranging for someone to pick this Hermandez up."

"Eh, it may not be as simple picking him up from the apartment. It's got reasonable security . . ." She trailed off uncertainly.

"It's all right Officer Carvello, I recognize the address. You can leave the pickup to us. We do have a certain degree of 'expertise' in these matters."

It took her a moment to realize he'd just cracked a joke. "Of course," she said, feeling strangely depressed, even though she'd asked not to be involved. Still, she hid it with a smile, and a polite nod to the Officer. "Agent Mathews, if you'd like to accompany me to the Agency's offices, I can arrange to give you a copy of my notes."

17

Some Party

(Monday: New York, Commonwealth of America, Mainline)

Carlos surveyed the devastation of the flat. Luckily, he had been out when Imp-Sec's thugs had come calling, but the evidence of their visit was clear. Both tables had been tipped over, one of them was now missing a leg, and leaflets covered the floor like confetti. The duplicator was lying on its side on the floor; the ink had leaked out of the machine and had created a soggy patch on the mat. Its stink filled the air and the first thing he'd done when he arrived back was to open the windows. Even with the windows open the stench was still giving him a headache.

It had been obvious that too many of the security team hated the Anarchists and had taken the opportunity to let their frustrations out. Most of it had been wanton waste; opening and dumping all the tins of dried food onto the floor, then turning all the clothes drawers upside down and strewing their contents on top. Both beds had been stripped, the mattresses sliced open, and their contents mixed into the sheets and blankets that had been dumped beside them.

'Come the revolution,' he thought with a wry smile, as he turned a chair right way up. He wondered how they'd have felt if they'd known that one of the team had actually been an Anarchist. And all because of Hermandez.

And just where was Hermandez, he wondered. His flatmate had left a message on Sunday that he wouldn't be back for a couple of weeks. Carlos suspected he was off line, but which one? The Anarchists' Armed Action Wing was pretty tightly compartmentalized, for obvious reasons, and questions about their activities were not welcomed. Particularly when those questions came from those on the more 'political' side of the movement. He remembered the last time he'd asked and how that particular point had been reinforced.

As a politician it wasn't that he disagreed with the principle of plausible deniability. If the politicians didn't know it made it easier to deny responsibility. The Action Wing on the other hand had a much more practical and paranoid reason for their secrecy, they simply didn't trust anyone who wasn't one of them. This time, however, he didn't have a choice, he had to know. And perhaps the raid had given him the excuse. After all, with Imperial Security involved, he had to 'warn' his flatmate. And if it got him out of printing more of those damn pamphlets . . . He nodded pleased, as he righted another chair. Yes, that would work.

Then he remembered Jade. Damn. If this was going to work, he had to disappear immediately, without letting her know anything, something he didn't like doing. There was a knock on the door. "Come in," he called.

It was Dario, one of Hermandez' fellow activists, and he paused in the doorway. "Some party!"

"Ha. It was Imp-Sec. According to those downstairs, they were looking for Hermandez." Carlos shook his head. "I have a feeling they'll be back, and I suspect it would be better if I didn't present myself as a punching bag for their frustrations."

"Where were you thinking of going?" Dario asked, as he looked around at the mess.

Carlos frowned. "Given it's Imperial Security, maybe a trip back home to Canada. Off line might be better but . . . ," he shrugged, indicating the difficulty that created. "Can you warn Hermandez Imp-Sec are looking for him?"

"Of course." Dario looked thoughtful. "Where will you be staying until you decide?"

"I'm not sure yet. I need to clean up here first."

Dario shook his head. "No, I'll get someone to do that for you. Here." He tore a corner off one of the leaflets littering the floor and quickly scrawled an address on the back. "This is one of our safe houses. Tell them Dario sent you. I want you to stay there for a couple of days. We might have a job for you that would get you off line."

Hoping the job involved getting a message to Hermandez, Carlos glanced at the paper. "The Bronx?"

"Is that a problem?"

"No, it's a bit of a walk, but I'll just grab a bag and head off, then wait till I hear from you."

"Walk?"

"I'd rather not use the subway. Walking gives me an opportunity to make sure I'm not followed."

Dario smiled. "Good thinking. I'll make sure I'm in touch in a day or so." He held out his hand. "Good luck."

***

Fifteen minutes later Carlos adjusted the weight of his duffel bag over his shoulder as he took a moment at the top of the steps to look around. He couldn't see anyone watching, but that didn't mean there wasn't. The safest approach would be to head to the restaurant first. He could leave a message there for Uncle, too. He wouldn't want him worrying, Carlos would do enough of that for both of them.

The staff were already in the process of preparing the restaurant for the evening meal. "Ah, Yvettia," he said to the waitress setting out the cutlery. "Do you know where Tove is?"

"He should be in his office," she said, looking up.

"Thanks," Carlos said, and headed toward the back of the restaurant.

"Carlos, what can I do for you?" Tove asked as Carlos knocked on his door. The restaurant's day manager was a large, rather fat man with a perpetual twelve o'clock shadow, and a rather interesting background in guns.

"I have to disappear for a couple of weeks," Carlos said. "I may have attracted the attention of Imp-Sec."

"Oh, anything we need to worry about here?"

"I don't think so. They're actually after Hermandez."

115

Tove nodded, unsurprised. "Well, if there's anything I can do?'

"I just need to write a note for my uncle in Montreal. I don't want him to start worrying if he doesn't hear from me for a while. Could you post it for me?"

"Of course."

It didn't take Carlos long to write the note, and address it, then grab a couple of pastries from the kitchen. Next, he headed down to the wine cellar. There, after a quick change of clothes, he wrapped the duffel bag into an old blanket before unlocking the small door on the far side of the cellar. Behind the door a short passage led next door, and then via a series of linked passages to a house four lots down.

Exiting the house via the coal cellar he let himself out into the lane that led down the back of the terraces. Taking a deep breath, he slung the blanket and its bag over his shoulder and headed down toward the Haarlem River and the 3rd Avenue ferry.

18

You are not the First to Find Themselves in This Position

(Monday: New York, Commonwealth of America, Mainline)

Jade cleared her throat, startling her boss who was lost in studying a file.

"Miss Carvello," Inspector Terrance said surprised, looking up at her. "What are you doing in the office today?"

"I'm sorry to trouble you Inspector Terrance. But Agent Mathews from Imp-Sec is here for a copy of my case notes."

"I hope there's nothing wrong?" Terrance asked, considering the stone-faced agent standing behind Jade.

Agent Mathews looked him up and down silently.

Pulling a face, the Inspector slid a thin file out of the middle of the tallest pile on his desk. He checked the title, then looked at Mathews. "I'm not being difficult Agent Mathews, but do you have a Search Warrant? Client-Agency confidentiality and all that."

"Sorry, no warrant," Mathews said, sounding not in the least sorry. "The information is required as the result of an ongoing investigation under the *Treasons Act*."

Terrance gave a small sigh. "Then I must regretfully inform you that without a warrant, or alternatively the authority of our principal, I am unable to provide you with access to the file."

"Inspector Terrance –" Mathews started.

"No," Terrance said cutting her off. "Last year's decision of the Supreme Court regarding section 13 of the *Treasons Act* made it quite clear that internal working files of this Agency can only be obtained on production of a Search Warrant, or on permission of the principal. I'm sorry, Agent Mathews, but my hands are tied." Terrance, contrary to Mathews, sounded genuinely apologetic.

"Fine. I'll get a Search Warrant."

"Agent Mathews, if we could have a minute," Jade said, her mouth dry. She hated this sort of confrontation. And being responsible for an inter-jurisdictional dispute wasn't going to look good on her file.

"Of course," Mathews said, and moved away down the corridor, leaving Jade free to talk to her boss.

"Inspector –" she started.

"Miss Carvello, I'm really not being difficult on purpose. There are real, and significant penalties, both legal and financial, if we start handing over documents to Imperial Security willy-nilly – simply because they ask for a copy."

"But you said we could do it with the permission of the principal . . ."

"Miss Peric. Yes."

"I'm sure if I asked, she wouldn't have a problem, given that Imp-Sec are actually working on her behalf. Or at least they're working with Special Agent Aife Schneider from the Comptroller-General's Office, who is."

Terrance considered her for a moment, then shook his head. "Miss Carvello, I have no idea how you manage to get into these sorts of situations."

And that wasn't the least of it, Jade thought, thinking about Carlos.

"Very well, if you would care to get Agent Mathews back, we'll see about getting Miss Peric's authority to release the information."

Jade nodded, her stomach still feeling queasy at the thought of what she had to do once this immediate issue was resolved.

"Agent Mathews," the Inspector said, when Jade returned with the Imp-Sec Officer. "Miss Carvello has suggested that we could resolve this stand-off expeditiously by seeking Miss Peric's authority to release the information to you. Under normal circumstances this authority should be in writing, but verbal approval can be given if witnessed by representatives of both parties. Would that be adequate?"

"I believe so," Mathews said, the stone-face starting to melt slightly.

"Good. Miss Carvello," Terrance said, indicating the phone. "If you would do the honors."

Jade checked her watch – almost one. She hoped Margaret would be at her desk.

"Miss Peric," Jade said, when Michael had put her through.

"Jade?"

"Yes, sorry to interrupt you. But it turns out my investigation into Hermandez Cortez *is* related to Aife's audit and Imperial Security are now involved. They've requested a copy of my case notes."

"And?" Margaret said.

"And the Agency needs your permission to release the notes. Otherwise Imp-Sec will have to obtain a Search Warrant, which would seem to be overkill."

"Wonderful, Bash and Crash are now involved." There was a moment's silence as Margaret thought about it. "No, that's fine. Unless you don't want me to give permission?"

"No, no. I do. Could you confirm that to my boss, he's just sitting here."

She handed the phone over thankfully.

"Miss Peric, Inspector Terrance of the Rucker's Agency here. I apologize for the interruption, but I hope you understand how seriously the Agency takes the confidentiality of our clients."

He listened for a moment.

"Thank you. So, just to confirm, you're happy for us to provide a copy of the case notes to Imp-Sec?"

"Excellent, and for the record would you be prepared to confirm that for the Agent concerned?"

He listened, nodded, then handed the phone across to Mathews. "She wants to speak to you."

"Miss Peric?" the Agent said, coming to attention. The Agent listened intently, then clicked her heels. "Thank you, ma'am." She handed the phone back to Terrance. "She said she expects a report from you when she gets home," she told Jade.

"Let's see about getting you a copy of this file then," Terrance told Mathews.

"Inspector Terrance, can I see you afterward for a moment?" Jade asked, trying to ignore the nausea she was feeling, and wishing she could just forget the whole thing.

Terrance gave her a puzzled look. "Of course, give me a couple of minutes."

It was closer to ten before he came back, leaving her plenty of time to worry about what could happen after her confession. She'd just mentally started to draft her resignation when he returned.

"Now, what can I do for you, Miss Carvello?" the Inspector asked, taking his seat.

"I think I've stuffed up." Her gaze was fixed on the wall above his head.

She heard him get up and looked down to see him closing the small office's door.

"Sorry." He resumed his seat. "So, what makes you think you've stuffed up?" he asked quietly. "I thought you handled that little problem we had with Imp-Sec quite well."

She caught herself picking at her fingernails and lifted her eyes to his. "Carlos Babineaux."

"Who is . . .?"

"The flatmate of Hermandez Cortez."

"And he is a problem why?"

"He was identified by the bank teller as the Anarchist paying off Markus Ackov's director to ensure any reports of possible eco-terrorism were filed and lost."

Terrance considered her thoughtfully. "And why is this a problem?"

She started to rub her thumb. "Because we're involved."

"Involved, as in . . .?"

"We've had an affair. Have an affair. Having an affair."

"And when did this affair start?"

"Last weekend." How could she be so stupid. Stupid, stupid, stupid.

She looked up when he didn't say anything to find him considering her pensively.

"If you need my resignation . . ." She could feel the sharp sting of tears.

"What? No. Of course not. You haven't spoken to him about the case, have you?"

"No. I'd never do that."

"Good." He nodded. "Do you intend seeing him again?"

She shook her head. She never wanted to see him again. Not after he'd put her in this position. "Should I tell Imp-Sec?"

"If they ask, yes. Otherwise I wouldn't volunteer the information. You've told me, so let's leave it at that for the time being."

"Thank you." She stood up to go.

"Miss Carvello," he said quietly. "You're certainly not the first Agency employee to find themselves in this position, and undoubtedly you won't be the last. The important thing is that you told me."

19

How Much Does a Housekeeper Earn?

(Monday [late]: New York, Commonwealth of America, Mainline)

"We're here, ma'am," the chauffeur said as the car pulled up outside the house.

"Thanks Rolf," Margaret said. She was exhausted. It had been a hard day and all she wanted was a bath and then, maybe, dinner. As expected, the Comptroller-General's audit was disrupting the Department, and everyone was looking over their shoulders, wondering what they were looking for. As a result, between the audit and the bomb attack, there were a significant number of people who had decided to simply not turn up for work. At least that meant that no one seemed to have picked up on Director Jones' absence yet. And she wasn't looking forward to having to go to Naisre tomorrow. Thirty-one hours in an airship was not her idea of fun. No baths, and although showers were provided the water never seemed warm enough.

She stepped out of the car to see the air filled with the late airborne fluff of the poplars that lined the drive. There was so much that it had formed thick drifts under the shrubs.

"Ma'am," the butler said, opening the door for her as she climbed tiredly up the front steps.

She looked up and gave him an exhausted smile. "Everything quiet on the home front?"

"Yes, ma'am," James said with a solicitous look. "Miss Carter is just having her tea and we've settled the other two officers into one of the spare rooms on the third floor."

"Thank you."

Mrs. Mack appeared from behind the butler's bulk. "Your bath will be ready in ten minutes, ma'am."

"Thank you, Mrs. Mack. Did you get my message about leaving for Naisre tomorrow?"

"Yes ma'am. We've packed your bags as you requested. And I left a message with your sister asking her if she would be able to move her next visit to Sunday."

"Thank you," she said, giving the tiny housekeeper a grateful look. "I really didn't want to put Louise off for two weeks." She started to turn away but then turned back with a request. "Could you arrange for a cup of tea and perhaps a couple of Cook's macaroons to be placed on the stand next to the bath?"

"Of course, ma'am. And Mr. Ackov asked if he could see you when you returned."

"Oh? Where is he?"

"In the back garden, ma'am."

"I'll see him before my bath then."

Margaret found her steps lightening as she made her way down the hall to the back garden. Outside, the sun was just starting to set, and the garden was bathed in its soft glow. The outside lights had been lit, and the gas lights cast a flickering radiance over the flowers.

Markus was sitting on a chair on the raised porch that looked out over the garden; a thick pile of files on the coffee table next to his chair, and a pad of lined paper in his lap.

He looked round as he heard the door open. "Margaret," he said, starting to stand.

"No, stay there Markus," she said. His wound was healing nicely, but she knew it still caused him pain at times, particularly when he had to get up.

He allowed himself to relax back into his chair.

"Where's Jessie?" she asked, taking the chair on the other side of the low table.

Around them the scent of gardenias lingered on the air, while the frangipanis in their wheeled pots lent their own heady fragrance. She'd been stunned to discover the number of plants which wintered over in the heated glasshouses, before being trundled out in their wheeled pots in spring. The garden had been a major inducement to accept Serge's offer of the house, but she'd had little enough time to enjoy it with the hours she'd been working.

"She's helping Cook," Markus said.

Even as he said that the door opened and Jessie appeared, an expression of earnest concentration on her face as she focused on carefully carrying out a tray bearing a tea pot, milk, and two cups. Behind her was one of the maids with a plate of macaroons, carefully trying to control her smile at the look on Jessie's face.

"Mrs. Mack suggested you might want to have the tea here, ma'am," the maid said.

"Thank you, Gwendelyn. And thank you Jessie," she said as the child carefully placed the plate on the table.

Jessie glanced up and gave her one of her dazzling smiles.

As Jessie and Gwendelyn headed back inside, Markus shook his head.

"What?" Margaret asked.

"Jessie told me at lunchtime she wanted to be a housekeeper when she grew up."

"And you had hopes of her becoming an academic?" Margaret guessed.

He gave a rueful smile.

"There's plenty of time for her to change her mind. But if she does decide to become a housekeeper, she could do a lot worse."

He didn't look convinced.

"Do you have any idea how much Mrs. Mack earns?" Margaret said, suddenly upset at his attitude.

"No," he admitted.

"I would guess somewhere around 45,000 pounds. And with a degree, a Steward for a Continental Leader is going to pull in a minimum of 90,000."

He looked a little sick.

"And what was your salary at the Department?" she asked, twisting the knife. "About 15,000 pounds?"

"Seventeen and a half actually," he said defensively.

"I rest my case."

He frowned. "Why so much?"

She shrugged. "Just think about it. Housekeepers are responsible for staff, in Mrs. Mack's case at least ten, and a significant budget. That's in addition to the requirement to providing, and ensuring, that a significant amount of discretion is applied in the running of the household. There's also a chronic shortage of labor with people constantly being drawn to other lines. Put all of that together and you've got a massive need to provide an incentive for those who are any good to stay with their current employer."

"I guess." His gaze fell on the tea pot. "Shall I?" he asked.

"I think I'd better do that," Margaret said, getting to her feet.

The tea poured; she popped a macaroon in her mouth before resuming her seat. She closed her eyes to better appreciate the almond flavor as it dissolved on her tongue.

"What?" she demanded at Markus' expression when she opened her eyes and saw him watching her.

"Nothing, it's just you looked completely relaxed then."

He smiled at her, and she was unable to resist smiling back at him. He had such beautiful eyes she thought. When she realized what she was doing, she quickly looked down and noticed the files on the table between them.

"I see you've been busy," she said, indicating the pages of notes he'd made, eager to change the conversation. She'd asked Sylvi to give him the files on the potato blight on Chikyù to have a look at after he'd asked her how the investigation had been progressing. He'd looked so much like a puppy she hadn't been able to resist his request to help. Besides, he might be able to suggest something, as Sylvi was finding it difficult to recruit investigators she could trust. Sylvi had ended up recruiting from the Department's field agent pool, but pulling those back from the lines they were stationed on was slowing things down more than either she, or Margaret, was happy with. Higher level policy officers were slightly easier to get hold of, she could recruit from other Departments. Although getting them released by their respective Departments had required Imp-Sec's assistance on at least five occasions.

He looked at the pile and nodded. "Thank you for arranging to get me the information. It was enthralling."

She raised an eyebrow, wondering how anyone could think trawling through files could be described as 'enthralling'. "Did you find anything?"

"Do you want the good news or the bad news first?"

"Let's start with the good news."

"First, the Chikyù's potato blight appears similar to the strain which devastated Russia ten years ago."

"You're sure?"

"Definitely, the morphology is quite distinctive."

"And how is that good news?" she asked, remembering the devastation the Russian Blight had caused.

"If it *is* similar to the original Russian strain, we know that didn't survive well outside its plant host and was killed by frosts, or very warm weather. The exception involved oospores and hyphae being present within the tuber. That's how we eventually managed to bring the disease under control on the Mainline; strict quarantine and the destruction and burning of all potatoes within the quarantine area."

She nodded. "The industry was virtually wiped out though."

"In Russia," he pointed out. "And the introduction of blight resistant species enabled the industry to be re-established. That might give us a chance in Chikyù but . . ."

"The bad news?" she guessed.

"It took three years for the Russian Blight to really bite. According to the files it looks like the entire European continent on Chikyù is already affected, despite the blight only being detected late last year."

"Where did it come from then?" she demanded. "I take it there's no sign of it elsewhere?"

He shook his head. "The first outbreak was identified near Parisii last year. But there were also outbreaks near Adair, which is the equivalent of Mainline Bremem, and Brangaine, Mainline Bologna." He showed her the map.

She shook her head disbelievingly. "France, Germany, and Italy. And with the Alps separating them. That can't be natural."

"No. And I suspect there have been several other outbreaks, but the subsequent ones may be hidden within the natural spread of the disease. And unfortunately, the news gets even worse; some of the areas affected seem to have been infected by a mutant strain with a virulence almost double that of the original variety."

"Double!"

"Here," he said, opening one of the files. "The field agent reported that within two weeks of the first signs of infestation in a field, all the plants were showing signs of infection, with total leaf loss within fourteen days."

"Gods," she whispered, remembering the accounts she had heard of the original outbreak in Russia. And this had the potential to be twice as bad. How many people would die from this?

"What do you suggest?" She took a sip of the tea only to discover it had gone cold. She considered the plate of macaroons, but her appetite had disappeared.

"I've already given my recommendations to Director Saito."

"And they were?"

He leaned forward earnestly. "To impose an immediate quarantine on all transfers on and off the line. Chikyù also needs to impose a quarantine line around Europe if it wants to protect its own crops."

"I wouldn't want to be the one to tell the World Leader," she said.

"If you don't, and a contaminated potato gets through to the Mainline . . ."

"I know, but while the war didn't hit Chikyù particularly badly, it is still recovering from the disruption it caused. And Mark only became World Leader four years ago . . . "What?" she demanded seeing him suddenly smile.

"Nothing, it's just the way you casually mentioned the Chikyù's World Leader by first name."

"He *is* my brother-in-law, but I can assure you that he puts his socks on in the morning like everyone else," she said sharply.

He held up his hands placatingly. "That's not what I meant."

She nodded, acknowledging her over-reaction. "To tell the truth, I actually don't know Mark that well. I only met him at my brother's wedding." She frowned. "So, I don't know if he even wears socks. But I did meet Hayden, his brother, a couple of times because he was close to my cousin Conrad . . ."

"I don't know if that actually makes it better, or worse," he admitted.

Suddenly feeling uncomfortable about the conversation, Margaret made to stand up, but Markus held up his hands.

"Look, I'm sorry. Really. It's just . . ."

She finished standing. "No, it's all right," she said, suddenly feeling exhaustion descend on her. "I need to get a letter off to the Undersecretary before I can change. And I've got an early start planned."

"Oh?"

She suddenly realized she hadn't told him. "I'm off to Naisre tomorrow. I really should be taking Sylvi with me, but at this stage she's still pulling her team together. I expect to be back Sunday."

A look of disappointment crossed his face. "I guess Jessie and I will be gone by the time you get back. The doctor was planning to give me a full bill of health tomorrow."

"I'd rather you didn't leave. Until we pick up your assailants you both remain a target."

"But all we do is cause you problems," he protested.

"I'm not sure I'd call it a problem. Besides, look what you've achieved here," she said, gesturing at the map still laid out over the top of the pile.

He looked embarrassed. "Anyone could have done that."

"Actually, they couldn't have, or they would have done it for me. So, let's not have any more protests. Mrs. Mack is enjoying have Jessie around, and I'm sure Sylvi has a lot more for you to do."

He nodded, and she wondered at the feeling of relief she felt knowing he'd still be there when she returned.

Leaving Markus to enjoy what remained of the evening light, Margaret headed inside. She was just on the first step when she heard the front door open and Jade's voice. With a small sigh she turned to find out what the latest news was on her investigations.

"Ma'am," Jade said, as she came in and saw Margaret standing at the foot of the stairs.

"What did you get?"

"Jones was definitely receiving money from the Anarchists."

"I guess that's pretty much what we were expecting then."

Jade nodded. "And Imperial Security tried to pick up Hermandez Cortez, the activist with the Anarchists' Armed Action Wing. Unfortunately, it appears he's disappeared again."

"Any idea where he might have gone?"

"None," Jade said regretfully.

"All right. I'm taking the six o'clock flight to Naisre tomorrow morning. I'll need you to escort me to the airpark, but then you can try chatting up that boyfriend of yours and see if you can find out where Mr. Cortez has gone."

"He's *not* my boyfriend," Jade snapped.

Margaret stared at her, surprised at the strength of her reaction.

"He was an undercover assignment, not my boyfriend," Jade said more calmly, although Margaret thought she sounded like someone trying to convince herself. "Besides, Imp-Sec want to talk to him."

"Why, what's he done?"

"He was identified by the bank teller as the Anarchist paying off Markus Ackov's Director to ensure any reports of possible eco-terrorism were covered up."

"Oh." She watched Jade twisting her watch around her wrist. "I'm sorry."

"Yeah, so am I." There was a hard edge to Jade's voice.

"Is there anything more then?" Margaret asked finally.

Jade shook her head.

"Then I'll see you at dinner."

20

Naisre

(Wednesday: Thursday: Naisre, Mainline)

Margaret followed the aide across Naisre's hard concrete shell, her heels sounding a sharp staccato with each stride. Behind her a steward maneuvered the low trolley carrying her bags, the trolley's wheels clunking as they hit each expansion gap in the concrete. Over the heavy stink of diesel from the airship's engines she could just make out the sharp tang of an early morning in the Rockies. The combination of pine, spruce, and diesel providing a unique welcome to the C-T E's capital.

Unfortunately, the flight had been every bit as long as she had anticipated and having to make polite conversation for two days to people she had no intention of ever meeting again had left her exhausted. The airship crew tried to make the flight as entertaining as possible, but after you'd seen the Rockies from the air for the umpteenth time there really wasn't anything to look forward to.

She'd been a little surprised at how crowded the airpark was. At least twenty airships swung gently from their masts in the early morning breeze while in the distance, just beyond the low roof of the departure and arrivals' hall, a further six or seven of the military's rocket planes stood poised to launch outside their angular hangers.

The aide who was leading the way held the door open for her and she acknowledged the gesture with a polite nod as she passed through. Inside she looked round worriedly for the steward who seemed to have disappeared with her luggage.

"My bags?"

"I've arranged for them to be delivered to your suite. The First Leader asked if he could see you immediately you arrived."

"Of course," she said, suppressing a sigh. She'd been hoping for the opportunity to freshen up first, but that was obviously out of the question.

"I understand you've been here before, Leader?" the aide said, gesturing toward the row of lifts at the back of the hall.

"Too many times."

"Then I won't bother with the guided tour," he said.

Margaret gave a polite nod in response.

In the lift, the doors closed automatically, and they began the long descent to what had once been the floor of the valley. When the doors opened, Margaret was once again engulfed by the distinctive, slightly stale blend of scents that was uniquely Naisre. Stepping out onto the empty station she felt the change in air pressure that signaled a train arriving at the platform in front of her.

"That's good timing," the aide said, waving her forward onto the train.

Margaret raised an eyebrow. Hardly good timing when trains on this particular line ran every five minutes, making a complete circuit around the city in half an hour.

Ten minutes later the train stopped at Hugle Station and she and the aide stepped out onto the crowded platform. Taking the lift down one level the aide's pass got them past the security checkpoint without Margaret even having to show her own.

"If you'd care to wait here a moment," the aide said as they entered the cavernous foyer, "I'll see if I can locate the First Leader for you."

She nodded, not really acknowledging his departure, once again struck dumb by the theatrical splendor of the foyer, that rose the entire seventy-one stories of the city to the concrete shell overhead. There, natural light streamed in through the plasteel glass windows that lined the ceiling. Over a yard thick, the windows were strong enough to withstand a direct hit from a small atomic warhead and had come close to bankrupting the Empire when they were fabricated.

There was no doubt about the foyer's Nayarit heritage. Gray and black flecked granite lined the walls, while smaller tessellated marble tiles in a variety of colors covered the floor in a series of repeating patterns. Large, square columns lined both long walls, while embossed stylized heads of Nayarit gods and their cohorts were carved onto each face. Above them, in alcoves set high into the granite walls, stood the demons of Nayarit theology. Stunted wings projected above deformed bodies that reflected a jaguar and winged serpent motif. Around their feet were scattered the skulls of their fallen enemies.

Engrossed in studying the statues, she failed to notice the arrival of the small boy pedaling a bright red pedal-car.

"Aunt Margaret!"

She looked round, startled. "Artos," she said, going down onto one knee as he pedaled madly toward her. For a moment she had a presage of what promised to be a very messy collision, but he suddenly put the car into a controlled skid that would have done an experienced racer proud and a moment later she had her arms round him and was hugging him hard.

He felt soft and quite squeezable, but when he started to struggle, she let him go and pulled back to have a look.

"You've grown," she said accusingly, wondering when he'd managed to do that.

"Of course, I'm seven now!"

Ah, the certainty of children. "Is your mother here?" she asked. He had his mother's eyes; limpid pools set in olive skin. With his blond hair, which he got from Donald, he was going to be quite the lady killer when he was older.

"Mama is having tea with Defella and Aunt Dymeka."

"Oh?" Margaret guessed that Dymeka must be one of Defella's sisters – she hadn't quite got her head around all of Defella's family. There was a banging from the far end of the hall and a protesting, high-pitched squeal as a blue pedal-car steered by a girl of perhaps two or three, and pushed by another girl of Artos' age, careered through the door at the end of the hall.

Artos gave them a worried look. "Got to go," he said, and pedaled madly away.

Another pedal-car, green this time, slid round the corner, propelled energetically by another girl of perhaps five.

Margaret blinked; all three girls were blond, with gray eyes, and the distinctive golden-hued skin of a Dynand. Their short tunics reminded Margaret of those worn by Roman nymphs. Both vehicles careered past without stopping.

"Slow down Dires," someone called, and Margaret looked round to find Defella had followed them into the room and was watching them with a fond smile. Neither vehicle seemed to slow.

"I take it they're yours?" Margaret said.

Despite having just turned thirty-three, and with a new role as consort to the most important individual in the Empire, Defella had not given up on her short, sleeveless tunic, which left most of her flawless olive skin uncovered. Indeed, she seemed to be setting a new fashion among those who should know better, Margaret thought. Not all of those wearing the new fashion could carry it off.

That was definitely not the case with Defella, and not even a hint of a bump marred her stomach as yet. Her hair appeared to be a slightly darker shade of green than Margaret remembered, and there was now a flash of black hair over one ear. The short dagger she had once worn tucked into the top of her right boot had been replaced by a considerably more effective automatic. The piercing green of her eyes were still as distinctive as ever, though.

"My sister's get," Defella said, crossing the room and, taking Margaret's hand in hers, pulled her into a hug.

Margaret returned the hug carefully. She wasn't much of a people person, and at times she found Defella way too touchy-feely. It made a nice change from the rest of her family though – sometimes.

"I've been told I have to congratulate you," she said.

Defella dimpled. "Thank you. That's why Dymeka is here. As soon as Mama heard, she had to send someone and Dymeka wasn't going to leave her daughters. I think Artos is finding them a little much."

"I wouldn't worry about it; it's good practice for when he's older."

"I think so too," Defella said, but Margaret suspected they weren't really talking about the same thing. On Dynand a genetic mutation had resulted in a serious imbalance of females to males, and to some unique social constructions. She could still remember Donald telling her of how Defella had proposed to him, offering herself as second wife to Matija, Artos' mother.

Margaret shook her head, trying to remove the image. "So, where's Donald?"

"He was just following me a moment ago," Defella said, peering around for her partner. "Someone must have grabbed him for something. Donald!" she called. "I'll go and get him," she offered when there was no response.

"No, stay," Margaret said, suddenly eager to keep her there. "Come on," she added, urging her toward one of the chairs. "You can bring me up to date on what's been happening before the esteemed First Leader deigns to make his appearance."

"He's not like that," Defella said defensively.

"I didn't say he was," Margaret said reassuringly. "Sit. Talk."

Defella allowed herself to be shown to one of the chairs that lined the foyer's wall. She seated herself demurely, as Margaret took the seat next to her.

"So, tell," Margaret said. "How did this happen?" She waved at Defella's stomach. Then she blushed as she realized what she'd just said. "Oh, I didn't mean. I meant . . ."

"It's all right," Defella said, dimpling again. "It was a surprise to us too. After what he suffered at Arnold's hands, and then the treatment he received for his new kidney we thought it would be impossible too. As it turned out we were wrong." She put her hand self-consciously to her stomach.

"Let's hope everything goes well. I know Ivy is hoping for as many little Clemhorns as possible, given that if anything happened to Donald she would have to step into the breach."

"No, I can't really see my sister-in-law wanting that responsibility," Defella admitted.

Margaret nodded. While Ivy had agreed to accept the position of World Leader of Etu, as the only remaining member of the Clemhorn family aside from Donald, taking on the role of First Leader would be a bridge too far. "Although she and Cador aren't doing too badly in that area themselves. I hear she's pregnant again."

Defella nodded. "I like Ivy. But I'd have given up after the first set of twins. Even with all my sisters and cousins around to help – two at once is just too much."

Margaret pulled a sympathetic face. "So how is Donald settling into his new responsibilities?" she asked.

Defella smiled. "I think he's starting to enjoy it. The first twelve months or so were horrific. He was only getting about four hours of sleep a night – there was so much to do. But over the last year he seems to have started to relax into the role."

"Rajko said the Council's much more settled. Apparently, they've even started to make progress on the new legislation Donald's proposed."

"And how long has that taken?" Defella asked. "All Donald wanted to do was to repeal the Edict against contact with lines with a Hallow Rating of more than 6.4. You'd think he was proposing the end of the world."

"Unfortunately, their concerns are not totally unwarranted," Donald said.

Margaret looked up to see her cousin. She got up and they kissed cheeks, before she stood back to take a look. "You're looking good," she said. He'd started to fill out – during the war he'd become positively emaciated. "And I like the gray, it gives you a statesmanlike appearance."

His hand unconsciously went to his hair.

"I told you," Defella gleefully told her partner. "He didn't believe me," she explained in an aside to Margaret.

Donald shrugged as he checked his watch. "I've ordered afternoon tea in the sunroom."

Margaret looked at Defella who rose gracefully from her seat.

"I believe my husband is hungry."

"It's all this thinking I have to do," Donald said. "And the arguing, don't forget the arguing."

"The little gods ever forgive us if we forget the arguing," Defella said with a grin, taking his hand. "And who have you been arguing with now?"

"The World Leader of Chikyù."

"Mark?" Margaret said. "What have you two been arguing about."

"You, or rather you and Sylvi's demand that we impose an immediate quarantine on the line."

"It wasn't quite a demand, more a request . . ." She trailed off as she saw his face. "All right," she conceded. "Perhaps it was a polite demand. Did he agree?"

"He didn't have any choice. I hope you know what you're doing."

"So do I, but given that the blight is even more virulent than the one in Russia fifteen years ago . . ."

Defella looked puzzled. "Blight?"

"Margaret's detected a new, virulent version of a potato blight on Chikyù."

"One of my agents," Margaret said, not wanting to take responsibility for doing everything herself.

"I've asked her to attend tomorrow's security meeting," Donald said. "There's evidence that someone is spreading the disease on purpose."

"Ah."

"About the Edict," Margaret said, returning to the original conversation. "You said the Council's concerns are not totally unwarranted?"

"Actually, no. If they were, I'd simply have repealed the Edict by Imperial Decree. But there *are* dangers in contacting an advanced line. The last war was a perfect demonstration of that."

Margaret nodded. It had been Miro's decision to contact a line technologically in advance of the Empire which had driven the Civil War into one that had risked the entire stability of the C-T E and prolonged the war by a further five years.

"We need to set safeguards in place before we lift the Edict," Donald continued. He paused next to a door and opened it. "Afternoon tea is served."

***

Margaret had just got back to her own rooms and was adjusting the temperature of the water in the bath when the phone next to the bed rang. She looked round doubtfully, then down at the water starting to pool in the bottom of the bath. She dithered for a moment, wondering if she could leave the water running, then with a sigh she flicked the taps off and walked exhaustedly over to the phone.

"Yes?" she said, picking the phone up, not inclined to be polite.

"Margaret?" a voice with a heavy Serbian accent said hesitantly.

"Markus?"

"Ah dobro, it is you."

"Is anything wrong?"

"No, well that is, Jessie has something to ask you. Can you hold on a moment, I'll just put her on."

"Hello, madam?" Jessie's voice curled down the phone, leaving Margaret feeling a little lighter.

"What can I do for you, Jessie?"

"Papa said I had to ask you."

"Ask me what?" she said, hoping to move things along before the opportunity of a bath before tea totally evaporated.

"There is a fete in Central Park next week. I asked Papa if I could go, and he said I would need to ask you."

"Do you know why?" Margaret asked, completely out of her depth.

"He said it was because of security."

Of course! Understanding was like a light bulb. "Can you put your papa on?"

Jessie said something softly to her father, and a moment later Markus came back on the phone.

"I'm sorry to trouble you, Miss Peric, but Jessie did want to go, and Karen pointed out the difficulty it would cause . . ."

"But Karen didn't say no?"

"No, ma'am."

Margaret suppressed a sigh. So, they were back to being formal again.

"All right, tell Karen that I said Jessie could go and she is to make all necessary arrangements for any additional security she feels is necessary." She felt the beginning of a headache at the thought of how much this might end up costing her. Then again, with Imp-Sec already providing some of the security round the house perhaps the cost wouldn't be that much. "Get her to liaise with the Imp-Sec's Troop Leader," she said.

That should keep some of the cost down.

"Thank you, Miss Peric."

"Margaret," she reminded him.

There was a pause. "Margaret," he said.

There was another silence, then the line went dead. Margaret studied the phone uncertainly. Just what had happened there? There seemed to be depths to that conversation she wasn't aware of.

Replacing the phone on its stand she headed back to try and run the bath again, a bounce in her step that had not been there before.

21

Vignette: What to See in Naisre

When refugees from the Nayarit Line escaped their own Earth to create a new Empire on the Mainline, an Earth with a history different to their own – they brought peace to an Earth that stood on the verge of war. In memory of their own world, they created a replica of their fortified, domed cities in the valley where they had opened their first portal. Since its foundation, Naisre has slowly expanded beyond its original confines to become the premier city of the Cross-Temporal Empire with over nineteen museums. Together, these museums contain the relics and spoils from all fifty-four lines of the Empire. Must-see museums include the Museum of Alternate Histories, the Imperial Portrait Gallery, and the Nayarit Memorial (a stunning recreation of the Temple of Xmal on the Nayarit Line). In addition, we strongly recommend that tourists allocate at least two days to visit Britain's reconstructed Albert and Victoria, and Russia's Fabergé Museums.

While hostel accommodation is limited, there are several cheaper hotels that cater for backpackers and offer reasonable rates.

A Backpacker's Guide to Naisre.
The Backpacker's Guide Press.

22

You Might Want to try Rucker's

(Thursday: Naisre, Mainline)

As Margaret was ushered into the conference room the next morning, she was surprised to find she was the first. She hadn't seen the room before, and her gaze was immediately caught by the massive aquarium that covered the entire length of one wall from ceiling to floor. Small, multicolored tropical fish moved through gently waving fronds of seagrass, while the light shining through the water gave the entire room the feeling of being in an underwater grotto. After placing her file toward one end of the massive table in the center of the room she drifted across to take a closer look.

She was watching a pair of zebra fish who appeared to have set up home among some purple and red coral when the door opened, and she looked round to see Donald.

"First Leader," she said with a wry smile.

"Madam Director-General," he replied, acknowledging the absurdity of where they found themselves. "Admiring the aquarium?"

"You'd have to be a fool not to. It doesn't make up for being so far underground though. How can you stand living here?" she asked, indicating the windowless walls that surrounded them.

"You get used to it."

"I don't think I could. I never liked it when I visited as a child, and it seems to be getting worse. Too claustrophobic. How does Defella cope?"

"She doesn't. That's why we built the house; it's about ten miles away, up in the mountains. If I'd thought about it, I'd have invited you to stay with us. Maybe next time. It's certainly got enough space. I modeled it after the house Nona designed on Etu."

Margaret nodded, remembering the house built into the cliffs near the Great Lakes where her cousins had grown up. "I'd like that," she said.

Donald checked his watch. "Everyone should be here in a couple of minutes. Do you want a cup of tea or something?"

"A hot chocolate please."

Margaret expected Donald would call for a servitor but instead he opened the two hatch doors in the center of the built-in bookcase that filled the far end of the room to display a small urn, percolator, and a hot milk dispenser. She watched him place two spoons of chocolate powder into two cups, mix in a little boiling water, then add some steamed milk, and a touch of cinnamon.

He took a sip from one of the cups, gave a satisfied nod and handed her the other cup.

"Ah – First Leader," a female voice said from the door. "If you're serving . . ."

"I *was* serving," Donald said, emphasizing the past tense. "*You* can get your own."

Margaret watched the woman pause to place the file on the table before crossing the room with a confident stride. She was perhaps Margaret's age, her makeup perfect, her silver hair worn in a short pixie cut that had been clearly chosen to emphasize her eyes. She was wearing a tailored silk blouse and a tight pencil skirt.

"Christobel Mullova," she said, holding out her hand. "Media adviser to the First Leader."

"Margaret Peric, Director-General, Department of Agriculture and Food."

"And here come the rest," Donald said.

Margaret looked round as a group of four entered the room behind her.

"Margaret, may I introduce you to Rajyeshwar Mitchel, our exalted Comptroller-General," Donald said.

"Not so exalted," said the brown-skinned gentlemen in a rumpled black suit. He carried the strong accent of the Indian subcontinent. "I hope our Ms. Schneider has been to your satisfaction?"

"To my entire satisfaction," Margaret said with a genuine smile. "I have to say I have been very impressed with your Ms. Schneider. She's certainly shaken the Department up."

"I'm glad you're pleased with her. Sometimes she can be a little too enthusiastic but given what she is uncovering it appears entirely justified in this case."

"Entirely," Margaret agreed with another smile.

"And our three representatives from the uniformed forces," Donald continued, indicating the three standing behind Rajyeshwar, all wearing the soft gray of the Imperial armed forces. Only the facings on their uniforms served to indicate their particular service.

"First, Cliff Lawrence, Head of Imperial Intelligence."

"Leader," Margaret said politely. She tried to maintain an outer calm, but a genuine smile reached her eyes. Finally, she had met the man who had held the post for most of the last fifteen years, except for the five during the war when he had been forced into early retirement by Miro. His face had the appearance of a revered grandfather, and his hair was a cloud of fine silvery threads.

"Milady," Cliff said, clicking his heels.

"Heidi Klume, Acting Head of Imperial Security," Donald continued, indicating the next officer who wore the Eye of Providence, the 'all-seeing eye', as a small badge on both her collar tabs. Despite her position there was no indication of rank on her uniform.

They both acknowledged the introduction with a polite nod.

"And finally, Leader Horatio Tuma, Military Chief of Staff," Donald said.

"Lady Peric," the tall, rather thin gentleman with a small, pencil thin mustache said. "I had wondered where you had disappeared to after the war, until I read your report."

"I'm surprised you remember me," Margaret said, startled. She'd attended several functions which Horatio had also been at, and they shared a number of mutual acquaintances, but they had barely talked.

"Naturally I remember you," Horatio said. "You were by way of being the prettiest woman at any of the balls you attended."

Margaret felt her face redden. Uncertain of how to respond she gestured to the table. "Should we start?"

"Leaders," Donald said, indicating the bar. "Help yourself to coffee, or chocolate."

There was a confused movement of bodies around the bar but within five minutes everyone had settled themselves around the table.

"Right," Donald said. "I assume everyone's read the information pack that was distributed three days ago." A nod acknowledged the files in front of everyone. "I'd like to give everybody the opportunity to bring their reports up to date. Madame Director-General?"

Margaret took a deep breath and opened her file. "There's not much to add. I understand from our conversation yesterday that the World Leader of Chikyù has agreed to an immediate quarantine of the line."

Donald gave a nod of confirmation. "I also understand that Mark has requested additional resources and Horatio has a fast reaction Force on the way to Europe as we speak. But I'm not sure that they'll be able to do much until we can stop whoever is responsible."

"And you're sure it's not natural?" Heidi asked.

"Everything points to a human agent," Margaret told the Security Chief. "I was speaking to Director Saito this morning. She's in charge of the project team I've set up to deal with this, and she's confirmed her team is now confident it couldn't be anything else. For the moment we're working with the World Leaders of Notway, Clyde, Huis, Kleng, and as I said Chikyù, to quarantine all infected counties, and to impose restrictions on inter-line transfers. In addition, we've now imposed mandatory inspections of all wheat crops throughout Mainline's American wheat-belt. But as the First Leader has said, none of that is going to mean anything if we can't find and counter whoever is responsible.

"Shit," Heidi said, obviously unhappy at the news.

"Anything more?" Donald asked, but Margaret shook her head.

"Just that I'd like to acknowledge the assistance of Imp-Sec in helping to set up the project team. It's taken much longer than I was hoping for, but without Imp-Sec's help we'd still be at first base."

"Heidi?" Donald asked, looking at his Security Chief.

"We're still trying to track down Hermandez Cortez, but unfortunately we're not having much luck. We're presently following up on a lead that he's already on Chikyù and are liaising with the World Leader's Intelligence Chief. It appears Carlos Babineaux, who was Hermandez' flatmate, has also disappeared. We had a tail on him hoping he'd lead us to Hermandez but he seems to have slipped his leash."

Margaret's ears pricked up at that, wondering whether Jade knew Carlos had disappeared.

"You've lost *both* of them?" Donald said, raising an eyebrow.

"I know," Heidi said sourly. "I've had words with my Sector Chief."

Margaret wondered whether some of Heidi's unhappiness was linked to the fact that she was only acting in her position and was therefore even more focused on doing a good job to prove she could do it on a more permanent basis.

"Anything on the letter bomb yet?" Donald asked quietly.

"It's still early days, but I've got a good team on it."

"I want whoever sent it, and I want them quickly," Donald snapped. "It was aimed for my cousin, and I'm taking it personally."

"Of course, First Leader," Heidi said, giving Margaret a nod.

"Anything else?" Donald asked, and Heidi shook her head.

"Cliff?"

The head of Intelligence shrugged. "We're trying to identify some sources within the Anarchists, but they haven't exactly been on our radar to date. That will change now, obviously. At present, we're putting feelers around the domestic authorities, but if they haven't already got someone undercover it's going to take a while to develop our own sources."

"You might want to try Rucker's," Margaret suggested.

"The Agency?"

She nodded. "They might have some sources you can use."

Cliff looked interested and made a note. "Thank you."

Donald turned to his Chief of Staff. "Horatio, what have you got?"

"Nothing," Horatio said. "Until you've got a definite threat that exceeds the capacity of Imp-Sec, I'd prefer to keep the armed forces out of it. Having said that, I've increased the GTG status of the RBG to two hours. And following our conversation yesterday I let Chikyù know we're prepared to lend them two Battle Groups, expense free, if they need further assistance to enforce an internal quarantine in Europe."

Margaret held up her hand. "GTG and RBG?"

"Sorry," Horatio apologized. "Good to Go, and the Rapid Response Battle Group."

"Thanks." And just who had decided that those abbreviations made any sense, she wondered.

"So what do we do?" Donald asked, looking around the table.

"It all comes back to those damn Anarchists," Heidi said, her anger appearing genuine.

Horatio nodded. "Why can't Security simply close them down? That would get rid of the problem."

A typical military response to a problem, Margaret thought, starting to open her mouth. Any sort of security crackdown was sure to pick up Louise, and she could imagine what Mama would say to her if that occurred. And obviously it would all be Margaret's fault, being the elder and supposedly more responsible sister.

"There are too many of them," the Head of Security said, beating her to the punch.

"And more importantly," Christobel, Donald's media adviser said, "you don't want to."

"Why?" Donald asked her.

"At the moment they serve as a useful pressure valve for the dissatisfied. Most of their members are not involved in anything illegal. But if you try and close them down that could change."

"You can't say that about the Anarchists' Armed Action Wing," Heidi said.

"No," Christobel agreed. "Those you need to take action against, but it would be easier if you could get their actions disallowed by their own political wing."

"You do realize that even the political wing espouses the overthrow of the State?"

Christobel rocked a hand. "There is some debate about that. Wilthur, one of their top intellectuals, has recently started to argue that it is actually unnecessary to overthrow the State – that it will simply wither away by itself."

"And he's had to survive, what, four attempts on his life from those who believe he's an enemy to the cause," Heidi pointed out.

"Exactly. The trick is to divide and conquer. But if you simply tar them all with the same brush then you're not going to be able to do that. And you have to understand they do represent a significant proportion of the working class in many Mainline cities."

"I can certainly confirm that about New York," Margaret said.

The conversation quickly evolved into a discussion about what they could do to put a spoke in the Anarchists' operations until Donald pointedly checked his watch. "All right Heidi," he told his Security Chief, "you need to locate Cortez, and what's his name . . ."

"Babineaux," Margaret offered.

". . . Babineaux. And we've agreed we're not going to close the Anarchists down, but that doesn't mean you can't kick some doors in."

Heidi looked a little happier at that.

"And I want twenty-four-hour protection for Margaret, Mr. Ackov and his daughter," Donald continued. "I do not want anything happening to any of them."

"Understood," Heidi said.

"Margaret, we need to get more information on how the blight might have been introduced. Pass any information you have onto both Intelligence and Security."

"Of course." As if she'd want to keep *that* information to herself!

"Cliff, I know I'm probably asking the impossible, but Intelligence has to get someone on the inside."

"You probably *are* asking the impossible," Cliff said sourly. "But we may not be the only ones with an interest in keeping an eye on the Anarchists, so I'll get feelers out. We may end up having to burn some perfectly good covers though."

"Just do it, and Heidi, make sure that your people are aware this is a joint exercise with Intelligence, and DoAF. I don't want any demarcation disputes. This is too important to turn into some sort of pissing contest."

"Understood."

"Until we've got more information that's probably it," Donald said, giving a nod of dismissal.

There was a confused series of handshakes as the others made their farewells then Donald and Margaret were left alone as Christobel pulled the door closed behind her as they left.

"So, how do you think that went?" Donald asked, tiredly rubbing the bridge of his nose.

"We knew there were problems. I was impressed by the way you handled your staff though."

"Thanks. Most of the time I feel I'm just playing dress-up."

"Snap," Margaret said with a laugh. "How do you think I feel? You at least won a war. Me, I got the job because my cousin is the First Leader."

Donald gave her a crooked smile. "There were other reasons. But I'm glad you did. If we hadn't appointed you, we'd never have discovered this . . . this mess. But this stuff," he pointed at the file in front of him. "This is serious. How the hell are they doing it?"

"Maybe if we had access to DNA testing facilities, I could tell you. Without it, unless we find the people responsible all we can do is guess."

"DNA?"

"Deoxyribonucleic acid. It's the molecule that provides the genetic instruction for all living organisms. The Nayarit had several advanced techniques that enabled them to directly map and manipulate it."

Donald nodded thoughtfully. "I'm pretty sure Sultan had the same technology. I think they used something similar to ensure the kidney they gave me wasn't rejected. I still can't understand the sheer waste of what happened there." His face showed a momentary pain and Margaret knew he was remembering the start of the war he had observed that had all but destroyed the Sultan line. He and Defella had got out through the gate a couple of minutes before it was destroyed by a Kinetic Orbital Weapon. That, from what Margaret understood, basically involved dropping a telephone-pole-sized tungsten rod from an orbiting satellite to impact the Earth with the force of a meteor strike. Simple, brutal, and from Donald's description of the bombardment, supremely effective.

"I might speak to Kaito," Donald said thoughtfully.

"Why, what's your tame inventor working on now?"

Donald looked around guiltily, and Margaret wondered what he was worried about. Kaito had shared an apartment with Donald before the war, and it had been his invention of the first re-usable portal that had saved the Clemhorn cause from destruction during the war. "He's ah . . . doing some initial work into trying to establish a direct link to Sultan."

"And I presume the Council doesn't know about this?"

"No."

"How's he doing?"

Donald pursed his lips and rocked his head. "But," he said, "this might be a good test."

"Oh?"

"I'll speak to him," Donald said. "In the meantime, why don't you assume that we have access to this DNA equipment and get a pack together of what you think we'd need?"

"And when I do, I presume you don't want me to put this through either Security or Intelligence?"

"I knew there was a reason I made you a Minister of the State. No, I'll get someone from my personal guard to you. Probably Colonel Ferai."

"Really, you've got him working for you now?" Margaret said, raising an eyebrow.

The massive African had been born on the Mmbuto é line before it had been absorbed into the C-TE. He had lost an eye while fighting pirates on a trireme early in his military career, armed with just a mace. He'd fought in the war using body armor and heavy assault weapons and was now in the Imperial Guard. Margaret had met him only once, but his size and the white tattoos that covered his face, meant she was unlikely to ever forget him.

"I know. I was surprised he accepted my offer, but I think Linele had something to do with it."

"How is your sister-in-law, and the twins?"

"They're all fine. That is . . . according to the last letter I got which would have been about two months ago. The twins are six now." He appeared surprised.

"Everyone gets older, Donald."

"I know, it's just that it's happening faster than I expected."

Margaret nodded, thinking of Artos, and Louise and the maturity she seemed to have acquired recently. "All right," she said. "I'll speak to Markus and we'll see what we can pull together for you."

"Thanks. Do you have time to join us for lunch before your airship departs?"

Margaret checked her watch. "I've got a couple of hours."
"Good," Donald said, pushing his chair back.

23

Travel Broadens the Mind

(Friday: New York, Commonwealth of America, Mainline)

Jade stood up from the chair and stretched. The windows in the front room were open, and the thin lace curtains billowed on the light breeze. Outside, dusk was closing in, and the room's two electric lights cast dim shadows on the walls.

"Tired?" Karen asked, looking up from the book she was reading.

Jade nodded. "It's been a long day."

"It's almost eight. Why don't you clock off? I can handle everything else until ten."

"Are you sure?" Jade asked uncertainly. She was certainly ready for a long soak in the bath.

"It's not as though either of us is really needed," Karen said, jerking her head toward the front door and the two Imp-Sec officers outside who were now tasked with external security.

Jade nodded. The additional security certainly made things easier. "All right," she said, deciding. "I'll see you in the morning."

Karen turned her attention back to her book.

Jade was just crossing the foyer to the stairs when the phone rang. Reversing direction, she picked it up. "The Peric household. Jade Carvello speaking."

"Ah, Jade, glad I got you." It was Inspector Terrance, her boss at the Agency. "I need to see you tomorrow morning in the office."

"Of course, sir. Can I ask what it's about?" Jade asked, already starting to wonder if Imp-Sec had found out about her relationship with Carlos. It had to be something fairly serious if she was needed in the office on Saturday. Or more worriedly, so important that the Inspector had to come in on the weekend.

"We might have a lead on Cortez."

At last! "What time do you want me there?"

"Nine o'clock will be fine."

"Nine it is then."

"Who was that?" Karen asked from the doorway as Jade replaced the handset in its cradle.

"Inspector Terrance," Jade said. "He wants to see me in the office tomorrow morning. Apparently, we have a lead on Cortez."

"Hermandez Cortez, the owner of the knife?"

Jade nodded.

"Let me know what you find out."

***

The front desk was unstaffed when she arrived at the building the next morning but the Security Officer who opened the front door for her simply waved her through. "Inspector Terrance is expecting you," he said.

It was the first time she'd been in the office on a Saturday and when she stepped out of the lift on the fifth floor she found the foyer in darkness. Cautiously, she made her way down the corridor to the Inspector's tiny office.

"Miss Carvello," Terrance said, looking up at her soft knock. "Come in. Take a seat," he continued, as he returned the file he'd been reading to one of the piles covering his desk.

He looked different without a tie, or his normal jacket.

"You said you had some news on Cortez?"

"Yes. He's on Chikyù."

"Chikyù! How did you find him there?"

"It turns out that the Anarchists are of significant interest to the First Leader. Unfortunately, Imp-Int doesn't have any information

154

on them and as setting up informers takes time, which they don't have, we were requested to provide access to any sources we might have."

Jade nodded, wondering where this was heading.

"As it happens, we did have the names of a couple of informants we could give them. Interestingly, and unusually when dealing with Imperial agencies, Imp-Int actually appear prepared to share *their* information with us."

"Really?" Jade couldn't hide her surprise. After the way Imp-Sec treated the information she gave them on what she'd managed to dig up on Hermandez she would have thought it would have been situation normal, with the information only flowing their way.

The Inspector smiled at her surprise. "I was speaking to the Section Chief's deputy last night. Apparently the First Leader made it very clear that he expects this to be a genuine joint effort. Having said that, when I asked how they'd located Hermandez on Chikyù she got a bit coy. My guess is they got word from another source that they either don't know or can't disclose."

"Chikyù," she murmured. That certainly put him out of reach. "I certainly appreciate you telling me this," she said. "But I can't see why it couldn't have waited until Monday."

"We thought you might prefer as much notice as possible."

"Notice of what?"

"You're going to Chikyù."

"I am? Why?"

"Semper ille nostram," he said, quoting the Agency's motto.

"We always get our man," she translated. "I'm not sure that applies when Imp-Sec is involved."

"They're not."

"Pardon. I thought that —" She stopped as he held up a hand.

"Under normal circumstances they would be. But they've been caught on the hop on this one. And the political situation appears . . ." he hesitated for a moment as he thought of the best way to express himself, ". . . difficult. While they're certainly liaising with Chikyù's own security on an official basis, the World Leader of Chikyù has made it clear that neither Imperial Intelligence nor Security are welcome on the line. There is still considerable bad feeling from the war. However, as it appears that Imp-Sec don't have much faith in

Chikyù's investigators they've asked if we'd be prepared to lend a hand. It seems you made quite an impression in the right places."

"I have?"

He gave her a small smile. "I haven't the foggiest idea why. More importantly though, there's now a reward of £75,000 on his capture which would more than cover any expenses on our part. And given your links with the Anarchists you already have an advantage. And of course, we do have the ability to work a little beyond what may be permitted legally."

"We?" Jade said, grasping at straws. *Links with the Anarchists* indeed.

The Inspector beamed at her. "The Agency. I've spoken to the Superintendent and she's more than happy with the suggestion."

"Hold on. You said beyond legal?"

He at least had the grace to look a little embarrassed. "We can't directly liaise with Chikyù agencies. To do so would imply that the First Leader doesn't have faith in the World Leader. Politically that's not a good idea. So, if you're picked up your actions will be disowned by the Empire."

"And the Agency?"

"We'll try to get you out."

Oh great, she thought. Try . . .

"And if I do find him, how do I get him back here?" she asked with more than a hint of frostiness in her voice.

"*When* you find him just hand him over to Chikyù authorities. You'll have letters providing authority to arrest him; it's just they don't have any legal authority off the Mainline. However, you will also be provided with papers authorizing his extradition which should be sufficient to keep him in jail, and you out of it." He gave her a reassuring look. "The mission isn't intended to be impossible, Miss Carvello, merely difficult."

She frowned. "And how do you expect me to find him? Chikyù is a little larger than New York."

"Imp-Int placed him at Genessee two days ago. That's near Mainline Memphis. You'll take a train to the portal at Chicago, with a direct connection to Genessee."

"And do I have any backup?"

"The Superintendent approved a two-person recovery team. Miss Carter will be accompanying you." He opened the top drawer on his desk and pulled out a thick folio. Half standing, he passed it to her over the files that covered his desk. "Yours," he said with a grin.

He was enjoying this way too much, she thought.

"Tickets and bank drafts for both you and Miss Carter," he said. "Also, the necessary letters of authority."

Jade opened it hesitantly. An artist's sketch of Hermandez stared up at her from the top of the file. She looked at him with interest. It was a good picture of him. They'd even got the small tattoo that looked like a tear on his cheek right.

There was also a considerable stack of cash that she riffled through quickly. Upon opening the sheet of paper marked itinerary she grimaced. "No, you haven't left us much time." They were booked to take the Chicago sleeper on Monday night.

"And what about Miss Peric?" she asked, realizing that with both Karen and her away Margaret would be left without personal security.

"Imp-Sec has already taken over that responsibility until your return. Miss Peric has been informed."

She nodded. "I'd better go and let Karen know then."

"Have fun," he told her as she closed the folio and got up. "And don't forget your receipts," he called after her.

***

She found Karen cleaning her revolver at the kitchen table. Bits of the revolver were spread out across the newspaper she'd laid out on the table in front of her.

"What did our lord and master want?" Karen asked, not looking up as Jade pulled out the seat opposite.

"We're off to Chikyù," Jade said, as she put the wallet down on the table.

"About time, too. I'm starting to find this babysitting boring."

Jade shook her head. She'd be quite happy never to leave New York. Obviously, Karen was not of the same mind.

"When do we leave?" Karen asked, reassembling the gun at a speed that implied she was ready to go immediately.

"Monday night. We're to take the sleeper to the portal at Chicago, transfer through, and connect to an express to Genessee."

"That's the Memphis equivalent?"

157

Jade nodded. "Apparently Hermandez was sighted there two days ago." She pulled the picture of Hermandez out the folder and passed it to Karen. "That's him."

Karen studied the picture closely for a moment before passing it back. "He shouldn't be too hard to find. What's our bonus?"

Jade frowned uncertainly.

"You didn't ask!"

Jade shook her head, embarrassed. She hadn't even thought about it.

"What's the bounty?"

"£75,000."

"That would be £25,000 then. Split two ways of course. I take it the Agency is covering all expenses."

Jade nodded, feeling more than a little under-prepared.

"And Imp-Sec are taking over here?"

"Yes. Inspector Terrance said they'd already started."

"Good, then I've got some business I have to attend to before we leave. Have you got my tickets?"

Jade opened the wallet and passed the tickets across to her, as well as half the cash the wallet contained.

Karen checked the tickets, then folded them up and put them away. "I'll see you at the station thirty minutes before we leave. Two words of advice – pack light. No more than a backpack and that satchel you call a handbag. We're not going to be away long."

"Uniforms?"

Karen thought about it for a moment, before shaking her head. "No, let's not advertise who we are."

As the door swung closed behind her Jade shook her head, a little bemused by her friend's reaction. Then, taking up the pad of paper on the table she started to make a list of what she had to pack. A moment later she drew a line down the middle of the page and started to list all the things she had to do before she left, including letting her mother know she was going off-line.

24

On the Run

(Sunday: Pittsburgh, Commonwealth of America, Mainline)

Carlos looked out of the window at the plain redbrick wall on the far side of the alley. Craning his head, he could just see the row of rubbish bins stacked along the foot of the wall. He was starting to get quite tired of that view. And just why was he in Pittsburgh? The only American portal to Chikyù was in Chicago and Dario had been quite clear that he'd be joining Hermandez on that line. He hadn't been able to see how they were going to get him through the portal, but now he couldn't even see how they were going to get him to the portal. At least he wouldn't be there much longer, as he'd been warned that morning that he was being moved.

His musings were interrupted by a hesitant knock on the door.

"Come in," he called.

Sandi, the pretty young Anarchist responsible for maintaining the house poked her head round the edge of the door. At eighteen, she was between boyfriends, and would not have been averse to keeping him company while he was here. He'd learned that in the first five minutes of his arrival in the house. Gods she could talk. It had taken all of his diplomatic skills to let her down gently. Apart from her being a little too young for his tastes, he had the feeling that if Jade ever found out he'd been dipping his wick in someone else's honey pot any chance for their relationship would come to an abrupt, and very painful end.

"Herman's here," Sandi told him.

"Thanks." He waited until she'd closed the door before picking up his backpack. He took a last look round the room to make sure he hadn't forgotten anything. As he did so, he caught sight of movement out of the corner of his eye in the alley below. Curious, he peered out of the window from behind the curtains.

He swore as he made out the shadowy form of a crouching figure behind one of the bins. There was no mistaking the figure's helmet and shotgun as anything but. He took the stairs down to the small kitchen on the ground floor two at a time.

"Carlos," Herman said, surprised, jumping to his feet as Carlos burst in through the door.

Tall and thin, with large spectacles and short, carrot-colored hair, Herman came across as a bit of a geek. One who had a bad case of hero worship when it came to Carlos.

"There are armed police outside!" Carlos said.

"You're sure?" Herman asked.

"Definitely. I only saw the one, but there'd have to be others."

Sandi was rummaging in the back of the cutlery drawer and as Carlos turned to ask what she was doing she produced a small pistol.

"No, no guns," Carlos said, holding out his hand for the pistol, even as Herman pulled out a much larger revolver from a holster in the small of his back.

Herman considered him for a moment, before nodding and replacing his revolver in its holster. "Give him the pistol, Sandi, we don't want you caught with it. Then go and make sure the bar is on the front door and the shutters are down. We'll get out via the loft."

Carlos held himself motionless, wondering if Sandi would refuse to hand the pistol over, but with barely a pause she passed him the gun and, picking up the keys, headed for the front of the house.

Carlos pocketed the small pistol thankfully. He really didn't like amateurs with guns. Herman worried him enough. Besides, he liked Sandi, and an armed encounter with police was guaranteed to end badly.

"Wait for us in the loft," Herman said. "I need to make sure the back of the house is secured."

Carlos nodded and headed up the stairs. He was just lifting the bar out of its supporting bracket that closed the door at the top of the stairs when Herman clattered up the stairs behind him.

"Where's Sandi?" Carlos asked.

Herman peered over the edge of the banisters. "Sandi," he called.

"Coming," came the answer, immediately followed by the sound of splintering glass.

"Sandi, now!" Carlos called as he pushed the door open and peered into the loft beyond. Light filtered in around the uncovered tiles overhead. Wooden boards had been laid over the exposed beams, the path they created disappearing into the dim distance.

Herman rested a hand on his shoulder, peering past him into the loft. "That way," he said, pointing to the right. "Keep going till you get to the end. You'll find another door similar to this one. Go through it and wait for me at the bottom."

"What if I meet anyone?"

"If you do, just ignore them," Herman said with a grin. "They'll ignore you. They're supporters."

There was another crash from downstairs, followed by a scream from Sandi.

"Go," Herman ordered.

Carlos headed off along the precarious pathway laid across the rafters, balancing himself by running his fingers along the underside of the tiles. At the far end he found the door that Herman had mentioned, and opening it carefully found himself looking down a mirror of the stairs he had come up. Cautiously he worked his way down, being as quiet as possible. At the bottom he found a coat rack and was just considering appropriating one of its coats when there was a creaking on the stairs, and he looked up to see Herman coming down the steps.

"You won't need the coat," Herman said.

"Where's Sandi?" Carlos asked.

"I don't know. She should be all right though. There's nothing in the house, and so long as we get away, they won't have any reason to hold her. I'll make sure I contact our lawyer as soon as I get back."

"And how do we get away?" Carlos asked. "They'll have blocked off the end of the street."

"Down here," Herman said, opening the door to what once must have been the coal cellar.

Carlos shrugged and followed him down. At the bottom of the steps, he found that the space had been converted to a wine cellar, with heavy, wooden wine racks lining the walls.

"Here, help me with this," Herman said, moving to an empty rack. "It's heavy."

Once they got it moving, the rack swung smoothly on oiled hinges, exposing a small, bricked tunnel that led off in the direction of the river.

"It was used by smugglers bringing in goods from the Ohio River to avoid duties," Herman explained.

"And presumably the reason you got the house?"

Herman grinned back at him. "Of course."

It took the two of them to pull the rack closed behind them and lock it into place. Then, bent double, they started down the tunnel. The air was warm and smelled of moisture and wet bricks.

It was fifteen minutes before they finally came to the steel grilled gate that marked the end of the tunnel. Herman fiddled with the lock for a moment and then leaned on the gate, forcing it open.

Stumbling out of the tunnel Carlos found himself on the edge of a small, deserted brick wharf overlooking the river. Grass had pushed up between the bricks and the shrubs growing around them provided cover from prying eyes. The sky overhead was a flawless blue, with not a single cloud to spoil the perfection.

"Nice," Carlos said admiringly, wincing as he straightened his back. "Pity the tunnel couldn't have been just a touch higher. What now?"

"We walk," Herman said, checking his watch. "Perhaps forty-five minutes?"

They followed the road up the hill, away from the river and its deserted wharf.

Sweat ran down Carlos' back under the heat of the sun, and his backpack chafed at his shoulders.

Finally, after forty minutes, the road they'd been following turned into a lane, shaded and dappled by mature oaks, that gave some relief from the heat.

The lane wound up a low hill that was crowned by a small, white, clapboard building with a wrap-around veranda. With a final, careful glance behind them, Herman opened the whitewashed picket gate and led the way up the flagstone path.

Carlos was expecting him to continue onto the veranda, but instead Herman followed the path around the house to where a large, shingle-clad, windowless barn was built into the side of the hill. The shingles that covered the barn had only just started to acquire the silvering of age, which probably meant the barn was less than five years old.

Carlos raised an eyebrow as Herman pulled out a rod of clear plastic attached to a chain around his neck. As Herman placed his thumb on the flat piece of plastic at the top of the rod it began to glow. Inserting it into the lock he pushed down on the handle and leaned against the door.

"Inside," he said, as the door swung open.

Carlos stepped through doorway into a tiny vestibule. He was not surprised to find that the next door was set at ninety degrees to the one he'd just come through. He tried the handle, but it refused to move. As Herman pulled the door closed behind them with a heavy thud there was an answering click under Carlos' hand, and as he pushed down on the handle, he found it opened smoothly. A little more substantial than required for a simple barn, he thought dryly.

Inside, the air was like a sauna, the floor of pressed clay filling the space with the stink of linseed oil. He froze at the sight of the shimmering soap-bubble of sparkling light, about ten feet across, hanging suspended in the air in the center of the barn.

"How did you get a portal?" he asked, stunned.

Herman shrugged. "Better you don't know."

"Carlos Babineaux?"

Carlos looked round at the new voice to find his attention immediately captured by the sight of the submachine gun lazily carried by a guard lounging against the side of the vestibule. Behind him a second individual kept his eyes on a number of screens showing the outside of the barn. At least these two looked like professionals

– he hated to think what might have happened if Sandi had had access to a submachine gun back at the safe house.

"Yes."

"Good. You need to change. Your clothes are over there." The guard indicated the table in the far corner.

There was no sign of a power supply for the portal, which meant it was on the other side. That made sense. Portals, even small ones, needed a lot of power, often enough to supply a small town. More importantly they needed a *stable* source of energy because what happened when the power failed didn't bear thinking about. Normally it involved a very large explosion.

As Carlos walked across to the table, he couldn't take his eyes off the portal. Just *how* had they got their hands on one?

The clothes laid out for him on the table included a coarsely woven, short-sleeved linen shirt and loincloth, with a sleeveless leather jerkin and leather kilt. There was also a long wallet next to a money purse with a strap to hang from his belt. A pair of moccasins completed the ensemble.

He looked around for somewhere to change but seeing nowhere shrugged and started to strip. Ten minutes later he had finished changing. The biggest struggle had been tying the loincloth and Herman had had to come across and demonstrate.

"So how do I look?" he asked.

Herman studied Carlos' frosted hair with concern and pulled out a box from under the table. Rummaging in it he retrieved a woolen bonnet of indeterminate heritage.

"It's clean," Herman said, when Carlos looked at it doubtfully. "Here," he continued, passing him the wallet. "You are now Mark O'Henry. There's identification, a map, and sufficient money to get you a ticket to Genessee by boat. You've got three weeks. Once there you need to book into the Continental Lodge. You'll be contacted."

Carlos thumbed through the thick wad of foreign banknotes. "I guess I'm ready then."

Herman handed him a blindfold and Carlos looked at it uncertainly.

"It's security," Herman said. "You need to wear it. And don't try to guess where you are."

"Need-to-know," Carlos said dryly.

"Exactly. I'll take you through and walk you through to the Chikyù portal."

Carlos felt a thread of fear. The idea of putting himself in such a position of utter dependence went contrary to almost all his training, but what choice did he have?

He slipped the blindfold over his eyes and soon he felt Herman take his arm and walk him carefully over to the portal.

"Right, one step and we're through," Herman said.

Carlos nodded and together they stepped forward. Suddenly, despite the blindfold, light flashed across his vision as he stepped into a vortex of swirling color that flashed and pulsated around him. Time hiccuped, and as chaos spat him out the other side, he stumbled.

"Careful," Herman said warningly.

"Is this Chikyù?" The room smelled of burlap and damp hessian, which probably meant the walls were either built with, or covered with sandbags.

"Next stop," Herman said.

"Carlos Babineaux?" a voice said. The voice had an interesting accent. There was some East-European in it, but it seemed mixed up with what might be Middle Eastern.

"Mark O'Henry," Carlos said, turning to face the voice.

The other muttered a curse in Arabic and spat.

'Kiss my arse.' Carlos winced as he mentally translated the phrase. He'd learned the language during the last war when the intervention of the Sultan Line risked the entire stability of the Empire. At the time he'd thought it would be a useful skill, but with the end of the war, and the apparent destruction of Sultan, he'd questioned the time and effort he'd put into learning the language. Now he suspected it was going to be time well spent, particularly as the accent was one that he'd had heard on the voice of at least two speakers from Sultan – and that meant big problems.

"This way," Herman said, leading him forward. They passed through an opening in the sandbags. Outside, the air smelled considerably fresher, with the scent of maple and birch on the breeze. They walked about seven yards and then made a sharp left. The ground was soggy underfoot, and mud stuck to the soles of his moccasins. As they turned Carlos stumbled in the mud, his hand catching himself on what felt like another sandbag wall.

"Careful," Herman said, warningly. "Not far." Another seven steps and there was another sharp left. "Three more steps, then through the portal."

As the vortex spat him out on the other side of the portal he swallowed heavily against the sudden surge of nausea. No one had warned him about that, although perhaps no one he knew had had to go through a portal wearing a blindfold.

"You can take it off now," a voice with a strong Brooklyn accent said.

Carlos cautiously lifted the blindfold to find himself in a small room with a single door on the far wall. The guard facing him was carrying the same model of submachine gun as those who had met him on the Mainline, although his kilt and leather jerkin reflected Carlos' own clothes.

"I take it this is Chikyù?" Carlos said.

"Indeed it is; Sonnontio to be precise. And you're Carlos Babineaux?"

"Yes."

"If you give me a moment to lock up, I'll walk you up to the train station where you can get your ticket."

"Train. I thought I was traveling by boat."

"You would have," the guard said conversationally, "if there was enough water in the river, but it's been a dry summer. Trains are faster, but riskier."

"How fast?"

"Just over a day via Scatchwah."

"That's Mainline . . .?"

"Chicago," the guard confirmed. "Anyway, as I said, just give me a minute and I'll walk you over."

"Thank you." This was Carlos first time off line, and the experience was a little overpowering. Having someone walk him through his first actions on Chikyù promised to make things a bit easier.

25

Vignette: Portals

Trans-Temporal Portals are specific occurrences of a 'wormhole' or an Einstein–Rosen-Podolsky Bridge that links two non-contiguous space-time points between parallel universes (or in this case: time-lines). The portal allows people and objects to pass through this gateway from one parallel dimension to another. The selection of the 'linked' lines depends on how the quantum state of the exotic matter making up the gate has been 'tuned'. Travel through a portal does not change the person's relative position in either time or space.

Because of random quantum effects within the event horizon, coherent energy cannot pass through the gate. This prevents electrical signals from passing through the portal. As a result, telex machines are now placed in proximity to all portals, which allows physical representations of the message to be passed through a gate before being re-encoded and passed on.

**Professor Kaito Langley, University of Constantinople.
Lecture Notes on Portals – an Introduction.
Unpublished.**

26

Departures and Arrivals

(Sunday: New York, Commonwealth of America, Mainline)

Margaret climbed tiredly out of the Rolls. It was only midday, although it was difficult to be confident of that given the gloom and the steady drizzle with which New York was welcoming her back. It had been a long flight, and the last two hours had been particularly rough. At one stage, the captain had even considered aborting the landing. Now the sound of the rain on the gravel and faint stink of wet coal smoke, heavy and cloying, caught at her memories and . . .

She found herself looking up through the drifting rain at the small hill in front of her, smoke drifting down from the village on its summit. Below it the newly reinforced and revetted earthworks of the rebels were surrounded by an abatis of felled trees, their branches and sharpened points directed toward the trenches of Margaret's own troops surrounding the base of the hill.

"Leader?" It was the artillery commander.

She gave a curt nod. "Fire at will."

There was a dull, double boom from the first howitzer, and she watched the shell explode in the air over the top of the village, the thud of its explosion muted by distance. The other guns followed in turn, and she tried to avoid thinking of the damage they were doing to those sheltering behind the village's earthworks.

A puff of smoke from an emplacement on the top of the hill was followed a moment later by a hissing, spitting noise from the incoming shell. She flinched at the horrific ripping sound from the shell as it exploded behind her. The sound was followed a moment later by the tinkle of falling earth and shrapnel. Straightening, she glanced back to where a soldier was screaming in pain from a missing limb, blood already covering the medics trying to hold him still so they could get a pressure bandage over the hole in his shoulder. Margaret turned her face away, straightening in pretended indifference.

"Ma'am?"

She turned her attention back to the footman who had hurried down the steps with an umbrella to keep the rain off her. She swallowed uneasily and, with a brittle smile, turned back to the chauffeur.

"Thanks Rolf, I won't be going out again today."

At the top of the stairs the single Imp-Sec Officer in heavy body armor gave her a polite nod as the footman opened the door for her.

Jessie and Mrs. Mack were waiting to greet her in the main hall. Swallowing, she put on her best face, hoping that her lack of color would be blamed on the trip.

"Mrs. Mack. Hello Jessie," she said. "How is your father?"

"Papa is at work," Jessie announced proudly.

"Oh?" No one had told her about Markus having a job. She looked questioningly at Mrs. Mack, the diminutive housekeeper.

"I understand he has accepted a contract with the Comptroller-General, ma'am. He started today."

"On a Sunday?" She held up a hand to forestall any explanation, disappointed that no one had warned her. "It's all right. Is Jade still here?" she asked.

"Yes Miss Peric," Jessie said. "Do you want me to go and get her? She's packing."

"No, I wouldn't want to interrupt her," Margaret said.

"She's been packing for *two* days," Jessie confided in a loud whisper, obviously surprised it was taking so long.

Margaret looked at Mrs. Mack again. The housekeeper gave a short nod.

"If it was my first trip off line I'd probably take as long to pack," Margaret told Jessie. "But perhaps, Mrs. Mack, you could tell Jade I'd like to see her before she leaves. And is there any chance of having a bath run for me? Coming into the airport was just awful."

"Yes ma'am, I've already ordered one."

"With double bubbles," Jessie announced.

Margaret gave the two co-conspirators a tired smile. "My thanks," she said. She started for the stairs, to pause at the housekeeper's, "ma'am."

"Yes, Mrs. Mack," she said, looking back.

"I thought you might want to be reminded that Miss Louise will be visiting tonight."

Margaret grimaced. "Thank you, I had forgotten."

"And ma'am, you might like to know that Jules has given his two weeks' notice."

"Oh, why?"

"I understand he's getting married, and he and his fiancée are returning to Greece."

"Jules is the second footman, isn't he?"

"Yes ma'am."

"I'd like to give him a wedding present. Would ten percent of his annual salary be sufficient?"

"It would be *extremely* generous, ma'am." From the housekeeper's expression Margaret guessed the offer might have been a little too generous, but then it was only money, and weddings were expensive.

"See me tomorrow and I'll arrange the bank check."

"Thank you, ma'am."

She was idly flicking bubbles from her fingers, trying to ignore the tremor in her hands, when there was a knock on the bathroom door. "Who is it?" she called.

"It's Jade, ma'a – Margaret."

Margaret smiled at her hasty correction and dropped her hands into the water to hide the tremors. "Come in," she called, sinking down farther under the bubbles.

Closing the door behind her, Jade took a cautious seat on the chair set beside the bath.

"I hear you're off to Chikyù?" Margaret said.

"Yes, I hope that's all right?"

"Of course it is," Margaret said. "This is your first time off line isn't it?"

Jade nodded, unable to hide her nervousness.

"You'll enjoy it," Margaret assured her. "And if you get the chance to have a look at the city of Yuchi, do it. It's at the intersection of the Missouri and Mississippi Rivers. Its Earth mounds are simply unbelievable. I was there, I think about five years ago."

Jade didn't look convinced.

"Karen is going with you?" Margaret asked.

"Yes, thank the gods."

Margaret had to hide a smile at the relief in Jade's voice. "Then when you're back, we'll discuss having you appointed to my personal household."

"Ma'am?"

Margaret was surprised at Jade's response. "I did tell you."

"But I thought . . ."

Margaret put her head on one side and considered her for a moment. "What, that I wasn't serious? Jade, I was never more serious. I owe you my life. More importantly I consider you a friend, and I don't have many of those."

She was amused to see the blush that rose from Jade's neck to cover her face.

"Thank you . . . Margaret."

"What time are you leaving?"

"About ten tomorrow morning."

"So, you'll be having dinner with us?"

"If that's all right. I've arranged to meet Karen at the station."

"I'd better get out then. Otherwise, I'll start turning into a prune. Can you pass me the towel?"

Jade averted her eyes as Margaret climbed out of the bath, bubbles dripping off her body onto the floor. As Margaret wrapped herself in the towel, Jade beat a hasty retreat.

Margaret spent the afternoon reading the files her Executive Assistant had sent her from the office. Unfortunately, her work didn't stop just because she wasn't in the office. At times she might be envious of those Departmental Secretaries whose offices were in Naisre, but then she had only to remind herself that she could look out her office window and see the sun. Something impossible for those who worked and lived under Naisre's concrete dome. And there was no question that she had a lot more freedom to make her own decisions than many of the cabinet who had their offices in the capital.

By five her eyes ached, and she had a crick in her neck from reading. As the front door opened, she heard the rush of small feet and Jessie's "Papa!" Deciding she had had enough she placed the last pile of files back into their box and stood up, straightening carefully. There was the sound of softer conversation outside, then a quiet knock on the door.

"Come in," she called.

Jessie appeared, towing her father behind her. "See, I told she was here."

Markus gave her an apologetic smile, his soft brown eyes sparkling as he saw her. "Miss Peric, I hope you had a good flight."

"Markus, I thought we'd agreed it was Margaret."

He shrugged, one of those apologetic Slavic shrugs that could encompass a world of meaning. "Margaret," he said, conceding.

"The flight was as awful as expected. The last two hours – horrific."

"My commiserations."

"And I hear you have a job now?"

"I'm working as an expert to the Comptroller-General's auditors."

"And they're paying you well?"

"Extremely well. But if you will excuse me, I need to change for dinner."

"Of course."

A glance out of the window showed that the storm appeared to have blown itself out, and Margaret decided to take the opportunity to enjoy the last of the sun and take a walk around the garden.

Louise arrived in a rush just as the household was sitting down to eat. "Sorry everyone," she announced as she took her seat and reached for a bread roll. "The owners were visiting, and we all had to stay back to meet them. What's for dinner?"

"Jessie?" Margaret asked. "Perhaps you could tell us." She knew the girl had spent the afternoon helping in the kitchen.

"Solyanka soup, Kotlety, which is like small meatballs, and a choice of two desserts," Jessie said, but she looked worried. "I'm not sure about the desserts," she admitted. "Cook was still deciding."

"Sounds good," Louise said, starting to butter her roll. "And sherry?"

Margaret sighed and rolled her eyes. "Please get a *small* sherry for my sister," she told the footman.

Louise gave a theatrical sigh, which Margaret ignored. "Louise, Markus has just re-joined you in the labor market."

"Oh?"

"Yes, he's got a contract with the Comptroller-General."

"Three months," Markus confirmed.

"Does that mean you can start paying rent now, instead of just sponging off my sister?" Louise asked.

"Louise!" Margaret exploded.

"Margaret, it's all right," Markus said smoothly.

"No, it's *not* all right," Margaret said. "Markus and Jessie are my guests, Louise. And can I point out that just staying here has made Imp-Sec's job considerably easier, as well as saving them a hell of a lot of money." She stared at her sister challengingly, then, not waiting for Louise's response, she turned to Jessie. "I understand you're looking forward to the fair on Wednesday."

Jessie had been looking worried, but now her face lit up with an enormous smile. "They have elephants, and camels, and acrobats, and fairy-floss toffee-apples."

Margaret's teeth ached at the mention of that sickly sweet concoction. She could understand Jessie's fascination for it though.

"They have a fair, where?" Louise put in, unabashed at Margaret's earlier putdown.

"In Central Park?" Margaret said, looking at Markus for confirmation.

He gave a small nod.

"So, what is your favorite?" Louise asked Jessie.

"The elephants," Jessie said, giving an emphatic nod.

"They're my favorite too," Louise said. "But I'll be working on Wednesday," she added, disappointed.

"I understand the fair doesn't close till ten," Markus told her.

"Oh?" Louise looked hopeful. "In that case, given you've got a job now, you'll have enough money to take me to the fair when I complete my shift." She fluttered her eyelashes at Markus, who looked very uncomfortable.

"Louise," Margaret warned, feeling an unexpected surge of anger at her sister. Markus was *her* friend.

"I was just asking," Louise protested.

"Then don't!" Margaret told her.

"Come on, Mags, lighten up," Louise said, rolling her eyes. "I was just joking."

Margaret glared at her sister as the soyanka, a thick, bitter-tasting cabbage soup, arrived to bring an end to the conversation, and the rest of the meal was taken in strained silence.

27

Vignette: Airships

In 1709, Ema Mazarović demonstrated the first successful ascension of a hot-air balloon in Zagreb. After her first balloon caught fire without leaving the ground, her second balloon rose to 237 feet. A small balloon, it was made of thick brown paper and filled with hot air. The hot air was produced by lighting a fire in a clay bowl embedded in the base of a waxed wooden tray.

The 19th century saw continued attempts to add methods of propulsion to balloons. Australian William Bland sent designs and a model for his "Atmotic Airship" to the Great Exhibition held in London in 1835. The Atmotic was an elongated balloon with a steam engine driving twin propellers suspended underneath. Bland believed the engine could drive the machine at 50 mph and fly from Sydney to London with a payload of 1.5 tons in less than a week.

In 1842, Henri Giffard built the first powered airship, which comprised a 143-ft long, cigar-shaped, gas-filled bag with a propeller, powered by a 3-horsepower steam engine. Development progressed quickly and in 1874, the Zeppelin company started construction of the Graf Zeppelin, the largest airship built to that time. The Graf Zeppelin had an impressive safety record, flying over 999,000 miles (including the first circumnavigation of the globe by airship) without a single passenger injury.

An airship's gas bags were initially constructed using several layers of calf's intestine folded together to give (in theory) an impermeable membrane. Goodyear soon replaced this with gelatinized latex, but the risk of leaks and explosions continued. The Nayarit's self-sealing, leak-resistant, multi-layered cross-linked nano polyurethane plastic films solved both the threat of leaks and explosions and ushered in the period of the great airships.

Marianne Henderson.
'Airships: Queens of the Skies.'
Perth: Hague Publishing.

28

The Start of Jade's Excellent Adventure

(Tuesday: Chicago, Commonwealth of America, Mainline)

Jade stirred from her sleep as the steady motion of the train eased to a stop. A carriage door slammed further down the car, followed by the whistle of a guard in the distance. As the train again lurched into motion, she plumped her pillow back up and tried to will herself back to sleep. Unfortunately, the small bunk's mattress was so thin as to be virtually useless.

A movement from the other side of the cabin disturbed her, and she cautiously rolled over, careful of the narrowness of the bunk.

"What's the time?" she asked drowsily.

"Just after twelve," Karen murmured.

"What's happening?"

"Customs just boarded, and I have to go to the toilet."

In the dim light from the corridor that leaked in around the small curtain blocking the window on the sliding door, Jade could just make out Karen's shadow on the far side of the cabin.

She watched Karen unlatch the door, and as she slid it open Jade had to shield her eyes against the glare that spilled in from the corridor outside.

Karen hesitated a moment, then Jade heard a soft step and a click as Karen slid the door shut behind her.

Jade dropped her head back on her pillow. She'd had less than four hours' sleep last night, and it appeared she was going to get even less tonight. The train was due to go through the portal shortly after twelve, after which time their carriage would be held to join the express due to leave for Genessee around seven. If they kept to schedule, they should arrive at Genessee around dinner time.

For the moment, however, it seemed customs would be shortly moving through the carriage checking for any undeclared items. The guard had their passports, and he'd told them customs probably wouldn't disturb them, but professional curiosity had her wondering how they did their job. This was, after all, the first time she'd been off line and she wanted to experience everything she could.

Swinging her feet over the side of the bunk she bent over to pick up her slippers but couldn't find them on the floor where she'd put them. They must have slipped under the bunk with the carriage's motion, she thought. With a soft curse she went to her knees to sweep the floor under the bunk with her hand. She had just found the first one when she heard the door slide open behind her. There was a double click followed by two soft phhfts, followed by what sounded like two coins hitting the floor outside the door. A moment later her mind had put everything together, and she realized someone had just fired a small caliber suppressed pistol into her bunk.

She froze. Her pistol was in her handbag which was on the shelf above her bunk, far out of reach.

She heard the door slide shut and as it did so, she jumped to her feet, hands scrambling for her handbag. Her fingers closed on the handle of the revolver and a moment later she was peering out of the door onto an empty corridor. Unfortunately, given the nightgown she was wearing, she was hardly dressed for a midnight gunfight she thought, even as a spur of heat burned her toe. She looked down to see a bullet casing. Point 22, she thought, picking it up. She tossed it thoughtfully, careful to avoid burning her fingers, eyes scanning for the second round. A glint of metal a short way down the corridor alerted her. She picked it up quickly and returned to the carriage.

She flicked the light on, and her eyes were drawn to two identical holes in the fabric covering the wall about a foot above the bunk.

Suddenly the enormity of what occurred struck her and she started to shake. Someone had shot at her!

When Karen let herself back into the cabin, she found Jade sitting on the bunk, her head between her knees, clutching her pistol in her lap.

"What's wrong?" Karen demanded, sliding the door closed and kneeling down to take Jade's hands.

Wordlessly Jade tipped the two cartridges into Karen's palm and indicated the holes in the bunk with a jerk of her chin.

Karen swore as she inspected the holes. "Did you see them?"

Jade shook her head.

"Are you all right?"

Jade nodded, then started to shake.

"Shit," Karen said.

There was knock on the door further down the corridor and some quiet voices. It appeared the customs officers had started to work their way down the carriage. Karen looked worried. "Here, get back into bed and get that gun out of sight."

"Shouldn't we tell them?" Jade asked plaintively.

"If we do that, they'll want to hold us for questioning and we'll miss our connection to Genessee. If they hold us too long there's a good chance we'll miss getting Hermandez. And there goes our bounty."

Jade nodded, happy for one of them to be thinking. Lying down she pulled the blanket up, and allowed Karen to tuck it in around her.

"We'll work out what we're going to do as soon as customs have finished with us," Karen promised.

A moment later even the meager moonlight from outside disappeared and Jade's ears popped as the train charged into a tunnel.

She was immersed in rolling thunder for a moment, then her ears popped again as the train rushed free of the tunnel, and there was a knock on the door. "Customs."

"Come in," Karen called.

The door slid open, and a customs officer came in. He held a clipboard in one hand and a screwdriver in the other. "Jade Carvello and Karen Carter?" he asked, checking his list.

"Yes," Karen replied.

"Customs inspection," he said. "Your bags please."

Karen gave a sigh and reached up to pull her handbag and backpack down for him. Finding nothing in either, he was just starting to undo the screws that held the cabin light's casing in place to check they hadn't hidden anything in there when there was a disturbance further down the carriage. Two officers ran past the door, and grabbing his clipboard he charged out after them.

"What's happening?" Jade asked, the strangeness temporarily penetrating her fog.

Karen poked her head out into the passage. "It looks as though they found something." Closing the door, she locked it and took her place on the bunk facing Jade.

Jade swung herself back up, wrapping the blanket around her shoulder. "What do we do now?" she asked uncertainly.

"If they made one attempt on us, there's nothing stopping them from trying again."

"But how did they know we were on the train?" Jade asked plaintively.

"Who knows?" Karen said. "It's obvious we need to get off it though, at least for a while. I've got a suggestion if you're interested."

"Of course."

"Let's get a hotel for tonight and try for a different connection tomorrow. That might throw them off our trail. At least for a day or so."

"Wouldn't it be better to use a different form of transport?" Jade suggested diffidently.

"It would be, but the train is going to take less than a day, even a local. Any other form of transport is going to take at least five times as long. And we can't afford that."

Jade's ears popped again as the train plunged into another tunnel, the thunder of its passage echoing off its walls.

"Portal," Karen said warningly.

Abruptly Jade found herself lost in a sparkling maelstrom of light, then time hiccuped and chaos spat her back out.

She swallowed convulsively. "Is that it?"

"That's it," Karen confirmed. "Welcome to Chikyù." She checked her watch. "We'd better get dressed if we're going to leave the train."

Feeling a little better now Karen was in control, Jade got up and retrieved her clothes from the top shelf. Karen had insisted they wear plain clothes for the mission. While Jade recognized the sense of it, wearing uniforms would merely serve to warn Hermandez if anyone saw them, she felt naked without its protection. Meager though such protection might be on Chikyù, particularly now people were shooting at her.

***

The station's gas lights barely provided enough light as Jade carefully climbed down from the carriage, breathing shallowly because of the stench from the city around them.

"Ah the smell of fresh horse manure and human dung," Karen said, as she passed Jade the backpacks, one at a time, then followed her down the steps. Moving away from the stairs and into deeper shadow they hoisted their packs onto their backs.

"Now where?" Jade asked.

"Let's try the Railway Hotel. It should just be outside, or at least it has been at any other station I've come through."

Outside Jade wanted to stop, to look around at her first sight of another line, but Karen grabbed her hand, quickly drawing her across the dung and straw strewn cobbled square to the four-story redbrick building that lined the far side.

As Karen held the lobby door open for Jade, she cast a quick eye back over those now hurrying away from the station.

"Anything?" Jade asked.

"I don't think so." Karen frowned uncertainly.

Despite the gas lights illuminating the lobby, Jade noticed several candles set on saucers burning around the room. The thick scent of rose and lavender gave a hint to their purpose.

The receptionist looked up from the book he was reading, his face lightening as he saw the two women. "May I help you?" he asked in heavily accented English.

At last, Jade thought, something exotic.

"A room with two beds."

"Of course. Your passports please."

"How much?" Karen asked, as the receptionist copied down their details into a large ledger.

"How long?" he responded.

Karen looked at Jade. "Just the one night?"

Jade shrugged.

"That's seventy pounds," the receptionist said. "You're in room 106 on the first floor. There's a shared bathroom and toilets at the end of the corridor. Soap and towels are in the room."

Karen handed over the cash and accepted the key in exchange.

Upstairs, Karen dumped her bag on the bed. "I'll head back and get the tickets," she said, throwing Jade the key. "Lock the door and don't open it unless you know it's me. I should be back in about half an hour."

With the door locked behind her Jade looked around the room in disappointment. Her first hotel room on a different line, and what a dump. The wood floor had gaps between its planks that were large enough to lose a coin in, while the wood itself was encrusted with dust and old wax. The carpet that covered the floor at the end of the bed was tattered and threadbare, and when she tried to sit on the bed the mattress collapsed around her leaving her in a deep valley. At least they weren't going to be there long.

She was still sitting on the bed, watching the bedside clock count off the minutes as she tried to make sense of why anyone would try to kill her, when there was a soft knock on the door. The problem was, she thought as she got up to answer the door, it didn't make any sense.

"Who is it?" she called softly, revolver in her hand.

"It's me, Karen."

Jade unlocked the door before stepping back. "Come in."

Karen came in holding up two tickets. "Got them. We'll be in separate carriages, but we leave at eight tomorrow."

"Oh great," Jade said sarcastically – another night without much sleep.

Karen gave her an understanding smile. "Why don't you have a bath while I unpack," she suggested. "It might help you relax."

Jade accepted the offer with a nod. Perhaps the bath would help.

29

Vignette: Backpacking on Chikyù

Backpackers should not travel alone outside Chikyù's major cities because of the significant risk of robbery. Sticking to the major cities and using railways (efficient and well maintained despite an absence of toilet paper) to travel between them will reduce the risk significantly.

While the KVirus provides protection against most diseases, contaminated water and malaria remain a significant danger on the line. We strongly recommend that besides at least one change of clothes, a rainproof poncho, and sleeping bag, your personal kit should include:

1: phrase book

2: toilet paper (useful on the trains which don't provide it)

3: water purification tablets

4: bug spray or repellant lotion

5: permethrin spray (once sprayed onto clothing, it will last for six washes).

6: malaria tablets

7: anti-diarrhea pills and constipation tablets (believe us, the native remedies are vile, and way too strong)

The Backpacker's Guide to the Chikyù Line.

30

That's Not Mine

**(Wednesday: Scatchwah, Chikyù line (Chicago equivalent),
enroute to Genessee)**

Jade fidgeted as she waited for Karen to return from sending the telegram informing New York that they'd run into some problems but would be in Genessee that afternoon. She checked her watch again. If Karen didn't hurry, they'd miss the train.

She pulled a face at the squalor that surrounded her. Last night, despite getting shot at, the platform had seemed a romantic place of light and shadow. In the light of day, it was obvious that coal smoke from the engines had coated everything under a thick layer of grunge, turning everything a dull gray. She grimaced as she checked the palm of her hand again. It still bore the stain of the residue she'd picked up when balancing against the side of the carriage to remove her shoe, which had somehow picked up a stone. She brushed irritably at the long denim dress she wore, wishing she could have at least worn trousers. But Karen had been quite specific about what they should wear, and it did seem to help her blend in.

There was a whistle from the guard and as the last stragglers picked up their pace, Karen finally appeared hurrying down the platform.

Jade waved to her urgently and Karen waved back, indicating she shouldn't wait. Clutching the handrail Jade pulled herself up the steep metal steps and into the carriage. As she did so, there was a shrill whistle from the engine and the train lurched into motion. Before she could check to see whether Karen had made it, she was forced to step back out of the way of a straggler clambering on board behind her. By the time she was able to look again, there was no sign of Karen on the platform. Relieved that her partner must have made it Jade checked her ticket and set off to find her compartment.

Her cabin was empty. Sliding its door open Jade gagged at the thick fug of stale tobacco that greeted her. Holding her breath she made a dash for the window, and after a moment's struggle managed to force it open a couple of inches. Not that that was much improvement she decided, as the compartment immediately filled with acrid coal smoke from the engine. She tried to close the window again, but it refused to move more than an inch, and finally accepting defeat she took the seat farthest from the window, holding the corridor door open with her knee to try and get some fresh air through the compartment.

As they traveled south, following the Illinois and then the Mississippi rivers, the carriage gradually filled with passengers. By lunchtime she was sharing the compartment with a family with five young children; a priest of one of the local religions dressed in a bearskin which he had laced around his body so he resembled a strange and very large teddy-bear, and who kept eyeing her off; and a traveling fabric salesman with an enormous suitcase of samples who insisted on showing her his wares. As none of the other passengers spoke English all she could do was shake her head and smile.

At one she was hungry enough to risk leaving the compartment. She went in search of the restaurant car, keeping an eye out for Karen on the way. There was no sign of her partner, leaving Jade concerned that perhaps Karen hadn't made the train in time. If so, there was nothing she could do until the train arrived at Genessee.

There was a limited choice of food in the restaurant; a couple of tired looking wraps, or the hot meal of mushed corn with a heavy chillied-mince on a flat bread. She'd opted for the corn and mince, given how hungry she was. Although she had had strong doubts about the meat as Karen had warned her they ate a lot of guinea pig on the line. It didn't look like guinea pig, but then she didn't have any idea what guinea pig would look like, or taste like, once it had been minced, and then drowned in as much chilli as this one had been. What she did know was that she'd have preferred a hot dog with mustard. Unfortunately that wasn't on the menu. Lunch didn't turn out to be that bad, despite her misgivings. The corn and mince were surprisingly filling, and the chocolate dessert, a sort of mousse made from llama's milk and eggs, more than made up for any other deficiencies in the meal.

Four hours after returning to the compartment Jade tiredly massaged her forehead. She hadn't been able to get back to sleep last night after the shooting and had been too worried to close her eyes on the train. Her exhaustion was now giving her a headache. The last half an hour had been particularly rough as the train plunged through what seemed a continuous series of tunnels.

The train lurched and she held back an oath. The young couple sitting opposite her with their five children nodded politely, and she gave a cautious smile in response. Now, as the train charged through another tunnel, the salesman stirred sleepily before pulling his hat further down over his eyes. With nothing else to do, she pulled the guidebook she'd purchased at Scatchwah out of the top of her backpack. Her eyes flicked to the door to make sure it was still closed, then positioning herself to make the best of the meager illumination from the overhead light, she settled down to read the guide's two-page history to the line.

She already knew that Chikyù's Point of Divergence had occurred when the Huns pushed into China, rather than traipsing west into Europe. The result had been a vast, but short-lived Hunnic Empire in central China. The Empire had collapsed after the Black Plague followed them off the steppes and devastated China. The result had been a series of independent warring states that in time had succumbed (in the south at least) to an expanding Burmese Empire. But that was as much as she remembered from school.

Someone made their way down the corridor, and she tensed until they'd passed the door. Letting out her breath she turned her attention to the book.

Apparently, on Chikyù, the Black Death had struck Europe in AD 570 (700 years earlier than it had on the Mainline). Over the next fifty years over eighty percent of Europe's population had been wiped out. Muhammad had died before he could receive his revelations, and without the threat of Islam to keep it together Christianity had schisimed, with Cathar heresies taking control of large areas of Western Europe. Lost in a series of crusades and counter-crusades, Europe's civilization had stagnated, never emerging from the Dark Ages.

America, with no Mainline Columbus, Drake, Ivanov, or Zheng, was left to its own devices. Several large cities eventually developed using intensive aquaculture, maize, and potato crops to feed their populations. The three largest were: Tenochtitlan (Mainline Mexico), Atakapa (at the mouth of the Mississippi), and Yuchi (at the confluence of the Missouri, Mississippi, and Illinois rivers).

There was a description of Yuchi in the guide, and remembering Margaret's recommendation to visit, Jade flicked to its section. Apparently, when the line had been discovered Yuchi had been the center of the Cahokia civilization. The civilization, which had encompassed the entire Mississippi basin, had boasted a population of just over half a million, and with 250 earth mounds, the largest of which surpassed even the massive temple mounds in Tenochtitlan, Yuchi had been the largest city on the line.

Yuchi and the rest of the line had been devastated by the diseases that had accompanied the discovery and assimilation of the line into the C-TE in 32 AE. Apparently, according to the guide, the city had never recovered, although it still served as a significant tourist attraction for those visiting from off line. Helpfully the guide then provided a useful list of activities, hotels, and favored eating sites.

She checked the guide's publication date. Ten years ago, which meant that its recommendations might be a little suspect, particularly as it predated the war. From memory Jade was fairly sure Chikyù had avoided most of the excesses of the last war, so perhaps the recommendations wouldn't be too far out.

There was a change in the rhythm of the carriage and she looked up as she realized the train was starting to slow. Beside her, the traveling salesman had woken up and was now gathering his bags.

"Excuse me?" she said uncertainly. "Genessee?"

He shook his head and held up a finger. "One more."

She bobbed her head. "Thank you." She could feel the reassuring weight of the automatic pistol in the handbag pressing down on her lap.

He nodded, slid the door open and started to maneuver his way down the corridor toward the vestibule as the gleam of lights from the platform outside streaked past the window. There was a squeal of brakes and the train eased to a stop at the station. She checked her watch – despite the best efforts of the driver and firemen it still appeared that they were an hour behind schedule.

The father of the young family opposite her tapped his pocket watch as his wife started to rouse their children. Seeing her looking, he opened and closed the fingers of one hand four times. "Genessee," he said.

"Twenty more minutes?" she asked uncertainly.

He nodded, giving her a broad smile, although Jade wasn't sure he'd understood her. Still twenty minutes sounded about right. Which meant she should probably go and freshen up as soon as they were moving again. The young family followed the salesman down the corridor, the parents chivying their children like ducks herding their ducklings. Alone now in the compartment she looked out of the window and noticed several soldiers moving along the platform beside the train.

She was returning from the toilet when she noticed two of the soldiers she'd seen on the platform entering the compartment at the far end of the carriage. They carried carbines and wore the dark green uniforms with the black shoulder straps and collars of the Military Police. The guide had been quite helpful in describing their uniforms, as regular soldiers wore yellow facings, and the police wore blue. She wondered what they were doing, before dismissing the thought with a shrug.

She'd just settled back into her seat when there was a knock on the door, and she looked up to see the two MPs standing there.

"Edina Child?" the first one asked, looking at a photograph he was holding.

"No," she said, surprised. "Jade Carvello."

"Your passport," he said, stepping into the compartment, while the second stayed back by the door, covering her with his carbine.

She started to stand up but, noticing them both tense, stopped. "May I?" she said indicating her backpack. "It's in the side pocket."

"Please pass," the first said, while the second continued to watch her nervously.

Jade started to get a very bad feeling as she carefully held the backpack out to him.

"On the seat," he said.

She placed it where he indicated.

"Please sit," he said. "This pocket?" he asked and tapped the side pocket where the passport was.

She nodded.

As he unlaced the pocket Jade noticed that he was careful not to block the line of fire from the other soldier still watching her stonily from the door.

Removing her passport, he glanced through it quickly. "It is her," he told the other guard who tensed even further. Placing the passport in his belt pouch he turned his attention back to the pack and started undoing the top clasp.

"What's going on?" Jade asked, but at a gesture from the one covering her from the passage carefully settled back. She had had way too much experience with guns recently.

The MP went through her pack efficiently, pulling things out quickly, obviously searching for something. Almost at the bottom he pulled out a package about the size of a box of cigars, carefully wrapped and sealed in waxed brown paper. A smile of satisfaction crossed his face.

"That's not mine!" she protested.

"Please stand," he said, a pair of handcuffs appearing in his hands.

"But it's not mine," she insisted, unable to think of how it had got there.

The hand with the handcuffs lashed out, striking her across the face. The metal hit hard, tearing her cheek, the pain causing tears.

"Stand!" he ordered again.

She clasped her cheek, shocked, but as he raised his hand again, she scrambled to her feet.

"Now turn."

She turned, not understanding what was happening, hoping it was some sort of misunderstanding.

31

Well Look Who's Here

(Wednesday: Scatchwah, Chikyù line [Chicago equivalent], enroute to Genessee)

Carlos checked his watch and frowned. They'd been late pulling into Scatchwah, but despite that the train seemed to be in no hurry to be on its way again. He was idly watching those waiting on the platform to board when the face of one of them caused him to do a double take.

It couldn't be! But there was no doubt. The young woman standing on the platform was either Jade – or her twin sister. There was no mistaking the short bob of dirty-blond hair, and that cute snub nose. She was wearing a long denim dress and loose cotton blouse, but he'd have recognized her anywhere. He lifted the newspaper he'd been reading to cover his face but continued to watch over the top of the paper, wondering what she was doing there.

A sudden memory of the Agency Officer he'd noticed standing behind Margaret Peric outside of Ag and Food after that debacle with the letter bomb caused him to swear. He'd thought there'd been something familiar about the agent; he just hadn't put the pieces together. Jade was a Rucker's Agent.

Damn, she'd lied to him, claiming to be in service. He considered confronting her, but there was too much at risk, no matter how much he might have enjoyed it. He'd put two years of his life into this operation – he couldn't take the risk of blowing it now. And then the hypocritical nature of his thoughts brought a rueful smile to his face. Talk about the pot calling the kettle black. Still, it didn't answer the question of what she was doing here, and whether it involved him.

He continued to study her unobserved, pleased to simply watch her without her noticing. It was definitely Jade but she appeared nervous, fidgeting, checking her hair. She was continually scanning around her as though waiting for someone and he wondered who she was traveling with. The Agency never put one of its agents out in the field by themselves; it was always a minimum of two. Yet here she was. All by herself.

There was a whistle from the guard and those waiting on the platform broke for the train. Jade at last seemed to see the person she'd been waiting for. She gave them a wave and headed for the next carriage down. As she disappeared, Carlos settled back in his seat. A young couple entered the cabin and Carlos gave them a polite nod before pulling his bonnet down over his eyes to try and catch up on his sleep.

He roused for lunch, and made his way down the swaying the corridor to the restaurant car where he bought a tasteless wrap and a bottle of small beer. He was heading back when he saw Jade coming out of her cabin and ducked into the toilet to avoid her. Continuing, he looked into the compartment she'd come out of. The occupants, a salesman and a young family, looked up as he poked his head round the door. There was no one he recognized though. He nodded pleasantly and went on his way, once again wondering just what Jade was doing there.

***

Five stops, two crosswords puzzles, and three hundred miles later dusk had fallen and a change in the carriage's rhythm prompted him to check his watch as the train started to slow. It was ten past eight, so they obviously weren't going to reach Genessee until half eight at the earliest.

The brakes squealed as the train eased into the station. The platform lights gleamed in the gathering night. Glancing out of the window he noticed the armed Military Police stationed along the edge of the platform. He watched, hiding his concern as they boarded the train, two to each carriage.

Time to leave, he thought, checking his purse.

Someone slid the compartment's door open. "Excuse me, sir."

He froze. His departure had obviously not been quite quick enough.

Putting on his polite face he turned, to find one of the MPs holding a photo out for him.

"Have you seen this woman?" the MP asked.

He studied it carefully. It really was a good photograph of Jade and he wondered where they had got it from. It would probably be counter-productive to ask for a copy, he thought. She really did have a nice smile though.

"Pretty," he said, not having to pretend. "But no, I haven't seen her." Carlos felt oddly reluctant to hand it back. "Can I ask what she has done?"

"She is a terrorist. She is carrying viruses to kill our plants."

Carlos didn't have to pretend to show the shock he felt. Jade? "I hope you find her quickly," he managed.

The officer nodded and headed down the corridor to the next cabin, as Carlos made his way in the opposite direction, toward Jade's carriage.

He found another two MPs in Jade's carriage, working their way down the corridor, checking in each cabin as they went. They were just about to enter Jade's compartment and he slowed uncertainly, but they waved him on, holding themselves against the corridor wall out of his way as he pressed past.

He slowed and looked back. The two MPs had entered the compartment and cautiously Carlos retraced his steps.

"Edina Child?" someone said.

"No, Jade Carvello." The voice was definitely Jade's. He'd recognize her Brooklyn accent anywhere.

He heard them check her passport then open her backpack. There was the sound of someone rummaging through the pack, then Jade's voice of shocked denial. "Where did that come from. That's not mine!"

He listened to the catastrophe happening in slow motion, then as he heard the sound of metal tearing flesh and Jade's shocked yelp, he reached for his flick-knife. A quick flip and the blade would lock in position, but it wasn't just *his* interests that he had to consider.

Peering around the open door he saw Jade's face had been forced against the outside window. The MP had his handcuffs out and was pulling her hands up and back to put the cuffs on. Jade screamed in pain and Carlos reacted instinctively. The second MP had his attention fixed on Jade. Dropping the knife back in his pocket Carlos slid up quietly behind him. One arm went round the MP's neck and he squeezed tightly, applying pressure to the carotid artery just as he'd been taught. He felt the MP drop. As the man fell, Carlos lifted the carbine out of his hand.

He looked up just in time to see the first MP start to turn.

"That is no way to treat a lady," Carlos said, the cold bite of his anger lending an extra edge to his words.

He saw the MP's eyes widen in surprise, just before his open palm connected with the MP's chin. He had wanted to hit him with the carbine, but just in case he could still save the mission he needed to minimize the damage as much as possible. Besides there was no need; his palm had perfectly connected with the MP's chin, snapping his head back, and slamming his brain into the back of his skull. The strength of the blow and his weight took Jade down with him, but Carlos was already turning back to the second guard who was starting to come to and was peering uncertainly around.

"Roll over," Carlos said, a quick gesture from the carbine reinforcing his command. Having handcuffed the man and gagged him with a handkerchief, Carlos turned back to find Jade still trying to struggle to her feet.

"Get him off me!" she snapped.

Carlos ignored her as he transferred her cuffs to the MP. This time the gag was one of Jade's socks that were strewn over the bunk. Then, and only then, did he help Jade to her feet.

"What are you doing?" she demanded, anger strengthening her Brooklyn accent. That was useful information he thought. You always wanted to know how you could recognize a woman when she was *really* pissed off.

"I could ask the same thing of you," he said, grabbing one of her stockings from the pile of clothes on the seat and starting to stuff everything on the seat back into the backpack.

"I asked first though."

"I'm busy saving your life. Do you know what this is?" He held the brown paper package up to show her.

"How would I know what it is?" she said furiously, snatching the package out of his hand and shaking it in his face. "I had everything under control until you did your macho bullshit bit."

He grabbed it back nervously. "It's a virus, probably tailored for plants." Nothing seemed broken and he placed it carefully on the top of the backpack, and laced the top flap closed.

He opened her passport and flicked through it, pausing as he came to her photograph.

"And how would you know that?" she asked.

"Because they told me so," he said, indicating the soldiers. "Well not these two, but the ones checking for you in the next carriage down."

She looked at him, eyes squinting at him angrily. "And just why did you have to hit them? My employer would have got me out?"

"The Agency?"

Her eyes closed dangerously, so he leaned forward and dragged his thumb through the blood running down her cheek. He held it up to show her. "I doubt it," he said. "You wouldn't have survived the night."

"They certainly won't listen to me now," Jade said, looking down at the two gagged and handcuffed soldiers lying on the floor of the cabin.

"They wouldn't have listened to you before," Carlos said. "I know these people. Guilty until proved innocent. Basically, they had you bang to rights as soon as they found the box." They'd been even worse than Imp-Sec, and that was saying something.

Jade didn't look convinced, and Carlos had the feeling that at least part of the reason for that was that she hated to be proved wrong.

"Besides, your passport's been doctored."

"What?" She seized it out of his hand.

"The photograph's been lifted then re-glued. Obviously 'you' tampered with it."

She cursed as she saw what he'd seen.

"You still haven't told me why you're here," Carlos said.

"I've got a warrant for your flatmate," she said curtly.

"Hermandez?"

"Yes, Hermandez. How many flatmates have you got?"

Carlos looked at her backpack, and a nasty thought occurred to him. "Are you sure?" he asked. "That one didn't seem to find anything when he was searching your bag."

Jade frantically reached into the pack's side pocket and found nothing there. "Shit," she said, ashen faced. "And this pocket had all my money."

"You've been set up," Carlos said. "Without your papers, and with that package you'd simply have disappeared, and the Agency wouldn't have known anything."

"That's rubbish," she protested. "Who'd do that?" She shook her head.

Carlos simply flicked his knife open and cut one of the stockings in half.

"Hey, what do you think you're doing?" Jade grumbled. "Do you know how much those cost?"

"If you'd rather be arrested for assaulting a public officer?" Carlos said, using the two halves to bind the gags in place.

"And just *who* assaulted a public officer?" Jade's voice rose an extra octave. "Well, lookie, lookie, it's Mr. Babineaux."

"Who are you traveling with?" he asked, ignoring the comment.

"Why would I be traveling with someone?"

"Agents always travel in pairs."

Jade sighed. "It was Karen Carter."

"Is she on the train?"

"I'm not sure," she admitted.

"The MPs were only looking for you so Karen should be fine. Come on," Carlos said, taking her arm. "We need to get out of here."

She touched her cheek with her finger and looked at the blood for a moment. Then she looked up at him tremulously. "I still don't think you should have done that, but thank you."

"You're welcome. Although to tell the truth I don't think I should have done it either." Bending, he picked up the photograph of Jade the first MP had been carrying and slid it into his pouch.

"What?" he demanded, seeing her looking at him.

"Nothing," she said, shaking her head.

"You're a dangerous terrorist," Carlos said. "I need to be able to recognize you again."

"*Me*? You're the one wanted by Imp-Sec."

"What?"

"Bribery and corruption of a public official. The bank teller recognized you when you deposited Mr. Jones's payoff."

Wonderful, he thought. His uncle was going to be so impressed. He slid the door open and checked the corridor, which luckily was still empty. Placing a hand on her back he guided her down the corridor.

"What's the plan?" she asked quietly.

"I don't have a plan," he admitted, wishing that he did. It would have been useful to impress Jade with, because he had the feeling that he hadn't succeeded in impressing her yet, despite the fact that he had impressed himself.

She rolled her eyes, which just proved to him he'd been right. "We'll be arriving at Genessee soon," she said warningly.

"I know." He checked his watch. "Less than five minutes." He paused. "Actually, I do have an idea."

In the vestibule the darkened countryside could be seen rocking past the small window.

Jade raised an eyebrow. "Let me guess. Your idea is we jump."

"If we jumped, we'd probably break something. No, I'm hoping Genessee is a terminal. If it is there's a chance the train will reverse into the station. If it does then it will need to change direction, and if it does that it will have to stop for a moment. That's when we jump."

"And if it doesn't?"

"We jump as soon as it starts to slow down. Those gags aren't going to last for long, And the station is going to be lousy with soldiers. We'll never get you off the platform."

Just then Carlos felt the train start to brake, and he leaned into the wall, reaching out to pull Jade against him as she almost lost her balance. The train continued to brake, then as its wheels passed over a turn-out Carlos opened the door and cautiously leaned out.

"Well?"

"Looking good," Carlos said, unable to see anything through the darkness ahead. There was a blaze of lights behind them though. "Get ready to jump."

"I like the kilt," she whispered in his ear.

He closed his eyes and offered up a silent prayer for patience.

"You still haven't told me what you're doing here," she said, as she wrapped an arm around him to keep her balance.

"I needed a holiday. New York was getting a little hot for me. Now I know why."

The train continued to slow until it finally ground to a halt with a squeal of metal and hiss of escaping steam.

Carlos clambered down and held up his arms to Jade who started to climb down even as the train gave a lurch. As she lost her balance Carlos captured her in his arms.

"Now what?" she said, somewhat breathlessly as he placed her on her feet, and they watched the train reverse away from them toward the lights in the distance.

"Now we walk," he said.

32

It Was Those Damn Elephants

(Wednesday: New York, Commonwealth of America, Mainline)

The crowd at the fete flowed over the edge of the path and onto the lawn on either side. On the far side of the Rose beds, children lined up impatiently with their parents, as they waited their turn to ride the four camels, now being led around the outside of the lawned area by their handlers. The high-pitched screams of the children who were playing tag on the lawn, had been audible from the other side of Central Park. In the distance, Jorg could see the crowd around the fete's promised two elephants.

"I don't like this," Jorg muttered, stepping aside just in time to avoid being run over by a father in hot pursuit of his toddler.

"Yeah, well neither do I," his wife, a tall, lithe blond, wearing a blue dress and matching scarf retorted. "But it's what we signed up for." She shifted uneasily under the weight of the heavy backpack she was carrying.

"I didn't," he muttered again, reluctantly tearing his gaze from the toddler who was now upside down in his father's arms. "They're just having fun."

"You can't make an omelet without breaking some eggs," she snapped.

"Just remind me why blowing up a bunch of civilians is going to help us overthrow the State."

"We are *not* going to blow up any civilians," she whispered back angrily. "And lower your voice." She peered around worriedly, but no one seemed to be taking an interest in them. "You know the plan. We plant the bomb, then phone in the warning. The park's evacuated and when Imp-Sec arrive *that's* when we detonate it."

"I still don't like it, Sofia."

"You don't have to like it," she snapped. "Just do what you've been told."

They'd reached the statue of Lord Washington and she slipped the backpack off and sat down on the statue's pedestal, the backpack between her legs.

"Sit!" she hissed.

He eyed the backpack uneasily, but settled himself beside her.

She checked her watch. "Five minutes, and we can leave."

"And why do we have to blow up Washington's statue?" Jorg whined. "Dad always let me climb up on his horse when he brought me to the park."

His wife rolled her eyes and shook her head.

"Stop it," she hissed, a short while later, when the nervous tapping of his fingers on his knees had got too much for her.

"I can't."

She frowned, catching sight of something behind him. "Time to go," she said, standing up.

He looked round to see what had startled her. "Fuck," he said, seeing the two Imp-Sec officers walking in their direction. They'd barely made it ten yards when he heard a young girl calling after them.

"Miss, miss, you left your pack."

Jorg looked over his shoulder to see a young girl, eight, maybe nine, with olive brown skin, staggering under the weight of the backpack containing the bomb as she tried to catch up with them.

"It's not ours," he said, not slowing down.

"But I saw . . ." the girl's voice trailed off.

"Jessie!" someone was chasing them, a small, compact woman, barely larger than the girl.

The two Imp-Sec Officers had increased their pace.

"Jorg, down!" it was Sofia.

He glanced back to see Sofia had stopped and was holding her revolver in the approved two-handed stance their instructor had spent so much time trying to drill into them. Without thinking, he threw himself at the girl, knocking her to the ground and covering her with his body as Sofia's revolver barked three times.

"Jorg, we've got to go!"

Jorg scrambled to his feet and yanked the girl up after him by her arm. He paused at the sight of the two black-clad bodies now lying sprawled on the ground, blood staining their shirts.

"Let her go," a voice screamed, and someone grabbed his arm.

He looked round to find the small woman, who'd been chasing the girl, clutching his arm. Startled, he shook her off, his fist accidentally hitting her in the face as she lost her grip.

The girl's brown eyes went enormously large. "Miss Peric is going to be *furious* with you."

"Jorg," Sofia screamed. "We have to go. Now!"

He glanced at the woman who was moaning at his feet, and then his eyes were caught by the backpack, mere feet away. Protectively he swung the girl up into his arms. "Who's Miss Peric?"

"The First Leader's cousin. Mrs. Mack's her housekeeper."

The First Leader's cousin, he thought hysterically. Of course she was! Could this day get any worse? He began to run, trying to keep up with Sofia. "And who are you?"

"Jessie. *Nous sommes des invités non payants.*"

Between the girl herself being out of breath, the French, the running, his rising hysteria, and the sight of three police officers now heading towards them from the left, their guns drawn; what Jorg heard was 'parent'.

"Sofia!" he screamed.

She slowed, turning to see what had alarmed him, and almost stumbled when she saw the three officers closing in on them.

Her revolver came up.

"No," he said, thrusting the girl at her. "Take this one and go! She's a Peric. I'll hold them off."

Her eyes flicked to the police, then back to his face. There was something there, something he hadn't seen from her for a couple of years – respect, pride? He wasn't sure, but it helped.

"Go!"

She nodded, taking the girl even as she gave him a sad, uncertain look. And then he was drawing his own weapon and turning to face the police.

He had fired four times before something slammed into his shoulder, knocking him off balance. Then something punched him in the chest, and as his revolver dropped from nerveless fingers, his knees buckled under him.

Sofia could always shoot better than he could, he thought, struggling to breathe, but his chest refused to move. He blinked, someone was crouching over him. A black uniform. There was something he had to tell them, but it was so difficult to remember. He smiled, remembering Sofia, and the way she had looked when he had seen her for the first time. The smile she had given him. Unconsciously, his lips mimicked the same curve.

The person crouching over him was tearing at his shirt, and then he remembered.

"Bomb," he murmured softly. "There's a. . ."

***

The phone rang and with a sigh Margaret turned her attention from the latest report from Sylvi's team and picked up the handpiece. "Yes Michael?"

"You need to take this call, ma'am. It's from your residence."

Margaret frowned. "Put it through."

There was a click. "Leader Peric?"

"Yes, who's that?"

"Force Leader Hore, Imperial Security. We have a situation."

"Oh?" Margaret said uncertainly. Why did the military always have to use such doublespeak? "And what situation might that be?"

"Miss Ackov appears to have been kidnapped."

Her mind was blank. Who was Miss Ackov? But then – "Jessie! Jessie's been kidnapped?"

"Yes, ma'am."

Her mind focused on the immediate tasks that needed to be actioned. "Has her father been informed?"

"No, ma'am, not yet. I thought it more important I tell you."

And just why was she considered more important than Jessie's father? She checked her watch – half twelve. "I'll do that. We'll be there in twenty minutes."

She put the phone down, closed the file, and stood up. "Michael!" she called as she grabbed her purse, automatically checking the revolver was still in its side pocket.

"Yes, ma'am?"

"Get hold of Mr. Ackov and tell him to meet me at the front door. Then get my chauffeur to pick us up from the entrance."

"Yes ma'am." For once Michael didn't pause to ask further questions but simply reached for the phone.

And the gods continued to watch over her as the elevator appeared as soon as she called for the car. As it grumbled its way to the ground floor Margaret felt a tic start to spasm in the corner of her eye. Gritting her teeth, she glared at herself in the mirror at the back of the car until the tic eased.

At the ground floor a huddle of security officers appeared to be getting a briefing from their sergeant, who looked round worriedly as she exited the car.

"You heard?"

"About the attack in Central Park, yes ma'am."

"Attack, what attack?"

"Two agents are down."

She shook her head, not really listening. Where was the car, and where was Markus?

The bell rang behind her and as the doors slid open Markus dashed out. "What's wrong?" he demanded as soon as he saw her.

"Jessie's been kidnapped. No, wait, I've already ordered the car," she said quickly as he made a start for the doors.

He hesitated, obviously not wanting to wait, but then the Rolls pulled up outside.

"Come on," she said, heading for the door. Out of the corner of her eye she saw the sergeant waving two Imp-Sec officers to follow.

"Is Jessie all right?" Markus demanded, hurrying to catch up.

"I have no idea," she said shortly. "I got a call from Imp-Sec at the house saying that she'd been kidnapped. The sergeant back there said there were two agents down." She reached for the handle of the car door, but Imp-Sec were already there and opened the door for her. She scooted across the seat as the second agent took the front seat.

"Residence," she said, as the doors slammed shut and the noise and clamor of the city was cut off. "And quickly!"

Rolf gave her a startled glance, but the Rolls accelerated away smoothly, and she turned to glare at the Imp-Sec Agent sharing the back seat with her and Markus. He was holding his assault rifle stiffly across his chest, his eyes nervously scanning the street outside.

"What happened?" Markus asked her plaintively.

"I don't know,. Demitri, what happened?" Margaret asked, leaning forward, and reading the agent's name off his tag.

"There was an attack in Central Park, ma'am. I don't know anything more," he said, not pausing in his scanning.

She gave an exasperated snort but leaned back into the seat. Taking Markus' hand she gave it a reassuring squeeze. "She'll be fine," she said, hoping that she wasn't lying. She felt him squeeze back and left her hand in his until they reached the house.

At the steps Margaret was out of the Rolls, even before the vehicle had come to a stop. Two steps at a time she almost ran up the stairs, arriving at the doors as they swung open, and Mr. Castles appeared.

"Good afternoon, Miss Peric," he said touching a finger to his bowler.

"Jessie?"

He shook his head, his red whiskers standing out from his face, and for the first time Margaret saw compassion in his eyes. "There's no news yet ma'am. I was just seeing to your housekeeper."

"Mrs. Mack?" The housekeeper had appeared at the top of the steps behind him. The small housekeeper's bronzed face was wet with tears, and a large white bandage covered up most of her gray hair.

Mr. Castles turned and, seeing the housekeeper, pointed back inside. "Did I say you could get up? Did I say you were to leave the house? No, I did not. Miss Peric, please see that Mrs. Mack stays inside and does not exert herself. She got a nasty knock to the head during the attack. Her staff were concerned for her and asked me to attend."

"Of course," Margaret said, casting a glance at the housekeeper.

"I'm sorry ma'am," Mrs. Mack said. "I tried."

"Oh fiddlesticks," she retorted. "Jessie had Imp-Sec looking after her; they're the ones who failed. And speaking of whom, where is Force Leader Hore?"

"I think he's in the dining room ma'am."

"Then we'd better see him," Margaret said, sharing a glance with Markus. "Thank you, doctor."

"I sincerely hope there is good news on Jessie in the near future," he said.

"So do I," she muttered to herself as she strode through the main entrance. She had expected the dining room to be full of large, burly Imp-Sec officers. Instead, there were just three officers clustered around a map laid out at the end of the table. A telephone line had been run in from the morning room next door, and two telephones had been set up on the table, about halfway down it.

"Force Leader Hore?"

A slim, bespectacled officer looked up, straightening when he saw Margaret. "Miss Peric?"

She nodded, and gestured towards Markus. "This is Mr. Ackov, Jessie's father. What happened?"

The Force Leader acknowledged Markus with a small, nervous nod before leading them to the far end of the table. He started to pull out a chair but when Margaret gave no sign of following suit, he ran a hand through his hair and squared himself. "We're still questioning witnesses, ma'am, but it appears that at, or around, 11:15 two armed individuals carrying a bomb ambushed the two agents accompanying Jessie after she had disembarked from the elephant ride. Both agents were shot.

"One of the agents managed to radio for assistance and agents from the house headed over to assist, but before they arrived the shots had attracted three local police who exchanged fire with those seeking to abduct Miss Ackov resulting in one of the abductors being killed, and two of police seriously wounded. By the time my agents arrived Miss Ackov and her abductor, who we believe is a woman, had disappeared."

Markus shook his head mutely, the pain in his eyes gouging a hole in Margaret's heart.

"So, what are you doing?" Margaret asked.

"At the moment I have a team trying to safely detonate the bomb the two abductors had apparently been carrying, while the local police focus on searching for the abductor and Miss Ackov. We have agents working to identify the dead kidnapper, and once we have a name, search warrants will immediately be issued for his home, and the homes of all known associates. In the meantime, as you can see, we've established a base here in case they call."

"Not enough," Margaret retorted. "There's a little girl's life at risk here."

The Force Leader drew himself up angrily, color draining from his face. "Leader, I have one dead agent, another seriously wounded, and two police officers in ICU. I am very aware that there is a little girl's life at risk. Rest assured that we will not leave any stone unturned in tracking down those responsible and recovering Miss Ackov."

Margaret glared at him, but he simply returned the gaze stonily. It was obvious he wasn't going to back down. "Who's in charge of the New York office?" she demanded.

"Ma'am, that would be me, Ma'am."

"And your sector chief?"

The Force Leader didn't even blink. "Group Leader Vasilievof. She's sector chief for the Commonwealth of America."

"Get her to phone me."

For a moment he simply stared at her, and she felt the tic in the corner of her eye start to spasm again.

Then, "Yes ma'am," he said with a curt nod. He turned back to the table and picked up one of the phones.

"Why would anyone do this?" Markus asked plaintively.

"I don't know," Margaret said. "This won't stop our investigation; it's already gone too far for that. I have no idea what they can hope to achieve."

"Ma'am . . ." It was Force Leader Hore, holding the phone out to her. "The Sector Chief wants to speak to you."

"Thank you," Margaret said, lifting the telephone to her ear. "Group Leader Vasilievof?"

"Leader Peric. You wanted to speak to me?"

"Correct. I wanted to know what you're doing to locate Jessie, because at the moment it doesn't seem that you're putting the resources into this case it deserves."

"Leader Peric, I can assure you that Force Leader Hore is one of my most experienced officers. He has immediate control of all Imp-Sec agents in New York and I am flying in additional agents from across the continent. He also has available to him the coordinated resources of all local police forces within the greater state of New York. As I am sure Hore has told you, we have one dead agent, another wounded and two police casualties. Neither Imp-Sec nor the local police will rest until the culprits are caught and punished."

Margaret shook her head, wishing Jade was here to cut through this bureaucratic bullshit. "Not enough. Have you considered obtaining additional resources from Rucker's?"

"No ma'am. In this case we already have enough people on the ground. Involving more, particularly from another organization, would simply create additional complexity, and run the risk of people tripping over each other."

"Then I'll need to speak to Heidi," Margaret said, referring to Heidi Klume, the acting Head of Imp-Sec."

"Ma'am, that is of course your right, but I can assure you we are doing all we can to find Jessie, and those responsible for her disappearance."

Margaret barely restrained herself from slamming the phone down into the cradle.

The sound of small arms fire could be clearly heard from the other side of the city as the rebels pressed the city's defenses and Margaret carefully replaced the receiver in its cradle. "Headquarters are unable to relieve us for another four days," she told her three Force Leaders, who'd crowded into the small room with her to hear the news.

"And just what do they expect us to do in the meantime?" Sharon asked.

"Hold," Margaret said dispassionately, too drained to think of anything more positive to say. This damn war had been going on too long. How many more people had to die? Both hers, and those she was fighting. "Sharon, tell your Squad Leaders to start digging in along the edge of the crest. Once they're established there, we'll pull everyone else back and bunker down. At least this time we have enough ammunition."

She shook her head; whatever platitudes Headquarters might offer her, it was never enough.

"Margaret?"

She realized Markus had followed her out into the hall and was staring at her, concerned. She tried to give him a reassuring smile but knew she'd failed dismally. "Sorry, just remembering some history."

He started to say something, but the house phone rang, and she picked it up quickly to avoid whatever he was going to say.

"Margaret Peric," she said.

"Margaret, it's Rajko."

"Rajko." Tears suddenly burned at the back of her eyes at the sound of her brother's voice and she rubbed at them with her free hand. "I'm sorry, Rajko, I'd really like to talk." And she was surprised at how much she wanted to just talk to her brother. To sit down and talk about happier days before the war. "But I need to keep the line free. One of my guests has been abducted."

"That's why I'm phoning. Donald wants me to ask you to just let Imp-Sec do their job."

"The way they did their job of protecting Jessie in the first place." Her voice tightened.

"Which is why you should let them do their job now."

"Rajko, she's only eight."

There was a moment's silence. "I know sis, but they *are* doing everything they can, and having you breathing down their necks is not going to help."

"I'll see," she said, not willing to promise but aware that if she didn't say anything he wasn't going to let her go.

"Look sis, I'll swing by New York on the way home. I'll see you in a couple of days."

"Sure," she said dully.

Hanging up again, she stared at the phone.

"It was those damn elephants," Markus said suddenly.

Margaret looked at him in surprise.

"If she hadn't wanted to see them so much . . ."

The elephants! Just how had they known where to seize her? She felt the tic on her bottom eyelid start to pulse as she remembered Sunday's dinner. "I'll be back in a moment," she said, starting for the front door.

33

Jessie's Gone

(Wednesday: New York, Commonwealth of America, Mainline)

"Stay here!" Margaret snapped to Rolf as he pulled the Rolls into the loading bay in front of Macey's. Without waiting for a reply, she opened the door and jumped out. Behind her she heard a muttered curse and the slamming of the car door as the Imp-Sec Officer who'd accompanied her tried to catch up. Lengthening her stride, she headed for the store's entrance.

"Lingerie," she snapped to the concierge who had opened the door on her approach.

"Straight ahead and down the stairs," he said, plainly taken aback. "But ma'am you can't leave your car there . . ."

She stormed down the stairs, to stop uncertainly at the bottom of steps. The lingerie counter was empty, the section apparently deserted. The faint scent of roses filled the air and – she sniffed – frippery. She heard boots coming down the stairs behind her and had half turned to tell the Imp-Sec Officer to stay upstairs when she heard soft footsteps followed by a startled "Margaret!" and turned back to find her sister staring at her from the entrance to the dressing room.

"How could you!" Margaret demanded.

"How could I what?"

"Tell the Anarchists about Jessie!"

"What? What's happened to Jessie?"

"Don't play the dumb blond with me," Margaret said, almost spitting. "You know damn well what happened. I invited you into my house and this is how you pay me back. I don't ever want to see you again." She turned away, then stopped as she felt a hand on her shoulder.

"Take – your – hand – off – me," she told her sister, very slowly and distinctly, feeling each word as carefully as though carving them from granite.

Stiffly she turned back to face her sister, the hatred in her face causing Louise to take a step back.

"You're talking about Jessie, your Jessie?"

"Yes, *my* Jessie," Margaret snarled. She could feel her anger rising and struggled to control the urge to wipe that fake look of concern off her sister's face.

"What's happened to Jessie?" Louise cried, panicked. "Margaret, tell me!"

"She's been kidnapped."

"Kidnapped!"

"From the fair you knew she was attending! At the elephants that she told *you* were her favorite. You told someone and they seized her. If she is hurt in any way, I swear . . . I swear I'll . . ." Suddenly, to her own distress, she burst into tears.

Louise stared at her in consternation. "Margaret. I swear I haven't done anything. I haven't talked to anyone. I haven't had time to attend any meetings for a fortnight."

Margaret rubbed the back of her hand across her eyes. Why was she crying – she never cried.

Something in her sister's eyes made Margaret pause, and she became aware they had attracted an audience, and two other staff were staring at them, fascinated, from the other side of the counter.

Margaret lifted her chin. "You swear?"

Louise gave a small, nervous grimace, and crossed her heart with her finger.

"Is there some sort of problem Miss Jones?" a male voice asked from behind them.

"No problem, Mr. Bannister," Louise said, flushing.

Margaret gave a sigh. If Louise hadn't had anything to do with Jessie's disappearance, then getting her sacked was probably going to be a bit unfair. On the other hand, if it turned out she *had* been involved in any way, then getting sacked from Macey's was going to be the least of her sister's problems. She'd make sure that Louise never had a job in New York, in America, or anywhere in the Empire for that matter, ever again.

"Mr. Bannister?" She put on her best professional face, turned and smiled at the small, dapper man peering uncertainly around her Imp-Sec bodyguard.

"Yes madam?" His tone indicated he was eager to know her name, and just as interested in knowing what she was doing here.

"Margaret Peric. I apologize for this interruption. A family matter. A child who was staying at my house has disappeared. I am perhaps a little overwrought."

A crease appeared on the manager's forehead as he tried to work out how that might involve his new sales assistant.

"Perhaps I could speak to my . . . cousin in an office?" Margaret suggested.

"Of course," Mr. Bannister said, obviously eager to get this whole unpleasantness off the floor and get everyone back to work. "Miss Jones," he said to Louise, indicating she should accompany them.

They followed Mr. Bannister up the stairs to his office on the second floor. Louise tried to catch Margaret's eye as they climbed but Margaret ignored her, her anger still too recent to make any effort at polite conversation.

He showed them in and was preparing to sit down when Margaret shook her head. "I'm sorry Mr. . . . ?"

"Bannister," he reminded her quickly.

"Mr. Bannister," she said with an apologetic smile. "The matter of the disappearance of the child has security repercussions. If I could just have ten minutes with my cousin alone."

"Of course," he said hurriedly, casting a quick, inquiring glance at the Imp-Sec Officer who was standing stolidly behind Margaret.

"Mr. Bannister," Margaret said as he started to pull the door closed behind him. "There will probably be something on the evening news if you listen to the radio."

He acknowledged the information uncertainly. He was still obviously wondering what his second assistant lingerie saleswoman had done to warrant this type of attention.

As the door closed behind him Margaret rounded on her sister, trying to ignore the sting of tears in her eyes. "So help me if it turns out you've lied to me."

Louise shook her head. "It's the truth. I haven't spoken to anyone outside of work since Sunday. I've been working double shifts for most of the last two weeks because Tiffany's been sick. I haven't been getting home till after nine."

"So how did they know?" Margaret asked bleakly. "If anything's happened to her, I don't know what I'd do," and helplessly she burst into tears again. "And Mrs. Mack feels responsible, but she's not. Jessie's my guest; she's my responsibility!" Margaret heard the start of a wail in her voice and forced herself to stop.

Louise gave her a nervous hug. "I'm sure she's all right."

"If you are, you're the only one who is," Margaret said bitterly.

She felt a concerned hand touch her shoulder and looked round to see the Imp-Sec Officer holding his handkerchief out to her uncertainly.

She took it with a nod and blew her nose. "I hate crying," she complained, tears continuing to stream down her face. "It hurts my nose and gives me a headache."

"Not forgetting it also shows you're human," Louise pointed out.

Margaret scowled at her through her tears. "I can't afford to be human!"

Louise frowned at this. "Fiddlesticks!"

Margaret couldn't help smiling. "But I can't do anything," she said a moment later. "Even Rajko has told me to leave it to Imp-Sec. And maybe they are doing their best," she said quickly, acknowledging the officer who'd given her his handkerchief. "But I have to do something. Jessie's *my* responsibility."

"So do something. Since when has our brother been able to tell you what you can and can't do?"

"But what?"

"Can't your Agency friend help?"

"Jade? If she was here, maybe, probably. But she's off line."

"Then talk to her boss."

"And offer him what?" she said angrily. "My credit's already maxed out."

"Look, if it comes to it, I could probably loan you twenty."

Margaret felt her eyes widen. "Twenty thousand. Where did you get that much money from?"

"I told you I cleared out Daniel's checking account –"

"But twenty thousand . . ."

"I didn't know it was going to be that much," Louise protested. "And I do want to pay him back so it can only be a loan."

"Maybe I won't need it," Margaret said, feeling a new hope start to rise as her desperation eased. "There's probably going to be a pretty massive reward offered by the police, that could defray some of the cost." She blew her nose again and dried her eyes. "I'll accept, thanks."

"And I'll ask around the movement," Louise offered. "But I'm not hopeful. I am very much still on the periphery."

"Will you be, okay?" Margaret asked, her hand uncertainly indicating the whole situation they found themselves in.

Louise nodded. "My cousin, yeah?"

"I thought it might be better than telling them I'm your sister. I know you're trying to hide any family connection. God knows at times I'd love to." She considered the now extremely wet handkerchief before placing it in her handbag.

Louise acknowledged the simple truth of that statement. "I'll be fine," she assured her.

"Then I'd better see about talking to Jade's boss. And this doesn't need to be mentioned to Force Leader Hore," she said, with a warning look at the Imp-Sec Officer.

"Wouldn't dream of it, ma'am," he assured her.

"Good," she said, casting a curious glance at him. He returned the look blandly. "Do you think your boss would mind if I made a call?" she asked Louise, indicating the phone on the table. "If I'm trying to do this without officially letting Imp-Sec know everything, I need to do it here."

Louise looked nervously at the door. "I'm not supposed . . ."

"And perhaps you could ensure we're not interrupted," Margaret said to the Imp-Sec Officer.

"Of course, ma'am," he said smoothly, opening the door.

Now that was someone who was going to go far, Margaret thought as she picked up the phone. "Zero for the switchboard?"

Louise nodded, still eyeing the door nervously.

"The Rucker's Agency, please," Margaret said, as the switchboard answered the call.

"Margaret Peric here," she said when she was put through, "I'd like to speak to Jade Carvello's supervisor."

"Jade Carvello?" There was the sound of rustling paper. "Just putting you through."

"Inspector Terrance's secretary."

"I'd like to speak to Inspector Terrance," Margaret said.

"I'm sorry. Inspector Terrance is in a meeting at the moment," came the answer. "Can I take a message?"

Margaret scowled. "I was hoping to see him. Would it be possible to make an appointment?"

"I'm sorry, but not today, ma'am. I can get you in for an hour tomorrow morning at ten?"

"Please."

"And your name?"

"Margaret Peric."

"And can I tell him what you want to discuss?"

"I'd prefer to leave that until I can see him."

"Of course, ma'am."

"Tomorrow," Margaret said her sister, as she hung up.

"We'll find her," Louise whispered fiercely, pulling her into a hug.

"I hope so," Margaret said, trying to ignore the prick of fresh tears in her eyes.

34

It's 'your' Virus

(Thursday: Genessee, Chikyù line)

Jade slowly came awake as the light, leaking in around the edge of the curtains, penetrated her eyelids. She stretched languidly, then froze as she remembered last night.

Last night? Oh gods! Why did she constantly let her attraction to Carlos have her ending up in bed with him? She couldn't even blame him for what had happened. It had been all her fault. He'd offered to sleep on the sofa. She'd been the one to tell him not to be silly. And then one thing led to another . . . She felt the corners of her mouth lifting at the memory of one particularly memorable moment.

Feeling the heavy weight of another body in the bed she rolled over to find Carlos watching her through lazy eyes. "What?"

"Nothing," he said, the exotic texture of his French accent making her catch her breath. "Just remembering last night. I've missed you."

"I've missed you too," she admitted, unable to avoid the truth, even though it would probably be better if she could.

He grinned and moved to kiss her.

"Oh no you don't," she said, holding up a hand to stop him. "Bed breath is bad."

"Bed breath?"

"Yes, you know. Morning breath." She waved a hand in front of her mouth.

"Ah, 'lit soufflé'."

"Pardon?" Unconsciously she had mimicked his accent.

"Bed breath," he said with a smile. "And you don't have it."

"Ah but *you* might," she pointed out, quickly inserting a hand between them to prevent him from kissing her. "Come on, up and at em, Tiger. You have a reputation to clear."

"And whose reputation is that?"

"Mine!" she said, quickly rolling over to avoid his lunge and falling out of the bed. She landed on her bottom on the wooden floor with a thud.

"Are you all right?" Carlos asked, peering down over the edge of the bed.

"Just peachy," she said scrambling to her feet, and giving a shimmy to drop the nightdress she'd been wearing back into place. It had ridden up a little more than was proper. Given Carlos' appreciative glance, however, she considered doing it again, but then her attention was caught by the beauty of their surroundings.

They'd arrived at the hotel after midnight last night, and while Carlos had diverted the receptionist with a request for an extra blanket, she'd sneaked up to their room without him seeing her. She hadn't really noticed the room's appearance last night, but in the morning light the room was delightful. It was a complete contrast to the dump she and Karen had shared in Scatchwah. The curtains were thin lace, the floor was polished black wood, covered with several brightly colored woolen rugs. The bed was a massive four poster, with heavy brocaded curtains that could be closed to further block out the light.

Carlos started to swing his legs out of bed and Jade made a dash for the bathroom. When she got back from doing her teeth she found Carlos, wearing only a loin cloth, studying the brown paper package that had been found in her backpack.

A cold chill ran down her spine as she remembered just how much trouble she was in.

Carlos looked up.

"You said it was a plant virus?" she said to cover her thoughts.

"I said I'd been told it was," Carlos corrected her. "I have no idea what it actually is." He reached for his switchblade, opened it and locked the blade with a flick of his wrist. Carefully he prized open the seal, trying not to damage the paper. Then, with the end of the package opened, he gently squeezed the box it was holding out.

For a moment the two stared at the simple wooden case.

"It's *your* virus," Carlos said finally.

With a snort Jade opened the case. Inside were two glass phials, both carefully stoppered, sealed, and cushioned in cotton wool. Carefully she lifted one of them out and silently considered the gray dust through the glass.

"I'd say that's probably enough virus there to get you hanged," Carlos said. Cautiously he lifted the phial from her fingers and replaced it in the box.

"Probably," Jade said. She'd been hoping it was all some sort of mistake but there was no getting away from the fact that she'd been implicated in the same plot she was trying to close down.

"But how did they get it into my bag? It never left my sight."

Carlos paused after he'd slid the box back into its waxed paper wrapping and considered her for a moment.

"What?" she asked when he gave no sign of telling her what he was thinking.

"You said you were traveling with another agent."

She conceded the point with a small nod. "But I can't see that — oh shit."

"What?"

"Two nights ago, she was looking after our luggage." It made sense, but Karen? That hurt — a lot. "I thought Karen was my friend," she added plaintively.

She stared at the box, then slammed her hand down on the bed and stalked across to look out of the window through the curtains. "She probably took my money too." She glared out at the view, stung by her friend's perfidy. A servant was hanging sheets up in the courtyard below.

"What happened to her?"

"We separated in Scatchwah. I was expecting her to board the train with me. I saw her on the platform, but I never actually saw her board." She swore as another thought occurred to her.

"What?"

"Just before we came through the portal someone tried to shoot me. Or at least I thought they'd tried to shoot me."

"Run that past me again," Carlos said. "I'm not sure I follow."

She turned back to face Carlos; eyes cold. "Just before we came through the portal someone put two shots into the paneling above my bunk."

"Did you see who it was?"

"No."

"And Karen?"

"She'd gone to the toilet. I thought the shooter had been trying to kill me, but perhaps they'd been just trying to scare me so that Karen could suggest we separate. If so, it worked a treat."

"Could the shooter have been Karen?"

"It's possible," she admitted regretfully. She straightened and folded her arms. "So what do we do?"

Carlos rubbed his chin, considering her doubtfully.

Jade frowned. "Just remember I'm the good guy here." She winced, recognizing just how much trouble she was in if she had to depend on someone presently wanted by Imp-Sec. The Gods know how Inspector Terrance was going to react to this.

He acknowledged it with a short, Gaelic shrug. "If we can get to Scatchwah, and I can contact my uncle, he should be able to get you back through the portal."

"Another uncle?" she said sarcastically. Just how many did he have?

He raised an eyebrow. "Both my mother and father came from very large families."

"And how will he be able to do that?"

"Uncle Pierre runs an import-export business."

"And just how are we supposed to get back to Scatchwah? Or have you forgotten that thanks to you beaning those two MPs I'm a fugitive from justice now?" she said.

"I think we can disguise you enough to avoid easy recognition," he said, ignoring her implication that he was responsible for the situation she now found herself in. "Change your hair color, or even better the length if I can find you a wig. Change your clothes. Maybe darken your skin, although I think you should probably be all right there. The problem is that without fake ID we're not going to be able to take the train and getting any sort of ID will take too long." He thought for a moment. "Fancy a romantic river cruise?"

"Well . . . if there's no choice . . ." Her voice trailed off suggestively. "It's a shame I couldn't get Hermandez though."

He held up the box containing the two phials. "I think this will probably more than make up for it."

She conceded the point. "Go on," she said, taking the box from him and giving him a small push toward the bathroom. "We can't stay here all day."

When he returned from his shopping, several hours later, he was carrying several packages wrapped up in plain brown paper and string.

"What did you get?" she asked, meeting him at the door.

"Have a look," he suggested, dumping the packages on the bed.

Bemused, he watched the childlike enthusiasm with which she sat down on the bed and started to rip open the packaging.

"What's this?" she asked, holding up a small, glass phial.

"Brown dye for my skin. The other one's for my hair," he said, as a second phial fell out of the paper and onto the bed. "And this," he said, pulling a wig out of a paper bag with all the aplomb of a magician, "is for you."

The black wig was long enough to cover her shoulders.

"I got this for you as well," he said, giving her a small hairband.

She wound her hair up onto the top of her head, pulled the wig on then froze, startled, as she caught sight of herself in the mirror. Staring back at her was her mother.

"What?" he asked looking over her shoulder when she hadn't moved for a minute. "Oh, you're going to fit right in."

She nodded. With her dark, tawny skin; almond shaped eyes, and long, black hair she looked like a native. "I didn't know I looked so much like my mother," she admitted. "I just hope she's not worried about me."

He winced. "This is also for you," he said, holding up another small parcel wrapped in brown paper.

"Not another plant virus?" she said, only half joking.

"No, go on. Open it."

Curious at his enthusiasm she carefully ripped the end of the parcel off to find something hard inside wrapped in tissue paper. Puzzled now, she opened the paper to find a chunky, sky blue necklace and matching wristbands.

"Very nice," she said neutrally. "Is it real?" The necklace, with its large chunky stones looked like some of the costume jewelry you'd buy in a swap mart back home.

"It'd better be for the price I paid for it. No, it's the real thing – turquoise. The style is pre-contact which is why I could afford it. Apparently, it's out of favor now. But –"

"Enough, Carlos," she said, putting a finger on his lips. "You're spoiling it." Holding the necklace around her neck she turned her back to indicate Carlos should do it up.

Head on one side she considered the effect in the mirror. The turquoise's soapy surface glistened in the light from the window, and she stroked the stones possessively. "It's beautiful," she said. Turning back, she gave Carlos a kiss. "Thank you."

She smirked at how relieved he looked.

"And I sent a telegram to my uncle. And here are our tickets," he said, producing two cardboard stubs.

The stubs bore the picture of a side-wheeler, and the title '*River Queen*' in ornate text over the top of the picture.

"When are we leaving?" Jade asked.

"Tomorrow morning."

"Then I guess we'd better make a start on your hair," she said.

***

Despite the sun being barely up, the wharf was crowded. The early morning mist still hid the far side of the river as they worked their way along the bricked surface of the wharf, trying to avoid the porters pushing their heavy trays filled with luggage or crates of fish.

Jade wrinkled her nose at the miasma rising from the mudbanks exposed by the low waters, which had trapped the raw sewage released by the city. Her ears were assailed by the cacophony from those already crowding the wharf, seeking to attract buyers for their goods.

Carlos forged through the crowd, heading toward the massive paddle cruiser towering over the wharf. At least four stories, its woodwork, freshly painted in cream and dark crimson, gleamed in the morning light.

As Jade struggled to keep up with him, she could just make out the sound of the small band on the boat's mid-deck, welcoming aboard those traveling with it today. It certainly looked and sounded promising.

They reached the gangway, and Jade appreciatively eyed the steward in his white naval uniform standing beside the arch with the *River Queen* ornately engraved over the entrance. She was so busy checking out the steward that when she looked round for Carlos, it took her a moment to find him among the crowd. He hadn't stopped, and she had to hurry to catch up with him.

"Where are you going?" she demanded in a loud whisper.

"To our boat."

"I thought you booked us on *The River Queen*?"

"Subterfuge," he said, not slowing down, and forcing her to hurry to keep up.

"I'll subterfuge you," she said. "What did you book us on?"

"I'll show you in a moment. Or at least I will if they haven't already gone."

"So where is it?" Jade asked quietly, pitching her voice below the clamor that surrounded them. They had almost reached the end of the wharf, and there was still no sign of anything that resembled a paddle wheeler.

Carlos looked worried, but then his face brightened as they made their way around a large pile of crates. "That's it."

"Where?" She was still unable to see anything.

"Down there," he said, pointing to the boat moored to the pier next to them.

"That! You've got to be joking," she muttered. The boat barely came over the top of the wharf. Certainly, it had two massive paddle wheels, and two stories, but the top floor looked to contain just the wheelhouse, with two cabins behind it. The ground floor was open with large bales of hay stacked on its foredeck, while a small flock of sheep huddled together in a tiny pen further aft. The large funnel protruding through the roof of the top floor emitted a thin trail of smoke.

"You said a romantic river cruise. There is no way that is going to provide anything romantic," she continued.

At least he had the grace to look a little bit embarrassed. "I thought this might be safer."

She rolled her eyes. He might be right, but she wasn't going to admit it. She eyed the wooden plank that had been laid from the wharf to the top of the wheelhouse roof. A rope provided something to hold onto.

"Come on," he said, taking her hand. "And remember, my name's Mark."

"Yes Mark, no Mark."

A small man, wearing only simple white cotton trousers, met them at the end of the gangplank. She tried not to stare at his moustache, which he'd grown from the corners of his upper lip, creating two long 'tendrils' that hung down past his chin with its single, straggly, goatee.

"Mr. O'Henry," he said. "And this must be your wife."

"She is indeed, Captain," Carlos said, giving her such an overacted fond look that Jade was tempted to shove him overboard.

The captain acknowledged Jade with a short nod. "Welcome on board the *Otsalanvily*. We were starting to worry you'd miss us." He turned and shouted some instructions over the side of the deck in what sounded vaguely Iroquian. Almost immediately the steady beat of the steam engine increased.

Two porters appeared and unwrapped the heavy mooring ropes from the bolsters on the pier, while a third untied the rope support for the gangplank.

"Celia will show you to your cabin," the captain said, turning his attention back to them and gesturing to the small girl who had appeared from around the corner of the wheelhouse. "I need to get underway, otherwise we won't make Ulilohi before dusk."

The girl watched them with large, kohl lined eyes, and peered nervously up at them when Jade gave her a reassuring smile.

Surprised as the boat's heavy wheels heaved within their cages. Jade grabbed for the rail as the backwash from the wheels threw them back against the wharf. There was a noisy squeal of wood moving over wood and the boat lurched into motion.

Glancing back at the pier Jade froze as she saw a squad of military police double-timing along the wharf toward them.

For a moment she couldn't remember the false name Carlos was using and tugged at his shirt to attract his attention.

"What?" he said, then following her gaze – "ahh." Those crowding the wharf were being forced out of the way. Jade could feel her breakfast settling in her stomach like congealed lead. As they reached the *River Queen*, however, the MPs dispersed along the front of the wharf, while their officer spoke to the steward on the gangway before heading on board.

"You knew," Jade whispered.

He shook his head. "I thought it possible when I made the booking in your name. But knew, no."

A whiff of the sheep from downstairs struck the back of her throat but Jade ignored it. The heavy stink of urine was suddenly easier to take. "You're a very clever man," she said into his ear.

"Perhaps you can show me how clever you think I am later tonight?" he suggested.

"Perhaps," she said, giving him a bump with her hips. "Come on, Celia's waiting." She nodded at the girl, now watching them with a shy smile.

35

The Bank of England is Hardly a Pawnshop, Ma'am

(Thursday: New York, Commonwealth of America, Mainline)

Margaret peered uncertainly into the small office. It was tiny, just big enough for the desk, two chairs, and the four-door filing cabinet it contained. It was made smaller by the files stacked so high on the desk they almost hid the small, stout man on the far side of the desk.

"Inspector Terrance?" she asked uncertainly.

"Yes?" The Inspector looked up, startled.

"Margaret Peric. I have an appointment."

"Miss Peric," he said, jumping to his feet. "I'm sorry. You should have said."

"I did," she pointed out.

"No, no," he said, obviously flustered. "I mean I didn't know you'd be coming personally, otherwise I'd have booked the conference room. This room is hardly suitable . . ." He looked round uncertainly.

"No, this is fine," she said, taking pity on him and waving off his concern to take the visitor's chair, carefully placing her briefcase on the floor beside her.

He looked nonplussed for a moment, before taking shelter in ritual. "May I get you a coffee?"

"Do you have hot chocolate?"

"I'm sure I can find something," he said, looking more uncertain than his words indicated.

As the Inspector exited Margaret took a moment to look around the office again. The desk was not only covered in papers; there was not a single spot of cleared wood on its surface. The lack of a window emphasized the general dinginess.

He returned about five minutes later with two mugs and a tray containing a bowl of sugar and a small flask of milk. Pausing at the entrance he looked uncertainly at his desk.

Margaret resisted the urge to raise an eyebrow. He placed the tray on top of the filing cabinet and moved one stack of files to the floor, before handing Margaret a mug and returning to his side of the desk.

"I really wasn't expecting you," he said, obviously still flustered as he took his seat. "The message was that you needed to discuss a job. I was expecting your agent."

She shrugged. "Jade has spoken very highly of you. I thought, given the situation I find myself in, that I should meet with you myself."

"Thank you. We have a great deal of respect for Jade."

"Indeed. However, I do not have much time before my Imp-Sec minders come looking for me so perhaps we could discuss the job I have?"

He placed a spoonful of sugar in his coffee and stirred it carefully before he looked up. "And what sort of job is it that you needed to see me personally?"

She opened her briefcase and extracted a broadsheet. This she balanced over the files between them and flipped open to page three.

"The killing of two Imp-Sec officers?" He raised an eyebrow.

"One Imp-Sec officer, and a police officer," she corrected him.

"And this would involve you how?"

"The officers died trying to prevent the kidnapping of a young girl staying in my house; Jessie Ackov. They failed. I want you to find her."

"You must pardon my slowness Miss Peric, but what do you expect us to do that is not already being done by those more inclined to take action following the death of two of their own?"

"I would expect you to find Jessie for me, Inspector Terrance."

He took a careful sip of his coffee, before looking at her over the top of his cup. "You must forgive my curiosity Miss Peric, but I have to ask why."

"I am not used to being on the sidelines. I feel powerless, and it is not a feeling I enjoy. I need someone on my side, on Jessie's side."

He sighed. "Miss Peric, I would not be doing my job if I did not inform you that this is likely to be expensive, and I can't guarantee that we will be able to locate Jessie, let alone return her."

"But you will take the job?"

"I will. However, given the cost, we should discuss finance."

"Will 100,000 pounds be enough?"

He froze, startled. "To begin with," he said, after a moment.

"I can place the amount into escrow to cover initial expenses within a week."

"Then I will arrange our accountant to contact your office tomorrow to confirm details."

"And you will arrange daily briefings on progress, starting tomorrow."

"Daily? That would be unusual."

"But you can do it?"

The Inspector nodded.

"Then we can leave it at that for the moment," Margaret said, rising to her feet.

"Indeed," the Inspector said, taking her proffered hand.

"Have you had any word on Jade?" Margaret asked, as she placed the broadsheet back in her briefcase.

"No. Not that I would expect to for another week or so. Why?"

"No reason. Just curious." She paused in the doorway. "Thank you, Inspector Terrance. I should warn you that I have been told by the First Leader to pull my head in and allow his security forces to handle it."

"Why am I not surprised?" the Inspector said with a half-smile.

"That won't cause any difficulties?" she asked.

"No, but I appreciate the warning."

Outside the building Margaret took a deep breath. The air smelled of roses from the florist shop next door, and the sky was a perfect cloudless blue, but without Jessie everything had a certain hollowness. She sighed, then, not giving her two Imp-Sec minders time to fall in beside her, headed down the steps to where the Rolls was waiting for her. Behind her she heard her two shadows pick up their pace.

"Bank of England, Rolf," she said, as she slid into the back of the limousine.

***

"Miss Peric for the Manager," she told the concierge on her arrival.

"Do you have an appointment, ma'am?" he asked, casting a nervous glance at the two Imp-Sec officers who had followed her through the doors.

"I do." She glanced at the two officers. "I'll ask you to stay here."

"Ma'am," the older said, stoically casting a look at the much-abused chairs lined up in the center of the bank's cavernous waiting room.

"Miss Peric?"

Margaret looked round, surprised, caught out by the sudden appearance of the runner.

"Yes."

"The Manager can see you now."

The Manager's office was considerably larger than Inspector Terrance's. It might even have been larger than her own, making her wonder if she'd chosen the right career. The Manager came round the desk to greet her. His immaculately coiffured hair and impeccably tailored suit with its wide Chelsea collar made her feel positively under-dressed in comparison.

"Miss Peric."

"Mr. Hastings. Thank you for seeing me at such short notice."

"It was no trouble, can I get you a tea, chocolate, anything . . .?"

"A glass of water perhaps."

"Janice," the Manager said, addressing the runner. "A carafe of water and two glasses please."

"Now what can I do for you?" he asked, gesturing Margaret to the small, round coffee table in a corner of the room.

Margaret opened her briefcase and pulled out a file. "I need to take a loan against my farm, and against personal jewelry. The need is urgent. I need 100,000 pounds within a week, and another 100,000 within four weeks."

The Manager looked puzzled. "That is a *little* unusual for this branch."

"The circumstances are a little unusual," Margaret said dryly. "It is made a little more interesting by the fact that my farm is on the Dontfrey Line."

"Dontfrey . . .?"

"Last year the farm had an annual income of approximately 30,000 pounds."

"The farm is unencumbered?"

Margaret nodded. "Proof of receipts, and free title are in there. In addition, I have documentary evidence of my present salary of 93,000 pounds a year as Director-General for the Department of Agriculture and Food. The jewelry . . ." She paused.

"The Bank of England is hardly a pawnshop, Miss Peric." The Manager looked affronted.

"But you do deal with high-end collateral lending," Margaret said, trying to ignore his arrogance. "The jewelry was valued about two years ago by Lloyds at approximately 230,000 pounds. I would prefer not to have to lose it . . . . If you're not prepared to cover the loan yourself, I am prepared to have you act as an agent on my behalf."

"If I could ask about the need for the money?"

Margaret shook her head. "It is a personal matter. It is, however, legal."

The Manager considered her for a moment. "If you're sure?"

"Yes," Margaret said, and gave a short, emphatic nod.

"Then I'll arrange for the application. Between the collateral you have nominated, and your salary, I don't have any doubt that I will be able to approve the initial 100,000 pounds. I can't guarantee the additional request until we've had the chance to crunch the figures."

"Thank you," Margaret said, feeling some of the tension binding her chest start to loosen. She hadn't realized how worried she'd been.

It took an hour to complete the paperwork, but when it was done and the forms were presented for her signature Margaret was surprised at her reluctance to sign.

"Miss Peric?" the Manager said.

With a surge Margaret scrawled her signature and slid the form across the table. "If that's all?" she said, standing and snapping the briefcase closed.

"Of course," the Manager said, surprised and rising to his feet. "I'll have the contract couriered round to your residence. As soon as it's been notarized, we'll arrange the transfer of funds into your account."

"You will remember how urgent it is?"

"I understand. I expect to be able to confirm the loan by Monday."

"Thank you," Margaret said, holding out her hand.

***

Margaret was sitting in the front room, the curtains closed, and the gas lamps turned down, nursing a whiskey-sour when there was a quiet knock on the door behind her.

"Come in, Markus," she said without looking round.

Keeping her gaze on her glass, she swirled the ice around in the top of the drink. There was the muffled sound of footsteps across the thick rug, and she looked up in time to see Markus lower himself into the chair opposite.

"Force Leader Hore told me what you'd done," Markus said softly.

"And what's that?" she asked quietly, as she returned her gaze to her glass.

"That you'd sold your farm to pay for the Agency."

"Mortgaged," she corrected him gently. "And the bank still has to agree."

"But why?"

"Because I need the money to pay the Agency, Markus. I don't know what view you might have of my wealth, but the farm makes less than 30,000 pounds a year, and most of that gets plowed straight back into it to pay for improvements. At the moment, my only source of income is my salary as a director-general. This house . . ." She looked up, meeting his eyes and seeing his embarrassment. "If Serge wasn't loaning me this place I'd probably be living in a flat in the Bronx."

"I meant, why employ the Agency?" he corrected her quietly. He shrugged. "You've got Imp-Sec and police crawling over each other. You don't need to do this."

"I don't like not being in control," she said.

As she entered the small, sandbagged command post Margaret could smell the stink of gunpowder, sweat, blood, and shit that permeated the whole bastion, but which for some reason had concentrated itself in the confined space of the bunker.

"Anything?" Margaret demanded, raising her voice to carry over the increasing rattle of small arms fire from outside.

The radio operator, looked up from her set in the corner, and shook her head. "Nothing, Leader."

It was taking too long. Command had promised they'd have the relief column here several hours ago. If they were much longer there wouldn't be anyone left to relieve.

The sudden whistle of an incoming shell made her flinch, and she looked up in time to see the ceiling come crashing down around her. Stunned, she dragged herself erect, to find sand pouring in through the remains of the wooden ceiling, and the operator pinned to the floor under the weight of one of the roof's supporting timbers. The remains of the radio were scattered among the debris around her.

"Medic!" Margaret called frantically, struggling to lift the beam enough to work the operator free. Finally, she managed to pull her out, but the operator was limp, and there was no sign of a pulse when she checked. Cursing, Margaret braced herself and knelt to press the heel of her hand against the operator's sternum. As she did so, she felt blood bubble up around her hand, flooding the front of the operator's shirt.

Scrambling back, she felt the hysteria starting to rise as her back hit the bunker wall, and two medics appeared in the entrance. "Leader?" one of them said.

Wordlessly she gestured to the operator, already knowing it was too late. And damn, she couldn't even remember the operator's name.

Stacy, she thought. It had been Stacy. She remembered finding that out two days after they'd finally been relieved. She had had to find that out to be able to write the letter to Stacy's parents.

"Margaret?"

She shook her head. "Sorry, just woolgathering."

"It's just . . ." He broke off and tried again. "It's just that if anything happened to Jessie, I don't know what I'd do."

Hearing the catch in his voice she looked at him in surprise. Tears were running silently down his face. The urge to comfort him was overwhelming. She placed the glass on the table and crouched next to him, placing an arm around his shoulders.

With a sob he broke into tears, and she gathered him into her arms, wishing that there was someone that could do the same for her.

36

Well That's New

(Friday: New York, Commonwealth of America, Mainline)

Margaret looked up, disturbed by the knock on her door.

"Ma'am?" It was Sylvi for her daily briefing.

"Come in," Margaret said, blinking as she realized she'd been staring at the open file on her desk for . . . she blinked again, fifteen minutes. "Michael not there?"

Sylvi shook her head. "Looks as if he's headed off for the weekend. His desk's been cleared." She caught sight of Margaret's face. "Are you all right? Do you want to cancel?"

"No. I could do with the interruption."

"Still no word?" Sylvi asked as she took the seat on the other side of the desk.

"Nothing." Margaret grimaced. "You'd think we'd have heard *something* after nine days."

"There's a lot of people rooting for you, you know."

"No, I didn't but thanks." Not that it was going to make any difference. She forced a smile. "So, what have you got for me?"

"Some good news for a change. In relation to the Mainline wheat rust outbreak, we think we've finally identified a variety of wheat that appears to show resistance to the fungus. I've got Alan coordinating the test plantings as a priority."

"So, how long? Three months? I've got the First Leader breathing down my neck for a solution."

"You've heard the saying – watching grass grow."

"Sorry, still in military mode. Yeah, done my share of watching grass grow, or in my case beets; it took us five years."

Her memory flashed back to the farm, and a simpler time before the war when she hadn't had millions of people whose lives depended on her – or even just one little girl with soft brown eyes and olive brown skin. She noticed Sylvi had frozen; her horrified gaze fixed on Margaret's hands. Margaret looked down and winced when she saw that her left hand had been pressing the point of the ballpoint pen into the back of her right hand, hard enough to draw blood. Well, that was new, Margaret thought, as she deliberately laid the pen back on the table, and ignoring the pain, looked up to meet Sylvi's eyes. "How long?"

"Twelve, eighteen months," Sylvi said, her face carefully blank.

"And how long to build up enough seed stock for distribution?"

"Alan estimates two years, minimum."

"That's quick."

"One of Alan's staff had the idea of using both the Northern and the Southern hemisphere's growing seasons."

It was a good idea and should halve the time to build up the seed stock, but Margaret couldn't marshal any genuine enthusiasm.

"In the meantime," Sylvi continued, "we're recommending farmers are required to withhold planting this year, and that next year any seed stock is treated with fungicide before planting. With luck, the year after that we'll have enough of the resistant variety for planting."

Margaret nodded.

"It's going to be expensive though," Sylvi warned her, and slid a one-page summary of costings across the table.

Margaret scanned the page: fungicide, resistant seed, import subsidies, and – "Non-planting subsidy?" Her eyebrows rose at the eyewatering amount at the bottom of the page.

"It's the only way to make sure we break the cycle."

Margaret nodded thoughtfully. "I'll speak to the First Leader. Anything else?"

"The Rice Blast. Apparently the Mainline successfully dealt with a similar outbreak in China just before the Nayarit invasion."

Margaret winced. "Yeah, sorry. I should have remembered that one. Didn't it involve a combination of chemicals and the crossbreeding for a resistant strain, or something?" Just where had her brain gone?

Sylvi nodded. "The fungus is a clever little bugger though and has established some resistance to both. As a result, the Chinese focused on developing an integrated solution."

"And the solution?"

"Eliminating crop residue after harvest to reduce the occurrence of fungal overwintering, managing the amount of water supplied to the crops to limit spore mobility, and the use of carpropamid to protect the grain from the fungus.

"At the moment, I'm trying to arrange for copies of their training sheets to be translated into English and Russian. The Chinese Emperor has also volunteered some of their field agents to assist with the dissemination of the information."

"And what do they get out of it?" Margaret asked.

"They're the largest manufacturer of carpropamid in the Empire."

"Of course." Margaret smiled tightly – money speaks.

"I think they're also hoping the publicity will lead to improved prestige and influence across the lines."

"That should make Notway, Clyde, and Huis happy. Rajko, particularly, as Notway's been anticipating a drop of over 50 percent compared to last year."

"He may not be happy with how much it's going to cost. Our projected budget anticipates a 50/50 split between the Mainline and the affected lines." Sylvi slid another estimate sheet across. The total was only marginally less than the estimates to deal with the wheat rust.

"And Kleng, and Chikyù's potato blight?"

Sylvi shook her head. "With the help of the military and local authorities, the quarantine zones appear to be slowing the spread. And we've got relief supplies being distributed to those affected. People may be hungry this winter, but no one should actually starve to death. It's only a stopgap measure though. If we can't find a solution, the blight is eventually going to spread – we can't keep it locked up forever. Particularly the Chikyù variety."

"I've spoken to the First Leader. He's aware of the need for a solution and has assured me he has several avenues of inquiry in train. I'll emphasize that next time I speak to him."

"Thank you." Sylvi closed the folder and slid it across to Margaret. "Formal recommendations, costings, briefing notes, and draft media releases; as well as the draft interim final report."

"Oh gods. Why did you say that? I was following you until then."

Sylvi looked puzzled.

"A draft interim final report. What, by the gods, is that when it's at home?"

Sylvi blinked. "It's the report you get while we're waiting for the final report, which probably isn't going to be even started for another year. And it's a draft, so you can make any changes you want, and we'll include them in the draft final report."

"Don't you mean the final interim final report?"

Sylvi shook her head. "No, it still remains a draft report to allow the First Leader and his office to make whatever changes they require."

Margaret gave up. "Okay. I'll have a look at it over the weekend and get it back to you on Monday."

"Thank you," Sylvi said. She pushed her chair back to stand up, then paused. "If you need to talk?"

"Talk?"

Sylvi's eyes flicked to Margaret's hand.

"I'm fine, Sylvi," Margaret told her, forcing herself not to look down. "But thank you for your concern."

Sylvi nodded uncertainly. "If you change your mind . . ."

"I know where to find you," Margaret said, forcing sincerity into her voice.

Sylvi hesitated for a moment, then with a nod, she rose to her feet. At the door she stopped and turned back. "Just remember, the offer stands." And then she was pulling the door closed behind her, leaving Margaret staring at the file Sylvi had left her.

37

What are you Doing With a Pistol in Your Bag?

(Wednesday: Mississippi River, Chikyù line)

Jade hid a smile as Carlos collected a sheep's foot in his mouth. Carlos was helping Ani, the captain of the *Otsalanvili*, and his two sons move the sheep ashore. As the sheep were unimpressed with the idea of walking across a narrow, bouncing plank of wood from the paddleboat, the four men were having to individually carry them down the gangplank. Understandably the sheep were making their protests clear at this indignity. Watching the men swearing as they tried to persuade the recalcitrant sheep to cooperate was quite entertaining – besides allowing her to watch Carlos, something she'd found herself doing more and more recently. Although not, she admitted, as he currently presented – stripped to the waist, sweat sheening his skin, muscles flexing as he seized another sheep and dragged it onto the plank.

A'no, Ani's eldest son and the boat's chief engineer, carried more muscle than Carlos but there was no doubt Carlos was more than keeping up with him.

She'd been surprised to find the boat was a family affair, but apparently that was common among the Kahnia, who filled the same niche on Chikyù as the Romany on the Mainline. As far as she could make out the Kahnia had been 'travelers' since being forced out of their traditional lands around the Great Lakes by the Siouan some 500 years before. Many had settled into the role of water workers along the Mississippi, living on the sufferance of their more powerful neighbors. That changed with the line's assimilation into the Empire, when their position as outsiders made them useful agents of the Byre family. The introduction of steam engines onto the line had allowed them to move from the oar powered boats they had used before the Decimation, to the paddle wheelers that now carried Chikyù's ever increasing trade.

She couldn't help an unconscious sigh as Carlos released his last sheep to join the rest of the flock already on the wharf and stretched. There was a giggle and she turned to find Tsisho, Ani's wife, standing beside her. Tsisho, a tall, regal looking woman with long, black hair that she wore in a plait reaching the small of her back, had an earthy sense of humor that seemed incongruent with her regal appearance. Celia was with her mother. The young girl smiled shyly up at Jade, her level of English still making her uncertain.

"It is good, is it not to watch the men work?" Tsisho said.

Jade blushed and shrugged.

Tsisho leaned on the rail next to her. "You are not wedded long, no?"

"No," Jade said. Not exactly a lie, given they weren't married at all. She didn't like lying to the Otsalanvili family. They were good people, who had opened themselves to their guests.

"I can tell. Tsi'tenha, says you still have the bloom of first discovery."

Tsi'tenha, the family's grandmother, was a small, hunched figure who spent most of her waking time spinning yarn in the corner. Despite the fact she moved with the aid of a cane, her mind was still razor sharp, with a carnal attitude to life.

Jade couldn't help blushing again. "How long before we reach Yuchi?" she asked to change the conversation.

"The place of the mounds?" Tsisho checked the angle of the sun. "Perhaps five days now. It depends on how long it takes us to pick up a new cargo."

"Will we stop there?"

"Yuchi? Probably not. There is not much there anymore for the likes of us. Mother remembers when it sat astride the three rivers like a colossus. But now . . ." She shrugged.

Jade nodded, trying to hide her disappointment. At least with the river running so low they were anchoring each night. Which meant they'd be traveling past it in daylight, but she'd still liked to have had a proper walk round. Margaret's recommendation still nagged at her.

Akweks appeared on the lower deck, leaning out on the lower rail to watch the scene on the wharf. A cousin, he undertook the role of the boat's night watchman. He was tall, with a quiet reserved nature that seemed to fit his role, and his appearance meant dusk would not be far off.

"I must start to prepare dinner," Tsisho said.

"Can I help?"

"I have potatoes to peel."

"Then I'm your woman."

***

Jade woke, and lay there for a moment listening to the quiet slap of the water against the hull as she tried to work out what had disturbed her. She could feel the gentle motion of the boat and frowned uneasily.

"Wake up," she whispered, as she poked Carlos with a finger.

"Huh." Carlos was not one of those who could instantly go from sleep to awake.

"Wake up!" she whispered again, digging an elbow into his side this time.

"I'm awake," he protested.

"Something's wrong."

"What? What's the time?"

"How would I know what the time is?" she muttered. "And if I knew what was wrong, I probably wouldn't be getting you up."

"Why do I have to do it?"

"Because you're the man." She gave him a push to emphasize her statement.

With a sigh he started to swing his feet out of bed, then froze.

"What?"

"Shh . . ."

Straining her ears Jade could just make out the quiet sound of footsteps on the deck outside their window. "Akweks?" she whispered, referring to the night watchman.

"Akweks doesn't wear boots."

Jade swung herself up and felt on the floor for her shift.

"What do you think you're doing?" he asked, pulling on his trousers.

"Coming with you."

"Of course you are," he said sarcastically. "How are you with a gun?"

"My target shooting's okay, but I've never actually fired one off the range."

She heard him rummaging in his travel bag. "Here," he said, passing her what, from the weight and feel, could only be a small pistol.

"What's this?"

"A pistol."

"I know that! What are you doing with one in your bag?"

"It's a pistol, Jade. Where else would I keep it?"

"But I told you I've only ever shot targets," she whispered, trying to pass the gun back to him – but he had already moved past her to the door.

"Carlos!" she hissed in protest, just before the door slammed open.

Instinctively she lifted the pistol, trying to cover the figure silhouetted against the light from the moon, but Carlos blocked her line of sight. There was a muttered exclamation, followed by a quickly muffled scream of pain as Carlos drove his knee into the stranger's groin. She flinched as Carlos tossed something back onto the bed. Reaching for the object she felt the hard metal of the barrel and recognized it as another gun.

"Light," Carlos muttered, as he pulled the stranger inside and sent him sprawling facedown on the hard wooden floor at the foot of the bed.

Suddenly Carlos swore and slammed the stranger's face into the deck.

"What do you think you're doing?" Jade demanded, as she fumbled for the matches to light the lantern.

"He tried to kick me," he whispered back, unrepentant.

With the lantern lit Jade cautiously slid off the bed, keeping back from the two men on the floor. Carlos was kneeling on the back of the stranger, who was lying facedown, one arm pulled back tightly behind him. A black bandanna covered his face.

"He doesn't look like police," she said.

"That's what I thought," Carlos said. "Have you got some rope?"

Jade rolled her eyes. What was she, a chandler all of a sudden? Leaving the gun on the bed she untied the stranger's bandanna and passed it to Carlos. "Use this."

It was only a moment's work to have him trussed securely then Carlos bent over and checked his breathing.

"How is he?" Jade asked.

"Breathing." Carlos said, dropping the stranger's head back onto the floor.

"Carlos!" Jade protested.

"He shouldn't have tried to kick me. You might want to get some trousers on."

Jade looked down and realized she was still only in her shift. "How many do you think there are?" she asked as she pulled her trousers on.

"No idea," Carlos said taking the stranger's revolver and checking the action. "Ready?"

"As ready as I'll ever be," she said, hefting the pistol he had given her.

Carlos listened at the door then cautiously opened it and slid out onto the deck.

Jade followed, her ears straining. She could just make out the whisper of water lapping against the side of the boat and squeak of the boat rubbing against the pylons.

She felt Carlos nudge her shoulder and looked round to see him pointing at the dark shape of something on the wharf.

"Stay here," he whispered.

She crouched in the shadow of the wall as Carlos vaulted over the side of the deck and onto the dock. He bent over the shape, then looked up and shook his head.

"Akweks?" she asked when he returned.

"Yes."

"How is he?"

"Dead. Unlike me they don't know how hard to hit someone without killing them."

Abruptly any sympathy she'd had for the person Carlos had hit disappeared.

The sound of crockery shattering in the main cabin made both their heads snap round.

"I'll go first. Follow me close," Carlos whispered.

They paused at the door to the cabin, which was half-open. "You go right," Carlos whispered in her ear.

Jade felt like throwing up and wished she could have peed before all this started. She felt Carlos take one step forward, pushing the door open as he did so, and followed him into the room, going right as he went left.

Her pistol up, her whole attention was focused on the near corner. She started to swing round to cover the rest of the room, and catching movement out of the corner of her eye sped up the process. Ani was on his knees in the center of the room, with a man standing behind him, gun in his hand. The gun was coming up on her, but Jade was already pivoting and instinctively pulled the trigger.

The explosion of the gun going off was echoed by Carlos' revolver beside her. Her bullet tore a hole several feet above where she was aiming. She dropped her aim and pulled the trigger again, although she was not quick enough to prevent her target from firing. He flinched, and she watched the puff of smoke rise from his gun, and saw the blossom of red burst from his firing arm. She dragged her aim across his body and fired again, and again, two shots in close succession, each time hitting her target dead center. As he staggered back, she continued her pivot to find Carlos' target lying across the bed, a gaping wound in his shoulder.

Tsisho was cowering in the corner, her nightdress had been torn exposing one shoulder and a breast.

"Jade, Jade!" Carlos' voice finally penetrated the buzzing in her ears, and she looked up to find him looking at her with concern.

"Are you all right?"

"I . . . I think so."

"These two are dead, but I need to check the rest of the boat. Are you okay to stay here?"

She nodded and swallowed convulsively.

Ani was cradling Tsisho and Carlos paused to pass him one of the intruders' guns before touching Jade's shoulder.

As Carlos ghosted out into the night, he pulled the door closed behind him.

Jade settled herself back against the wall, arms folded in a futile effort to stop her hands from shaking.

Tsisho was still crying softly to herself, Ani's arms wrapped around her, as they rocked themselves back and forth.

She was still watching the door when she realized that Tsisho's sobs had stopped, and she looked round to see Ani helping her to her feet.

"Thank you," Ani mouthed.

Jade nodded before transferring her attention back to the door. There was a quiet knock on the door, and her hold on the gun tightened.

"Jade." It was Carlos.

"Here," she tried to whisper, but her voice refused to work. She swallowed and tried again.

"Coming through," Carlos warned quietly.

The door opened and Celia slipped inside, followed quickly by her grandmother.

Celia ran straight to her mother's arms, but Tsi'tenha simply stopped and snorted when she saw the two bodies, before she sat down on the edge of the bed.

Carlos slid in after them. "Still all right?" he asked Jade.

She nodded, not wanting to risk speaking.

"A'no and Okwaho are safe," he told the room. "They're holed up in the engine room. I gave A'no the revolver, but I didn't want to bring everyone up in one group." He frowned and looked sadly at Ani. "I'm afraid Akweks is dead. I don't think there's anyone else on board, but I want to do one final check."

Ani nodded, cold anger showing in his eyes.

"How do you want to deal with this?" Carlos asked. "Jade and I would like to avoid . . . any official entanglements, and if you want to report this to the authorities we'll need to leave."

"No, no authorities," Tsi'tenha said, her voice strong despite her age.

"Mother," Ani protested.

Tsi'tenha prodded one of the bodies with her foot. "This one is the mayor's nephew. What justice do you think we will receive from the gadje if we report this?"

Ani looked at the body, then nodded reluctantly. "No authorities," he agreed.

"Then, perhaps we should leave," Carlos suggested. "We can dump these upriver."

"No," Tsi'tenha said.

Carlos looked at the aged figure sitting on the bed, a woolen shawl pulled tight over her nightdress.

"We must not seek to draw any attention to ourselves. We will leave at first light. In the meantime, you and A'no take the bodies south, beyond the edge of town. Leave them to be found after we have gone. Akweks we take with us."

Carlos considered her for a moment, before giving a curt nod. "It will be as you suggest, Auntie."

She looked up at him. "You are a true warrior of the people. And one who respects his elders. You could learn much from this one," she said, turning her gaze on her son.

Ani rolled his eyes at this familiar complaint.

"I'll be back soon," Carlos told Jade, before slipping outside again.

It was almost half an hour before he returned, and this time Okwaho was with him.

"It's clear," he said. "We've moved Akweks to the main storeroom. A'no's just getting the dinghy ready. He'll be here in a moment."

Even as he spoke, A'no appeared in the doorway. A pistol was thrust down the front of his trousers. He checked the room, then at a nod from his father, he bent down to take the dead man's shoulders. Carlos took the feet and together they lugged him out of the room.

Tsi'tenha prodded the bloodstained rug beside the bed with her foot. "You need to burn this."

Tsisho looked at the rug. "Yes Mother," she said, her voice heavy with regret.

On Carlos' next return Jade followed them as they made their way carefully down to the stern where the dinghy was tied up. There were already two bodies in the bottom of the boat, but Jade didn't say anything. They had killed someone in cold blood, and who knew what they had intended for the others.

Jade watched as the body was lowered into the dinghy. Once Carlos had climbed inside, A'no pushed the dinghy off into the still waters of the river.

By the time they returned the sun was just starting to appear over the top of the distant hills.

"Everything all right?" she asked.

Carlos nodded, clearly exhausted as he hauled himself back onto the rear deck. "We set up a little scenario they might buy, a falling out between friends. Even if that doesn't work there's nothing to link them to the Otsalanvilis."

"Come on, we have a bath waiting for you," Jade said sympathetically. At least on a paddle wheeler there was never any shortage of hot water.

38

Don't Cry Miss Peric

(Saturday: New York, Commonwealth of America – Mainline)

Margaret was in the conservatory re-potting some herbs while Markus paced up and down next to the window. Normally she found the routine of potting relaxing, but not this time.

"Oh, for goodness' sake, sit down, Markus," she said finally. "You're wearing a hole in the lino."

He grimaced and collapsed into one of the two cane visitors' chairs, burying his face in his hands.

"I'm sorry," she apologized, "I shouldn't have . . ."

As he waved it off, she frowned. "How much sleep did you get last night?" she asked. He looked exhausted.

"An hour, maybe two."

"You're not going to be much good to Jessie if you can't sleep," she pointed out.

"I'm no good to her now," he said bitterly.

"Do you want some sleeping pills? I can give you a couple until you can see Mr. Castles and get your own."

He shook his head. "No! I had to take sleeping pills after Adriana died. I hated them. They just left me feeling dead."

She couldn't argue with that, but when the alternative was lying awake night after night, or alternatively suffering through an endless series of nightmares she'd take the deadening effect of the pills any time.

"Why haven't we heard anything?" he asked, staring out of the window. "It's been ten days."

She didn't know what to say to that. There was nothing she could say. For a moment she simply stared at the tray she was holding, then angrily slammed it down on the table. The wood splintered and clay pots toppled off the table, shattering as they hit the floor.

They stared at the debris in shocked silence. There was the sound of racing feet from inside the house and an Imp-Sec Officer burst into the conservatory, gun in hand.

"It's all right," Margaret said tightly. "An accident. I dropped the tray."

Uncertainly the officer holstered her weapon. "Should I send someone to clean it up?" she asked cautiously.

"No, I can do it," Margaret said.

"If you need anything, just call," the officer said, backing out of the room.

Margaret bent and started to pick out the larger pieces of pottery from the soil. As she straightened, she banged heads with Markus, who had brought a bucket over for the debris.

He grunted. "Sorry," he apologized.

Margaret simply grimaced and dropped the pieces of pottery she was holding into the bucket.

There was a knock, and she looked round, startled. "Yes, James?"

"Inspector Terrance is here, ma'am," the butler said.

She stood up, frowning at Markus.

"Why?" Markus asked.

It was a fair question. They'd received a full briefing yesterday, and it had been agreed their next briefing would be Monday. Still, there was only one way to find out.

"Show him through, James," she said, stripping off her gloves.

"Inspector Terrance," she said holding her hand out for him when James brought him in.

"Miss Peric, Mr. Ackov," the small, stout Inspector replied, shaking their hands in turn.

"May I offer you anything?" Margaret asked, gesturing him to a seat.

The Inspector shook his head. "No, this is just a flying visit. I was on my way home from the office and thought I'd better let you know."

"Is it about Jessie?" Markus asked.

The Inspector shook his head. "No, I'm sorry, we still don't have any news."

"Then what?"

"Markus," Margaret said warningly. "Inspector . . ."

"From the way you've spoken of Jade I gather you were fond of her."

"Were?" Cold dread seized her heart. "What's happened?"

"She's disappeared."

Margaret collapsed onto the bench. Could things get any worse? She felt Markus rest his hands gently on her shoulders.

"Disappeared? Where was she?" she asked.

"On Chikyù."

"What happened?"

The Inspector looked puzzled. "That's what's strange, I don't know. We got a telegram from them from Scatchwah a week ago saying they'd run into problems but would be in Genessee that afternoon, and they'd let us know if they had any other issues. Since then, nothing."

"Scatchwah is the equivalent of Mainline Chicago?" Margaret checked.

"Yes," the Inspector said. "Unfortunately, what with the search for Jessie I wasn't able to follow up as soon as I should have, and I only started to make some initial inquiries yesterday about their progress. And then I got a courtesy note from Imp-Sec this morning informing us that she's 'disappeared', though they won't tell me how they know."

Margaret frowned. "That seems . . . unusual."

"It is."

"Anything else?"

"They're still trying to confirm this, but it seems she was caught carrying potato virus. When the local police tried to arrest her, she knocked two of them unconscious and made a run for it."

"Jade!"

"That was my reaction," the Inspector said with a tight smile.

"That's ridiculous! I've never known anyone who's a greater stickler for the rules than Jade. There's no way she'd have assaulted two police officers."

"My thoughts precisely."

"What are you doing about it?"

"At the moment officially nothing. Until I have some form of official confirmation, I can't do anything. And then there's the little problem that Imp-Sec were quite emphatic we weren't to put our oar in. They seem to feel they have everything under control."

"And just how would they know that?" Gods, she was so frustrated. She considered picking up a pot and throwing it through the window. It would be satisfying but probably a little bit extreme. She felt her eyes prick and clenched her jaw angrily. She was *not* going to be one of those women who was always crying.

"As I said they were quite emphatic we weren't to do anything. They don't seem very impressed with the fact that we accepted a contract with you."

"Tough," Margaret snarled.

"Exactly."

"So, what *are* you doing?" Margaret asked, catching his tone.

"I'm positioning a recovery team at Chicago, and I've briefed senior counsel. She's pulling together the necessary documentation for a snatch if we need it. That's what I was doing in the office this morning."

Margaret felt some of the tightness in her chest ease. "Thank you, Inspector. It seems Jade's faith in you is not misplaced." She suppressed a smile at the Inspector's sudden flush.

"Miss Peric," the Inspector said, rising to his feet. "I should leave now. I promised my son I would be back in time to take him to softball."

"Please let us know if you hear anything further," she said, ringing the bell.

"Of course."

"What was that all about?" Markus asked, as James closed the door behind the Inspector.

"I'm not sure. It's obvious something went wrong on the trip. But to think that Jade would do that . . ." She shook her head disbeliev-ingly, then paused as she realized the depth of feeling she was experiencing over Jade's disappearance. Perhaps it was because she considered Jade a friend, and she didn't have many of them, acquaintances, yes, but her friends she could probably count on the fingers of one hand. She winced when she realized that was literally true. Well, she was damn well not going to lose this one.

"I need to speak to Donald," she announced.

Markus looked a little worried. "Now? It's just that with the three-hour time difference it's only eight in Naisre."

"And if I wait, I might miss him. If he's not available, they'll tell me."

Markus still didn't look convinced, but Donald was her cousin not his.

As it was Donald was having breakfast and she got put straight through to him – well as straight as one could when one wanted to talk to the First Leader.

"What's up Margaret?" There was a reassuring solidity in his voice when he came on the line.

"Donald, have you heard anything about Jade?"

"Jade?" There was clear puzzlement in his voice.

"My bodyguard. The one who saved my life from the letter bomb."

"No, what's happened?"

"She went to Chikyù to try and arrest the Anarchist who attempted to kill Markus and she's disappeared."

"Do you want me to ask Brian to try track her down?" he asked, referring to Chikyù's World Leader.

"I suspect Brian's already trying to find her for evading arrest. According to Imp-Sec the locals tried to arrest her for carrying potato virus, and she knocked two of them unconscious before disappearing."

"And just what do you want me to do?" he asked plaintively.

Margaret sighed. "I'm really not trying to make your life difficult on purpose."

"The gods help me if you ever do that."

She couldn't help smiling. "I was hoping that you could put some pressure on Imp-Sec to find out why they think they have the situation under control. And just who their source is that they're not disclosing."

Donald sighed. "And just why do you want me to put more pressure on Imp-Sec? They're already chasing their tails trying to locate your

Jessie. They've made fifty-one arrests so far, and still aren't any closer to finding her."

"Jade's a friend, Donald."

There was a moment's silence. "And neither of us have so many of those that we can afford to lose any more, do we?"

So, he did understand.

"No," she said softly.

Donald gave another sigh. "I'll see what I can do," he promised.

"Thanks Donald. Give my best to Defella."

"Will do."

She replaced the phone in its cradle and looked up at Markus who was watching her with worried eyes. "He said he'll see what he can do."

"I'm sure Jade will be all right," he said kneeling down next to her and taking her hands in his.

"I know, it's just . . ."

"I don't think I've said how much you've helped me about Jessie. If you hadn't been here . . . I don't know how I'd have coped."

"You'd have coped," Margaret said. "We all cope; it's just the damage that occurs while one is coping."

"Perhaps," he agreed, thought about it, then shrugged.

"Ma'am." It was James again.

"Yes," she said, looking up as Markus got to his feet. Markus started to withdraw his hand, but Margaret closed her fingers on it.

"Miss Louise is here."

Margaret shook her head. "It's starting to feel like Central Station. Show her in, James."

Even as she spoke, Louise bustled in, took one look at the tableau and raised an eyebrow.

Margaret ignored the unspoken question. "It is the polite thing to wait until invited to enter a room that is not your own."

Louise made a face. "This is too important for that. I might have word on Jessie."

"What?" Margaret and Markus said simultaneously.

"I have a contact — a friend of a friend. But she wants a guarantee of the reward, and a new identity before she'll talk to anyone. Her boyfriend runs a safe house for the Anarchists' Armed Action Wing. She's been looking at leaving him for some time. Apparently the relationship is abusive, but she's been worried about what her boyfriend would do to her if he ever found her again. And from what my friend told me she has every right to be worried."

"Of course," Margaret said, not even bothering to think about it. "How do we contact her?"

Louise reached into her handbag and pulled out a visiting card. "This is Mureal's, my friend's. Call her between four and six this afternoon and she'll put you in contact."

Margaret took the card. At last! "Thank you," she said gratefully.

Louise shook her head. "Just get her back safe." She gave Margaret a crooked smile. "I need to go. Take care, Mags."

"Always," Margaret said.

Louise studied her for a moment, her head on her side and Margaret wondered what she was looking at, but then she seemed to shake her head and turn her attention to Markus. "I hope this helps."

Markus merely nodded.

James had been standing unobtrusively by the door, and he trailed Louise out as she headed off.

"The Inspector's son will be disappointed," Markus said.

"Pardon?" Margaret said, still staring at the card Louise had given her.

"The Inspector's son. The Inspector said he was going to go take him to softball."

"I thought you would want me to tell Imp-Sec and let them deal with it."

Markus shook his head. "It turns out I trust your instincts. I think the Inspector may have a little more . . . finesse." Then he shrugged. "I'd probably prefer it if both were involved but I think you need to let the Agency know first."

Margaret felt her mood lighten at Markus' words, and his trust in her judgment. "Then let's try and track him down. The Agency will know where he is."

***

It took two hours before the Inspector returned to the house, and on his recommendation Force Leader Hore was in the small group clustered round the phone at four p.m.

At his nod, Margaret picked the phone up and dialed the number on the card. The phone rang six times before it was picked up and she heard a cautious "Hello?"

"Mureal? This is Margaret, Louise's sister."

"Margaret, I'm glad you called. You're happy with the request?"

"Absolutely."

"Then we can meet you at the main information desk in Macey's in an hour. I'll be wearing a red and white dress."

There was a click and Margaret looked up at the expectant faces. "I'm meeting them at Macey's in an hour," she said.

"I must protest, ma'am," Hore said. "Having you meet this woman is too dangerous."

Margaret sighed. "Force Leader, during the insurrection on Dontfrey I saw more combat than I hope you ever will. I have a far better idea than you what constitutes danger, and meeting two women in Macey's hardly classifies as such. So, this is what I need, Force Leader Hore – firstly an armed, female agent in plain clothes. Secondly you need to have your Hostage Rescue Team ready to go as soon as I get the address – we'll discuss their deployment on my return. Inspector, I also need Rucker's to supply me with one of your female agents."

"In plain clothes, of course," the Inspector said with a smile on his face from the putdown Margaret had just administered to Hore. "I'll see to it immediately."

Margaret turned her attention back to Hore.

"Ma'am," he agreed stiffly.

***

"You're going to have to lose that stiffness," Margaret remarked casually to the Imp-Sec Officer Hore had found her, as they approached the entrance to Macey's.

"Ma'am?"

"She means you going to have to lose that poker up your arse," the Agency officer told her. The Agency rep was a petite blond who despite looking barely old enough to have a driving license had been highly recommended by the Inspector. He had assured Margaret that her shooting skills had been unparalleled in her class.

The Imp-Sec Officer frowned, and Margaret hid a smile.

Inside the store the crowds were starting to thin, and Margaret quickly led them across the floor to the Main Information Desk. The desk was deserted when they arrived, and Margaret was looking around for their contact when the Agency officer touched her shoulder.

"Ma'am," she said, nodding toward the door.

Margaret followed her gaze to see two women walking toward them. One was wearing the red and white dress she'd been told to expect. Both looked around Louise's age, and the woman with Mureal was wearing large sunglasses and a high-collared, long green dress that covered her arms and looked far too hot for summer. There seemed something vaguely familiar about her.

"Mureal?" Margaret asked, as the two women approached.

"Yes. You must be Margaret?" the woman in the red and white dress replied. "And these two I take it are your friends?"

"Indeed. Could I suggest we discuss this over a coffee?"

Mureal looked at her companion, who gave a single, uncertain nod.

"Sibilla, perhaps you could grab us a table?" Margaret told the Imp-Sec Officer.

Sibilla's smile faltered, but she headed off to see to the task. Margaret did consider heading off in the opposite direction, just to see what she would do, but that was petty, and Jessie's safety was too important to play games with.

"Please," Margaret told them.

Upstairs the coffee lounge was almost empty, and Margaret could see the relief on Sibilla's face as they appeared. Obviously, the idea that Margaret would take the opportunity to disappear had occurred to her as well. After ordering, Margaret led her small group over to the table Sibilla had requisitioned.

"Now, perhaps you could introduce me to your friend," Margaret said to Mureal when they were all seated.

Mureal looked at her companion. "This is Adeline," she said, as Adeline warily took off her sunglasses.

"Pleased to meet you, Adeline," Margaret said, holding her hand out, and feeling the start of a slow burning anger at the large black eye Adeline was sporting. She was fairly sure she could also see the green stain of an old bruise over the top of the dress.

Margaret considered her for a moment. "I'm sorry, but you look familiar. Have we met before?"

"No, ma'am. But I work for your Department. In Records."

"Of course," Margaret said smoothly, deciding that she'd need to speak to Aife about that. The audit was starting to wind down but checking out what files Adeline had had access too might suggest a useful course of further investigation. That was for the future though. "I understand you know where Jessie is?"

"You know my requirements?"

"A guarantee on the reward and a new identity. Yes. I can guarantee the reward if it leads to the safe recovery of Jessie. The new identity I will guarantee personally regardless of what you tell us."

Adeline flushed, embarrassed, and looked down at the table for a moment before flashing a glance back up at Margaret from under long lashes.

"I'd like to introduce Sibilla, who represents Imp-Sec," Margaret continued, "and Special Agent Constello from the Rucker's Agency." She indicated each of the officers, then paused as the waitress delivered their drinks.

"Now perhaps you could tell us what you know," Margaret said when the waitress had gone.

Adeline took a breath, then straightened her back.

"My boyfriend is František Lanfear. He runs a safe house for the Action Wing."

"Address?" Margaret prompted.

"It's a terrace house at 73 Sir William Howe."

Margaret frowned – that wasn't that far away.

"Why do you think Jessie is there?" Sibilla asked.

"I saw her a couple of days ago. They have her in one of the spare rooms on the second floor."

"Is she all right?" Margaret asked.

Adeline nodded.

Margaret slid a paper napkin and a pencil across the table to her. "Can you draw us a plan of the house?"

Adeline nodded again and started to draw. When she had finished Margaret considered the plan carefully. "So, just front and back doors? No other exits?" she asked.

"No, ma'am."

Margaret slid the plan across to Sibilla.

"How many people are in the building?" Margaret asked.

"Just František and Sofia."

"And you saw Jessie in which room?"

Adeline pointed out the room on the plan.

"Sibilla?" Margaret said. "Any questions?"

Sibilla had a couple, then looked at Margaret. "That's it," she said simply.

"Constello?" Margaret asked.

The Rucker's agent shook her head.

"Then Adeline, if you go with Special Agent Constello she'll make sure you're safe."

Adeline gave her a tremulous smile. "That's it?"

"For me," Margaret said, giving her a reassuring smile. "Sibilla may have some more questions for you later."

***

Markus was waiting for them at Imp-Sec headquarters. He looked up nervously as they came into the conference room.

"We've got the address," she said. She waved him back into his seat as Sibilla, Force Leader Hore, and the Inspector followed her in.

"What's wrong?" Margaret asked, noticing Hore's worried expression.

"We've just received word that we have a mole in Imp-Sec."

"Who?"

"Our source doesn't know."

Margaret threw her hands in the air. "So, they might have already moved Jessie?"

"No," Hore said. "The only ones who know anything about what we know are in this room."

"I would have suggested we use Agency personnel on the recovery," the Inspector said. "But if Imp-Sec have been penetrated I can't guarantee our own personnel haven't been as well. However, if we pair each of our staff with someone from the other group our . . . mutual dislike and . . ." he paused, "distrust of each other, should serve to keep one another in line."

"It's going to be difficult relying on a team that hasn't worked together," Hore pointed out. "But given the alternatives I don't see we've got any choice. Pulling a new Hostage Recovery Team in from out-of-state would take at least a day, and by then they might very well have moved Jessie and we'd have to start all over again."

"When do we go in?" Margaret asked.

"One a.m.," "Three a.m.,", Sibilla and the Inspector said simultaneously.

"Split the difference," Margaret suggested.

Hore looked at the Inspector and the two seemed to come to a silent agreement. "Two it is," Hore said.

***

Margaret waited in the back of a baker's van parked at the end of the lane. Markus occupied the bench next to her. There'd been some argument about that, resolved when Margaret pointed out that having him with the team would be safer than having him wait at headquarters where he might be recognized. The Imp-Sec officers wore black coveralls over the bulletproof vests that had come into vogue during the war, and heavy combat helmets. Besides them Agency officers wore their much lighter blue overalls tucked into black battle boots, along with heavy belts with batons and sprays. Both groups carried the short-barreled shotguns preferred for this type of restricted space work.

Sibilla was listening to the radio; the crackle of sound from the receiver turned down to a quiet hiss.

"That's it," she whispered. "Go!"

The door swung open and the team of six slid out and quietly slipped down the street. Margaret followed them to the edge of the seat and peered around the door. At the other end of the street, she saw another team exiting a similar vehicle. On the street behind the building, she knew another two teams were setting up a perimeter.

As the first officers reached the door, one slid something into the lock and there was a flash of light followed by a muffled thud. Pushing the door open, the team entered. The second team following them in. Four minutes later there was a muffled shot, then silence.

"What's happening?" Markus demanded.

Margaret shook her head. "Quiet."

The scent of the pine forest reminded her of happier days celebrating Christmas with the rest of the family. But now the sound of the family's laughter as it gathered together had been replaced by the subdued sound of her Battle Group moving silently into position – or as silently as 1,000 soldiers can through open forest. She half-expected the hill fort to prove as deserted as the other two they'd stormed over the past month, but there'd been rumors that Jhansi and the other remaining members of the Charterists' Management Committee, had been seen in the area and this was their best chance to bring an end to this eternal war.

She checked her watch. Still an hour till dawn.

"Shit!" one of her officers exclaimed as the crest of the hill was lit up by a sudden glare. A second later the dull thunder of an explosion rolled down the hill, followed by the shockwave that caused the ground to heave beneath them.

Margaret stared at the top of the hill, fear constricting her throat.

"What was that?" someone whispered.

Margaret shook her head, hoping she was wrong about what she thought had just happened.

"Do we go in straight away?" someone asked.

"No," she replied. "We're going to need light for this. We wait for dawn."

Half an hour later a breeze sprang up, driving the scent of roasting flesh down the slope. As it filled her nostrils Margaret retched, leaning against a tree for support.

"Leader?" It was her aide, holding out a flask of water.

With a nod Margaret accepted the proffered flask, took a mouthful of water and swilled it around before spitting it out.

Finally light cautiously eased its way over the trees and the Battle Group launched its attack. The defenders had already taken an alternate path, and when news of her fears was confirmed, Margaret slowly climbed the steep slope of the hill by herself. At the top she paused and stared down into the massive crater that now filled its center. As smoke drifted up from the pit, it carried with it the stink of burned flesh to claw at the back of her throat. Around the crater the greensward was blackened and pitted by the fire created by the explosion. The ground was bloodied with dismembered bodies, the last of the Charterists, entangled in death. Women, children, and fighters. She washed her mouth out again and spat, knowing she would never be able to forget the stink of gunpowder and burned flesh that surrounded her, wishing she could purge her lungs. Then the anguish, and the anger at the injustice of it all hit her and she vomited again, and again, until there was nothing left, and she simply turned her back on it all and walked away down the hill.

She wanted to scream, to shake those responsible until they felt her pain, but they were now beyond her reach. And as she reached the bottom of the hill, she started to strip off her uniform.

Beside her, she heard a sharp gasp of breath from Markus. For a moment she was still lost in the memory. But was it a memory? She couldn't remember stripping off her uniform so where had that come from? She could remember the pain she had felt, and she remembered turning away, but then there was nothing. Just a hole in her memory.

She became aware of two officers appearing at the front door supporting a man wearing a singlet and short underwear. Jessie . . . She breathed out, hoping against all hope. A moment later a woman was led out by two officers. She had a bag over her head and her hands were handcuffed behind her back.

Thirty seconds, she forgot to breathe, a minute, and then a female Agency officer appeared in the door, with Jessie holding her hand. An Imp-Sec Officer looming over them both protectively.

"Jessie," Markus whispered, and then he was running and as she followed him, walking slowly, measuredly, she saw him reach the small group and kneel down to sweep Jessie into his arms.

When she reached them, Jessie looked up over her father's shoulder.

"Hello, Miss Peric," Jessie said. Her small face was solemn. There was a smudge of dirt on her face and a weariness in her eyes that made Margaret cringe inwardly. "I knew you'd find me," she added, and then she held up her thin arms to Margaret and Margaret bent over to feel them around her neck. As she did so, she felt tears course their way down her cheeks.

"Don't cry, Miss Peric," Jessie said.

Margaret's voice choked with tears, and she simply shook her head and buried her nose in Jessie's hair, breathing in her scent.

39

Captain, We Might Have a Problem

(Monday: Yuchi, Chikyù line)

The light cotton shift clung to her skin as Jade leaned over the side of the paddle wheeler, watching the approaching mounds of Yuchi that could now be seen over the top of the distant trees. The tallest of the mounds was almost 100 feet, edged with flat slabs that had been mortared in place. Decay was already visible, however, with greenery encroaching on the mounds and small shrubs appearing between the slabs.

Beneath the boat, the river was a deep, chocolate brown, barely moving between the piles of silt that protruded above the surface on either side. Jade wrinkled her nose at the stink of rotting vegetation, and the heavy scent of coal smoke from the boat's engines.

"Penny for your thoughts," Carlos said.

"Just wishing for some rain," Jade said, resting her chin on her hands.

Carlos nodded. "I've asked Ani to drop me off here for an hour. I need to check if Uncle Pierre has replied to my telegram yet."

Jade sighed. "I don't suppose I can come. I'd really like to get a closer look at the mounds after Margaret's recommendation."

He shook his head. "It's too risky."

"Just how did I know you were going to say that?" she asked, leaning against his shoulder.

The relentless threshing of the paddles caused a continuous vibration underfoot and she shifted irritably. The paddles created a thin mist which helped a bit with the heat, but there was little shade on the deck to protect her from the sun. And after five days, despite the cream Tsisho had given her to protect her skin, she was peeling badly. Carlos, on the other hand, had simply developed a rich, golden tan – which she thought completely unfair. Unfortunately, the only alternative for her was staying undercover where the temperature was at least ten degrees higher because of the engines.

Beside her, Carlos stiffened.

"What?" She looked up at the approaching pier in the distance.

"I'm not sure," he said, "but there seems a few too many people on the pier."

She shaded her eyes. The crowd at the end of the pier did look larger than they would have expected.

"Come on," he told her. "And don't rush."

She followed him back to the wheelhouse where Okwaho was manning the wheel under the careful supervision of his father.

"Captain, we might have a problem," Carlos said.

"The police?" Ani spat the wad of tobacco he'd been chewing over the side of the boat. "I noticed."

"You're not expecting anything?"

"No, and a bit of a surprise, given we weren't planning to stop here."

"Can we just keep steaming?"

"Not if they order us to stop."

Carlos nodded. "Then perhaps it might be better if Jade and I weren't here when they come on board."

Ani shook his head. "This close they'd see you leaving. You two had better come with me. Okwaho, just take her in real slow; I'll be back in a couple of minutes."

Okwaho looked nervous at the responsibility his father had dumped on him.

"Tsisho," Ani called.

His wife poked her head round the corner.

"I'm putting our guests in the bolt hole. Can you clean out their cabin?"

They followed him down the ladder at the back of the boat into the engine room.

A'no looked up as they entered, sweat glistening from his heavily muscled torso.

"We need to use the bolt hole," his father told him. "We might have visitors."

A'no simply nodded, and Jade wondered at his lack of surprise. After closing the bunker door, he assisted his father to move the kindling, then quickly lifted the three wooden planks at the bottom of the store to demonstrate a narrow space that ran off under the deck.

"In you go," Ani said. "If you need to, there's a hatch at the back of the space that will drop you into the water. I wouldn't advise using it, but if you need to . . ."

Carlos thanked him and helped Jade down.

Crouching, Jade peered farther into the hole. It smelled of damp wood and heat from the boilers.

"Here." It was Tsisho, with their two backpacks.

As Carlos took the packs Jade bent and slid into the space. It ran for about twelve feet under the deck and would be just wide enough for Carlos to lie down next to her. The bottom of the space was padded with an old rug to give some protection from splinters. Craning her head back she could just make out what might be a door at the end of the space, a bar running across the block at the end.

"You need to lock the planks in place," Ani said, passing her two short beams that she saw would fit into slots on either side of the opening.

As Carlos lay down next to her A'no laid the planks back in place then started to replace the kindling. As he did so, the meager light that had leaked in around the edges of the planks was snuffed out.

"Pass me one of the beams," Carlos whispered.

Jade carefully maneuvered the beam over their bodies.

"Ow."

"Sorry," Jade whispered as the end of the bar connected solidly with his chin.

They quickly forced the beam into position, then Carlos wriggled down to place the second. When Jade tried to assist him, she found her way blocked by their backpacks.

"You'll have to try do it yourself," she whispered.

It was more difficult with just the one of them to force it into place, and unfortunately the weight of the kindling on top of the planks made it almost impossible. "Merde," he swore softly after he'd tried to bang it into position with his hands.

"What?"

"Skinned my palm," he said.

She felt him working his way back level with her.

"Careful," he said, as he braced his feet against the beam and shoved it into place.

They were just in time as the threshing of the wheel eased into silence.

Jade felt for Carlos' hand, and as he took it, he gave it a reassuring squeeze.

Despite the danger Jade found herself dozing off. At one time she half-roused to hear voices and feet overhead as they moved the kindling to check for anyone hiding beneath.

Finally, she roused to hear the paddles starting up again, and Ani's voice softly letting them know it was all right for them to come out.

"How was it?" Carlos asked the captain as they emerged to find they'd been confined to the bolt hole for two hours.

"Thorough. Tsisho and her mother are still cleaning up."

"What were they looking for?" Carlos asked, stretching out some of the kinks in his spine.

"Two fugitives. Here." Ani passed him a photo. "They had this for the woman."

Carlos passed it across to Jade, who gave it a quick glance. It was the same picture the police had been using when they searched the train.

"Unfortunately, none of us had seen her," Ani said with a smile.

"And they have no description of her companion?"

"Nothing specific. Average height, wearing a kilt. Nothing like yourself."

"I presume it's no longer safe to drop me off for an hour?"

"Probably not," Ani said.

"How much farther are you planning on traveling before stopping for the night?"

"Not far. There is a widening in the river just ahead. We were going to anchor there overnight. It is a gathering place for other Kahniakenhaka on the river."

"If I hike back to town, do you know whether the telegraph office will be open? I still need to check to see if there is a telegram for me from my uncle."

Ani looked at his son. "It should be . . ." he said. "Is it important?"

Carlos gave Jade a look that had her wondering what he was thinking. "Very," he said.

"It will be five miles when we anchor. The railway is only a short distance away. If you follow that you can't get lost. We will wait for your return."

"Thank you," Carlos said. Reaching into the bolt hole he lifted their two packs out. "In the meantime, we can settle back into the cabin."

There were two other vessels already moored in the bay, and as Carlos slipped away into the dark to work his way back into town Jade joined the others in an impromptu gathering of Kahniakenhaka.

The Kahniakenhaka were a closed, secretive clan, but once Jade's role in saving the Otsalanvili had been explained she was immediately accepted as part of the wider family.

She was cradling the youngest member of the clan in her arms, playing peek-a-boo while watching the dancing occurring out on the deck, when she became aware of someone watching her and looked up to see Carlos.

"Hi," she mouthed.

When he simply continued to look at her, she returned the baby to its mother and stood up.

"What's wrong?" she asked.

He didn't bother to ask why she thought something was wrong, but simply took her arm and drew her away from the others.

"My uncle has confirmed that, if we can get to Genessee, he can get you through the portal," he said when they were far enough away that they could speak without being heard.

"But?" She could still sense there was something wrong.

"Jessie's disappeared."

"Jessie?" she said uncertainly.

He held his hand up about belt height from the deck, and Jade felt sick. "What happened?"

Carlos held up his hands. "It was a telegram, so there weren't any details, but my uncle obviously thought you needed to know."

She frowned, because there was something he wasn't telling her. "What?"

"That's all my uncle said."

"But there's something you're not telling me." She glared at him. "Did you have anything to do with this?"

"No. Definitely not," he assured her.

"How long ago did it happen?"

"He didn't say, but the telegram was two days old."

"Gods, Margaret and Markus must be frantic."

She chewed her bottom lip. She had to get home, now. Not least because she had to warn Inspector Terrance about Karen.

"I need to get back," she said.

"*We* need to get back," he corrected her. "I'm the one whose uncle has to get you through the portal."

"Fine," she said shortly. "But how? I don't imagine we can just buy a ticket."

"Hop a train. There's a sideout only a short distance away. We can catch one from there."

"A sideout?"

"It's a passing track. Freight will pull off onto it to allow other trains to pass."

"They won't be checking?"

"I don't think so. They've probably set up a cordon around Yuchi, but we're outside it now. I expect there'll be more checks at Scatchwah, but most likely nothing before then."

"Then we'd better leave," she said. She pulled his face down to hers and kissed him lightly on the lips. "Thank you. But if I ever hear you had something to do with Jessie's disappearance . . ."

He nodded. "We'd better get our stuff together."

***

Two days later Jade watched Carlos carefully slide the freight door open another inch. They'd pulled into the yard at Scatchwah approximately half an hour ago and given the way he was now treating her with kid gloves she could tell he'd got the message loud and clear that if they didn't make a move soon, she'd explode. She knew Carlos had been hoping to wait for nightfall before they made their move, but she felt a sense of urgency that didn't allow further delay. Outside, their view was blocked by another line of wagons. Carlos crossed his fingers, showed them to Jade, then heaved at the door. The squeal of metal on metal echoed along the long line of wagons.

"Could you have made it any clearer we were here?" she snapped.

Wisely he ignored her and jumped down. He held up his arms for her. Taking hold of his hands she slid down him to the ground.

"There, that wasn't too bad, was it?" he said.

"It would have been better if I could have had a proper seat, and maybe a window," she told him.

He gestured up at the door above them. "You could see out of that."

"It wasn't a window."

"Are you never satisfied, woman?"

"Never," she said stretching up to give him a quick kiss. "So where now?" she asked when he would have tried for another one.

He looked around uncertainly, but they were completely blocked in by wagons on either side. Bending over, Jade tried to peer under the wagon but all she could see was more wheels.

"We need to get to the Railway Hotel," Carlos said, as she straightened up. "My uncle said our contact will be in room 102."

She frowned.

"What?" he said.

"We stayed at the Railway Hotel on the way down here. That's probably where Karen slipped me the package."

"Well, I certainly won't slip you anything," Carlos said reassuringly. "Unless you want me to," he amended quickly.

She rolled her eyes. "Men! Anyway, the hotel is back that way," she said, pointing back along the train.

"And how would you know that?"

"We passed a station signpost about five minutes before we pulled into the yard."

"See, I told you we didn't need a window."

She punched his arm. "Come on," she said, taking the lead. She felt his eyes on her and added an extra swing to her hips, smiling to herself as she did so.

They'd just reached the end of the line of wagons when they were hailed by a lone railway worker.

"What are you two doing here?"

Jade sensed Carlos trying to work out how to get close enough to knock him out.

Deciding she'd better take charge if she didn't want another offense added to her charge-sheet, Jade simply walked up to him, and looked up at him from under her eyelashes. "We're lost," she announced.

"Lost," the worker said, uncertainly.

"Lost," Jade confirmed. "My *hero* here," she indicated Carlos with a jerk of her chin, "said we could just follow the railway to get back to the city, but it doesn't seem to have worked."

The worker nodded, pretending to understand. "Scatchwah's that way," he said, pointing down the track. "If you take the track about twenty yards down there it leads to the road. Just follow that and you won't get lost."

Jade turned and glared at Carlos. "I *told* you we were going in the wrong direction," she said, and headed off in the direction she'd been given without giving him the chance to respond.

Giving an apologetic, what-can-you-do shrug to the worker, Carlos followed her, having to hurry to catch her up.

"Very impressive," he said, under his breath.

"Thank you," she said, glancing at him out of the corner of her eyes.

The marshaling yard turned out to be at least five miles out of the city, and with the temperature making walking uncomfortable after the first two miles Carlos waved down a hay cart and they rode into the city ensconced in some comfort on the back of the cart pulled by two of the largest Clydesdales Jade had ever seen.

Waving goodbye to the driver and his son just inside the city gates, they'd merged into the crowd, just another two Kahniakenhaka. Now they stood off to one side of the station forecourt, looking up at the Railway Hotel on the other side of the street. Dusk had added a certain softness to the city's harshness, hiding the thick layer of dust and horse manure that covered the forecourt's cobblestones.

"You're sure your uncle said the Railway Hotel?" Jade said.

"You're not nervous, are you?"

She scowled at him and checked the pistol in the small of her back. "Let's just get this over with," she said, hoisting her backpack higher onto her shoulders.

Inside they headed straight for the stairs, bypassing the concierge. On the first floor Carlos motioned Jade back from the door and knocked softly.

There was a movement from inside and as the door opened Carlos stiffened, shock visible on his face.

Out of sight, Jade carefully started to work the pistol free of her belt.

"Carlos Babineaux?" someone said.

"Why?" Carlos asked.

"Because if you are, your uncle asked us to arrange your return."

"Do you have some form of identification?" Carlos asked.

"He said you'd appreciate the latest pinot noir champagne."

"Only if it's from the Montagne de Reims," Carlos replied.

Jade frowned. That sounded suspiciously like a coded phrase, and if it was it seemed obvious from the relaxation in Carlos' shoulders that it had been answered correctly. Carlos gestured her over with his fingers before stepping out of sight into the room. Cautiously she allowed her blouse to fall back over the pistol before following him in.

There were two men in the room, and she stiffened momentarily at the sight of the automatics both men were re-holstering. Both were stocky, fit, and heavily set.

"Jade Carvello?" the first said, doing a double take at seeing her.

"Yes," she replied cautiously.

"Milosh Nikolić," he said, flipping open his wallet to show the Eye of Providence, on its mother-of-pearl shield. "Imperial Security. This is Pavlo." The other officer nodded in greeting. "It's a good disguise. You've got the virus?"

"Yes," Jade said, shrugging off her backpack, more than happy to be relieved of responsibility for it.

"No," Milosh said, holding up a hand to stop her. "Let's get you back the Mainline first. You've seriously pissed off a lot of the locals here and I'd rather you were back in our jurisdiction first." He checked his watch and looked across at his companion. "Half an hour?"

Pavlo nodded, and disappeared into the bedroom, reappearing a moment later with two heavy duffel bags.

"What's happening?" Carlos asked.

Jade felt slightly nonplussed with the calm way he was now dealing with the situation, especially given his initial reaction and shock at seeing the two Imp-Sec officers.

"You two head across to the station," Milosh said. "Pavlo and I will follow. We've got first-class return tickets for you on the Chicago shuttle. Here . . ." He picked up two cardboard tabs from the table and handed one each to Jade and Carlos. "Seats are on a first come first served basis so we'll just have to hope we can get a cabin to ourselves." He picked up two folders from the table and gave one to Jade. "New passports," he said as he handed the second to Carlos.

Jade opened it. Her face stared up at her, minus the wig.

"I'd leave the wig on until we're on board," Milosh said, answering her unspoken question. "It's too good a disguise."

Jade noted that apparently, she was now Kada Foreman. She showed the passport to Carlos.

Milosh handed them their tickets and Jade started to feel some of the constant anxiety she'd known since the shooting begin to ease.

"Now, why couldn't you be this organized?" she asked Carlos.

"I'm the one who arranged this," he reminded her.

She rolled her eyes. His uncle must certainly have some pull.

"Everyone ready?" Milosh asked.

"Is there time to use the toilet?" Jade asked.

Milosh checked his watch. "Five minutes."

When she reappeared, face and hands washed and feeling almost ready to face the world, Pavlo had disappeared and Milosh and Carlos were waiting for her by the door. Milosh was carrying one of the bags and was obviously anxious to be off.

"Ready," she confirmed.

Pavlo was waiting for them at the top of the stairs, accompanied by another four extremely fit young men, all carrying the ubiquitous duffel bags slung over their shoulders. For what was obviously supposed to be an undercover operation, the demeanor of all six Imp-Sec officers screamed 'heavy'. Still, it did make her feel safer.

"Right, good luck," Milosh said. "We'll be following you so don't worry."

Right, don't worry, Jade thought, hoping they weren't going to be famous last words.

Leading the way, she and Carlos started downstairs. The reception was temporarily unstaffed and outside the gas lights were now lit, the warm glow adding a romantic tone to the street.

Carlos gave her a reassuring smile and she took his hand as they headed across the street, dodging a horse drawn tram following the rails laid into the cobblestones.

"That's it," Carlos said, reading it off the overhead display. "Platform Two."

They threaded their way through the late crowd and followed the sequence of platforms down to number two. A guard on the front gate punched their tickets with bored indifference and Carlos led the way down the carriages to the front of the First-Class section, about halfway down the train. Jade glanced behind them as she followed Carlos up the steps. Milosh and Pavlo were about twenty feet behind them.

Carlos checked the cabins as he led the way down the corridor. At the third door he motioned Jade inside and as she settled her backpack into the overhead storage he waited by the door. A moment later the two Imp-Sec officers followed them in, sliding the door closed behind them and placing their not inconsiderable mass between it and the two fugitives.

Milosh looked at his watch. "Five minutes," he said.

"Are the other four coming with us?" Jade asked, surprised when they hadn't appeared.

A face looked in through the window but quickly moved on to the next cabin at a glare from Pavlo.

"If things go well. They're providing outer protection."

There was a knock on the outside window and Jade looked round in time to see one of the four moving off toward the front of the train.

"Damn," Milosh said, looking out of the window.

Jade followed his gaze to see a squad of six military police running down the platform toward the train.

"Arm up," Milosh told Pavlo.

Pavlo pulled the barrel of an automatic carbine out of the top of his bag, quickly followed by the stock and magazine, and assembled them efficiently.

"Hmm, guys?" Jade offered uncertainly, as another automatic carbine appeared from Milosh's bag. "Is this necessary?"

"First Leader's orders. We're to get you back to the Mainline asap." Milosh slipped on some body armor, the padding clearly marked with the black and silver of Imp-Sec. He tightened the straps with a jerk.

Jade felt sick. The First Leader. What had she done to attract his attention? She gave a wan smile at Carlos who was watching her with calculated interest. She blew out her breath.

Milosh checked his watch. "All right, Pavlo. It seems this is where we earn our pay."

"All 450 pounds of it a year," Pavlo said, cocking his gun.

There was the sound of a disturbance outside and the door slid open. The officer who'd opened the door flinched at the sight of the two guns trained on his chest. Or it might have been the sight of the two Imp-Sec officers blocking the doorway. Jade knew she'd have been very nervous in his place. Milosh and Pavlo seemed to exude danger.

"Force Leader . . ." Milosh peered at the MP's name tag " . . . Johnathon. Group Leader Milosh Nikolić, Imperial Security. Can we help you?"

The Force Leader frowned. "We have a warrant for that individual. She is wanted for assault of an officer in the line of his business, and for terrorism."

"I am afraid you can't have her. The First Leader personally gave me my orders."

"And I have my orders from the World Leader."

"Personally?" Milosh asked, showing his teeth. "In any event it doesn't matter – you're not having her. And if your World Leader has some sort of problem with that, he will need to take it up with the First Leader."

"And just how do you propose to get out of here?" the Force Leader asked.

Milosh showed his teeth again, as the train suddenly gave a lurch, and the Force Leader looked around wildly. As he did so, Pavlo took a single step forward and jammed the barrel of his gun under the Force Leader's ear.

"Tell your soldiers to stand down," Pavlo said slowly.

The Force Leader looked round out of the corner of his eyes. "Stand down," he told his troops.

"How?" Jade whispered to Carlos.

"They probably have two in the train, and another two in the signal box. At least that's how I'd have done it."

She remembered the one who had knocked on the window, then did a double take at what Carlos had said – *if* he'd done it?

The rest of the trip was rather anticlimactic. In Chicago, the six Chikyù MPs were released, and Jade and Carlos were ushered through to Immigration where she found a lawyer and two Agency agents waiting to escort her back to New York. She'd barely had time to hand the package containing the virus over and get a receipt before she was being escorted out the door to the express that would take her back to New York. She had just reached the door when she noticed Carlos still standing between Milosh and Pavlo.

"You're not coming?"

He shook his head regretfully. "I don't think I can," he said looking meaningfully at his two companions.

Jade was suddenly reminded that despite everything he had done he was still an Anarchist, and probably still of significant interest to Imp-Sec. "I'm not leaving you," she said.

"Miss Carvello," her lawyer protested.

"No. He saved my life. I'm not leaving him."

"I'll be fine," Carlos said reassuringly.

She looked at him, and he returned her gaze levelly.

"Go on," he said. "I'll catch up with you in New York."

She was torn, but Margaret needed her, and with a nod she turned back to the door.

"Jade," Carlos called.

She looked back.

"If you haven't heard from me within three days, phone the French Embassy and ask to speak to Uncle Babineaux. Tell him his nephew Carlos still needs his help."

"Should I ask if he'd appreciate the latest pinot noir champagne?"

"It probably wouldn't hurt." He gave her the grin that would have won her heart, if she hadn't already lost it.

Her heart, oh dear when did that happen, she thought. She gave Carlos a lopsided smile, realizing that it didn't really matter when — it had happened. "Three days," she said, and allowed the lawyer to lead her outside.

40

Welcome Home Miss Carvello

(Thursday: New York Grand Central Station, Commonwealth of America, Mainline)

Margaret was staring at a hoarding on the platform opposite when there was a soft cough and she looked round to find Inspector Terrance standing just behind her.

"Miss Peric," he said, touching a finger to the peak of his bowler hat.

"Inspector," she said politely.

"I wasn't expecting to meet you here."

Margaret gave a tired smile. "I wasn't expecting to be here either," she admitted. In fact, it was only two hours ago, after her conversation with Donald, that she'd decided she would.

The station lights flickered into life as dusk continued to descend over the city, and the Inspector checked his watch. "Shouldn't be long now." He leaned forward to peer down the track. "And here it is."

The locomotive pulled into the station in a billow of coal smoke and steam, causing Margaret to take a step away from the edge of the platform. Even before the train had eased to a complete stop,

281

passengers were already opening their carriage doors, ready to disembark as soon as it had stopped moving.

Margaret kept her eyes peeled, but it was the short Inspector who spotted Jade first. "There she is," he pointed out, as Jade stepped down from the carriage, backpack slung over one shoulder. She looked around uncertainly and Margaret waved to attract her attention.

Jade saw her and, giving a short wave in response, headed in their direction. She blinked as she came close enough to notice the Inspector standing next to Margaret.

"Sir." She sounded surprised.

"Miss Carvello," the Inspector said, holding out his hand.

Jade returned the shake then turned to Margaret. "Is there any news on Jessie? Carlos got word in Yuchi she'd disappeared."

"She's safe," Margaret said, pulling Jade into a hug. "And just as importantly, so are you." For a moment she felt Jade stiffen with shock, before returning the embrace.

As Jade pulled back from the hug the Inspector stepped forward to take her backpack. "Miss Ackov was rescued Sunday morning in a joint exercise between Imp-Sec and the Agency. Quite a remarkable success."

"And she's all right?" Jade asked.

"She's fine," Margaret assured her. "Come on, I've got the Rolls waiting. Inspector, will you be accompanying us?"

"Just to the vehicle," he said. "I'm on my way home but I felt it was my duty to welcome Miss Carvello back."

"Why thank you, Inspector." Jade sounded surprised.

How typical of Jade, Margaret thought, that she didn't know how many people cared for her.

"I received a briefing from Imp-Sec this morning based on Mr. Babineaux' testimony last night," the Inspector continued. "I'm glad you survived. There were times I was concerned for your safety."

"So was I," Jade said forcefully.

"As was Miss Peric," he said.

Margaret raised an eyebrow as she noticed the Inspector glance at her out of the corner of his eye, the hint of a smile on his lips.

"I understand she spoke to the First Leader on your behalf when we first became aware of your . . . difficulties . . . with the authorities on Chikyù."

"Really?" Jade said. "At least now I know why the Imp-Sec snatch team received their orders direct from the First Leader. Those poor guys."

"Oh?" Margaret said.

"Long story. I'll tell you later." Jade turned to the Inspector. "Any news on Karen?"

The Inspector shook his head. "No. And no word on Hermandez Cortez either. They both appear to have vanished. Still, if they reappear on the Mainline, they are now on Imp-Sec's wanted list. And the Agency's Board have agreed to place a reward on Karen's capture. The Agency doesn't like agents who go rogue."

"If I see her, I'll make sure to tell her," Jade said tightly. "She may even survive that conversation."

The Inspector frowned. "Miss Carvello," he told her warningly. "Please remember we must at least attempt to adhere to the rule of law."

Margaret snorted.

The Inspector shook his head. "That isn't helping."

"It wasn't supposed to. Besides if I see Karen first you can also rest assured that she may not necessarily be alive by the time the law arrives." She stared at him, until he sighed and nodded.

They'd reached the front of the station by now and Rolf, who was leaning against the Rolls' passenger door, drew himself up as he saw them approaching, touching one finger to the peak of his cap as he opened the door for them. "Welcome back, Miss Carvello."

"Oh, aren't we lah-di-dah," Jade said, giving him a warm smile.

Rolf winked at her as he took the backpack the Inspector handed him and placed it in the boot before returning to the driver's seat.

"I'll leave you here," the Inspector said. "I would like a full report, Miss Carvello, but it can wait until Monday." He swung the door closed, and with a jaunty wave headed off to find a cab.

Jade pulled a face. "Right, so now I've got to write my report over the weekend."

Margaret frowned as Rolf pulled out into the traffic. "Are you sure? I thought that meant you didn't need to start until Monday."

"You don't know the Agency," Jade said. "Complete paperwork is next to godliness. It used to drive Karen mad." She froze, and Margaret patted her hand. "All I'd like to know is why she did it," Jade said plaintively.

"Money? Revenge?" Margaret shook her head. "You might never know." She frowned at the look Jade was now giving her. "What?"

"I didn't want to say in front of the Inspector, but you look terrible. Are you okay?"

Margaret jerked her head warningly at Rolf, and Jade looked mortified, realizing that was probably not something she should have said to her principal before one of her staff.

"I'm fine," Margaret said. "Just haven't been sleeping properly. Probably worrying about you and Jessie."

Jade nodded, although it was clear she wasn't convinced. "You can stop worrying now," she said brightly. "We're both home."

"And how are you?" Margaret asked.

"Tired and filthy. It was twenty-four hours in the train. But . . ." she peered around at the scenery of New York scrolling past outside the Rolls' window. "I'm home!"

Margaret nodded. She could understand the feeling, but it had been some years since she could admit to having a home. Not since before the war. "And the trip?" she asked. "Did you manage to see the earth mounds?"

Jade shook her head regretfully. "Unfortunately, at the time Carlos and I were lying in a priest hole in the keel of a paddle steamer, under several layers of firewood."

"Sounds like an exciting sixteen days."

"Only sixteen days?" Jade sounded puzzled. She frowned as she counted up the days on her fingers. "No, it must be –" she stopped and shook her head. "It felt much longer than that."

"It can," Margaret said. Her own war had seemed to last a lifetime.

"I'm worried about Carlos though," Jade admitted. "When we arrived in Chicago his relationship with Imp-Sec seemed . . . complicated."

"I can try and find out for you," Margaret offered.

Jade frowned thoughtfully. "He did say that if I hadn't heard from him within three days, I was to phone the French Embassy and ask to speak to his uncle. But it's only been one day." She looked at Margaret uncertainly.

"The French Embassy? I wonder why?" Margaret considered the matter for a moment. "Let's give him another day then. After that I'll phone Donald and see if he can't wring some information out of Imp-Sec about your boyfriend."

Turning into the drive that led to the house, Jade watched with interest as the vehicle and its contents were carefully checked by the two Imp-Sec officers on the main gate before it was allowed through into the grounds.

"I know, it does rather seem like locking the stable door after the horse has bolted," Margaret admitted.

"Given the mailbomb, and Jessie's kidnapping, you probably should have been doing something a little earlier," Jade agreed, as Rolf pulled to a halt at the foot of the main steps.

Upon opening the door, the scent of frangipanis swept into the vehicle, and Margaret watched Jade take a deep breath in obvious enjoyment.

"Come on," Margaret said, climbing out of the car. As she did so, the front door of the house opened, and a small body flew down the steps to throw herself into Jade's arms.

"We were so worried about you," Jessie said, her face buried in Jade's shoulder.

Jade patted her reassuringly.

Margaret shook her head. After all Jessie had been through, she had still worried about Jade.

Jade looked rather surprised as the same thought must have occurred to her too.

"Well, I'm here now," Jade said.

Jessie loosened her hold and slid down Jade to take her hand. "Come on, Miss Carvello, everyone is waiting for you," she said looking up at her with her large, serious eyes.

Jade looked across to Margaret, who waved her up the steps. As Jessie led them through the door and into the main hall, Jade found the whole household lined up to greet her, with Markus at the top of the line. Jade stopped dead.

James, the butler, started to clap and the others joined in enthusiastically. As they did, Margaret slipped up beside her and gave her a hug. "Welcome back," she whispered in her ear.

"Thank you," Jade said, overcome with emotion.

Margaret gave her a reassuring pat. "Go and have a bath. Change, then come and talk. I have something to tell you." She looked down at Jessie. "Jessie, please take Miss Carvello to her room."

"Come on Miss Carvello," Jessie said, tugging on her hand.

Margaret watched Jessie lead Jade up the stairs, then with a sigh decided she'd better see about clearing some of the reports Michael had forwarded to her for her attention. She was halfway through Aife's draft final report, red pen in hand, when a particularly obtuse piece of writing had her wrinkling her forehead. After a couple of re-reads she was no clearer on what Aife was trying to say and decided to ask Markus for his opinion.

She found him in the front room reading a newspaper while Jessie was busy on the floor next to him coloring in a picture book with some crayons.

"Have you got a moment Markus?" she asked as Jessie looked up at her with a happy smile before returning to her coloring.

"Of course. What do you want?"

"It's Aife's draft report. I'm just up to some of her preliminary findings, but I can't make head nor tail of what she's actually trying to say."

"Where?" He accepted the report she handed him.

She leaned over his shoulder to point out the problem paragraph.

"Margaret . . ." It was Jade, paused uncertainly in the doorway. "You said you had something to tell me?"

"Come in," she said, straightening, but leaving her hand on Markus' shoulder.

Jade raised an eyebrow at the gesture.

Margaret ignored that.

One of the serving maids appeared as Jade sat, pushing a trolley bearing a teapot, cups, milk, and a small plate of sandwiches.

Margaret passed Jade the plate before taking her own seat. "We thought you'd probably be hungry."

"Thank you," Jade said. "I ate on the train but that was . . . what . . ." She looked up at the clock. "Gods, eight hours ago."

"Tuck in then."

Jade didn't need a further invitation, and, obviously starving, she'd devoured one of the delicate triangles in a single mouthful before apparently remembering where she was. After that she kept her bites small and even, chewing carefully between each bite as Margaret poured the tea.

"I thought I'd better warn you that my cousin will be here on Saturday," Margaret said conversationally. "He wants to thank you personally for your actions with the letter bomb."

Jade was swallowing at the time and the shock sent a piece of the sandwich down the wrong way. "The First Leader?" she said, when she'd finished coughing and could take a breath.

"The same," Margaret confirmed. "Here, have some tea," she said, passing her the cup.

Jade looked at Markus as if to make sure it wasn't some form of weird joke on Margaret's part. But seeing as Markus was looking rather wan himself . . .

"I have a netball game," Jade said, obviously casting around for an excuse that might get her out of this.

"They can afford to play without you for one game," Margaret said calmly.

"They've already had to do without me for two."

"Then one more won't make any difference," Margaret pointed out.

Jade looked at Markus for support. But all he did was shrug. Jade looked at the sandwich in her hand and took another bite.

41

There's a Gentleman to See You

(Saturday: New York, Commonwealth of America, Mainline)

"Ma'am."

Jade looked up from the report she was working on. She hadn't been the only one worried by the First Leader's visit, and the house had been at a constant level of frenetic activity for the last two days as Mrs. Mack drove the staff to distraction to ensure the house was perfect for his arrival. Jade had even seen James polishing the balustrade on the main staircase, a task normally so far below the responsibility of a butler that she'd actually stumbled when she saw him. The only two not affected were Margaret and Jessie: Jessie because she was too young, and Margaret because, well, because she was Margaret. As a result, Jade had settled herself into a corner of the kitchen to work, out of the way of the frantic activity that filled the rest of the house. The quiet, controlled bustle of the kitchen, and the warm scent of fresh bread cooking were soothing after the chaos of her life on the run over the past weeks. It didn't stop all the interruptions though, she thought with a sigh, looking up to see Gwendelyn, one of the under-maids, standing uncertainly by the door.

"There's a gentleman to see you, ma'am."

"Me?" Jade paused. "It's not the First Leader, is it?" she asked, warily. It wouldn't have been past Margaret to dump him on her like that.

"No ma'am."

Puzzled, Jade followed the maid to the entrance to the drawing room. A familiar figure was staring out the window over the front garden.

"Carlos?" she said, stunned. "What are you doing here? Did Imp-Sec release you? You can't stay – if Miss Peric finds you here . . ."

Carlos turned, a rueful smile on his face. "I'm actually here to see Miss Peric."

"Why?" Just what did he think he was doing?

"That's also my question," Margaret said, appearing in the door behind her. "Mr. Babineaux, I believe?"

"Ma'am."

"I understand I owe you my thanks for Jade's safe return."

"No thanks are necessary. It was my genuine pleasure," Carlos said, flashing Jade one of those grins that caused her heart to miss a beat.

"So I can see," Margaret replied, as she seated herself and adjusted her dress. "Am I right that your visit has something to do with the phone call I just had with the Head of Imperial Intelligence?"

"Ma'am."

Jade furrowed her brow as her head swung between the two of them. What was going on?

"Cliff was a little cryptic," Margaret continued dryly. "But apparently he had phoned to let me know you were going to call, and he was confirming your credentials."

"What credentials?" Jade demanded.

"Your boyfriend's an agent of the Agence Nationale de la Sécurité, the ANS – the French Secret Service," Margaret said.

"What!" Jade exclaimed. "Why didn't you tell me?!"

"I was undercover, Jade."

"So? You should have told me." Jade was furious. Didn't he know how confused she'd been when she'd thought he was an Anarchist?

"And when was I supposed to tell you?" Carlos asked. He paused for a moment. "And why am I the one in trouble? You never told me you were working for the Agency."

"I couldn't."

Carlos raised his eyebrows. "And I could?"

"Children, children," Margaret admonished them.

Jade narrowed her eyes.

"Look. I'm sorry," Carlos apologized. "You know now though."

Jade scowled. He should have told her. With a tilt of her nose, she sat down on the couch.

Margaret looked at her, then rang the bell. The under-maid appeared almost instantly. "Gwendelyn, could we have tea please?

"So, Mr. Babineaux, what did you want to see me about?" Margaret asked as the maid disappeared.

There was the sound of the front door opening and voices from the hall. Margaret looked around and got to her feet. "Excuse me for a moment."

Jade watched her leave the room.

"You got back all right then?" Carlos said, sitting down next to her.

"I did."

"And Jessie's all right. I heard Imp-Sec got her back."

"Apparently, it was a *joint* Agency and Imp-Sec operation," Jade said a trifle sharply.

"Ah, I didn't hear that," Carlos said, "but my source was Imp-Sec, so they might have just forgotten."

"And I heard Imp-Sec had an Anarchist mole. You wouldn't know anything about that, would you?"

"I might have mentioned something to them about that. So, forgiven?" he asked.

She sighed. "Forgiven." It did seem ridiculous to remain angry with him when they'd been on the same side, even if he should have told her. She found her attention focused on his mouth and unconsciously ran her tongue over her lips, watching his eyes widen.

There was a cough from the door and, startled, both looked round to find Margaret watching them with interest. Beside her was a vaguely familiar figure; blond hair, medium height, and wearing a dark-colored suit of military cut. Behind him hovered the slim, bespectacled figure of Force Leader Hore, looking uncharacteristically nervous and clutching what looked like a thin cigar box to his chest.

Carlos leaped to his feet. "First Leader!"

Jade tried to follow his lead but stumbled and fell back into the sofa. Ignoring the hand Carlos put out to help her, she pushed herself to her feet, feeling her face flush with embarrassment, and wishing the ground would open up and swallow her. How could she have failed to recognize him!

"Miss Carvello," the First Leader said, ignoring her faux pas and holding out his hand. "You have my personal thanks for your actions in saving my cousin."

Jade took his hand, then stood there frozen, trying to work out what she was supposed to do with it. Did she curtsy or bow? What was she supposed to say? The Agency induction course on etiquette simply didn't cover this situation.

The First Leader rescued her by taking her hand in both of his before turning back to the Force Leader and clicking his fingers. Hore opened the flat box he was holding, and Jade saw that nestled inside the black velvet was a small, red enameled cross with black borders. Attached to the cross was a ribbon of red and black fabric.

The First Leader gave her a broad smile. "And I am also happy to convey the official thanks of the Empire by providing you with the Order of Saint Vladimir, second class. The Empress Catherine II established the award in 1782. Traditionally, recipients are entitled to hereditary nobility, but unfortunately that is now more honored in the breach than in the observance." He gave her an apologetic grin.

"I'm sure I can survive without that particular honor, sir."

"It certainly makes a pleasant change to give the award to someone who actually meets the technical requirements."

"First Leader?"

"That 'whoever at the peril of their own life saves ten lives from fire or water'. If I may?" He gestured at the tray.

"Of course," she told him, not really understanding what he was asking.

Lifting her collar, he removed the tie she was wearing, and replaced it with the small red and black necklet that was attached to the cross. After closing the stud at the back, he stepped back and saluted her. "Congratulations Dame Carvello."

Automatically, Jade snapped an answering salute.

"I understand Margaret has arranged with her redoubtable Mrs. Mack for a dinner in your honor tonight. I look forward to hearing of your experiences on Chikyù. Unfortunately, it is not a line I have ever visited."

"Of course, First Leader." Jade's hand unconsciously rose to touch the small cross.

"Donald, please," the First Leader told Jade. "And Mr. Babineaux," he said, turning to Carlos. "Heidi has asked me to tell you to look her up next time you're in Naisre. I understand she wants to pass onto you her personal thanks."

"Heidi?" Jade said, bristling jealously. She wasn't aware she'd said this aloud until Donald smiled at her.

"Heidi Klume is my acting head of Imperial Security," he said. "And your Mr. Babineaux has agreed to continue to assist Imp-Sec with their investigations."

Jade flushed, and then shot a glance at Carlos, wondering what it was he'd agreed to help with.

"It wasn't as if I had much choice once my uncle signed off on it," Carlos said.

"Your uncle?" Jade said, starting to feel like an echo.

"The head of the ANS."

Jade rolled her eyes. Of course. Who else would he be?

"Come in Markus," Margaret called.

Jade looked round to see Markus hovering uncertainly in the doorway.

If Jade had thought the attention she had received from the First Leader worrying, the attention he focused on Markus was positively disconcerting.

Fortunately, Markus seemed oblivious to the glance, and Donald quickly hooded his interest.

"Mr. Ackov," Donald said, offering his hand. "I understand we have you to thank for discovering this plot against the Empire."

Markus gaped, but took the hand when Margaret elbowed him in the side.

"And I trust your daughter has recovered?" Donald asked.

"Sir. Quite well, thank you."

"Did you want to meet Jessie?" Margaret asked, preparing to ring the bell. "I'm sure we can tear her away from Fresia for a couple of minutes."

Donald looked puzzled. "Fresia?"

"A cat who appears to have adopted the household," Margaret explained. "She's due to have kittens any day now, and we promised Jessie she can keep one."

"Not just yet," Donald said. "There are still some things we need to discuss. I'm not leaving for Baltimore until after dinner, so there's plenty of time."

"And how is Artos?" Margaret asked, reminding Jade that the First Leader's son lived with his mother in Baltimore.

"He sounded fine when I spoke to him earlier by phone. Apparently, he's just started dance lessons, much to his disgust. Too many girls if I understood his complaint."

"That will change," Margaret said.

"Undoubtedly," Donald agreed, taking one of the chairs and gesturing for the others to sit.

As Jade resumed her place on the sofa, she wondered what Donald wanted to discuss, and why it would involve her. One hand caressed the cross, now hanging from her neck. A noble! Her father would have been so proud, her mother – probably wasn't going to believe it. As Carlos sat beside her, she found herself leaning into him.

Hore was left without a chair but at a 'join us' gesture from the First Leader quickly found a stool in the hallway and joined the circle.

"Thanks to the intelligence Carlos provided," Donald said, "it appears clear Sultan is involved."

"And that intelligence is what?" Margaret asked.

Donald nodded at Carlos.

"My transfer to Chikyù was accomplished via a black-portal operated by the Anarchists," Carlos explained.

Jade winced. She should have picked up on that when he'd appeared on Chikyù, but she'd simply assumed the Anarchists had been able to bribe someone to let him through the Chicago portal. Obviously, she'd been wrong.

"The technology, and the sophistication of the operation exceed anything the Anarchists would be capable of without outside help.

More pertinently, the portal operator spoke Arabic with a mid-European accent."

"You speak Arabic?" Jade said, surprised, in Arabic.

"A little," he replied in the same language. He looked so smug at having confounded her, that she felt like thumping him.

Margaret nodded. "Sultan."

"But of course, we don't know whether it is the Junoobil, or the Sho'mali alliances. The Sho'mali supported Miro during the Civil War, but my brother's actions at the end of the war could just as well mean it's the Junoobil."

"And what did Conrad do?" Margaret asked interestedly.

"After the cold war on Sultan went hot, Junoobil bases off line started to coordinate a response against Sho'mali resources still on Sultan," Donald explained. "Unfortunately, that would have meant the portals wouldn't have been available to us, which would have stopped our offensive dead in the water. Conrad ordered a commando raid to seize their main portal and sent their technicians packing."

Conrad! Oh, little gods and fishes, Jade thought. They were actually talking about the hero of the war who'd died during the assault on Cape Town. And not just as a historical person, but as though they actually knew him. She stopped herself when she realized how ridiculous that sounded. Naturally they'd known him. He had been Donald's brother.

"Well, that could have done it," Margaret agreed.

"It doesn't have to be just those two either," Donald continued. "The politics of Sultan were complex enough before the war. I can't imagine it's got any better since. The problem is we don't know what is going on there, which in hindsight is a clear oversight, and something I intend to remedy immediately. And this is where you two come in," he said, looking at Margaret and Jade.

Margaret raised an eyebrow. "Oh, how?"

"You, dear cuz, are going to lead a diplomatic mission to Sultan to establish an embassy there."

"You've got to be joking, Donald! I don't have the experience for something like that."

"I wasn't expecting you'd do it without an experienced deputy."

"So, I'm just going to be a figurehead?" Margaret didn't sound any happier at that suggestion.

"No! Look, Margaret, you're ideal for the role. You've got combat experience from the last war. You've proved your ability to handle large Departments. And you're my cousin, which will give you extra credence." He ticked the points off on his fingers.

"And what happens to my Department? I can't just leave them. Jeffries only left a week ago. Regin hasn't even had time to get his boots under the desk."

"I'm sure Acting Deputy Director-General Regin Marchetti is fully capable of doing the role *you* appointed him for."

"And the Director-General?" *Her* position, dammit.

"I was thinking of Sylvi Saito."

"What!? Donald, she'll be eaten alive. She's been a Director for *four* months. You're bouncing her over the heads of five, considerably more experienced Directors."

"She's done very well on that task group you gave her. And she's impressed both Heidi and Cliff."

"You've already spoken to them about it!?"

Donald made a placating gesture. "Look cuz, Sylvi was only ever going to be a Director in Ag and Food for a year, two at most. I'm just moving her promotion up."

Jade watched Margaret's eyes narrow angrily. "She was your source, wasn't she?"

"Not as such."

"And what does *that* mean?"

Donald sighed. "Your brother asked me to find her a job. Apparently, her brother's just married Kaius, who's the only child of one of Notway's Continental Leaders."

"I know who Kaius is!" Margaret snapped, her eyes hard. "So, you just dumped her into my Department because Rajko asked. I'll kill him."

Donald ran a hand through his hair uneasily. "I'm not explaining this properly."

"No, you aren't. I know the Empire works on nepotism but there *are* limits." She shook her head angrily.

"Look, Margaret," Donald said, trying again. "Sylvi is actually *over*-qualified for the position of Director. Before we dropped her into Ag and Food she'd been acting as Notway's Chancellor for the last two years and making a good fist of it. Rajko wants to make the position permanent, but we thought some experience on the Mainline first would be useful."

"And you didn't think to tell me. You were taking a hell of a risk. What would have happened if she'd flopped? The Mainline is *not* one of the other lines; even one as large and as complex as Notway."

Donald scrubbed his face. "I was going to tell you, it's just . . . I honestly forgot. This whole thing about the viruses and possible food shortages just drove it out of my mind, and then when I remembered I thought that because you'd put her in charge of the project of coordinating our response, Rajko must have spoken to you. It's obvious he didn't now, and I apologize."

Margaret closed her eyes. Donald wasn't wrong in thinking that giving Sylvi some experience on the Mainline within the Empire's bureaucracy would benefit her as Notway's Chancellor, but he should have told her, warned her. Given her the chance to make sure that Sylvi *was* coping. Although, given the way Sylvi had handled everything that had been thrown at her, she suspected Donald might already be trying to work out how he could poach her from Rajko.

"But Margaret, I really need *you* as the Ambassador. I don't have anyone half as qualified, or suitable. Maybe if you hadn't been as successful as you were in dealing with the crisis, or if Mr. Ackov hadn't been able to warn us about the plot . . . But he did, and you were. And for the moment you are far more useful to me as an Ambassador than in your present position where your own success has made you dispensable."

"And just where is this mission going to go?" Margaret said icily. "As you've pointed out, we don't exactly know who our friends are on Sultan, or even if we have any."

"I'm not suggesting you leave next week," Donald said plaintively. "We need to find out what's been happening on Sultan first. There's no sense in you heading off without knowing what you're getting into."

"Leader?"

Margaret, who'd been watching her troops shake themselves out into a loose skirmishing line along the track at the foot of the hill, gave the Force Leader a nod.

Behind her, the sun had almost disappeared behind the line of hills, leaving the horizon a deep, fiery red.

"Have we got any more information?" she asked.

The Force Leader shook his head. "The auto-giros won't get here for another half an hour. There was a delay in refueling them."

"And half an hour puts it well after dusk. They won't see a thing. Still no sign of our scouts?"

"Nothing."

"I don't like it."

"Neither do I," he admitted.

"Unfortunately, we don't have any choice. We have to clear the hill by dawn, so the rest of the Army has a clear path to Cresolate in the morning."

She turned back to the hill. "All right, send the skirmishers in and get the main battle-line ready to advance when I give the word."

She heard the bugler signal the advance and watched as the skirmishers scrambled up the steep slope, using the shrubs to pull themselves up between the granite slabs that lined the hill. The skirmish line had almost disappeared when an explosion shredded the foliage around them. The explosion was quickly followed by a second.

"Claymores," the Force Leader swore, as the rapid staccato of individual aimed weapons told her what had probably happened to her scouts.

Margaret winced, as the first mortar rounds blossomed along the main battle-lines.

"Signal the advance," she said, already knowing that they were going to take heavy casualties.

"Margaret?" Donald prompted.

Margaret shook herself. "No," she said. "There's no such thing as too much information."

Jade looked at her, troubled. Something wasn't right.

Donald nodded. "Cliff believes he can remedy that situation if he can borrow Miss Carvello for a couple of weeks."

Jade's attention shot back to the First Leader. "And just who's Cliff when he's at home?"

"The Head of Imperial Intelligence," Donald said with a twinkle in his eyes.

"Oh."

"He was very impressed with the way you handled what happened on Chikyù."

"Oh," she said again, then cringed at what she must sound like.

"He was also very impressed with the report he received from the Agency on your skill with languages. Arabic, Russian, Spanish, Nayarit? Why did you learn that one, by the way?"

"It's a family tradition on the female line. My great-grandmother came through the first portal from Nayarit with Iapura."

"That would explain it. It's not exactly a popular language," Donald said. The First Leader turned his attention back to Carlos. "And Mr. Babineaux, I understand you'll be returning to Chikyù tomorrow."

Jade looked at Carlos, disappointed. "Why?" She'd been hoping to spend some time with him.

"We need to identify the line from which the Anarchists are operating their portal. Apparently Imp-Int have something that will do that, but I have to be on the line to operate the device." He shrugged. "At this stage, I'm still undercover. So, all I have to do is turn up to the portal on Chikyù and ask to be transferred back."

"And how are you going to explain your failure to contact Hermandez?" Jade asked.

"I'm just going to blame you."

"That story has got more holes in it than Swiss cheese," Jade said angrily.

He opened his hands, placatingly. "There isn't anyone else who can do it."

Jade threw up her arms in disgust.

"Is there anyone else from my household you want to steal?" Margaret asked icily.

Donald gave her an unrepentant grin. "I'm hoping you'll also let me borrow Mr. Ackov for a week. I've taken your advice on board and I'm organizing a conference in Naisre to discuss the potato virus."

Jade saw Margaret give Markus a look which almost amounted to panic.

"Ah, First Leader, I have a daughter," Markus said uncertainly.

"It's all right Markus, Jessie can stay here," Margaret offered tightly. "You wouldn't want her to miss the birth of Fresia's kittens." She turned back to Donald. "And that's it?"

"For the moment," Donald said with a grin. "Although I'm hoping you'll be able to show me the gardens you've told me so much about."

"I think we can manage that," Margaret said, ringing a bell for the maid. "Ah Gwendelyn," she said, when the under-maid appeared. "Please tell Mrs. Mack we'll take afternoon tea on the terrace."

Ten minutes later, Jade stood on the terrace with Carlos watching Margaret and Markus show Donald round the garden below,. While Gwendelyn and Jessie set out afternoon tea at the other end of the terrace under the careful supervision of Mrs. Mack.

"You know, now you're a noble, you're going to have to select a motto," Carlos whispered.

"Give me a moment, Carlos," Jade protested. "I haven't been a noble for even an hour yet."

"So, have you got any ideas?"

She shook her head.

"How about: 'ego sum vestrum semper'?"

"Which means what?" she asked suspiciously.

"I am always right."

She punched him. "So how long have you been a member of the French Secret Service?"

"The Agence Nationale de la Sécurité? Sorry, for the French, the name is very important. It is perhaps because we are such small players in the Empire, no?" He seemed to be adding something up. "Just over five years. My uncle recruited me after I completed my apprenticeship, when I was undertaking a sabbatical to France. They were looking for fresh blood."

"Your uncle – the head of the ANS?"

"That's the one. Yes."

"And you are from Canada?"

He nodded. "My family immigrated to Canada from France when I was four. I don't think I've told you any lies. I've been very careful about that."

And just what did he mean by that, she thought. "When do you have to leave?"

He looked at his watch. "In about three hours."

"Three hours!"

"I've already been off line for three days. Much longer than that and it's not going to be worth me going back at all."

She pouted. "But I wanted to show you my new negligee." She saw indecision warring on his face, and she stretched up and whispered in his ear. "And then I was going to do things to your body that were going to blow your mind."

He almost choked. "We've still got three hours," he said hopefully when Jade had finished pounding his back.

"Not long enough for what I want to do to you," she said regretfully. "And not with him in the house." Her eyes flicked to the First Leader now making his way up the steps to the terrace. "Just make sure you don't do anything stupid."

"Since when have you known me do anything stupid?"

She simply looked at him.

"All right, all right – although we might have different views of stupid."

"And don't do anything that gets you killed."

"For the promise of a night of unbridled debauchery – I think you can count on it."

"And make sure you come back to me," she said, finally unable to ignore her true feelings.

"Always," he said, with such sincerity that she froze for a moment.

"Carlos," she said finally. "How do you say, 'Fidelity and Love' in Latin?"

"'*Fide et Amore*', why?"

"Think about it," she said, before pressing her lips lightly to his.

42

Vignette:
On Portals, Princes, Peasants, Pigs, and Plague

A century ago, Iapura led 53 survivors through a portal to escape a dying Earth. They had expected to emerge on Alpha Centauri but instead found themselves on an alternate Earth. An Earth where in 1884, Russian and English armies faced off across America's Great Plains, unprepared for the technological prowess of the conquering Nayarit.

Within six months, the 53 refugees had seized control of the Mainline, and over the next 100 years expanded their empire across the multiverse, eventually including 54 alternate Earths within the Cross-Temporal Empire (C-TE). Over time, two theories rose to explain the factors that had shaped the differences between these different Earths, and what had made the Mainline what it was.

The first, Individual Causation, argues that it is the action of decisive individuals that shape history, with the decisions of one special individual setting the course of history. For example, the actions of pivotal figures such as Alexander the Great, or the first Han Emperor Liu Bang, could cause branches in the multiverse, creating vastly different historical outcomes based on their choices.

On the other hand, Historical Inevitability suggests that impersonal forces, such as economic trends, social movements, technological advancements, climatic variations, and pandemics drive history by creating a series of paradoxes over an extended period that lead to inevitable shifts in historical trajectories, independent of individual actions.

In 1985, Professor Feryal Özel of the University of Constantinople proposed a fresh approach. By combining the two theories and creating a single weighted index which identifies key individuals whose actions could significantly influence events, as well as the buildup of paradoxes within a society.

For example, if a key leader made critical decisions during economic crises and social upheaval, the combined index would show a high probability of a split.

Professor Özel recently pinpointed such a split or Point of Divergence (POD) on the Mainline during the reign of István Dragutin, King of Serbia (1276–1349). The alliance he created between serfs and nobles set the scene for Serbia's victory over the Turks at the Battle of Kosovo in 1389. A victory that propelled Serbia to the forefront of European humanist thought and sparked the 'Serbian Renaissance', locking the door on the nascent Italian city-states.

People quickly dubbed this split the 'Princes, Peasants, Pigs, and Plague POD. "Princes" refers to Dragutin; "Peasants" to those freed from land ties by Dragutin who moved to cities; "Pigs" to the development of the Manguliica variety in Serbia, which improved pig size and boosted food production, and "Plague" to the Black Death, which devastated Italy but spared Serbia due to Dragutin's strict quarantine measures.

Thus, the convergence of princes, peasants, pigs, and plague irreversibly altered history, leading us to the world we know today.

Donald Clemhorn. PhD Alternate History.
An Early History of the Cross-Temporal Empire.
Unpublished.

Be Kept Informed

Thank you for reading FOR THE HONOR OF THE AGENCY.
We hope you enjoyed it.

If you would like to be kept informed of further releases from
Hague Publishing, and get a free copy of Carlos' recipe for his
'Lemon Sponge' why not subscribe to our newsletter at:

www.HaguePublishing.com/subscribe.php

And if you loved the book and have a moment to spare we
would really appreciate a short review. Your help in spreading
the word is gratefully received.

Now read on for an extract from:

FOR THE HONOR OF
THE EMPIRE

BOOK 2 in The Honor Series

FROM
FOR THE HONOR OF THE EMPIRE

CHAPTER I
IS MISS PERIC GOING TO BE ALL RIGHT?

(Sunday: Mainline New York)

"Good morning, Miss Peric," the chauffeur said, as he opened the front door for her.

Louise turned away from her study of Central Park's elm forest drowsing in the warmth of the early morning sun, just beyond the long, graveled driveway that led down from the house to the Avenue that ran along the side of the park. "Rolf, what are you doing opening doors? Shouldn't you be polishing the Rolls or something?"

"This is one of those 'somethings'," he explained with a smile and closed the door against the screech of a tram turning into Fifth Avenue from its route down Seventy-seventh.

"Are they in the dining room?" she asked, starting for the open French-doors on the far side of the main hall, and ignoring the massive granite staircase that rose three stories from the floor.

"They are."

"Don't bother announcing me," she said over her shoulder.

"Morning, Markus," she said, as she breezed into the room. She inspected the spread laid out on the sideboard for breakfast, wondering if she'd have time for a danish. "What are you doing here? I thought you were still in Naisre."

Markus looked up from the coloring book Jessie, his eight-year-old daughter, was working on from his lap. Given that the table was large enough to seat twenty-four, and they were the only two in the room, the room appeared, to say the least, underutilized. She wondered why they weren't using the smaller dining room. The answer, she suspected, was Mrs. Mack. The diminutive housekeeper had a powerful sense of propriety.

Markus blinked at Louise's appearance. Despite the earliness of her arrival, she was wearing a long black beaded net evening dress. "I got back last night," he said. "It's a bit early for you, though, isn't it?" He glanced at the clock on the mantelpiece that still showed eight. "Or is it late?"

"The dress? I have the day off, so I thought I'd take Margaret shopping. And as it's such a beautiful day, I thought it deserved a beautiful dress." She glanced at the windows, where the silk brocade curtains had been pulled back and the windows opened to let in the early morning breeze. The dining room's polished oak floor glowed gold in the sunlight.

Jessie gave Louise an enormous smile. "Have you seen the kittens yet, Miss Peric?"

"Not yet, sweetheart. I hope you'll show them to me before I leave."

Jessie nodded and returned to her coloring.

"So, is Mags up?" Louise asked.

"I haven't seen her yet." He frowned. "I would have expected her to be up by now, though."

"No problems. I'll wake her."

At the top of the stairs, she rapped smartly on the door to her sister's third floor bedroom. "Margaret, come out, come out, wherever you are."

Her call was met with dead silence. After thirty seconds, she knocked again. "Mags?"

When there was still no response, she tried the door, only to find it locked. Her hands suddenly felt cold. "Margaret!" she called, rattling the door. "It's Louise, let me in."

"Louise?" It was Markus at the foot of the staircase. "Is everything all right?" Jessie clutched his hand as she stared up at Louise with wide, concerned eyes.

"No," Louise said. "The door's locked." She was aware of how stupid that sounded, but to put into words what she was afraid of . . .

Markus hurried up the stairs. "Margaret. Miss Peric?" he called, trying the door.

Louise bent to look through the lock, but the key was in it, blocking her view. Damn! Backing away, she looked over her shoulder to the ground floor where one of the ImpSec officers who'd been stationed at the house since the mail bomb attempt on her sister's life was looking up at them.

"You!"

The officer started.

"I need you up here," she told him. "Now!"

Behind her, Markus was rattling the door handle, presumably trying to force it open by sheer willpower.

The ImpSec officer took the stairs two at a time, talking into his radio as he did so.

"My sister's not responding," Louise said, as he arrived, slightly out of breath. "You need to break the door down."

"Are you sure?" Markus asked uncertainly.

"Yes — something's wrong."

Markus gave a nod and stood back from the door.

The officer lifted his foot and kicked at the solid, wood-joined door, causing the plate to splinter away from the jamb. Another kick and the wood around the plate and its reinforcement shattered, and the door slammed open.

Louise was through the door before it even had time to bounce back. Inside, she gagged at the stink of stale vomit. "Margaret!" she whispered at the sight of her sister lying in the large four-poster bed. Her sister's face was white, and vomit stained the bed-sheets.

She didn't remember moving, but somehow, she was across the room and checking her sister.

"She's still breathing," she said, relieved to feel the soft flutter of her sister's breath on the side of her cheek.

Markus had picked up the empty medicine bottle from the bedside table. "Sleeping pills," he said. He sniffed at the glass on the bedside table. "And vodka." He shook his head. "Oh, Margaret," he said, tenderly brushing a lock of her limp black hair away from her face.

"We need the doctor," Louise told the ImpSec officer, who had just returned from checking the en suite.

The officer nodded and headed downstairs at the run, calling loudly. But Louise was too busy trying to roll her sister onto her side to make out what it was he was saying.

"Jessie, out," Markus snapped to his daughter, and Louise looked up to see Jessie watching them from the doorway.

"Is Miss Peric going to be all right?" Jessie asked.

"I hope so," Louise said. "But you need to wait outside."

Jessie nodded reluctantly.

Louise and Markus shared a worried look.

"Miss Peric?" It was James, the butler, hovering in the doorway as he tried to take in what he was seeing.

"Tell one of the maids to get some fresh linen, and we need some light in here," Louise said, gesturing at the heavily curtained windows.

The butler nodded.

As soon as he'd gone, Markus looked at her.

"What?" Louise demanded.

"You don't seem very surprised by all this," Markus said.

Louise shrugged, unwilling to say anything.

Markus looked at her steadily, then nodded. "I'll get a cloth," he said, turning for the en suite.

He was still tenderly wiping Margaret's face when there was the sound of voices from downstairs. "That would be Doctor Castles," Markus said, a moment before the doctor with his bushy ginger sideburns bustled in.

Doctor Castles nodded curtly at them before pulling out his stethoscope to check on Margaret's breathing and heart. Apparently satisfied with what he heard he picked the medicine bottle up to check on its label. "Barbiturates," he said, making it sound like some sort of swear word. "Yes, that would do it." He peered at the vomit still staining the sheets. One finger prodded the remains of what looked like half-digested tablets. "Lucky she vomited, and lucky she didn't suck it back in."

"And who are you?" he asked, turning on Louise.

"Her sister."

"And has Miss Peric attempted suicide before?" he asked.

Louise hesitated for a moment, then shrugged. "I don't know," she admitted. "I know something happened at the end of the war that involved her in some sort of breakdown. But I was on the Mainline at the time, and Mama and Papa never talked about it."

"The war." He frowned, then shrugged. "Right, well, there's nothing more I can do for her at the moment. You'll need to have someone with her at all times. I'll arrange for a nurse to be sent round. She'll need to stay on the premises — I presume that won't be a problem, Mrs. Mack?" he asked the diminutive housekeeper, who had followed the butler back into the room.

"Of course not," Mrs. Mack said.

"Shouldn't you pump her stomach, or something?" Louise asked.

"There wouldn't be anything left in there to pump," he said. "This occurred when . . ." he poked at the stains again " . . . sometime last night. If you want to make yourself useful, get her into a clean bed and air this room. It stinks."

Louise watched him re-pack his bag sourly. As he closed the latch on his bag, he looked up.

"Assuming there's been no permanent damage, you may want to get your sister into see Doctor Helen Rubenstein. She's a psychiatrist who's done a lot of work with returned soldiers. I can give you a referral if you want one."

"Thank you, that would be helpful," Louise said. She frowned, working through what he'd just said. "Permanent damage?"

"I don't think there will be, but we can't dismiss the possibility until she wakes up."

"And when might that be?" Markus asked worriedly.

"Hard to say. It might be tonight or it might not be for a couple of days. The nurse will monitor her for me and will call me if there's any change." And then he bustled out again.

Louise scowled after him. "Oh crap," she said. "I'll need to tell Donald and get a message to my parents."

The piercing ring of the downstairs telephone interrupted her. "I'll see about moving her into one of the spare bedrooms while we get this one cleaned up," Mrs. Mack said.

Louise nodded, not really listening.

"Miss Peric?"

Louise looked to see one of the underhousemaids standing uncertainly by the door. "Yes?"

"It's your cousin, ma'am, the First Leader. He wants to speak to you."

"I'll keep an eye on her," Markus assured her.

"Thanks," Louise said, getting to her feet, wondering at the relationship between Markus and her sister. He *had* been staying at the house for six weeks now. Well, well, the ice princess had an admirer.

Downstairs, she took a deep breath before taking the telephone from James. She watched the butler leave the room, pulling the door closed behind him as he did so.

"Hello Donald."

"How is she?" her cousin and, for the last three years, First Leader of the Cross-Temporal Empire, demanded.

"Still asleep," she said, wondering why only bad news traveled so quickly. "The doctor said we won't know if there's any permanent damage until she wakes up, and that might not be for a couple of days."

"Do you know why? Was there a note?"

"I didn't see any note. And no, I don't know why."

"She didn't seem depressed?"

"No. I had tea with her a couple of days ago and she seemed fine."

There was silence for a moment. "You'll let me know as soon as something happens?" Donald asked. "I just can't get away at the moment. The Council of Leaders is debating rescinding the Edict on contact with advanced lines this week. And numbers are much too close for my comfort."

"That's fine. There's nothing you could do here even if you could," Louise said honestly. Having Donald here would probably make it easier to deal with her mother, but it would be unfair on him.

"Well, take care. And Louise — thank you."

Louise hung up the phone. Then, after staring at it for a moment, she picked it up again. "Notway embassy, Naisre," she told the operator. The sooner she let their parents know, the better.

FROM
FOR THE HONOR OF THE EMPIRE

CHAPTER 2
WELCOME TO BEAUTIFUL PESH

(Wednesday: Sultan, Pesh)

The hotel bedroom smelled of rosewater and sandalwood. Jade considered the telephone on the side table nervously. "Are you sure this is going to work?" she asked in Arabic. "I mean, the number is almost four years old. Anything could have happened. He could have changed houses, or desks. Why would he still have the same number?"

Colonel Ferai considered her for a moment before shrugging his massive shoulders. "Apparently phone numbers are mobile here and stay with the individual. But we certainly won't find out if you don't try it."

His Arabic was atrocious, Jade thought as she nibbled her bottom lip. Jade knew the Colonel's first language was Phoenician, which Ferai claimed was quite close to Arabic, but Jade couldn't detect any similarity, and she'd understood Arabic was a pre-requisite for this mission. Ferai's home-line was the Mmbuto é, where the Phoenician civilization had escaped destruction during the third Punic war by establishing a colony in South Africa, but she had no idea why Imperial Intelligence had insisted on pairing her with him. She liked the man, but the one-eyed former colonel in the Mmbuto é Imperial Marines hardly merged into the background. His dark, almost blue-black skin was covered in intricate white tattoos and his height and sheer size made him stand out in any crowd. Though perhaps that was why — he intimidated people. Jade had watched with interest how much effort people went to in pretending he wasn't there.

Taking a deep breath, she picked the phone up and dialed the number she'd memorized.

A cultured voice answered. "Yes?"

"Emre Binbasi?" she asked uncertainly.

"Emre Kaymakam," he corrected her.

"My apologies, Kaymakam," she said. His new title of Kaymakam would make him the equivalent of what . . . a Corps Leader? "We were not aware of your promotion."

"Who is this?" Emre asked. "And how did you get this number?"

"My name is Jade Carvello. Donald Clemhorn asked me to phone you."

There was a moment's stunned silence, then — "Where are you?" Emre asked.

"I'm at the Ayasofya Hotel — room 503."

"Are you alone?"

"I have one companion."

There was a pause, and Jade could hear Emre talking to someone in the background. "I'm in the car," he said finally, "just picking my sister up from her school. I can be there in thirty minutes. How do I recognize you?"

"We'll be in the foyer. You'll recognize my companion. A large gentleman with white tattoos." She grinned at Ferai, who looked at her impassively.

"Don't move. I'll be there in thirty."

"Well?" Ferai said, as she replaced the phone.

"He'll be here in thirty minutes." She stopped, suddenly wondering how he'd answered the phone from his car.

"So, we're got time for a coffee," Ferai said.

"Why not?" After exchanging four diamonds for the local currency at a jeweler a couple of hours ago, they could certainly afford it. She smiled at the memory of Ferai simply standing in the doorway, arms folded, as she negotiated a price. His presence had disconcerted the buyer so much that the whole haggling process had moved with commendable speed.

After purchasing their coffees, they took a window table in the hotel foyer which overlooked the street and the Danube just beyond it. They'd come through the portal a short distance outside Pesh that morning and had walked into the city. Jade had been too nervous to pay much attention to their surroundings, although she couldn't avoid noticing the damage from the last war. Now, with nothing to do but wait until the Kaymakam arrived, she had the time to properly consider the city.

It looked . . . sullen. The sky was leaden, and the Danube, gray-skinned and sodden, ran morosely between high embankments just beyond the street. On the other side of the river, Pesh's massive parliamentary building stretched itself along the water, while beyond it the Great Mosque was missing half its dome, an ugly reminder of the last war. At least the scaffolding erected around it promised some hope for the future. For some reason it made her wonder how Carlos was faring on Chikyù.

"There is no joy here," Ferai said quietly.

Jade nodded, tearing her mind away from her concern over Carlos, and back to her own worries. There were few cars on the road, and what people were out hurried past, heads down, their pinched faces drained of color. A squad of eight soldiers in tired looking fatigues trotted grimly past.

She had just taken her last swallow of coffee when a large silver vehicle pulled up in front of the hotel and a young man in a silk, dust-orange uniform stepped out. He was wearing pince-nez spectacles, a Cossack style cap, and a serious expression. Two motorcycles pulled in behind the vehicle, and at a nod from the young man, their two riders dismounted, unslung their assault rifles and came into the hotel. After a quick look around, one returned outside to report while the other took up position by the hotel's front door, his back against the wall.

Outside, the young man gazed at the hotel for a moment before bending down and helping a young girl out of the car. The girl was wearing trousers under a white ankle-length skirt and as she emerged, she adjusted her red fringed headscarf. She had short boots under her trousers. A dark felt sleeveless jacket decorated with golden embroidery covered her long white blouse and completed the ensemble.

Putting a protective arm over her shoulders, the young man ushered her toward the hotel.

"Looks like our contact has arrived," Jade said, rising to her feet, recognizing Emre from the description the First Leader had given them.

Ferai hoisted himself to his feet as Emre, now Kaymakam, entered the hotel lobby. As he noticed Ferai, Jade saw Emre's eyes widen momentarily. Then, seeing Jade, he came across, holding out his right hand. "Salaam," he said. "Jade Carvello, I presume?"

Jade nodded. "Emre Kaymakam?"

"The same. May I introduce my sister, Darda."

Jade took her hand. "I'm glad to meet you, Darda. Donald asked me to inquire as to your health."

Darda looked wide eyed at her, and Jade couldn't help a pang of jealousy at her gloriously large eyes set in a model's face.

"You may tell Donald she is well," Emre said on her behalf. "Her school was outside the main target area so avoided any significant damage. And how is Donald?"

"The First Leader is well. I understand he and Defella are expecting their first child."

The only sign of surprise Emre offered at the news that the penniless adventurer he had known less than four years ago was now First Leader of the C-T E, was a slight twitch to his left eye.

"Please pass my personal congratulations on to the two of them when you see them," Emre said, recovering quickly.

"And we should congratulate you on your promotion," Jade said. "May I ask what your new command entails?"

"My brother commands the entire Janissaries Corps," Darda said proudly.

Emre looked embarrassed.

"A significant posting indeed," Ferai said. Jade nodded. The Janissaries served as the elite units of the Ottoman Empire and, given their primary base was in Pesh, also served as an equivalent to the Roman Empire's Praetorian Guard, with the power of hire and fire over the Sultan.

At Emre's puzzled glance at Ferai, Jade realized she had not introduced him yet.

"My apologies," Jade said quickly. "Can I introduce you to my companion, Colonel Ferai."

"Of the Mmbuto é line?" Emre asked.

Ferai nodded, surprised at being recognized. "Imperial Marines," he confirmed.

Emre salaamed shallowly. "I am pleased to meet you. Donald spoke highly of your ability." He looked around. "Do you have any bags?" he asked.

"Backpacks in our room," Ferai said.

"Would it be presumptuous of me to offer you rooms at our house? It's on the base and it would be more secure than here."

Jade looked at Ferai, who nodded. "I'll get them," he said.

"So, how badly was the city hit?" Jade asked as they waited. "It looked pretty bad as we were walking in."

"Ah, I was going to ask where your portal was," Emre said with a smile, before turning serious again. "Bad enough. We avoided getting hit by any biological or chemical weapons but got plastered by the kinetic weapons. The death toll wasn't quite up there with the Great War against the United Christian States, but it was close."

"That was what, thirty million people killed?"

"You know our history," Emre said, surprised.

Jade shrugged. "It was required reading during the war."

"We avoided those sorts of figures this time, but I suspect it was more by luck than good management."

"It still looks pretty bad," Jade said.

"If you think this looks bad, you should see the other guy. Cadiz was destroyed."

"So, what happened? We've always thought your war destroyed the line."

"About two hours after the destruction of our Moon Base, there was a coup in the United Tribes of the Great Plains which pulled them out of the war. There was some talk about a negotiated truce, but then those idiots on our esteemed High Command decided to ramp up the pressure and launched a raid on Cadiz. They detonated five thermobaric bombs over the city."

Jade frowned uncertainly. "Thermobaric?"

"It's a fuel-air bomb," Emre explained. "They were developed after the Great War as an alternative to nuclear weapons. As it turns out, it's a particularly effective weapon, so no more Cadiz. Spain immediately declared itself neutral, and the Angevin Empire followed suit."

Jade looked puzzled.

"England and France," he explained. "With the Angevins gone, the Etehad Sho'mali panicked and responded by pasting Prague and Berlin. Fortunately, we managed to hit them hard enough that their central command structure collapsed, and the war just sort of petered out. We certainly took a lot of damage, pretty significant damage," he admitted. "But at least we avoided the use of nuclear weapons this time." He broke off as Ferai reappeared, carrying the two backpacks. "Come on," he said, "let's go."

As they emerged from the hotel, the armed guard who rode shotgun in the front passenger seat opened the doors for them, then popped the hood on the back storage for the bags Ferai carried. Jade climbed into the car as the door closed behind them with a heavy thud. As she settled back into her seat, the car slowly pulled out from the curb. Jade was not entirely unsurprised at its lack of speed, given the amount of armor it was probably carrying.

As a thick panel of darkened glass rose to close the passenger compartment from the front of the vehicle, Emre adjusted his pince-nez. "So," he said, sitting back into the thick leather upholstery of the seat facing them. "Why are you here?"

Jade looked uncertainly at Ferai, who made a 'tell him' gesture with his shoulders.

Unfastening her jacket, she reached into her breast pocket and produced the small glass vial ImpSec had given her.

"What's this?" he asked, eyeing it uncertainly as she held it out to him.

"It's a particularly virulent potato virus," Jade said.

"And you give it to me, why?" Emre asked, making no effort to take it from her.

"Because we think it came from Sultan," Ferai said, his deep voice echoing around the back of the vehicle. "Ms. Carvello recovered it from some local terrorists, but intelligence indicates it came from Sultan. And given its particular . . . efficacy, we believe it may have been genetically modified. If so, the First Leader is hoping you can identify who might have produced it, and if there is an antidote. We simply don't have the technology."

"The tech any more," Jade corrected him. "The Hraffor from the Nayarit line who established the Empire could undertake quite sophisticated genetic manipulations. That was a hundred years ago, though."

Emre accepted the vial reluctantly, holding it up against the light to examine the dried dust it contained. "I can run some checks, but I may not be able to identify the source," he warned.

"That's all we can ask," Ferai said.

"There is another thing," Jade said.

"Oh?"

"The First Leader is interested in establishing diplomatic relations with Sultan."

Emre looked interested.

"The question, of course, is with who?" she continued.

"I see, I think."

"Our job is to establish where that embassy should be situated," Ferai said.

Emre's expression cleared. "Welcome to beautiful Pesh," he said, airily waving a hand at the ruined city outside the grayed windows. "Capital of the much reduced Ottoman Empire, the Northern Caliphate, and former member of the Etehad Junoobil."

TO BE CONTINUED

About the Author

Andrew spent much of his high-school years lost in the school library, exploring the worlds of Andre Norton, Robert Heinlein, and Isaac Asimov. His first commercially published series, The Portal Adventures (Peasantry Press), began as bedtime stories for his two sons. Now, with his children grown, Andrew lives in Perth with his wife and a fluctuating number of goldfish, writing science fiction, fantasy, and alternate history.

He has worked widely across the literary field, including as Principal of the Davies Literary Agency, editor and publisher of The Western Australian Year Book, and editor/writer for Afterlife—the online magazine for Atmosphere users.

Andrew's first published short story, A Messenger to the Dragon, appeared in Aurealis in 1992. His debut novel, Trouble on Teral—the first of The Portal Adventures, blending the spirit of Caroline Lawrence's Roman Mysteries with Andre Norton's juvenile speculative fiction—was released in 2018 by Peasantry Press. His adult alternate history series, The Clemhorn Trilogy, launched with Nightfall in 2019 (Zmok Books).

His alternate history short story 1827: Napoleon in Australia was shortlisted for the 2021 international Sidewise Awards for Alternate History and won the Tin Duck Award for Best WA Professional SF Short Work the same year.

For more information, and/or you'd like a copy of the recipe for Carlos' Lemon Sponge why not subscribe to his newsletter at: www.andrewjharvey.com.

Hague

Publishing

www.HaguePublishing.com

PO Box 451 Bassendean
Western Australia 6934

www.ingramcontent.com/pod-product-compliance
Lightning Source LLC
Chambersburg PA
CBHW070831190726
48292CB00006B/2192